For a Dream

For a Dream

A novel of the Great War

Anthony Kirby

ISBN 978-1-7382160-0-0

eISBN 978-1-7382160-1-7

Any references to historical events, real people,
or real places are used fictitiously.
Names, characters, and places are products
of the author's imagination.

front cover photograph – trench in the Somme
taken by John Warwick Brooke (Lieutenant &Photographer) (1916Jul)
Soldiers of 'A' Company, 11th Battalion, the Cheshire Regiment, occupy a captured German trench at Ovillers-la-Boisselle on the Somme.

photograph of Anthony Kirby, back cover – by Liam Maloney

photograph of Thomas Michael Kettle
from *The Ways of War* By T M Kettle (1917)

photograph of Lt. Michael Higgins: the Kirby/Higgins families archive(1917)

book design by Antoine Maloney

First printing 2024

Publisher: Anthony Kirby Publishing at Kirby.For.a.Dream@gmail.com

For **Bernard 'Ben' Queenan**

1920 - 2008

Born in Ballymote, Co. Sligo in 1920, Bernard's family emigrated to Glasgow later that decade. Brilliant both in high school and university, he shocked his parents by joining a Scottish Regiment at the outset of World War II. He quickly became a Lieutenant, and because of fluency in five languages became an intelligence officer. He ended the war with the rank of Major, and then completed his university studies.

He worked with the Decca London media group, and later with John Grierson in setting up Scottish Educational Television. He directed and edited the renowned short film *The Rime of the Ancient Mariner (1967)* and with Phillip J. Sleeman and Francelia Butler contributed to the classic volume *200 Selected Film Classics for Children of All Ages: Where to Obtain Them and How to Use Them.*

He directed the Audio Visual Department at Concordia University from 1972 until his retirement in 1985. Generous to a fault, he encouraged the undersigned in pursuit of excellence.

Anthony Kirby 2023

[Source of the title, and the poem extract on the rear cover]

Thomas Kettle (from All Poetry)

1880-1916

Thomas Michael Kettle, the Irish nationalist poet, politician, and soldier, was born in Co. Dublin the son of one of the founders of the Land-League, Andrew Kettle.

Following an education at North Richmond Street Christian Brothers' School, Clangowes Wood College and University College Dublin (UCD) Kettle was called to the bar in 1905. For the next three years he practiced law until he received an appointment in 1908 at UCD as its first Professor of National Economics. It was during this period that Kettle's nascent nationalist views flowered. For a brief period during 1905 he edited *The Nationalist*.

Kettle died with conspicuous gallantry in the attack on Ginchy at the battle of the Somme; Sept. 1916. His war journalism was posthumously published in collected form as The Ways of War (1917).

"Five days before his death in France on 9 September 1916, while leading his men at Ginchy, Thomas Kettle wrote to a friend in Dublin:

> *This note is really a conditional "good-bye" to you all. We have been on the march for days, sleeping on the bare ground, eating what we could ... and are moving up to-night into the battle of the Somme. The bombardment, the destruction and bloodshed are beyond all imagination. Nor did I ever think that the valour of simple men could be quite as beautiful as that of my Dublin Fusiliers. I have had two chances of leaving them – one on sick leave, and one to take a Staff job. I have chosen to stay with my comrades."* *(from the History of Parliament)*

To my daughter Betty, the gift of God

In wiser days, my darling rosebud, blown
To beauty proud as was your mother's prime,
In that desired, delayed, incredible time,
You'll ask why I abandoned you, my own,
And the dear heart that was your baby throne,
To dice with death. And, oh! they'll give you rhyme
And reason; some will call the thing sublime,
And some decry it in a knowing tone.
So here, while the mad guns curse overhead,
And tired men sigh, with mud for couch and floor,
Know that we fools, now with the foolish dead,
Died not for flag, nor King, nor Emperor,
But for a dream, born in a herdsman's shed,
And for the secret Scripture of the poor.

Written in the field before Guillemont, Somme,
on 4 September 1916,
by Lieutenant Thomas Michael [Tom] Kettle,
9th Royal Dublin Fusiliers, 16th (Irish) Division.
Killed in action, 9 September 1916.

Table of Contents

Preface:

Living in Canada, away from my native Ireland, I nonetheless developed a keen interest in three aspects of early 20th Century Ireland: the participation of two of my uncles in WWI; the terrible effects of that Great War on the Irishmen who survived it; the tumultuous political events in Ireland starting with the attempt to enact Irish Home Rule, and then the Easter Rising in 1916, and the role, albeit small, of my maternal family in the political life of Ireland's evolving Free State.

As a child growing up in rural Co. Mayo following WWII, I was conscious of my father's annual observance of Remembrance Day, but he died before I was old enough to have a proper conversation with him about it. My siblings and I did know that two of our uncles had served in WWI.

In the '70s my brothers John and Denis began to research the lives of our uncles, and some of the material they collected found its way to me and stoked my interest. In the early 1990s I learned more details about my mother's brothers Jack and Michael from a sister of my mother.

My Uncle Jack Higgins was Medical Officer on HMS Ocean, a large battleship that, with two smaller vessels, steamed up the Gallipoli straits in March 1915. Uncle Michael Higgins was an officer with The Prince of Wales's Leinster Regiment (Royal Canadians).

Lt. Michael Higgins

In the early '90s I became fascinated with my Uncle Michael's life and decided I would perhaps attempt a biography of my uncle. My friend Ben Queenan of Concordia University urged me instead to write a novel that would be loosely based on Uncle Michael's life. He worked with me to develop a two-page outline that became my touchstone for writing this novel.

The Irish fatalities in WWI were grievous, and many who were not killed, came home physically and psychologically damaged. There were two Great War veterans in my hometown. The first, Billy Sheridan, seemed unaffected, while the other, Jonny Ward, appeared to be shell shocked; he kept repeating the phrase 'How are ye, how are ye,' over and over again. He was harmless, but as ten and eleven-year olds, we tormented him, without any realization of what he had gone through.

As an adolescent living in Dublin in 1955, I occasionally read *The Sunday Press* a paper that ran a series of cartoons making fun of a local character called 'Bang-Bang' who would jump on and off double-decker buses with his hands raised as if he was holding a rifle, and shout 'Bang-Bang'. Even as a teenager, I couldn't see any humour there. I was in my mid-teens and was coming to understand 'shell shock'. While 'Bang-Bang's mental state was not a result of the Great War, I reacted to the cruelty of those cartoons, and inevitably my thoughts turned to our cruelty to Jonny Ward. It had become evident to me that Jonny Ward, and many others, had come out of the war suffering from shell shock, a form of Post Traumatic Stress Disorder.

My Uncle Michael was a junior official in the Munster and Leinster Bank in Skibbereen, Co. Cork. He closely followed the efforts of Irish Leader John Redmond in support of Home Rule for Ireland which had again been delayed due to the outbreak of WWI.
He heeded Redmond's call that Irishmen fight for 'Little Belgium and freedom for small nations'. Promised that his position at his bank would be preserved, he volunteered for The Prince of Wales's Leinster Regiment, in October 1914.

Michael served in Ypres, and all the major battlefronts of the early stage of the Great War, especially at the Second Battle of Arras, known in Canada as the Battle of Vimy Ridge, where he was killed.

Throughout the 1990s and early 2000s I visited the WWI sites of Ypres, Hooge, Beaumont Hamel, Arras, Messines, and Vimy Ridge, and many military libraries, trying to satisfy my deep curiosity. All this led to this book now in your hands.

Introduction:

This novel opens in Dublin and Cork, Ireland, as the Home Rule Bill is about to pass, giving the Irish, parliamentary control within Ireland. At the same time the Great War in Europe is newly underway, and much of the novel is set in the company of Irish soldiers, fighting on the side of Britain, in the trenches of Flanders during WWI. With the recent history of the 'troubles' in Northern Ireland in our memories, it's worth asking why these Irishmen were wearing British colours, and parts of the answer are fascinating.

In 1166, Dermot MacMurragh, the deposed King of Leinster, travelled to England, and then France, to track down and meet with Henry II, the first of the Plantagenet monarchs, in order to seek help in restoring himself to his king-ship in Leinster. He had been deposed that year by the High King of Ireland, Rory O'Connor. MacMurragh had family relations in the court and believed that could secure him an audience with the King.

Henry II gave Dermot permission to find support among knights in England who would agree to be mercenaries for his cause in Leinster. Dermot returned to England and to Pembrokeshire to meet with Richard de Clare (in Wales, aka "Strongbow") and his local Norman knights and supporters ...among them, mercenaries from Flanders.

While Henry II was occupied in France, securing his kingdom there, he remained conscious that Pope Adrian IV, the first and only English Pope had issued a Papal letter in 1155, a year after Henry's accession to the throne, giving Henry a license to bring the Irish 'Celtic Church' under conventional Anglo-Christian control. It could be seen as a grant of License to Invade Ireland for the King.

In 1166, Dermot was working to find English (Norman) knights to come to his aid in Ireland. Dermot was not asking the English to invade Ireland, but that was the outcome. In 1167, Dermot returned to Leinster with Richard Fitz Godebert, a Flemish mercenary knight, and several foot-soldiers.

His attempt to regain his kingdom soon came to a halt when High King Rory confronted him; Fitz Godebert returned to Wales to report the outcome to his lord, "Strongbow".

"Strongbow" honored his commitment to Dermot, and a second group accompanied him back to Ireland, a force Robert FitzStephen organised from English and Welsh mercenary knights and soldiers. They landed in Bannow Bay, and laid siege to Wexford, which fell in May 1169.

The Norman presence, fed from "Strongbow's" forces in South Wales, was strengthened in 1170 by the arrival at Wexford in May 1170 of Maurice FitzGerald and a force of 10 knights, thirty men-at-arms, and a hundred archers and foot soldiers. Friendly help had become an invasion which expanded further.

After "Strongbow's" successful invasion, Henry II, concerned that "Strongbow" was supplanting his right to rule over Ireland, mounted a second and larger invasion in 1171 to ensure his control over his subjects, which succeeded.

There now stretched 850 years of English, become 'British', control over Ireland, punctuated by repeated rebellions and uprisings. Henry II, from his arrival, attempted to introduce British Common Law as a replacement for the Celtic Brehon Law, but with limited success, and none outside the Pale, the area in proximity to Dublin (thus the phrase 'beyond the Pale').

England sought to assert the supremacy of its Parliament, and of English law, over any Irish Parliament or Irish legislation, by enacting the Statutes of Kilkenny in 1366. In 1494, at a Parliament in Drogheda, two statutes, that became known as Poyning's Law were enacted which provided that the King's Privy Council must agree to any assembly and legislation of an Irish Parliament, and that all laws passed in England applied to Ireland; the English Parliament effectively took control of Ireland.

Despite this, by 1500 English law was confined to an area known as the Pale, made up of Dublin and the east coast. Beyond the Pale, Brehon law continued to be applied. It was only during the reign of King Henry VIII in the 1500s that English law had a wider sway.

Poyning's Law, and the associated lack of parliamentary control within Ireland, was a progressively greater irritant, planting the seed for what instigated repeated rebellions, and became the drive for Home Rule in the late 1800s.

The English Parliament repealed Poyning's Law under the Irish Appeals Act, 1783. From that time until 1800, the Irish Parliament (known as Grattan's Parliament) sought to improve the situation of Catholics through the enactment of the Roman Catholic Relief Act, 1793, which conferred a limited right to vote and admission to practice at the Bar. However, in light of the French and American revolutions and the failed rebellion of 1798, the Act of Union, 1800 was passed, and this short-lived move towards home rule was quenched.

This Act dissolved the Irish Parliament and established the Westminster Parliament in London as the sole legislative body of the United Kingdom of Great Britain and Ireland. This Act centralised government power in London until the establishment of the Irish Free State in 1922. The Crown's representative in Ireland was the Chief Secretary for Ireland, who was a member of the cabinet. The British administration had its Irish headquarters in

Dublin Castle, under the control of the Under-Secretary and the Crown's official representative in Dublin, the Lord Lieutenant.

Calls for the repeal of the Act of Union became the core of political resistance in Ireland. Home Rule was the initial objective of Irish nationalists, but in the first half of the 1800s, the Irish were preoccupied with establishing the Land Law Act. However, by 1870, the return of Parliament to Dublin, the return of Home Rule, dominated political action, but the Government of Ireland Act enacting Home Rule was not passed in the British Parliament until 1914, just as WWI was starting. That led almost immediately to the Act, to Home rule, being suspended as Britain entered WWI in earnest, with substantial support for enlistment within Ireland.

As WWI got under way, Ireland, still without Home Rule, continued to pursue Home Rule or indeed complete independence from the United Kingdom, and headed toward the Easter Rising of 1916, the Irish War of Independence from 1919 to 1921, the creation of the first truly Irish Parliament, the First Dáil, in 1919, and Ireland's Civil War in 1922-23.

Notwithstanding this growing momentum, enlistment in the British forces was seen as something that could prove Ireland's loyalty to the United Kingdom, and could speed the enactment of Home rule.

You've been reading 'WWI' here, which we all use as commonplace, but within the British Isles, it was referred to as the 'European War' or 'the Great War'; WWI did not come into common use until WWII was breaking out. Within Germany, there was occasional use of 'World War', perhaps reflecting their sense that the combatants, England and France, had, as colonial powers, parts of their empires spread across the world.

A good sense of the Great War, and of its position in this novel, can be conveyed by briefly considering the major sites of conflict through the war, and by that measure it was indeed a European War, and a Great War.

I'll punctuate the survey with mentions of the casualty and death rates in some of the campaigns; this represented a huge shock to the citizenry of these countries as they were confronted by the horrors that modern weaponry were able to render. Some of the single-battle, single-day, single campaign totals have yet to be surpassed. Many of the scenes in this novel convey that horror.

The Great War started with the assassination of Archduke Franz Ferdinand and his wife; in a little more than a month, Europe was at war, a series of dominos falling as countries went to war to support their allies. It took a month for Austria-Hungary to issue a declaration of war against Serbia, and within days, all of Europe was at war.

There would be a Western Front, with the battle names that still resonate for the British, Irish, and Scottish, for Canadians and Americans, and for

Australians and New Zealanders, and equally in France, Belgium and Germany, and an Eastern Front, with its separate demands on Germany, and on Eastern Europe, Italy, and Russia; the Ottomans fought British and An-Zac forces in and around Gallipoli. At sea, massive British and German Navies were in combat at Dogger Bank and Jutland, with similar horrendous loss of life. Despite the lack of obvious victories by the British, by the middle of 1916, Britain controlled the North Sea, and enforced a blockade of German ports, a decisive measure in the final outcome of the war.

A Great War, a European War, a World War that wore on for four years, ending on November 11th, 1918. It claimed an estimated 40 million military and civilian casualties, including 20 million deaths, much of the war fought in trenches.

Hostilities broke out almost immediately after treaties of war were declared in 1914. By the third week of August a substantial contingent of the British Expeditionary Forces (B.E.F.) had joined French forces along the Belgian frontier and were at Mons when the Germans began their advance. The B.E.F., overpowered by the larger German forces, were nonetheless able to delay their advance, and while it was a German victory in the moment, Mons took on the colours of a heroic resistance among the British public.

At the same time, the Battle of Tannenberg in East Prussia was underway with the Russian Army attacking German forces. What started well for the Russian forces, turned ultimately into a rout, the Russian armies collapsing, with 30,000 casualties and 90,000 taken prisoner.

Both the Battles of the Belgian Frontier, and Tannenberg, were battles of mobile forces. That form of warfare was soon to be replaced by long-term trench warfare. This was a response to the massive casualties inflicted by modern weaponry on mobile forces. The retreat of the British in front of the German advance at Mons did not halt until the Battle of the Marne.

During the Marne Campaign, the failure of discipline at the highest levels of the German Command created an opening for a counterattack by French and British forces. It was mad maneuvering on both sides, with at one point a portion of the Army of Paris being rushed from Paris to the front in taxicabs. The Germans were driven back, took up a defensive position, and the conventional mobile combat had now become a war fought from trenches, and remained in that form until 1918.

The casualties on both sides in this First Battle of the Marne were enormous, reflecting the effects of modern weaponry on mobile forces. The public was shocked, and the armies were compelled to abandon mobile warfare, and resort to trench warfare. The casualties were heavy, with 263,000 Allied soldiers wounded, among them, 81,000 that died; the total of casualties in the German forces was 220,000.

As the historian Barbara Tuchman wrote as a conclusion to her book The Guns of August (1962): "The Battle of the Marne was one of the decisive battles of the world not because it determined that Germany would eventually lose or the Allies ultimately win the war but because it determined that the war would go on. There was no looking back, Joffre told the soldiers on the eve. Afterward there was no turning back. The nations were caught in a trap, a trap made during the first thirty days out of battles that failed to be decisive, a trap from which there was, and has been, no exit."

The battles went on, with the names engraved on monuments, and filling history books: the Allies had kept the Germans from Paris, but now came the First Battle of Ypres, still in 1914, the Battle of Verdun, the longest battle of the war, occupying virtually all of 1916, the Battle of the Somme, also in 1916, and the Third Battle of Ypres, the Battle of Passchendaele in the Allied Battle of Arras in the middle and latter half of 1917.

There were any number of other smaller battles on these and other fronts; some of them have a place in this novel. Vimy Ridge, where Canadian Forces made their mark and the Allied Battle of Arras are where much of the action in this novel takes place.

The Great War continued to grind on past these battles, finally ending November 11th, 1918.

CHAPTER ONE

Dublin 1914

Michael Sullivan's hair had wilted. Beads of sweat kept finding their way off his forehead and down his nose. He stole a quick glance at the large ticking clock across from his cashier's window: 2.45 p.m. Fifteen minutes to closing. Only four customers left.

Sergeant McGinley of the Dublin Metropolitan Police stepped up to the bar in a beige alpaca suit. Obviously off-duty - or working undercover, thought Michael with a small smile. He had come to know the sergeant well since moving to the College Green branch of The National Bank two years ago. In fact, the sergeant had been in his thoughts often the past week, given the shootings at Bachelors Walk the previous Sunday. A platoon of Scottish Borderers, recently arrived for training, had been dragged into haphazard civic duty and had fired into a demonstration, killing three.

—Bray sounds like an ideal holiday, said Michael. Richly deserved given the recent events.

—Thank you Michael. It's a miracle more blood wasn't shed.

—Indeed.

—Those damn Borderers are confined to Beggar's Bush. May they rot all summer in their stinking barracks.

—Exactly my feeling, Sergeant. How would you like your withdrawal, five fivers, ten sovereigns?

—That'd do fine.

—The National has a branch in Bray. Should the need arise.

—Thanks. As long as the weather holds and there's no war.

—Take care Sergeant.

A short, lean co-worker in a green visor walked over.

—Good chat with Dublin's finest? said James Lally with a wink.

—Oh, I've known him for years Jim. He's a good customer.

Michael looked up from the money he was counting, saw the broad smile on Lally's freckled face, and laughed.

—I have a crow to pluck with you, Jim. How about a pint in Mulligan's?

—That'd be grand, Mick. But aren't you seeing Virginia?

—No, she's on night duty. But we've something planned for the weekend.

1 - Dublin 1914

By 3.45 p.m. Michael had finally balanced his daybook, a respectable 15,000 pounds. Perspiration filled his forehead; his collar stud dug into his throat. The prospect of a cool pint of cider in Mulligan's filled his thoughts. A door opened behind him, and the Belfast accent of his manager echoed off the bank's high ceiling.

—A word with you Sullivan.

—Certainly Mr. Moore, said Michael, sealing his deposit envelope and walking briskly into the manager's office.

—Smoke? asked Moore, gesturing toward the chair facing his desk.

Michael accepted and leaned in towards the lit match, drawing the smoke into his lungs. Moore studied him for a moment.

—Michael, how long has it been since you transferred from Athlone?

—It will be two years in October Sir. Five years with the bank all told.

—Are you happy?

—I enjoy my work, and I love Dublin.

—Where do you see yourself in five years' time Sullivan?

Michael pondered the question, and his manager's interest.

—Well, I'm taking accountancy courses at Rathmines this autumn. Home Rule will make Ireland a center of commerce.

—Indeed.

—I see myself in head office, helping to grow local business. But if I am needed in Cork or Belfast, I could see myself in either place.
In a management capacity.

Mr. Moore seemed pleased.

—Excellent, Sullivan. I have something I'd like to propose to you right now.
Mr. Cleary and I have noticed your efficiency, your good relations with Lally, O'Riordan, Miss McNaughton. You're well liked Sullivan. Mr. Cleary and I agree that you might continue to flourish, given more responsibility. We'd like you to manage personnel training. You can take up these duties after the holiday weekend.
There would, of course, be an increase in salary. In the amount of...

He glanced down and shifted some papers.

—...a hundred fifty pounds a year. Would you be interested?

Michael took a quick breath.

—I would Mr. Moore.

Then his heart sank as he remembered Virginia.

—There's only one thing, Michael said. I have a leave of two weeks. Starting Monday, returning the 17th.

—Ach, sure that'd be perfect Sullivan. There's some red tape to be sorted out in any case.

With that Mr. Moore stood up, shook Michael's hand, and guided him towards the door.

—Have a great holiday then son. We'll see you in two weeks.

Michael bounded down the limestone steps of the National Bank. Here was a career breakthrough. And he not yet twenty-four!

He walked across College Green. The trams, drays, and traps, a happy confusion of traffic and sound.

At Westmoreland Street Constable Maloney waved Michael across. Passing Trinity, he crossed D'Olier to Hawkins and Poolbeg Streets. At the Theatre Royal, across from Mulligan's, a large hoarding announced Harry Lauder and his variety show. Inside the bar smelled of stale stout, sawdust and tobacco.

—What took you so long Mick? asked Lally, emerging from a pall of smoke and giving him a friendly nudge. You scheming with Moore, you devil?

—Meet your new director of staff training, said Michael.

Lally looked at him agog for a moment, then seeing Michael was serious, smiled broadly.

—It couldn't happen to a nicer fellow. When do you take up the new job?

—After my holiday. I'm bringing Virginia to meet my family. Then we go up to Sligo to meet her people. That's why I asked to see you.

—You want me to cover for you tomorrow morning?

—Exactly.

—That'll be a pleasure, Michael. I still owe you for Easter Saturday. Well, this requires something stronger than Guinness! Brandy? Lorcan, two large Hennessy's please, he said to the barman.

Michael hummed a tune softly.

—Is that *The Man Who Broke the Bank at Monte Carlo?* Lally asked.

—It is. It just popped into my head.

—Coincidence? laughed Lally.

—It's true. Providence, luck, whatever you care to call it, is smiling on me today.

—Well. Here's to your health.

—*Slainte* Jimmy, I hope the next promotion will be yours.

—You and me both, Michael.

The cognac burned the back of their throats.

—Gosh that's good stuff, said Michael hoarsely.

He looked around the bar: assorted couples in small booths, sipping long drinks: actors, chorus girls, dockworkers, bank workers, and insurance functionaries like himself.

The dark wood varnish was worn, the countertops burnt, but Mulligan's represented for Michael all the warmth and friendliness of Dublin.

—Not to mar the mood Michael, but I'm still terribly upset over the Bachelors Walk shootings, Lally said, his colour and voice rising. Three killed, fifty injured.
Where's the justice in that?

—I'm upset too, Jimmy. But we must remain calm. The whole country feels as you do. The man who called in the Scottish Borderers has been suspended and Sir John Ross has resigned. Redmond is doing his best for us.

Lally guffawed and drew in his breath, ready to run down the leader of Parliament. Michael put his hand on his friend's shoulder to stay him.

—No matter what's done, it won't bring these three back.

Lally dropped his head, and exhaled.

—I suppose you're right Mick. More violence will only make things worse ... except for that captain of the Borderers. Hanging's too good for him.

As they clinked and drank, Michael thought about the captain. Faced with an angry mob, he had panicked and given the order to shoot. Why shoot to kill? He should have told his men to shoot in the air. The Orangemen and Conservatives were taking up arms again, using Bachelors Walk as a pretext to stop the Home Rule Bill coming into force.

—Why wouldn't the King just sign and let Ireland go its way?

—So there we are, Lally said. Let's have another and then head home. Lorcan, a pint of Smithwick's, and what for you Mick?

—Mine's a Smithwick's too.

They drank their pints in gulps.

—Well I'm off Mick, said Lally. I have a couple of lads to see in Drumcondra about the football championships.

—*Slan leat.*

—*Slan agus beannact.*

It had cooled down outside. To the west the sky was a mass of red and gold. Saturday promised to be beautiful.

The bronze statues of Burke and Goldsmith gleamed as Michael made his way past the university to Grafton Street. Feeling hungry, he glanced at his fob watch. Almost 7.30 p.m.

His landlady would never cook supper this late. Bewley's Coffee Shop was halfway up the street.

The aroma of fresh-ground coffee assaulted his senses as he went through the door. He ordered a glass of milk and salmon mayonnaise, and glanced at the *Independent* from that morning. Belgrade had been captured by the Austrians. If it came to war, Ireland would be part of it. The British would likely not force conscription, yet all able-bodied men would still be required to do their part. To volunteer, Michael sighed. There was nothing he could do. Better men than he were trying to resolve the problem.

He pulled out a small pad and indelible pencil.

Dearest Virginia,
Lally has agreed to cover for me tomorrow morning. I hope to see you outside the nurse's residence at 8.15a.m. We'll try for the nine o'clock train to Maryborough.
All my love, your Michael

He folded the note and put it in the top pocket of his jacket. As he paid for his meal, the refrain from *The Man Who Broke the Bank at Monte Carlo* returned to badger him softly.

So he sang it to himself:

As I walked along the Bois du Boulogne
With an independent air
You could hear the girls declare
"He must be a millionaire"
You can hear them sigh and wish to die
You can see them wink the other eye
At the man who broke the bank at Monte Carlo

Michael walked to Lower Baggot Street, gave his note to Patrick the porter, and with a three-penny bit for a tip asked him to deliver it to Virginia. Then he caught the tram to Ranelagh, made arrangements with a hackney driver to pick him up at eight the following morning, and walked the short distance to his digs on Belgrave Square. The Rathmines Town Hall Clock struck ten as he climbed the steps of Number 48.

—Is that you Mr. Sullivan? asked a grey-haired woman.

–Yes Mrs. Byrne. I'm sorry to be a bit late.

–So, you're away tomorrow. Would you need breakfast before you go?

–No, only a cup of tea.

–What time would you like your tea for?

–At half seven, thank you. I have a hackney cab coming at eight.

–Half seven it is. Sleep well Mr. Sullivan.

–You too, Mrs. Byrne. Good night.

He climbed the stairs to his room, pulled out his suitcase and packed for the journey: two cotton shirts, an extra pair of trousers, a rosary, his shaving gear. In bed, reading Conrad's *The Secret Agent*, he longed for Virginia. He would kiss her lips in a few short hours.

He closed his eyes. Sleep came quickly.

Chapter Two

Rosnua, Queen's County, August 1914

Virginia looked agitated.

–Don't worry, said Michael. Everyone will love you.

Virginia sat back in her plush seat, laid her head on the embroidered headrest and closed her eyes. She thought of the little gifts she had purchased last week for Michael's younger brother and sister: *What Katie Did* for Rosemary, *A Child's Garden of Verse* for Brian.

–Ah, something for the mind, Michael had said approvingly when she showed him.

Perhaps he was right. In the nine months since she had known him he had been right about almost everything. If his family didn't like her it wouldn't be for lack of trying.

The Liffey shone like a silver thread in the early morning. Through the window of the moving train a barge could be seen puffing fully laden through the blue-white waters.

On a dock nearby, men rolled barrels up a gangplank while a huge wooden box hung suspended from a chain above them. The train pulled slowly out of Dublin.

–Newbridge! All for Newbridge!

She must have dozed off. Opposite her, Michael was reading *The Leinster Leader*.

–Newbridge! the conductor shouted again, in the passageway outside their berth.

If Michael noticed her stirring, he did not speak. How considerate, she thought. She had worked the night shift at the hospital well past midnight and risen earlier than he, to look fresh and ready: a new pink dress and white shawl, her ash-blond hair combed and clean, a light scent of lavender, no trace of fatigue on her face. She drifted back to sleep.

The train stopped briefly at Portarlington. The countryside was more rugged now. Soon after, the heavy sway of the tracks woke her fully.

–We'll be there in about twenty minutes, said Michael gently.

Outside were fields with cattle, then another with three mares and their foals, all running for a moment beside her window. Then empty fields.

–Maryborough! shouted the conductor.

2 - Rosnua, Queen's County, August 1914

As the train pulled in a man waved at Virginia from the large crowd on the platform.

—That's father, said Michael, excitement in his voice The man's auburn hair and full beard were flecked with grey. He looked to be in his mid-fifties.

With a hiss of steam, the train came to a halt. Michael reached up to the luggage rack, took down both of their suitcases, and practically leapt down the train steps. Virginia waited at the top for a moment as Michael and his father hugged. She looked away. Her own parents were more reserved; she felt a little uneasy at open displays of emotion.

Dr. Sullivan offered her a hand down.

—Virginia. What a pleasure to finally meet you girl.

Dr. Sullivan kissed her lightly on the cheek.

—Now, the motor is parked just behind the station.

He gently placed his hand on Virginia's forearm, guiding her through the crowd. Michael followed with the suitcases.

—Son, can you turn the starting crank?

The doctor drove skilfully through the town's crowded streets, and soon they were on the road to Rosnua, Co. Laois, and Athy. To the north were rugged hills, to the south the occasional forest and golden wheat fields rippling in the wind.

—Most of this land is owned by Major Cosbie and his family, said the doctor. They've been here for five generations now. They're Unionists of course, but we like them.

—Do you see that large ruin on the left?

—Yes, said Virginia.

—That's The Rock of Dunamase. It was given to Strongbow, the Norman prince, as part of his dowry in 1170. Cromwell conquered it in 1650. Today it is the historic home of the O'More family. Don't go home or back to Dublin without visiting it. Michael, you'll make sure Virginia sees Dunamase, won't you?

—Of course father.

Some minutes later they reached Oaklands, a solid two-gabled house. It stood near a mill and a swift stream, about fifty yards in from the road. A blond-haired girl and a red-haired boy weeded the flowerbeds in front of the house.

—It's Michael and father! the children cried, throwing down their hoes and running to open the gate.

–Rosemary, Brian, your older brother's home on holiday, said Dr. Sullivan. This is his friend, Virginia Martin.

The children greeted Virginia shyly.

–Brian, run and get your mother, there's a lad.

–Michael, I've an awful lot to tell you, said Rosemary, taking her brother's hand, and leading him towards the house.

A screen door slammed, and a small woman appeared from the back. Her dark red hair was heaped in folds on her forehead, her hands had a light dusting of flour that she wiped on her apron as she walked.

–Virginia, you're very welcome, said Mrs. Sullivan, embracing her, and then Michael.
I'm making a sponge cake for the evening and must look a sight.
Come inside now and we'll have lunch.
You both must be famished.

Once inside, through open French doors, Virginia saw an oblong garden full of gladioli, rose bushes and carnations.

–Oh, what a lovely garden! Are you the gardener Mrs. Sullivan?

–Yes, I plant the gladioli every spring. P.J., our handyman, helps me with the work. And Tom here lends a hand sometimes, she said, laying her hand on her husband's wrist.

–Oh, don't be talking now, Annie. You're the one with the green fingers. Haven't you grown carnations, lupines, and pansies from seed? Not to mention your vegetable garden and the lettuce we're about to eat.

The family said a brief grace and started eating: salad with nuts and berries, plus bread and cheese.

–So do you like nurse's training, Virginia? asked Dr. Sullivan.

–Well, it can be trying, with the long hours and shift work, and giving patients enemas and bed-baths. But seeing them smile and recover is something I love. I wouldn't leave nursing for anything.

–This past week, Bachelors Walk, can't have been easy, said Dr. Sullivan.

–I was finishing my shift when most of the casualties came in. The worst were taken to the Mater. Most just had cuts and bruises...well, that I saw. And the shock of it. I think that was worse. We kept about half of them overnight.

–Mmm, nodded the doctor. How do you find the Irish Sisters of Charity?

–They're strict, but kind.

–I'm glad to hear that, Virginia. I spent a year at Vincent's just after I became a doctor in 1882. I think it's a great hospital.

–I want to be a nurse when I'm older, said Rosemary.

–You will too, girl, you will too. But first I want you to do your best at the convent school here, and then with the nuns in Rathfarnham. You have to have high marks if you want to do nursing.

–I will, father.

The door opened and a tall young woman with auburn hair and a pale freckled face entered.

–Sorry to be late, father. Choir practice went on and on. I came as fast as I could.

–Oh! that's all right. We know you didn't do it on purpose. We're only having salad anyway.
Meet Virginia, she's almost like one of the family already.

–I'm Deirdre, Virginia, she said, shaking hands.

Virginia saw the shyness in Deirdre's green eyes.

–I've heard a lot about you Deirdre. I know we'll be great friends.

–Sit girls, sit, said Dr. Sullivan. Enjoy your lunch.

There was a knock at the door. A girl of about fifteen dressed in black with a white apron entered.

–Can I take away the salad plates, Ma'am?

–Yes Brigid. We'll have our coffee and dessert on the veranda.

–Yes Ma'am.

Sitting in a lounge chair in the garden, Virginia saw a hawk high in the sky. It hovered against the wind, almost perfectly still, then tipped its wings and fell like water off a cliff, crashing down into a bush nearby. There was a brief squeak and brief flurry, and the hawk took off again with something in its talons. No one seemed to notice. Mrs. Sullivan had already taken up her embroidery, Deirdre was reading a musical score, and Michael and his father were sipping coffee and smoking.

–Virginia, would you like to see some of my watercolours? asked Rosemary.

–Yes dear. Very much.

–Here they are, she said moments later, pulling the tapes off a portfolio. That's the Protestant church just across the stream from our house. That's Miss Fisher's house, and that's an old mill near here.

–These are very good, Rosemary. Who taught you to paint so well?

–Mother. And the nuns in Rosnua.

–You've got a lot of talent. Do you enjoy sketching?

—I love it. Would you like to come with me? We can draw the swans in the lake.

—Now, Rosemary, Virginia is probably tired from her journey, said Mrs. Sullivan without raising her head as Rosemary showed her disappointment. Would you like to lie down for an hour or so, Virginia?

—Yes, perhaps I will.

—Your bedroom is the second room at the top of the stairs. Michael has already put your suitcase there and you're just two doors away from the bathroom. Have a good rest. We'll call you well before teatime.

Virginia unpacked quickly, placing her clothes in the dresser and her brushes, perfume and dusting powder on top. She lay on the firm bed and closed her eyes. From the garden came the murmur of conversation; from farther off, the call of a cuckoo.

She was in the emergency room of the hospital and the casualties were stumbling in, young men with missing limbs and head wounds. She watched the train of men dispassionately, holding a bottle of iodine. Please, came a voice. An ashen-faced youth looked up at her from a stretcher, his lips purple. Blood oozed from a gash in his neck. Secure that dressing, Nurse Martin said another voice sternly, followed quickly by another, Stop wasting your time, fetch the Father.

Waking from her dream Virginia went into the bathroom, splashed cold water in her eyes and went downstairs. The clock said five-thirty.

—Virginia! said Michael, as she rejoined them in the garden.

He got up and took her hand.

—Here's Chris, just in from Cork.

Chris was the same height as his brother, his hair a little darker, his face a little fuller.

—Virginia, said Chris, shaking her hand. You're every bit as beautiful as Michael's letters attest.

She blushed and looked away uncomfortably.

—Chris completed his law degree earlier this year, said Michael. He's working in the south with the firm of Tim Hickman and Brother.

—Do you enjoy the study of law? asked Virginia.

—Yes, tell us about the law Chris, grinned Michael. How many widows and orphans did you save this month?

—Oh, I won't be drawn into that. Michael's quite a gay blade isn't he, Virginia?

–I've known worse, she said smiling.

–Like who? said Michael with mock indignation.

–Never mind, I'll tell you later.

–I had a letter from Jack on Wednesday, said Chris. He's on manoeuvres.

–Why must a doctor go on manoeuvres? No one is firing upon them, said Michael.

–It appears this exercise is quite secret, said Chris sighing heavily.

–Where are your parents? Virginia asked Michael.

–Father is at the dispensary in Rosnua. Mother is in the kitchen with Brigid.

–I'll see if I can help her, said Virginia.

–I'm afraid it's salad again, Virginia. But this time it's salmon salad, said Mrs. Sullivan.

She placed a poached salmon on a bed of lettuce and garnished it with sliced tomatoes and potato salad.

–But it's perfect for this hot weather, said Virginia.

–We've everything arranged, haven't we Brigid? Perhaps you could help Brigid set the table?

–By all means Mrs. Sullivan.

Virginia picked up several knives and forks in a dishtowel and returned to the dining room.

The crunch of gravel signalled the return of Dr. Sullivan. Chris went out front and hugged his father.

–Busy day? asked Chris.

–No more than usual, son. I've put Mrs. Feeney on a strict diet. She's so heavy now that it's affecting her heart. Other than that most people in Rosnua are well.

When they had gathered at the table the doctor continued.

–Hasn't this been a wonderful summer so far? We've already cut our oats and barley. I've asked Tommy Murtagh to come with his threshing machine. You'll be back in Cork by then, Chris, but Michael, I'm counting on your help.

–Of course Father. You know I enjoy farm work, especially at harvest time.

–That's settled then. And you'll help with refreshments and sandwiches, Virginia?

–That would be fun, Dr. Sullivan.

After supper Michael, Virginia, Chris and Deirdre walked through the fields towards the small lake at the foot of the farm. A heron moved silently in the reeds, its eyes on the water below. Every few minutes its head stabbed downward and emerged with a silver sprat in its beak. In the middle of the lake, two swans and a half-grown cygnet swam slowly.

–Are there many fish in here, Michael? asked Virginia.

–Lots of perch. Father fly-fishes here in spring and always catches a few trout. There's a family of otters on the far side that no doubt eat most of the fish.

Chris and Deidre went for a walk, leaving the young couple lying on the bank as twilight faded into night. A brace of snipe flew low over the water towards their nest in the bull-rushes.

A water hen dove for grubs. Removing some twigs, Virginia lay back, rolling onto her side and looking up at her beau.

–This is safe and nice, Michael.

He lay beside her, looking at the curve of her cheek. After a while he touched her hand and felt her fingertips press his. He felt his throat tighten.

–You are my love, Virginia.

He reached forward and kissed her on the lips. Her mouth opened slightly, and he tentatively caressed her tongue with his. She responded with caresses of her own.

He felt her fingers on his chest. He kissed her on the neck and lips again, and cupped her breast with his hand. He felt her breasts become firm. Then suddenly she became rigid in his arms.

–We can't go further, Michael. Let's compose ourselves.

Michael groaned, not letting go.

–You know I care for you very deeply, she said.

He lifted his head and kissed her again. She kissed him back, then broke off again.

–Michael, there's an end of it. Stop.

She broke away, stood and smoothed her blouse and frock. He felt a brief flare of anger. Then remorse.

–Virginia, I didn't mean to go quite so far.

–No, there are two of us here, you're not to blame, she said, offering him her hand. We'd best make a move.

Michael looked at his watch.

–It's almost ten thirty.

They walked up through the fields to the house, silhouetted against the low sky. Inside, at the foot of the stairs, Michael kissed Virginia goodnight.

—I take it you'll do communion and skip breakfast?

—Right, just a glass of water. Don't forget to call me in the morning.

—I'm very happy you're here, Virginia.

In his homily the next morning, the parish priest, Father Fogerty, asked the congregation to pray for peace in Europe and continued good weather until the harvest was in.

The choir sang *Salve Regina*.

—Do you hear that high soprano? Michael whispered to Virginia. That's Deirdre. Voice of an angel.

Virginia nodded in reply.

Dr. Sullivan left his weekly envelope in the collection, and the family walked to lunch at The Coach House, an inn about a mile outside town.

—Was this really a Coach House, Dr. Sullivan? asked Virginia.

—Yes, up to about fifteen years ago, coaches going to Cork and Waterford stopped here regularly. Now all that traffic is by train. Mrs. Sullivan and I stayed here for several weeks when we first came to Rosnua. We have happy memories of this place, don't we Annie?

—We do indeed Tom. Though that was a long time ago, said Mrs. Sullivan.

—True. Almost thirty years.

After lunch, there was Peach Melba and tea on the terrace. Dr. Sullivan, Chris and Michael had brandy and coffee at a table in the orchard farther below.

—It looks terribly like there will be war in Europe, said Dr. Sullivan quietly. I didn't want to say this earlier as it upsets your mother. If France is attacked, then Britain will be compelled to intercede. So Jack will be involved.

—England's wars are not our wars. Why must he fight? We're a separate country, said Chris.

Michael felt the blood rush to his face. His father spoke for him.

—What you say is partly true Chris. But as a member of the United Kingdom, we will be involved. There's no getting away from it. We must enjoy this peaceful weekend. It may be our last for some time.

They pondered the notion in silence.

—You're travelling to Sligo on Wednesday, Michael? asked Chris.

—Yes, by Limerick Junction. Virginia's parents are expecting us. It will be good to meet them.

—I'm sorry to miss the threshing, father, said Chris.

—No apologies, these early days at Hickman's are very important. You must establish yourself. I wouldn't dream of having you miss a day of work, said Dr. Sullivan.

That evening Tom Murtagh arrived with his threshing machine. They heard it puffing half a mile away, then caught the heavy whiff of coal fumes. Brian and Rosemary ran outside.

—You've come a day early, Tommy, said Dr. Sullivan.

—Yes, I have doctor. I've got my dates mixed up. The great weather has me busier than I expected. I hope it's all right?

—Of course. Thank you for serving us first.

—That's a pleasure, Doctor.

—Oh, Michael, Virginia. This means you won't be able to go on that picnic to Dunamase. I'm terribly sorry, Virginia, I know you were looking forward to seeing the ruins, said Dr. Sullivan.

—Not to worry, Dr. Sullivan, although I will miss our picnic lunch.

—Oh, and Chris will be able to help for a couple of hours.

The high pink-timbered machine belched smoke and steam and seemed top heavy. Tommy and his helper had trouble getting the machine and its paraphernalia into the back area of Oaklands, but finally, after much discussion and pacing off distances, the most suitable position was achieved. The thresher was set and ready for action the following morning.

Just after dawn, the engine was coaxed into life. As it coughed and roared, the smoke brought neighbours from the entire area. Mr. and Miss Fisher brought their hayforks and a flagon of cider.

Other neighbours came from across the lake and river, each with their own hayfork. They were weather-beaten, hardened men who walked quickly with a hunger for work in their stride.

Murtagh's helper, Jimmy Gordon, opened the reek and threw the sheaves of oats to others on top of the thresher. At the front of the thresher stood Dr. Sullivan and his farmhand Seamus.

They held jute bags below the little trap door of the machine. As the first of the golden grains poured out, Dr. Sullivan scooped a handful into his fist and examined them in the palm of his hand.

Then he put a few grains into his mouth and chewed them slowly with his eyes closed.

—Great stuff, that, he declared, a broad smile on his face.

Michael stood at the back of the machine where the straw poured out. Using his hayfork on the straw, he built the circular base of a reek (*rick or stack*). There was a certain skill in this, but Michael had done it many times before. A stream of sweat formed at the nape of his neck and flowed down his back. His tongue stuck to the roof of his mouth. He stole a quick glance at his father, who also seemed to be in a lather of sweat. Then, as if by telepathy, his mother, Virginia, and Deirdre came with glasses and jugs of cider. The work paused for a moment as everyone slaked their thirst.

When the grain in a bag reached within four inches of its lip, Dr. Sullivan and Seamus quickly changed it. Chris and other men carried the full bags to the loft, a long low stone building with a wooden floor.

Starting at the back wall, they poured the grain out onto the floor. Since the bags were open, the men just bent forward and the grain poured over their shoulders. Back at the thresher, Rosemary gathered the bags for her father and Seamus to reuse.

Around one o'clock, they paused and went inside for a meal of cold chicken, potato salad and cider. The children drank buttermilk. A sense of teamwork and good humour dominated the long kitchen table. All were conscious of work still to be done. The pause was brief.

—We'd best continue, said the doctor, rising from the table at a little after two.

The thresher droned on into the evening. Michael, high atop a second reek, saw it was time to begin another. He jumped down and began placing the straw in another circle.

At twilight there were four reeks of straw and the barley and oats had disappeared. The threshing wound down. Getting the machine out from the back of the house was as complicated as getting it in.

After much backtracking, pushing and shunting, the thresher finally rounded the side of the house, crossed the gravel path and exited the front gates. Brian and Rosemary followed it down the road.

—Come on in now, the two o' ye, Mrs. Sullivan called. You've done great work. It's time for milk and biscuits and bed.

—Mother, I want to see the new grain, said Rosemary.

—Of course you can Rosemary. Michael will show you.

—May I come too? asked Virginia.

—By all means. It's a sight to see.

—Come here, Rose, said Michael, leading her up the stone stairs to the loft.

The rich-coloured grain gleamed darkly in the twilight, covering the floor and rising halfway up the walls. All three stood entranced, afraid to break the spell.

—It's really beautiful, Michael, said Rosemary finally. We've lots of food for the chickens and the cows.

—Yes, and lots for us as well Rose. Father will take about half of it to the mill.

Tuesday morning the family saw off the young couple at Maryborough station.

—We don't want you to leave Virginia, said Mrs. Sullivan. But of course you must. Your parents will be anxious to see you.

—Come back soon Virginia, said Dr. Sullivan as he kissed her goodbye.

—I will Doctor.

—You'll send Brian and me cards from Sligo? said Rosemary.

—Of course. We both will.

With much steam and smoke, their train moved out to open country, and they began their journey.

—We'll be in Sligo by half-four Michael. Just in time for tea.

It was the first time Michael had seen County Clare. Ruined castles seemed to appear every three miles or so.

—Clare has been ruled by many chieftains, said Virginia. But nearly all were dispossessed by Cromwell. The ruins remain.

—Good farming country this, said Michael. I wouldn't mind owning 50 acres or so here said Michael as they reached East Galway.

—But what about your career at the bank? You're not going to give that up, are you?

—No, of course not. But I'm a farmer at heart Virginia. Perhaps in the future I'll transfer to Tuam or Loughrea and be able to combine careers as Father has done.

—Yes, though you'll need someone to share your life and the farm-work.

—Well, I may have already found her. I think perhaps you know her.

—Who is the vixen?

–She's sitting quite close to me right now.

–Ah! said Virginia, poking him in the ribs.

While they waited at Claremorris for the Dublin train to arrive, Michael read a loose copy of *The Irish Independent*. The Government proposed to put the Irish National Volunteers on a military footing until the European crisis was over. A hundred thousand rifles would be given out to the Volunteers.

–An awful lot has happened over the last three days, said Michael, shaking his head.

–But Michael, does it really affect us?

–I'm afraid it does, Virginia. Or at least it will.

–Can't we forget it for now and enjoy the rest of our holiday?

–Of course we can, love.

The train from Dublin arrived, and with it, fresh copies of the *Independent*. **England declares war against Germany** screamed the headline. Michael's stomach dropped like a lead weight.

Virginia took the paper from him and read aloud:

–"Owing to the summary rejection by the German Government of the request made by his Majesty's Government that the neutrality of Belgium be respected, a state of war exists between it and Great Britain as from 11.00 p.m. on August 4th."

The platform whistle blew, doors slammed, and the train lurched forward.

–Michael, what does it mean? Should we change our plans and go back?

–Certainly not. This is our holiday.

The train sped northwest through acres of heather and yellow gorse. They spoke little.

But when the train passed through the low grey granite of the Ox Mountains, their good spirits returned. Below was the unspoiled inlet of Sligo, green pasture flowing down to the shore, the tabletop of Ben Bulben off to the right, all bathed in sunlight.

–I've never seen beauty like this Virginia, he sighed, linking her arm.

–Now you see why I love home so much Michael. I really don't want to live anywhere else.

They disembarked and waited for Virginia's parents. Some minutes later, a pony and trap clopped up to the now-quiet station. Virginia waved at her mother and sighed.

But as her parents got down, and Virginia introduced them to Michael, there was a noticeable sadness.

–Mother, what is it? said Virginia.

Mr. Martin handed his daughter a telegram, already open.

```
MISS VIRGINIA MARTIN THE DEATH OF MARTINA
RYAN'S FATHER LEAVES US SHORT STAFFED AT
VINCENT'S STOP REQUEST YOU RETURN TO WORK
IMMEDIATELY STOP PLEASE ADVISE STOP MOTHER
DYMPHNA STOP
```

Virginia handed the slip of paper to Michael.

–What will you do? asked Mr. Martin.

–They wouldn't telegram unless it was an emergency, she said.

She looked at Michael.

Crestfallen, he nodded.

–Father–please reply Yes, said Virginia.

Mrs. Martin began to cry.

–Oh daughter, you've only just arrived. This is your holiday.

Her father put his arm around his wife and put his lips to her lowered forehead.

–We will miss you greatly. he said to his daughter. Perhaps it will be good for your reputation.

Recovering herself, Mrs. Martin asked what train Virginia would take.

Virginia looked at the date on the telegram; it had arrived two days ago. The hospital would be expecting an answer by now. She knew the train schedule by heart; in an hour or so, the carriage they had just stepped off would be travelling east again through the night.

–This is the one, she said. Michael, you could remain here for some days, to meet my family.

–Virginia, I would love to, but I go where you go.

The four stood in silence. The pony pawed the ground.

–Then let us enjoy the time we have, said Mr. Martin.

He gestured to the station restaurant, and they walked slowly in.

The door closed quietly in the dark.

Chapter Three

Mansion House, Dublin, September 1914

Michael yawned. His first day back at the bank had felt longer than his whole holiday. Without much forethought he had been thrown into training the new recruits in the basics of customer service: how to balance their deposits and cash floats. He even taught a little bank history, how it was founded by the Liberator Daniel O'Connell. The trainees were eager, but Michael still felt the effects of two straight days of travel.

After work Michael took the cross-city tram and was soon drifting in and out of sleep. The dulled voices of balladeers in the street passed through the window: new songs about Home Rule, kicking the Kaiser back home and the greatness of Redmond. Recruitment posters with Lord Kitchener's eyes and moustache, and fat commanding finger were everywhere.

One poster had a sad woman–Ireland–playing her harp while men in khaki gathered protectively around her.

Deciding to walk the rest of the way to Belgrave Square, Michael noticed, as he crossed Portobello Bridge, a parade of young women with Union Jacks and green Irish flags.

Were they demonstrating for the vote? he wondered. No. They were chanting about freedom for Belgium and small nations. He increased his pace to get away from them, but to no avail. A woman broke away from the group. She pressed a small Union Jack and a white feather of cowardice on him.

–Excuse me. Sir. Why are you still in civilian clothes? The Germans are racing through Belgium, raping nuns and killing children. To fight for Belgium is to fight for Ireland.

Michael felt both anger and shame. What right had this woman to question him and his motives? Certainly, if the newspapers were to be believed, Belgium was suffering.

But was that his concern?

Feeling the blood rush to his face, he made an excuse and rushed into Church of Our Lady of Refuge. Holy hour was coming to an end. He knelt and prayed for guidance.

He had to make a decision soon. After he'd placed the blessed sacrament back in the tabernacle, Father Menton, who had served in the parish for two years, raised his hand to address the congregation.

–Forgive me. I'd like to speak to you of a personal matter. I won't keep you long.

3 - Mansion House, Dublin, September 1914

Expressing his shock at the atrocities committed by the German army in Belgium, Father Menton announced that he'd be leaving the parish to serve as an army chaplain.

—I cannot in good conscience stand by while soldiers of the Dublin Fusiliers and other Irish Regiments face the hardship and horrors of war, he said. So I've applied to serve as a chaplain at the front, preferably with an Irish Regiment. My offer has been accepted and I leave on Tuesday.
I've made many friends during my service here in Rathmines. I shall miss you all. However, I feel called to bring Christ's comfort and sustenance to our soldiers. I ask a remembrance in your prayers. I will remember you in my Masses.

The congregation broke into spontaneous applause. Blushing slightly, Father Menton led the acolytes towards the sacristy. Michael wondered if the priest's courage and devotion to duty wasn't somehow a sign to him as to the decision he should make.

The next morning *Freeman's Journal* told of thousands of refugees arriving in Brussels. Many of the reports were written by Thomas Kettle, the barrister and Nationalist M.P.

> ...
> The following day Belgium transferred its seat of government to Antwerp. On Thursday, August 20th, a procession of German soldiers in green-grey uniforms proceeded to the accompaniment of military bands along the Chaussée de Louvain and the Grands Boulevards toward Brussels' Gare du Nord. A crowd, stunned speechless, glared at the goose-stepping troops.
> The German forces had now reached the Athens of Belgium—the university city of Louvain. Their soldiers behaved in exemplary fashion, buying postcards and souvenirs, standing in line with civilians and paying for their purchases. However, on the 24th, a German soldier was shot in the leg. Tensions grew.
> On Tuesday the 25th the Belgian army at Malines made a sudden sharp attack on the rearguard of the German army, flinging them back in disarray on Louvain. In the city there was gunfire and confusion when German soldiers felt they were being shot at by civilians. In retaliation, and as a gesture of German might, Louvain was set ablaze street by street. Its

> churches, university and priceless library were destroyed.

Two days later in Parliament John Redmond said that in no quarter of the world had the heroism of the Belgians been received with more genuine enthusiasm than in Ireland.

> ...
> The spectacle of a small nation making these heroic sacrifices in defence of their independence and honour, against overwhelming odds, appeals in a very special way to the sentiments and feelings of Ireland, he said. 1 wish to make it clear that with all their hearts, the people of Ireland are in sympathy with Belgium, and that they are willing to do what rests with them to assist her in the maintenance of her independence.

Kettle's reports appeared in *The Freeman's Journal* and later in *The London Daily News*. He told of crowds of refugees in the streets of Antwerp and of Belgian troops arriving there, blood, dust and sweat mingled in a hideous paste of war on their unshaven faces.

On September 6th the Germans sacked Termonde, another university town, and bombarded Malines and its cathedral. The barrister journalist described a train journey from Ghent to Termonde, the countryside colourful with gardens: The geraniums will never again look like fire. They will look like blood. At the bridge of Termonde, beauty was replaced by a town withered by war, its streets transformed to a tumbled avalanche of brick, stone, twisted iron and scattered glass.

General Sommerfeld had demanded a ransom of two million francs to save the town. When this was not forthcoming, he ordered his soldiers to spray the houses with benzene and set them ablaze. He spared only the museum and the Hotel de Ville. The hospital, orphanage and convent were burned.

On Friday September 4th *The Independent* reported that the French government had transferred all administrative functions to Bordeaux. The defence of Paris was to be handled by General Gallieni, the Military Governor. *God, things are going from bad to worse*, thought Michael as he read.

It was low tide on Sandymount Strand. The sun shone brilliantly on the shallow water. In the distance, off Howth Head, a yacht race was in progress. Michael told Virginia of Father Menton's announcement as they walked on Sunday afternoon.

—He is a man of great conviction, who's seen his duty and isn't losing time Virginia. I wish I'd his courage.

—You do, Michael, I know you do.

She kissed his cheek.

—Thanks for your confidence, Virginia. I know Belgium is suffering terribly. Irishmen have already fought at the Marne. But is this war really our war? Chris says it isn't.

—Mr. Redmond says one should volunteer for the defence of Ireland, but if I volunteer, I want to do more than that. There's talk of a '*Pals battalion*' in the Dublin Fusiliers, and if there's the same thing for the men of the Queen's County area, I'd volunteer love. I'm going to visit my parents next weekend to hear their views.

—Well Michael, personally I'd prefer you stayed here as part of Mr. Redmond's National Volunteers for the defence of this country. But if you decide to volunteer for service in an Irish Regiment, I'll be very proud of you. Let's put this aside for now and enjoy the day.

They continued walking along the strand, had afternoon tea at the Pavilion Gardens in Kingstown, and watched the new Chaplin comedy in the cinema there.

The following Friday, Michael was supervising one of his new charges as he balanced his drawer, when a tremendous roar rose from College Green. He looked out to see The Viceroy and Lady Aberdeen, sitting stiffly in their official state carriage, headed by outriders as it swung past the Bank of Ireland on its way to Dublin Castle.

But the Viceroy and his Lady took this route nearly every day, Michael thought. Most days they were virtually ignored. What was different today? Michael glanced quizzically at Lally.

At that moment John Joe, the bank porter, shouted excitedly.

—The Home Rule Bill has been passed! The Home Rule Bill has been passed!

The Viceroy and Lady Aberdeen bowed wearily and perfunctorily to the cheering throng. Had it not been for the bodyguard of cavalry clattering over the cobblestones to the front and rear, the carriage would have been enveloped by the tributary streams of enthusiastic masses converging simultaneously from Grafton Street, Dame Street, Westmoreland Street and Brunswick Street upon College Green.

—What a great day for Ireland, said Mr. Moore. If you cashiers can balance your tills accurately, you may take off early.

—Three cheers for Mr. Moore, said Lally.

–Enough o' that, Mr. Lally. Enough o' that, said Mr. Moore as he retreated flush-faced to his office.

Later, in O'Neill's, Lally passed Michael a tattered copy of *The Evening Mail*.

–The two earlier editions are completely sold out. Martin here loaned me the house copy.

Michael gave Martin McGlinn a wave as the elderly publican approached them through the crowded bar.

–Good to see ye back again lads, said McGlinn. It's a great day for the country. I'm thinking it's the greatest since the Liberator was elected. What'll ye have there lads? It's on the house.

–Two pints then, Martin, and thank you very much, said Michael.

–Ye'll have something stronger, or ye're not my friends.

–Two Redbreast then, followed by two pints, said Lally.

–My tab, said McGlinn. I'll talk more to ye later, I have a few people to say hello to.

–Thanks again, Martin. Your very good health.

–No, Ireland's. God save her.

–Amen.

Pressed against a comer of the crowded bar, Michael read *The Evening Mail*. The details were sketchy, but the gist of the story was that, anticipating parliamentary defeat, Law, Carson and the Conservative opposition in the House had abandoned the Chamber. Prior to the Bill receiving Royal Assent Redmond had issued an official declaration to the people of Ireland. *The Mail* carried the statement, and Michael read it before reading the events of the day.

> ...
> The democracy of Great Britain listened to our appeal and have kept faith with Ireland. It is now a duty of honour for Ireland to keep faith with them. A test to search men's souls has arisen.
> The Empire is engaged in the most serious war in history. It is a just war. It is a war for the defence of the sacred rights and liberties of small nations (...) Involved in it is the fate of France, our kindred country, the chief nation of that powerful Celtic race to which we belong; the fate of Belgium, to whom we are attached by the common desire of a small nation to assert its freedom; and the fate of Poland, whose

> sufferings and whose struggles bear so marked a resemblance to our own. It is a war for high ideals of human government and international relations.
>
> Ireland would be false to her history, and to every consideration of honour, good faith, and self-interest, did she not willingly bear her share in its burdens and its sacrifices. We have. always given our quota, and more than our quota to the firing line, and we shall do so now.

Requesting that Irish recruits be kept together in an Irish Brigade, and pointing out its advantages with regards to national pride and the formation of a home army following the war, the article continued:

> ...
>
> I feel certain that the young men of our country will respond to this appeal with the gallantry of their race.

Redmond concluded his statement with an appeal.

> ...
>
> Countrymen of a different creed (...), accept the friendship we have so consistently offered, to allow this great war to swallow up all the small issues in the domestic government of Ireland which now divide us; that, as our soldiers are going to fight, to shed their blood, and to die at each other's side (...) their union in the field may lead to a union in their home and that their blood may be the seal that will bring Ireland together in one nation, and in liberties equal and common to all.

—This statement by Redmond is eloquent, don't you think Jim? asked Michael.

—It is indeed Mick. But you know Johnny Red has said this several times already. However, this speech conveys the heart and soul of '*the Dollar Dictator*'. I'm sure it will have a profound effect here.

The newspaper contained further bulletins.

Following the release of his statement Redmond and other Members of the Commons went to the House of Lords for the proclamation, returning from the Lords at 12:22 p.m.

The Deputy Speaker informed Members of the Commons, of the Royal Assent to the Police Constable (Naval and Military Service Act) other acts and the Government of Ireland Act.

The announcement was greeted by Nationalist, Ministerial, and Labour cheers. The Chief Whip, Mr. Crooks, rose and asked if it would be in order to sing *God Save the King.*

Permission was granted. Crooks sang the first note, then members of the House joined in singing the first verse lustily. Mr. Redmond called for three cheers. After the cheering, Mr. Crooks called out God Save Ireland, to which Mr. Redmond instantly replied God Save England Too. Members then filed out, first shaking hands with the Deputy Speaker, then the Clerk of the House. Proceedings ended for the day at 12:30p.m.

–So Home Rule is law, stated Michael.

–Yes, finally Mick. It's too bad though that its implementation is to be postponed for the duration of the present world crisis.

–Yes, it is Jim, but it doesn't look as though this war will last long. After all, we've won the Battle of the Marne and if the Expeditionary Forces and our Allies can continue to contain the Germans, the war could be over by Christmas.

–That's a big if, Mick. You saw how quickly the Huns swept across Belgium.

–Yes, but the Belgians were badly armed. The French will beat them back with our help.

–What about yourself, Mick are you still thinking of joining up?

–Well, now that Home Rule is law, Britain's crisis is our crisis. I'm going to Rosnua tomorrow evening to talk the matter over with my parents. If Queen's County has a Pals Battalion, I'll probably go.

Someone began singing *A Nation Once Again* and everyone joined in. This was followed by *Ireland Boys Hurray, The West's Awake*, and *God Save Ireland.*

Lally signalled for sandwiches. McGlinn himself brought them, still in a highly elated mood.

–You know, this is the most crowded this place has been since I bought it.

–Well I hope you're not giving too many drinks on the house, Martin, said Michael. As an Aunt of mine in your business used to say, "Let no talkin' stop the drinkin'."

–Ah sure, don't be talking, Mr. Sullivan. We're almost after running out of porter. I haven't sold so much drink in years, and if I give the odd one on the house, I won't go bankrupt.

Towards 9:00 p.m. Michael looked at his watch. The skin on his face felt quite tight now.

He was merry, not drunk. However, he realized he was nearing his limit.

—Gosh, I'm going to have to go Jim. If I don't get seven hours sleep I'll be no use tomorrow morning, and I want to be in good shape when I see my parents tomorrow evening.

—Say no more Mick, I'm in the same boat myself. We may as well call it a night. I'll walk a bit of the way with you.

Wishing McGlinn a good night, the two friends walked out to Fleet Street.

Michael felt tired at work the next morning, but the day was not too busy. He balanced his cash at midday and caught the 1:30 train.

His parents met the train. As they motored to Oakland's, Michael sensed that his mother was tense.

—How is Virginia? she asked as they ate a mixed grill and drank strong tea.

—She's tired at times, Mother. But her training is going very well and Mother Dymphna and those in charge in Vincent's seem happy with her.

—We're delighted, said his father. She's a kind and giving person Michael. You're lucky to have found her.

—I count myself very lucky Father.

—But you didn't travel all this way to talk of Virginia, did you Michael? asked his mother.

—No, Mother. I'm trying to make an important decision. I'm thinking of volunteering. I'd like to join the Leinsters. Many of the lads I went to school with here in Rosnua have probably already joined.

—I'm completely against this, Michael, his Mother said instantly. I don't want you fighting in Belgium.

—Mr. Redmond says that in fighting for Belgium, we're fighting for small nations, meaning Ireland, said Michael in confusion.

—Both your father and I have seen the cost of war Michael. Your cousin Jack Healy died in the Boer War. Your Uncle Chris Sullivan fought in that same war and has never been the same.

—But Jack my brother is involved?

—Of course he is. As a naval surgeon. He has to be. But as a doctor he's removed from day to day combat. As a soldier you'll be in the thick of things.

His mother's face had caved in. He had never seen her lose control this way before. It was only when he saw the first tear hit the side of her nose that he realized how deeply she felt. Her voice trembled.

—I don't want you to die in a foreign land, she sobbed.

He rose from the table and kissed her on the cheek. She melted into his arms.

His mother began to cough her way through some incomprehensible sentences. He shushed her, told her to take her time.

—It's all right Mother. It's all right.

—It's not all right, she sobbed. You're my son. I don't want to lose you.

—I'm not going to die Mother. I'll take every precaution. Besides, Mr. Redmond says it will be a short war.

His father rushed over and held both of them in his arms.

—There, there, Annie. Stop crying. It's going to be a short war. If Michael feels that he must volunteer, we can't stand in his way.

—He's our second son, Tom. We've loved him from the day he was born. Why does he have to fight? Why isn't Redmond himself part of the fighting force?

—I can't explain this, Annie. There is talk that the leader's son and his brother have volunteered.

—That's their business Tom. I don't want Michael in the army.

—But he's of age Annie, almost twenty-four. If he feels he should enlist we must respect his wishes.

His voice breaking, Michael interjected.

—Mother, I've prayed and thought deeply about this. Belgium is being overrun by the German army. Priests and nuns are being murdered. Redmond says that Ireland and Belgium have deep ties and that we must help them now in their great need. It's something I feel I have to do. The bank says they'll hold our jobs for the duration of the conflict.

His mother finally regained control. Wiping her eyes, she managed a weak smile and drank the last of her tea.

Late that evening Michael walked the bottom fields near the lake with his father. They discussed things further.

—I never expected mother to be so upset.

—Nor did I son. She's only behaving as any mother would. Jack has to serve. You don't. Don't worry too much about her. I'll talk with her in the coming days. She'll come round Michael.

—I think Redmond has a valid point here. This is as close to a just war as I've seen. Your mother and I sensed the reason for your visit. Neither of us are political, you know. As you say, the Home Rule Bill is now law. This is a war in defence of small nations. You've said you feel you should volunteer. As a matter of fact, you'll make us very proud. There. I've said my piece. I want you to enjoy the rest of your time with us.

Sunday, following mass, Michael found out from Tommy O'Gorman, an old school friend, that there was a Pal's brigade from his area.

–You'll have to report to Birr to sign up, Tommy said. But training is in County Cork. A lot of the lads have joined up already.

That evening, his parents accompanied him to Maryborough, where he caught the train.

–Thank you both for your help and advice with regards to my decision, he told them. I probably won't see you both again 'till I'm leaving to enlist. I love you very much.

–We love you and we're proud of you Michael, said his father.

–Mind yourself now, and we'll see you soon, said his mother. Give our love to Virginia.

–I will, mother.

Michael mounted the train quickly and went directly to his compartment. He hated farewells.

Next day the papers told of a speech Redmond had made to a group of Irish Volunteers at Woodenbridge, County Wicklow. As in his Commons speech, Redmond appealed to Ireland's sense of duty, and in conclusion advised his listeners:

> ...
> Go on drilling and make yourselves efficient for the work, and then account yourselves as men, not only in Ireland itself, but wherever the firing-line extends, in defence of right, of freedom, and of religion in this war.

Overnight, posters appeared throughout the city, announcing...

> Public Meeting at The Mansion House on Friday,
> September 25th, at 8:00 p.m.
> Mr. Asquith, The Prime Minister,
> Mr. Redmond, Leader of the Irish Party,
> Their Excellencies - the Viceroy and Lady Aberdeen -
> the Lord Mayor, and other dignitaries will attend.

This may be just another recruiting rally, but it's not to be missed, thought Michael. But there was another happy event taking place at the Mansion House, and he wasn't going to miss it for the world. A surprise concert in aid of the Relief Fund.

He left a note at the hospital for Virginia, arranging to meet her at the Shelbourne that evening.

They had a light supper at the hotel and then went down Dawson Street.

–I want you to close your eyes for the next hundred yards now, said Michael.

–What are you up to, you imp? she asked, linking his arm.

–You trust me, don't you?

–Of course.

–And I've never treated you badly?

–No.

–Well trust me now.

The concert was in the Supper Room of the Mayor's Residence. Virginia kept her eyes closed until they reached the entrance.

–All right, you can open your eyes now, said Michael.

When she did, Virginia saw posters of a white-haired man, heavily moustached, wearing a slouch-hat and plus fours: the composer and folk singer Percy French.

–Gosh you're a devil. That's what you are, Michael Sullivan. You know I've always wanted to see Percy French perform.

–Well, there you are Virginia. You people from the West have to support each other.

The elderly troubadour had the energy of a man of half his years. Accompanying himself on mandolin and guitar, he sang *Abdul Abulbul Amir*, *Eileen Og*, *Carmodies Mare*, *The Emigrant's Letter* and two recently written songs, *All by the Baltic Sea* and *Am Tag*. He ended his concert with a plea for contributions to the Relief Fund and said that all the proceeds of his concert would go towards it.

–Gosh. This is an evening I'll always remember, said Virginia as they walked back to her room on Baggot Street.

–We'll have many more, Virginia. We both have an early start in the morning, so we'd best say good night now. See you tomorrow, dearest.

–What will we do?

–Oh, I don't know. Perhaps we could see another Chaplin film or listen to a band concert in the Green.

–Yes, a band concert would be lovely Michael. See you at the Shelbourne at 6:00, then?

–6:00 it is.

3 - Mansion House, Dublin, September 1914

The following Friday Michael finished work a little after 3:00 p.m. Mr. Moore had given him permission to leave early. Expressing satisfaction with the way Michael was fulfilling his new responsibilities the manager enquired about several of Michael's charges. Then suddenly he confided that he had complimentary tickets for the Prime Minister's speech.

—How do you feel about the current world crisis? he asked Michael.

—Well, I feel it's pretty much a just war sir. What right have the Germans to march across Belgium pillaging and destroying churches and universities just so they can subdue France? The paper on Monday reported the destruction of Reims' Cathedral. Most of this is unnecessary.

—Yes it is Sullivan, but then war is dreadful. Let's hope it ends very soon.

The manager offered Michael two tickets for the Mansion House Meeting.

—Thank you sir. I'll take just one. I can only speak for myself.

—Fair enough then. I'll probably see you there.

Mr. Moore handed him a ticket.

Michael knew the crowds at the Mansion House would be large. He also wanted to buy some new shoes and decided to go to Gleeson's on Upper Sackville Street. He made his way quickly up Westmoreland Street and had just reached the Sackville Street end of O'Connell Bridge when the gestures of an orator standing on an improvised platform at Bachelors Walk caught his attention. There was a guard of honour of National Volunteers surrounding the platform, and the orator's words were punctuated with enthusiastic cheers from the enormous crowd that spilled across the bridgehead and down Eden Quay. The members of a piper's band who had played the speaker to the platform were leaning against the windows of Keogh's public house, popping in and out of its swinging doors.

There was something familiar about the speaker. That he was a Monsignor or bishop was clear from the purple below his roman collar. Pushing through the crowd, Michael recognized Dr. Duggan, the administrator of St. Mary's Pro Cathedral.

The tumult and the clamour died down. Dr. Duggan wheeled round and his hand floated in a rhetorical gesture towards Aston's Quay across the Liffey, where along the embankment, just a few feet above high-water mark, a gigantic poster proclaimed in heavy red lettering on a green field:

Join an Irish Brigade today and avenge Belgium.

Michael followed the direction of the priest's pointing finger. Simultaneously there arose another roar of applause, which ceased as Dr. Duggan motioned for silence.

—People of Dublin, just imagine how you would feel if the Huns came goose-stepping along the quays from the North Wall. (Dr. Duggan's left hand shot out dramatically eastwards, towards the mouth of the Liffey). Just imagine that, and you will realize how the towns and cities of poor little Catholic Belgium have suffered. Just imagine how you would feel if the Huns outraged the privacy and sanctity of your convents and treated your Irish nuns as they have treated the good Belgian sisters. Would you like to see them hacking the hands off your little children as they did to the little babies in Belgium?

—Citizens of Dublin, you have heard how the mayors of Belgian towns were shot in cold blood by these brutal Huns. Do you think they would spare our Lord Mayor?

—Do you think they would have any mercy on him and the other members of the Corporation, who had the public spirit and patriotism to strike the name of Professor Kuno Meyer off the roll of freedom of the city? Thank God that Hun has gone back to fight for the Fatherland. But I'll stop speaking now for a few minutes as I hear a band coming along, playing another contingent of our gallant Dublin Fusiliers to the North Wall. These men are going across the sea to avenge Belgium, to avenge the violation of Belgium's neutrality, to—

—What about the violation of the Treaty of Limerick? cut in a voice from the crowd.

Immediately there was a chorus of angry protests against the interrupter.

—He's a Sinn Feiner!

—He's a German spy!

—Hand him over to the polis!

—What's the polis doing?

The crowd swayed to and fro like a rugby scrum. Dr. Duggan gesticulated frantically, but his voice was drowned in the babel of protest. Michael regretted that he had plunged so deeply into the crowd. He tried to edge his way back to the pavement.

—Hold onto him and give him over to the polis! shouted a workman beside him who reeked of porter.

Michael was surprised at the change of attitude of the average Dubliner towards the police. The Dublin Metropolitan Police were liked by the people of Rathmines and Rathgar, not by the average Dubliner. Now these people of Smithfield wanted to hand over a heckler to them. Things had certainly changed since the Bachelors Walk shootings.

Yielding to the pressure of the crowd, Michael climbed the nearby bench and from this vantage point, he surveyed the core of the seething, swaying crowd.

Then suddenly a youth—hatless, his clothes in tatters, his face bleeding—darted out of the vortex, almost pulverizing Michael in his flight towards Sackville Street. Just before rounding the plinth of the O'Connell statue the runaway wheeled round, shook his fist at the crowd, and yelled.

—Up the Kaiser!

—That fellow's a German spy, I know him, yelled a young woman smelling of musk and stale porter.

—Ah go on, Mary Agnes. It's coddin' yez are, chuckled a blowsy elderly woman in a moth-eaten, black-beaded dolman of the pre-Boer War era and a black bonnet with three twisted feathers.

—Have a sup o' this.

She produced a quart jug of foaming porter from under her dolman. The younger woman grabbed the flagon and drank long and lustily. Then with a sigh of satisfaction she handed it back to her friend.

—It's a bit late in the day meh-be to be praying that you may never die in childbirth, Mrs. Casey, ma'am, but may himself and the chisellers come back safe from the wars.

—I was middling drought, ma'am, and that's grand creamy porter.

—It's from Keogh's beyond, Mary Agnes, said Mrs. Casey. Keogh's pull the best pint in Dublin. But Mary Agnes, how do you know that lad is a spy?

—Don't I know him, Mrs. Casey, ma'am? All of them Sinn Feiners is spies, and they're all for the Kaiser. I seen him in O'Riordan's and him reading *An Toglac*, that rag that was oppressed by the polis yesterday and the printers took away in the Black Maria, an' as they stepped into the Black Maria the crowd was set to kill them.

—Oh! the dirty scut, Mary Agnes. Tis a pity the crowd didn't massacre him. And do you know what, Mary Agnes, it's just dirty begrudging spite against me and you and the likes of us who has the government separation allowance, that makes them say they're for the Kaiser?

—Well anyways, isn't it grand to hear Father Duggan. They say he's a doctor too, and can cure soul and body. It's grand to hear him shaming all the scum o' the city into fighting for the poor little Belgians. The priests is against the Kaiser, Mrs. Casey, ma'am.

—All them 'circular' priests, like Father Duggan, that darlin' man, is for the war Mary Agnes, and it's only a few men from the orders is for the Kaiser; priests like the Abbot of the Cistercian monks in Mount Melleray. Them's the priests that take an oath on joinin' the order never to open their mouths 'til Ireland gets Home Rule.

—Well Mrs. Casey, ma'am, isn't it you that's knowledgeable in theology? But why wouldn't the priests be for the war, and the farmers getting' forty pounds for a bullock wouldn't sell for seven pounds a month ago? And you and me and the likes of us that has husbands and sons gettin' the separation allowance, and us able to take our sup o' porter at our ease, and read in the papers the grand news about the bloody wars is goin' on in Europe, and Berlin, and Paris and them other foreign parts.

—That's a grand day, Mr. Sullivan.

This was the slow drawl of a lean loose-jointed man in rough brown tweeds emerging from the crowd. He sported a bowler hat, with a high complexion, corn-coloured hair, a firm jaw and sagging shoulders. It was Michael's customer Sergeant McGinley of the D.M.P., the Dublin Metropolitan Police. He towered above everyone in the throng.

—Who are you on the lookout for, Tim?

—Quietly Michael. I'm on undercover duty here.

As if a man of that size could be inconspicuous, thought Michael.

—Sinn Feiners and Fenians who might disrupt this meeting, McGinley whispered.

—By the way, how was your time in Enniskerry?

—Very good, Michael, but far too short.

—People of Dublin, continued Dr. Duggan in a strong voice, I regret that some of you were so exasperated a few minutes ago by the ignorant remarks of a youthful heckler that he was in grave peril of being lynched. I implore you not to let me hear a repetition of such incidents. One word more. Mr. Asquith, the Prime Minister, is to address a meeting tonight at the Mansion House. I understand that the Citizen Army have threatened that they will not allow him to reach the Mansion House. I have been told that some of the good women of Dublin, whose husbands and sons are fighting the Huns at the moment, have threatened to box the ears of these tin soldiers and to throw them into the Liffey. I beg these patriotic women to leave the Citizen Army to the police. I shall now conclude by appealing once again to all the young men listening to me to join an Irish Brigade today and avenge Belgium.

Loud and prolonged cheers followed as the cleric waved to the throng and retreated to the rear of the platform. The pipe band of Trinity College, resplendent in their ancient Irish kilts, struck up *Let Erin Remember the Days of Old* and the crowd began to break up.

—What's the next public demonstration you have to observe, Tim? asked Michael.

He and the policeman were moving on, yielding to the pressure of the dispersing throng.

—Well, there's supposed to be a meeting of National Volunteers, that's Redmond's volunteers, at the Rotunda. There may be some trouble there, as John MacNeill of the Irish Volunteers split from them yesterday evening.

—Oh. I'm on my way to Gleeson's to buy shoes, so we're going the same way.

—You know Michael, even with this Home Rule Bill, Dublin is becoming a difficult place to maintain order.

—How is that, Tim? The crowd just now at Bachelors Walk seemed quite friendly.

—The mood here has changed since July, I'll grant you that. But if there's another incident of the type we had eight weeks ago the whole mood of the country could change again.

We, and the powers that be, could be in real trouble. Ye see every second woman in this part of Dublin is getting some kind of separation allowance at the moment. They all have either a husband or a son in the Fusiliers. You heard the two women talking there during the meeting.

—Yes.

—And what they were saying is no more than the truth. But what's going to happen if a lot of these men die in battle? The mood could change overnight. Besides, too many people have guns here.

Do you recognize the stocky man with the set jaw? There he is now at the comer of Prince's Street. That man with a rifle on his shoulder.

—Oh yes, that's Pearse the teacher and writer, isn't it? He does write well. Isn't he allied with John MacNeill?

—Yes, we're keeping an eye on him. However, he's such a dreamer we don't expect him to do anything impulsive.

There seemed to be some sort of a commotion over at Nelson's Pillar.

—What's going on over there, Tim?

—Well, you know what that is now Michael. That's the Citizen Army, coming along in its full strength of sixty from Liberty Hall. Isn't it a funny sight to see them having to get police protection? Do you see the constables walking in front of them and alongside them? Well, they're just seeing them past the gaggle. The fisherwomen around the Pillar always attack them when they pass that way. Oh Jesus, do you hear the screeching and cursing of them women? Them women is that wild, they'd think nothing of clawing the eyes out of them. And do you see how the constables have got between the women and the

Citizen Army? Now see them trying to break through the cordon. Be Christ they'll get through too.

Tim McGinley's commentary on the Citizen Army was drowned out by a chorus of shrill invective. One overweight woman threw a couple of mackerel at their leader and hit him directly on the jaw.

–To hell with the Citizen Army. Why aren't they fightin' for the Belgians in the Dublin Fusiliers? the woman shouted.

Not missing a step, the red-haired NCO wiped his face with a large handkerchief.

–God her aim is good, Michael. Ye see now why they need our protection? said McGinley.

–Indeed I do, Tim.

–Right wheel, shouted the red-haired NCO as the Citizen Army swung down Sackville Street.

–You know that fellow has a fierce look about him. He's rearing for a scrap. I think I'd better walk behind them. The crowd might attack them at the bridge. I wouldn't put it past some of them lads that was at Dr. Duggan's meeting to throw the lot o' them into the Liffey.

–You're a hundred per cent right, Tim. Well. Perhaps I'll see you later at the Mansion House.

–That's if you can get in, Michael. There's bound to be five thousand people there.

–Well I'll try and get there early. Good luck.

McGinley's normal pace was a kind of shuffle, but as he walked behind the Citizen Army his disordered movements became more pronounced in contrast with the military precision of the rag tag group he was protecting. It was a deliberate gesture. He wanted to show that mentally and physically he was out of tune with Liberty Hall. The Citizen Army had just reached the comer of Prince's Street when they struck up their anthem to the air of *Tipperary*:

Tis the wrong way to crush the workers,
Tis the right thing to do
Tis the right thing to hate the bosses,
And ould Birrell and his crew.
Onward, Workers Union,
Forever we'll be true,
And we'll all join up behind Jim Larkin,

3 - Mansion House, Dublin, September 1914

And the Red Flag Aboo!

Well Larkin's a good man, thought Michael, remembering the Dublin Lockout fifteen months earlier. It was a long strike and caused a lot of hardship, but it did help the lot of the suffering labourer. It's a pity, though, that they had to arm themselves.

He was now at Gleeson's. The shoe salesman was efficient and outfitted Michael in a pair of black oxfords within ten minutes.

–Is there anything else you'd like to try on, sir? he asked, as Michael paid.

–No, but I see that you have equipment for army volunteers. So I may be back again after I enlist.

–Well, you know where we are.

–I do indeed. Thank you very much for now.

It was approaching 5:30 p.m., and the meeting at the Mansion House was to begin at 8 p.m. It would be best to get there at least an hour before. Michael stopped at a tea room near the Capitol Theater for a sandwich. Then he made his way back down Sackville Street and across the bridge. Westmoreland Street was crowded with people, most of them heading south.

At College Green an enormous gathering lined the sidewalks at the Bank of Ireland and at Trinity College. Straining for a better vantage point, fearless youths stood on the plinths of Goldsmith's and Burke's statues, and on Grattan's statue directly opposite.

Walking purposefully and proceeding at the back of the throng, Michael continued in the direction of the Mansion House. Entry to Grafton Street was blocked by a cordon of D.M.P.

The crowds were orderly and relaxed. Many made jokes with policemen. All smaller streets connecting to Dawson Street were also cordoned off. Both ends of Dawson Street were protected by a strong force. The Mansion House was guarded by 400 Irish Volunteers, all fully armed. Rival interests were represented among the crowd. On one side, 'sandwich men' carried placards urging recruits to the Royal Dublin Fusiliers, and directing them to the recruiting office on Grafton Street. On the other side of the street handbills were distributed for a Nationalist Rally in St. Stephen's Green at which Jim Larkin and others were to speak.

Arriving at the Mansion House, Michael had to present his ticket at least three times before being admitted to the Round Room. The large hall was already two-thirds full. At the far end, a 'veteran table', draped in green velvet, covered the width of the room. Behind it were three rows of formal chairs. The six centre chairs in the first row were draped with red taffeta canopies. The arms of the city of Dublin and its French motto, *Prêt pour mon pays*, fronted the canopy above the center chair.

The wall behind the stage was draped in Green Irish, and Red Imperial Standards. To the right of the stage Michael recognized Tom Kettle, whose journalism he admired, chatting quietly with John Redmond's son. Both were already in army uniform. Near centre stage parliamentary leader John Dillon was in earnest conversation with Redmond's younger brother Willie. There were rumours that Willie, M.P. for Clare, had taken a commission and was eager to join the fray.

The room was filling up quickly; soon every available inch of space both there and in the gallery was occupied. Looking around Michael realized that he was among the few people of military age.

A few minutes after 8:00 Mr. Asquith—accompanied by his daughters Violet and Elizabeth, the Lord Lieutenant of Ireland, the Lord Mayor, the Home Secretary and others—entered the hall. The audience rose and cheered vociferously. Many clasped the Prime Minister's hand as he passed down the hall.

Minutes later, as Mr. Redmond took his place beside Asquith, the audience rose again and cheered with even more enthusiasm. Then the Lord Mayor, Alderman Lorcan Sherlock, rose to introduce Mr. Asquith.

—As Lord Mayor of Dublin and irrespective of my duty as chairman I take the liberty of telling the Prime Minister, with all deference, that the causes of this war and the issues involved are understood in Ireland.
As we understand it, this is a fight between honour and dishonour, a fight for the principle of the sacredness of contracts as against the policy of 'To hell with contracts.' Speaking in the name of the citizens of Dublin I say that the interests of every man in Ireland are vitally involved in the fight that is now going on. While we as Christians earnestly pray for a speedy cessation of the war, and are aghast at the terrible incidents which arise from it, we are sane enough also to recognize that there can be only one plausible solution and that is a satisfactory termination. With these few observations I now beg to introduce the Prime Minister.

There was a commotion at the front of the audience. A bearded man in a black frock-coat was shouting.

—This war is ungodly and unjust. It is not Ireland's war. It serves only the interests of British Imperialism.

The man was quickly subdued and forcibly removed from the room. As he passed, Michael thought he looked a little like the pacifist journalist Frank Sheehy Skeffington. But would Skeffington be so foolhardy as to proclaim his views to a convinced gathering of unionists?

Ignoring this incident, and smiling benevolently, the silver-haired Prime Minister began his speech.

—My Lord Mayor, I am here not as a partisan, nor even as a politician. I am here as, for the time being, the head of the King's Government, to command a land loyal and patriotic to take her place in defence of our common cause. My Lord Mayor, it is not part of my mission tonight, and at this time wholly unnecessary, to justify and still less to excuse the part of the Government of the United Kingdom at this supreme crisis in our national affairs. There have been wars in the past in regard to which there has been among us diversity of opinion, uneasiness as regards to the wisdom of diplomacy, anxiety as to the expediency of our policy, doubt as to the essential righteousness of our cause. This, My Lord Mayor, as you have said, is not the case today.

—We feel as a nation, or rather I ought to say here, looking round at our vast Empire in every quarter of the globe, as a family of nations. We are united in defending principles and in maintaining interests which are vital not only to the British Empire, but to all that is worth having in our common civilization and all that is worth hoping for in the future progress of mankind. What higher cause could arouse and enlist the best energies of a free people than to be engaged at one and the same time in the vindication of international good faith, in the protection of the weak against the strong? I am sure you agree with me. This demonstration proves that you believe that Imperial Germany is the author of this war. The proofs are manifold and overwhelming. I will not spend my time outlining them here.

The atmosphere in the auditorium was electric. The Prime Minister was sweeping his listeners along on a wave of emotion.

—The facts of this war ought to make a special appeal to the people of Ireland. Ireland is a loyal country. She would, I know, respond with alacrity to any summons which called her to take her place in the assertion and defence of our common interests. The issues raised by this war are of such a kind that, unless I mistake her people and misread her history, they touch a vibrant cord both in your imagination and in your conscience.

—How can you in Ireland, with the call of smaller nations, deny help to them in their struggle for freedom? Whether, as in the case of Belgium, to maintain that which she has won, or as in the case of the Balkan States, in regaining what they lost or in acquiring and putting upon a stable foundation what has never been fully theirs? Nor again can you Irishmen sit by. How could you, in cold detachment and with folded arms, in the company of our gallant Allies in France and Russia and Japan with whom we are opposing with worldwide resistance the pretensions which threaten the best hopes of mankind?

–During the last few weeks Sir John French and his heroic forces have worthily sustained our hopes. Losses have been heavy. Ireland has had many in this total. Over half a million recruits have joined the colours here at home and I come to ask you in Ireland, though you do not need my asking, to take your part. But we ask you, here in Ireland, for your help today. We ask Ireland, though smaller in number, to volunteer your sons and daughters for the common good.
We are promising the formation of an Irish Brigade, Mr. Asquith concluded.

–We shall, to the utmost limit that military expediency will allow, see that Irishmen, who have already associated in any district in training and in common exercises, shall be kept together and continue to recognize the corporate bond that now unites them. I do not say and I cannot say under what precise form of organization it will be, but I trust and believe, indeed I am sure, that the Volunteers will become a permanent, integral, and characteristic part of the defence forces of the Crown. What we want, what we ask, what we believe you are ready and eager to give, is the offering of a free people.

Acknowledging the applause with a broad smile and waves to the audience, the Prime Minister resumed his seat.

A stocky grey-haired man then strode confidently to the podium. The entire audience rose to its feet in sustained applause. Shouts of *Hurray for John Redmond!* and *Home Rule!* filled the auditorium.

The clamour lasted more than five minutes. Raising his hand high and thanking the assembly for its tremendous welcome, the leader began.

–A little more than a week ago in the House of Commons I took the liberty of saying to the Prime Minister that I hoped he would soon come to Dublin. I have come here tonight to join with the representatives of all parties, and of the citizens of the Metropolis of Ireland, to tell the Prime Minister, and through him, the people of Great Britain, that Ireland is in heartfelt sympathy with the objectives of this war, and that you will bear your share of its burdens. Already, as you are no doubt aware, I have declared in the House of Commons that in my judgement Ireland was bound to take this course.
Her right to autonomy has been conceded by the democracy of Great Britain. Therefore Ireland will feel bound in honour to take her place side by side with other autonomous nations and the King's Dominions in upholding her interests. Further than that, there is this consideration–that the heart of Ireland has been profoundly moved by the spectacle of the heroism and the suffering of Belgium.

This elicited sustained applause.

–I have heard some people speak of this war as an English war, and not an Irish war. This is absolutely and fundamentally untrue. Ireland's highest interests are at stake. For forty years of infinite labour and sacrifice we have been toiling, and slowly winning for our country, by the repeal of unjust laws, by the enactment of ameliorative measures, at least a chance of progress and prosperity. When I look back on the days of my boyhood and remember the appearance of Ireland and the Irish people—the cottages in which they had to live, the fields they were afraid to till for fear the toil of their labour would be taken away from them—when I remember all that, and travel through the country today and see the smiling face of a country filled with a prosperous and hopeful peasantry, I find it difficult to realize all that has been won for Ireland by those forty years of toil and labour in Parliament, and out of Parliament.

—All religious opinions, every one of them, is at stake in this war. It is hard to realize here in this delightful autumn weather. It is hard to realize in the midst of this apparent peace that Ireland is at war.
But that is so.

—It is true our cities are not being sacked. It is true our cathedrals and our universities have not been burned to the ground. It is true our peaceful and happy villages have not been levelled. It is true our women and children have not been slaughtered before our eyes. Why is that so? Under God, there is only one reason, and that is the Army and the Navy and the brave men, many of them gallant Irishmen, who are by day and night risking and giving their lives to defend our property, our liberty, and our honour. Withdraw this barrier, tomorrow, and in forty-eight hours, the liberties of Ireland will be annulled.

—Our country will be devastated, our cities sacked, our women and children slaughtered. Under these circumstances, is this not an Irish war?

Yes! cried everyone in the assembly.

—And what is Ireland's duty in this war?

—To fight! answered Michael and the assembly at the top of their lungs.

Redmond continued.

—May I, without offence, point out how Ireland has fulfilled military duties in the past? In the House of Lords, fourteen years after Waterloo, Wellington said: 'At least one half of the troops whom our Gracious Sovereign did me the honour to entrust to my command, were Irish Catholics, and without their valour, no victory could have been obtained, and the first military talents might have been exerted in vain.' In the year 1840, in the entire British Army, sixty per cent were Scotch or Irish. And of these two-thirds were Irish. In 1853 the proportion was forty-four per cent. In 1868 it was forty percent and in 1877 it was thirty per cent.

—Why these figures? One of the most tragic incidents in our history supplies the answer. The population of Ireland has gone down in fifty years by four million. In spite of the fact that there are fewer young men between the ages of eighteen and forty in proportion to the whole population than in any country in Europe, owing to emigration—in spite of that the proportion is kept up and that proportion is high in the army today. I take leave to say that in proportion to our population we have a larger quota serving in the firing line than any other part of the United Kingdom.

—And as for quality, let Sir John French answer for that and let the Irish Guards marching into battle singing *God Save Ireland*, and the Royal Munster Fusiliers, the Dublin Fusiliers, the Inniskilling Fusiliers, let them answer. I was delighted to hear the words of the Prime Minister with reference to the proposed treatment of Irish recruits in the future. A Welsh Army Corps has already been created.

—I asked for an Irish Brigade, I meant an Army Corps. We have got an historical liking for the phrase Irish Brigade.

—I receive innumerable letters from officers, most of them young enough still to give good service, asking to be attached to the new Irish Brigade. It is not enough to tell us that there are Irish Regiments recruited in Ireland and by sentiment they are Irish and therefore they form an Irish Army Corps. We want the thing done specifically. An Irish Army Corps created so that their deeds and valour in the field would be able to be gathered by us, as one of the treasures of our nation in the future. I tell the Prime Minister that he will get plenty of recruits, and of the best material.

—In conclusion I say this to the Prime Minister, and through him to the people of Great Britain: You have kept faith with Ireland. Ireland will keep faith with you.

In unison with the whole audience Michael rose and applauded. He knew he had witnessed the apex of Mr. Redmond's career. He was more eager than ever to serve Ireland in her new Army. Acknowledging the applause, Redmond pointed to Tom Kettle and others in army uniform, then returned slowly to his seat.

John Dillon, Joe Devlin and Secretary for Ireland Augustin Birrell spoke briefly following Redmond. Michael, still lost in the leader's eloquence, hardly heard them.

The Lord Mayor then proposed a vote of thanks and the meeting adjourned with the entire assembly singing *God Save the King*. Then, cheering loudly, all sang *God Save Ireland*.

Hoping to avoid the crowd, Michael left via a side door and spoke to the commander of the National Volunteers. The officer waved him across the still heavily patrolled area and he found a vantage point at the corner of Duke and

Dawson Streets. Crowds were still three deep. Playing *God Save Ireland* and *The Boys of Wexford*, the Trinity College Officer's Band led the procession returning to Phoenix Park. In the rear of the band followed a torchlight procession of Volunteers in green uniforms.

As the cortege rounded the juncture of Dawson and Nassau Streets, several loud booms could be heard. From behind Trinity College and further north on the Quays, hundreds of red, blue, and vermilion fireworks illuminated the September twilight. Proceeded by outriders, the Lord Lieutenant's carriage followed the Volunteers, then Asquith and Secretary Birrell's carriage, then Redmond and Joe Devlin in an open car, and behind them a large contingent of National Volunteers. Michael and many members of the public marched behind them down Dawson Street, as far as O'Connell Bridge.

Michael dropped out at the bridge, leant on the parapet, and inhaled the bracing sea-breeze blowing up the Liffey from Dublin Bay. Beneath him a barge pitched and rolled in the rising tide. Across its bow, partly above water, was a yellow poster with heavy green letters: **Join an Irish Brigade today and avenge Belgium**.

The fireworks display seemed to be reaching a crescendo now. Seagulls, startled by the jets of flame, whirled and eddied over the surface of the river, their mournful cries ringing a weird antiphony to the confused babble of the crowd, and the fitful strains of the military band wafting ever more faintly from the direction of the Four Courts.

Then, suddenly, this cacophony of sound was drowned by the strains of mass singing. *The Internationale*. Turning around, Michael saw the Citizen Army again, equipped with ancient rifles, coming up Westmoreland Street flanked on either side by Dublin Metropolitan Police. At the head of this rag-tag group was a red banner, the words **Long Live the Worker's Republic** inscribed in gold letters on it. Catcalls and booing greeted these Communists born out of their time.

–Tis well yez have the polis to protect yez or I'd massacre the lot of yez meself, screamed an old man as he flung a bottle of Guinness at the leader.

–Mark time! shouted the commandant, in panic at seeing the old man lurch into the street, another bottle in hand.

–Old man, you'll have to stop that, or I'll have to take you to College St. Station, said a policeman in a kindly Galway accent.

–Is that the way of it, Sergeant?

–It is. Off home to your bed now.

–Just let me at these gobshites. I fought in the Boer War meself. Two sons o' mine are fighting for the 'Beljums' and I can take that squinty-eye four tip soldier with me left hand tied behind me back.

–Off home with ye now. Let these men pass, like a good man.

The old man lurched slowly to the sidewalk. People slapped him on the back and he became the centre of an admiring crowd.

–Up the 'Beljums'! they yelled. To hell with the Kaiser and Jim Larkin!

–Quick march! barked the commandant of the Citizen Army.

They marched in silence until their leading file was abreast of Mooney's on Eden Quay. And then, with a note of defeatism, they once more struck their marching tune to the air of *Tipperary*.

Michael watched the soldiers of the Citizen Army lurching along dejectedly, the reaping hooks and improvised pikes dotted among their ranks gleaming silvery in the moonlight.

They disappeared round the corner of Beresford Place and thence to Liberty Hall.

The sea breeze was beginning to blow rather sharply from the mouth of the Liffey. Fireworks were still soaring from the cupolas of the Custom House, the Four Courts, and the G.P.O., but the crowd was rapidly melting away. Anticlimax ensued after the passing of the vice-regal cavalcade and the heckling of the Citizen Army. Michael was feeling tired and was about to board a tram car when the rhythmic thump of marching feet struck his ear. Vaguely wondering if these were regular soldiers or another of Dublin's private armies, he turned round and recognized John MacNeill's Volunteers.

A yard ahead of the foremost file plodded the writer and teacher Padraic Pearse, his lips tightly compressed, the glow of a fanatical faith illuminating his pale priestly face. Beside him was the scholarly MacNeill, the setting sun highlighting his blond hair and steel-rimmed glasses. Among those who followed Michael recognized the animated features of the poet Thomas MacDonagh and the sickly figure of Joseph Mary Plunkett.

Though he had no thought of it then, he would hear these names again under very different circumstances.

CHAPTER FOUR

Recruiting office, Birr; Basic training, Cork, Oct / 1914 - April 1915

The recruiting office was in a corner of the Leinster's Regimental depot, just off the barrack square. Michael entered quickly, saying to the desk sergeant that he wanted to volunteer.

He was given an official application form and told to wait his turn.

The office smelled of new paint and paper. The olive-green walls, part wood and part plaster gleamed. Shafts of autumn sunlight slanted through the windows of the room, highlighting a poster of four soldiers with the flags of the United Kingdom in their rifles and the caption beneath them.

Who can beat this Plucky Four?
But all the same We're wanting more.
See your local recruiting officer today!

A score of men his age were seated in the middle of the room. Michael took his place beside a small man with a warm smile, open face, and wavy brown hair.

–Here to do yer bit for King and Country? the man asked in a broad Northern accent.

–You might say that, Michael replied, though Redmond says we'll really be fighting for Ireland.

–Och, I've no quarrel with that at all. I'm a follower of Joe Devlin the Belfast Nationalist M.P. meself. My name's Jamie Deegan. I'm from Cookstown, County Tyrone.
I believe in Home Rule for all of Ireland. I've come here to Birr to sign on in a Catholic regiment. There's lots of others feel like me. We'll not be part of a Protestant regiment.
So there'll likely be a few of us coming down here.

Jamie went on to tell Michael of his job in the Borough Health Department in Belfast. He felt that he had been passed over for promotion more than once.

–It's something subtle, ye know, nothing I can put my finger on. But if ye're not in the right clubs or a member of the Orange Order, ye only reach a certain level.
I'm thinking when this is over, that's if I get through it, I'll move to a city down here.

–You'll get through it all right, Jamie. Sure, it's only going to last six months. A year at most. Aren't the Germans on the run at the Marne?

–That may be the case. But don't forget the Hun is a clever devil at soldiering and has a card or two up his sleeve.

—You may be right there. Well as long as we get a chance to have a crack at them.

—We'll get that chance, never you fear, said Deegan.

The line had moved quite quickly and there were now just two people ahead of them. He took out his fountain pen and began to fill in the application form, the story of his life to date.

He hesitated at one question, sucked the top of his pen for a moment, and then read the question aloud.

—*Why have you volunteered to become a member of His Majesty's Territorial Army?*

He'd already discussed this in numerous arguments with his brother Chris.

—*To serve Great Britain and Ireland in their hour of need*, he wrote decisively.

The medical part of his induction was brief. The doctor simply checked his respiration, blood pressure and eyesight.

—You're in good shape, young man. You'll fight well for the cause. Now put your clothes back on. Colonel Jordan would like a word with you.

He pointed to a varnished door at the rear. The colonel sat at an oak desk beneath a portrait of the King in army uniform. He seemed deeply engrossed in some papers in front of him.

—Ah, Sullivan. Won't be a moment. There's just one small thing I have to finish up here. Sit down, please.

Minutes later Michael was conscious of grey eyes regarding him. The colonel moved his papers to one side.

—Now Sullivan, I've looked over your application form and noted your background. You're the type of recruit we're looking for. I wonder if you're aware that a highly respected general, who hails originally from Birr, is organizing a division here in this part of Ireland, distinct from the Ulster Division?

—Well yes, there's been some mention of this and of the officer who's to command it in the papers Sir.

—Yes, Lord Kitchener has asked Lieutenant General Sir Lawrence Parsons to take command of this new division. He took over late last month. This new division will have need of officers and my feeling is that you'd make an excellent junior officer. However, this is all contingent on you doing well in your basic training. So do your level best in the next six weeks and your immediate superiors will advise you then. You know that you've joined a regiment with a very proud history. You're the third person in today's group that I feel is officer material.

–The best of luck to you.

He shook Michael's hand warmly as he guided him towards the door.

The regimental headquarters at Birr was not equipped as a training centre, so Michael and the other seventeen new recruits were transported in two lorries to Camp Shanbally, Monkstown, County Cork. On arrival they were greeted by a tall athletic man with a clipped heavy-brown handlebar moustache and a staccato North-of-England accent.

–Men, welcome to Camp Shanbally. I'm Sergeant Major Dixon. My job is to make first-class soldiers out of you lot. I'll be very tough on you at times, but it's so's you'll be fearless in the front lines. Follow me.

Dixon brought them to three small huts which slept six soldiers each.

–Make the most of this night's sleep. It's the last good one ye'll have for the next six weeks. Store your personal belongings in the locker beside your bed, suitcase under your bed, and toilet articles beside the wash-hand basins in the centre of the dorm. Reveille is at 06:00 hrs and I expect to see ye all on parade at 08:00hrs. Lights out will be in twenty minutes, so be quick about it. Good night, men.

–Good night Ser'nt-major, they said as one.

Next morning they rose gingerly at 06.00 hrs.

–After you've shaved, you'd best make your beds immediately, said Dixon.

He seemed to have been awake long before them. This was followed by stretching, running in place, thirty push-ups, and arm exercises. They washed again and repaired to the mess hall for breakfast at 07.00hrs. This was followed by general barrack cleaning and kitchen fatigues. At 08.00 they reported by company for roll-call in the barrack square.

–Men, you're aware that as of Tuesday the 4th of August we have been at war with Germany and her allies, said Dixon, his handlebar moustache gleaming in the autumn sunshine. You've all answered Lord Kitchener's call to serve your Country in her hour of need. All very commendable I might say, very commendable. Being at war is no picnic, no Sunday outing. I want to turn you lot into the finest company of fighting men in the King's army. To do this I must determine your present level of fitness. I want all of you to get into uniform, then run six laps round that field over to the left. You'll reassemble here in forty minutes. Is that understood?

–Yes Sir.

–I can't hear you.

–Yes Sir!!

–That's better. Now get to it.

Michael, still in good shape from the divisional bank tournament three weeks earlier, completed the run easily. Deegan, his newfound friend, had trouble and walked the last two laps.

–It's the flaming fags, he said between gasps as they returned to the parade ground. I'm up to twenty-five a day. I'm thinkin' I'll have to cut back.

–Ah, that'll take care of itself Jamie, ye won't be able to afford them on Army pay, answered Michael.

As the weeks passed, Michael and his comrades gradually settled into the modified routine of basic training. Parade at 07.00 hrs, then ten minutes of laps - twenty minutes on Saturday, the day after payday, 'to sweat the drink out', then to the mess hall for breakfast. Squad drill was from 09.00 to 12.30 hrs, then they had lunch and lounged until 14.00: cleaning rifles, 'whiting' belts, and reading. Last drill ended at 16.30. After tea at 17.30 many took the tram into Cork to see a review at the Palace or The Opera House. Invariably most drifted into the pubs along the quays.

Michael became proficient at trench construction and drainage, map and compass reading, and signalling. He and Deegan also became known as crack shots because of their ability on the rifle range.

Michael's body became taut and lean. He felt alive when reveille sounded each morning. Route marches with full pack were less tiring than a month earlier.

In early November, the weather changed from sunshine to incessant rain which seemed to move gathering moisture across the Bay of Biscay and hit Cork and its suburbs, the nearest land. Several leaks developed in the roof of their living quarters. Michael, Deegan, and the others put their wash hand basins in strategic positions under the drips to little effect. New leaks kept developing. In the practice fields surrounding Camp Shanbally, their whole trench system became waterlogged. The men did their best at drainage, to no avail.

There always seemed to be at least seven inches of water on the floor of the trench.

–Now you get the real feel of trench warfare, said Dixon as he handed them yards of duckboard. I told you it was no bloody picnic, didn't I?

Even with the duckboard in place Michael's boots still squelched with every step he took. Dampness seeped through the soles of his boots. His socks became sodden, his feet always seemed to be wet. Yes, Dixon was right, this trench warfare was no picnic. Could he put up with two or more years of this type of existence, or were other choices open to him? Yes, there were. Colonel Jordan had said that he was officer material. While life as an officer involved more responsibility, he would also be using more initiative, more of his natural intelligence.

He saw his immediate superior. Captain Crawford next day, had an interview with Colonel Canning O.C. of Victoria Barracks in Cork the following week, and was accepted as an officer cadet almost immediately. His good friend Jamie Deegan was also accepted.

Life as an officer cadet meant a transfer to the New Barracks at Fermoy. Conditions there were little better than at Camp Shanbally. His quarters were damp, his bed covered by two thin blankets.

He informed Virginia of this.

New Barracks
Fermoy
10th October 1914
Dearest Virginia,
This new barracks is larger than Camp Shanbally. There's dampness everywhere, condensation gathers on walls and window panes. One has to sleep in vest, pants and shirt to keep warm.
Yet my work and new responsibilities are invigorating. There are sixteen recruits aged between nineteen and fifty. We are each responsible for a squad of twenty men. We are driving the men for all their worth, lecturing them on soldierly spirit, discipline, smartness and the rest. We're busy from dawn to dusk, dear one, but I wouldn't have it any other way. Our captain is a Canadian and four of our group are straight from university. Deegan, the Tyrone man I mentioned in an earlier letter keeps, us in good humour.
I miss my lissom sweet blond colleen terribly. I ache to be in her arms again and to receive her tender kisses.
Tell me how things are in your world, my love. I hope it's not all work and no play, sweetheart. Love is free, as a French philosopher said. I want you to meet other people.
But keep these beaus at arm's length.
I think of you first thing in the morning and last thing at night. I see your sunny face right now and can't wait for your reply to this billet doux.
Your own,
Michael

Michael found he liked the new rituals of life in Fermoy. The evening meal in the mess hall. The Colonel at the head of the table, the second in command at the other end, then the captain, the senior subaltern and all the cadets in order, down to Deegan and himself. The toast to the King and to Ireland at the end of the meal moved him. In a letter to his parents, he wrote:

> *Over coffee and cigarettes the pipers come in and march round the table playing Irish airs. It's all wistful and nostalgic. Then the CO goes out, and everybody rises to their feet respectfully, and in some curious manner the whole atmosphere gets to one, most indescribably.*

The men in his squad were shaping up well, advancing from squad to company drills. Route marches of six to eight miles were made throughout the surrounding countryside. Trenches with all types of traverses were dug around the barrack complex.

> *St Vincent's Hospital*
> *Nurses Residence*
> *Baggot St,*
> *Dublin*
> *15th October 1914*
> *Dearest Michael,*
> *I received your letter of the 10th inst. and am delighted to tell you that Sr. Dymphna has approved my request of several days ago for a transfer to the North Infirmary Hospital in Cork City,*
> *Nearer my love to you,*
> *Your Ginny*

Michael was surprised to receive another letter just days later.

> *16 Wellington Rd.*
> *Cork City*
> *18th October 1914*
> *Dearest Michael,*
> *I arrived here yesterday, but found these digs near the hospital this morning and have already done a couple of things to make my room a home, I must admit I'm a little tired and planning an early night. I'll report to Sister Columba, the sister in charge of the hospital nursing staff, at 9.00 a.m., tomorrow morning.*
> *All my love my dearest,*
> *Your Ginny*

Taking a suburban train from Fermoy, Michael met with Virginia as frequently as possible in the ensuing weeks. His almost daily letters were full of longing. Then authorities made a decision moving the 2nd Battalion of The Prince of Wales's Leinster Regiment from Fermoy to a new facility. Michael informed Virginia of this.

Camp Kilworth,
Co. Cork
5th November 1914
Dearest Virginia,
Our brief trip and stay at Acton's Hotel, Kinsale at Halloween will remain in my memory forever, I keep remembering the masks you'd bought in advance, The beautiful dinner laid on by the hotel and the lively music by the resident musical group, That new American song "Alexander's Ragtime Band" certainly kept us on our toes, Then your butterfly kisses as we bid each other a tender good night.
Yesterday, as I felt we might, we marched with full pack from the overcrowded barracks in Fermoy to these recently built quarters in the folds of mountains. The camp consists of a small central columned administrative building of Greek Design with a drilling square in front. To the rear there's a rifle range with targets where we practice rapid fire. Yours truly is really accurate now and fires twenty shots a minute, A little above average, even if I say it myself. Wee Jamie Deegan, Frank Hawkins and Jim Lavelle are in the same league.
The land surrounding the barracks is rugged and of course perfect for training from a military point of view. To tell you the truth, Virginia, it's the back of beyond, five miles from Fermoy and seven from Mitchelstown. We've been assigned to small huts which have sleeping quarters for eight men. Though the huts are well built they're badly heated, with a fireplace at the end of each room and a stove in the centre. Our uniforms, socks, salt, sugar and even matches have become damp. The nearest public house is Blue Dragon and is only open to officers, which is leading to quite a lot of unrest among the men, The CO, Colonel Crawford, will have to sort this out, otherwise he'll have a mutiny on his hands. He is a traditionalist, and we have formal dinners at H.Q. on Sunday evenings. He sits at the head of the long table with his assistant Colonel Murphy at the other end and all of us cadets squeezed in between. We eat well. usually mutton, sometimes roast beef accompanied by red wine. Then toast the King, then Ireland over coffee and cigarettes. Then pipers enter the mess hall and march round playing Irish airs. It's impossibly loud yet it moves me almost to tears.
I miss you terribly, my darling.
Your Michael

Michael's basic training continued into November, then on Friday 20th November, Colonel Crawford called him to his office.

–At ease Sullivan, at ease. I have the duty and honour of telling you that you've scored highly in all aspects of your officers training, especially marksmanship. These are your formal papers signed by Colonel Murphy and by me. Your rank is now that of 2nd Lieutenant. Your formal insignia will be given to you at a later date. You have my congratulations and those of Colonel Murphy. Dismiss.

Camp Kilworth
County Cork
20th November 1914
Dear Father,
I write in haste, but have wonderful news. Colonel Crawford called me to his office today, I have made the grade. My new rank is 2nd Lieutenant 2nd Battalion Leinster Regiment.
My friends Hawkins and Deegan are also in the programme. I am responsible for sixteen cadets now, aged nineteen to twenty five. But there are older men too, much older than me, in the company.
Tearing a strip off a man twice my age feels strange and unnatural, as if I were reprimanding you. But I hear your voice telling me 'You are an officer now. You stand for more than the Sullivan family.
Age does not matter. Instill discipline and attention in the men.'
Thank you Father for everything,
Your son,
Michael

Orders of the day for Thursday the 24th of December announced that a number of cadets would have seven days leave. Scanning the notice board Michael saw that both he and Deegan were on the list. A brisk wind blew across the barrack square. Temperatures were below freezing, skies were clear. Deegan came to his side, rubbing his hands together.

–Jamie, forgive me, I have to go immediately to the communications office and telegram both Virginia and my parents. I wasn't sure until now if I'd be given leave for Christmas.
So I need to send these messages. See you in a tick.

–Fine, Sulli. You know where I am.

Michael wrote two short telegrams.

```
NURSE VIRGINIA MARTIN C/O NORTH INFIRMERY
HOSPITAL, CORK CITY, DEAREST VIRGINIA STOP HAVE
```

```
BEEN GIVEN SEVEN DAYS LEAVE STOP
PLEASE LET ME KNOW IF YOU CAN JOIN ME AND THE
FAMILY FOR CHRISTMAS STOP LOVE MICHAEL
```

```
DR SULLIVAN, OAKLANDS, ROSNUA, QUEENS COUNTY,
FATHER HAVE BEEN GIVEN A SEVEN DAY PASS FOR
CHRISTMAS STOP AM TAKING THE AFTERNOON TRAIN
FROM FERMOY TO ATHY STOP
IT ARRIVES AT SEVEN STOP HOPE YOU CAN MEET ME
STOP MICHAEL
```

He met Deegan at their hut a little later.

–Well, I'm off on the evening train. Sure you wouldn't like to spend Christmas at my parents'? he asked.

–Och no, Sulli. Sure, I don't want to impose.

–You wouldn't be imposing, Jamie, my parents' motto is 'the more the merrier.' They'd only be delighted to see you.

–Yes. But imagine the delight of my mother and the young ones when they see me at the door Christmas morning.

–Oh, you're right there Jamie. I hadn't thought of that.

He packed only essentials, reasoning that all his civilian clothes were at Oaklands.

He put the men through their paces in a perfunctory fashion, his mind already in Rosnua. Minutes seemed like hours. He was going home. Home to his parents, Rosemary, Brian, and Deirdre. Home again to his own room, his favourite books. Home for the first time as a soldier. He couldn't wait for 16.30 and freedom.

He stopped again at the telegraph office.

–There's been a reply to both your telegrams said the communication's officer.

```
DEAREST MICHAEL STOP BECAUSE I'VE ONLY BEGUN
HERE I SHALL BE ON DUTY AT THE HOSPITAL FOR THE
NEXT SIX DAYS STOP
ALL MY LOVE YOUR VIRGINIA STOP
```

Though he understood, Michael was sad that Virginia couldn't be with him. There would be many other holidays. The reply from his father said he'd meet him in Athy.

The 4.30 train from Waterford was a half-hour late and crowded. He and Deegan found a place for their valises on a baggage rack and repaired to the dining car.

—I'm only having a sandwich, Jamie, they'll probably feed me at home. Would you like something heavier? My treat.

—Ach no, you can't be doing that, Sulli. I'll pay my own way.

—But I'm not going to see you for a week and it's Christmas. You can return the favour in the New Year.

—All right, so. But I'll buy you a meal sometime in January.

—You will indeed. I'll hold you to it.

Making good time, the train pulled into Athy towards a quarter to seven in the evening. Picking up his holdall, Michael wished Jamie a quick and safe journey from Dublin to Belfast and Cookstown. The platform was crowded as he exited the car, but he saw his father immediately. They embraced warmly.

—Let me look at you, Michael, Dr. Sullivan said, holding his son at arm's length. My God you look handsome in your new uniform. You've lost weight. Right, I've the new Model T parked about fifty yards from here. The town is quite crowded with shoppers, but we should make good time. All right?

Michael placed his bag in the boot and went to the front of the Model T. The engine caught at the second turn of the starting crank.

—Put this blanket around you, son. The seal on the doors isn't that good. It gets quite chilly when I hit higher speeds on the open road.

—Right you are, Father.

Though he'd been driving for only a year his father easily negotiated the narrow, crowded streets of the town. The rutted, second-class roads were virtually free of oncoming traffic. Twenty minutes later Michael heard the familiar sound of crunching gravel as his father drove up the short driveway to Oaklands. He was home at last. He bounded out of the car and took his holdall from the boot.

—Welcome home, Michael, said his mother opening the door and hugging him tightly, a dishcloth in her right hand. My, you look elegant in your Sam Brown belt and new uniform. Doesn't Michael look handsome, children?

—Yes, he does Mother. Can Michael help us with the dinner preparations?

—Of course he can. But not in his new uniform. You've got your regular room, Michael. Go up and change now. Put on some old trousers and shirt. We need your help here.

—Right away, Mother.

His room seemed smaller than he remembered it. He quickly changed and put on a worn pair of trousers. It seemed strange that the trousers were loose around the waist, he'd either lost weight or turned fat into muscle.

—Michael, could you wash and clean these Brussel sprouts? Then later perhaps you could clean and dice some celery.

—Certainly, Mother.

The sprouts were green with few yellow leaves. He quickly cleaned them in the kitchen sink. Though the kitchen was warm, Michael's hands became very cold because of the ice-cold water.

He washed and chopped the celery quickly, put the vegetable into a smaller pot and began to quickly rub his hands.

—Feeling cold, Michael? asked his mother.

—Yes, a little.

—Come over and stand by the range a while. I wish I could offer you whiskey or even tea, but you'll have to be fasting three hours if you're going to Midnight Mass.

—No, standing by the range should do the trick, Mother. I want to be part of the full celebrations at Midnight Mass.

He stood by the cooker for several minutes, his hands over the centre grate. The deep heat quickly restored his circulation. He looked at his watch. It was a little after ten.

—Mother, perhaps we should all change. It's gone ten o'clock. It'll take us a half hour to get to church. There are bound to be an awful lot of people there.

—I'm sorry, I lost track of time. Just let me baste the turkey again. It'll only take a minute. Rosemary, perhaps you should wear that lilac dress. You look so beautiful in it. Brian, wear that flannel suit you bought in September. Michael, I leave it up to you as to whether to wear your uniform or civilian clothes. Perhaps a suit might be better. After all, you're on holiday.

His mother was right. Why be conspicuous in his uniform? He picked out a dark blue suit he'd worn the previous spring. In his chest of drawers, he found a cream shirt and sky-blue tie.

The church, in half light, was already quite crowded when they arrived at 11.15. Many in the congregation smiled or nodded to his parents as they made their way as a family towards a bench on the right of the altar. Looking towards the left, Michael saw that, as in previous years, the manger had been set up, the crib empty awaiting the arrival of the Christ Child, which would be placed in it at the offertory of the Mass.

The service began promptly at midnight after a selection of seasonal carols and airs by Bach and Vivaldi. After the celebrant Father Fogerty, resplendent in gold vestments, had read the Christmas gospel. He emphasized God's great love for mankind in giving us his Son as our Redeemer.

—In Belgium and Northern France two great armies face each other, he continued. Many in the British Army are volunteers from our country. We pray that the Prince of Peace will give them solace. We wish the soldiers in the opposing army peace also. Peace begins with the self. So we wish both armies peace in themselves, peace for their families, and pray that by this time next year hostilities will have ended and Christ's Peace will reign throughout the world. God bless all in this assembly and grant you every blessing this Christmas and throughout 1915.

At the Offertory the younger primary school children brought the Christ Child to the crib while the older students brought the bread and wine to Fr. Fogerty. At communion the choir sang Franck's *Panis Angelicus.* Michael felt a gentle dig in his side.

—That's Deirdre as solo soprano, whispered his father.

Deirdre's voice was truly beautiful. With training she could have a concert career, thought Michael.

With the singing of *Silent Night* and *Away in a Manger* by both choir and congregation, and the final blessing by Father Fogerty, the celebration came to an end.

Outside, the weather had turned cold. Her choir uniform in a paper bag, Deirdre joined them.

—You were in great voice tonight, love, said his father. Wasn't she, Annie?

—She was, Tom. We must try and get you a really good voice coach, Deirdre. Sister Columba has little more to teach you.

—You really think that Mother? Deirdre blushed deeply.

—Yes dear. I'll try to get the names of voice coaches from the aunts in Dublin. Now tighten that scarf around your throat and let's get in the motor. You've a lot of singing to do tomorrow.

We don't want you catching cold. Excuse me, there's something I must check in the kitchen right away.

Mrs. Sullivan rushed to the kitchen range, grabbing a dry cloth as she opened the oven.

—The turkey is almost cooked. I'll baste it one more time. It should be ready in about fifteen minutes. Tomorrow all we'll need to do is reheat it. Deirdre, open the cold press.

I have ham and cheese there that I prepared earlier. Perhaps we could have it for supper.

—You're a wonder, Mother, said Deirdre. When did you find time to prepare this?

—Oh, I prepared the serving dish when your father went to Athy for Michael. You were already at choir practice. Now there's an Oxtail soup in that copper pot at the side of the range. It just needs to be reheated, move it to the centre ring. Tom, Michael, Brian and Rosemary, amuse yourselves in the drawing room. Supper will be ready in a few minutes.

—Can we open our Christmas presents, Mother? asked Rosemary excitement in her voice.

—You may open one and only one present, Rosemary. Choose carefully. That goes for you too, Brian. Off with ye now, the two o' ye.

The high-banked coal fire in the living room glowed. The only other light was a votive oil lamp in front of the small Christmas crib.

—Let me light a larger lamp, said Dr. Sullivan moving to the sideboard. You children will have a lemonade, won't you? Michael, how about a small glass of Tio Pepe while we wait?

The dry sherry was refreshing. Michael watched as Rosemary and Brian both drank a little of their lemonade and then burrowed into the presents at the base of the ornate tree.

Rosemary picked a flat package wrapped in dark green paper. She briefly looked at the small attached card.

—It says from you and Mother, Father. I wonder what it is. Oh, it's watercolours and a sketching pad! How did you know I'd like them?

—Simple. We both can see how much you enjoy sketching in summer, dear.

—Thank you very, very much Father.

She rushed towards his open arms and kissed him on both cheeks.

—It's a pleasure, love. Happy Christmas. Don't forget to thank your mother.

Meanwhile Brian had picked out a large thick package.

—This looks like a book, father.

—It probably is son. It probably is. We hope you haven't already read it.

Brian tore the wrapping paper.

—It's *The Riddle of the Sands*. Several of the lads in Castleknock have read it. Thank you Father.

—I hope you like it, son. Thank your mother when you have a moment. Happy Christmas and many more.

Dr. Sullivan gave Brian a quick hug.

There was a rustling from the kitchen. Deirdre entered the room carrying an ornate soup bowl, ladle, and cutlery on a breakfast tray. Mrs. Sullivan followed with the ham and cheese sandwiches.

—Help yourselves. I think this is what they call 'A cup in the hand' in Dublin and London, said Mrs. Sullivan.

She and Deirdre placed the food on a low coffee table.

—This is really wonderful Annie. Just what the doctor ordered, said Dr. Sullivan as he ladled the soup. Haven't I always told you children what a great cook your mother was?
Thank you Annie.

—Thank you mother, and you too Deirdre, said Michael, Brian and Rosemary.

—Go on now, eat up, said Mrs. Sullivan.

Michael's father was right, his mother's food was wonderful. The soup was the Oxtail soup The ham and cheese sandwiches were on home-made whole-meal bread.

Everything tasted especially good after mess food in Fermoy.

—I don't know about the rest of you, but I'm for bed. It's been a long day, said Mrs. Sullivan as she finished her meal. Deirdre, you'd best go up now as well. You have to be in good voice for eight o'clock Mass this morning. You'll have to leave here at a little after seven.

—I'll go up now Father, said Michael as he dried the last of the cutlery. I was up with the larks this morning. The train journey's left me tired.

—Of course Michael. It's just so good that you're here. Sleep as late as you like. That's what we're going to do. At all events we can't begin our special dinner 'til Deirdre returns from last mass. That won't be before two in the afternoon.

After the heat of the drawing room and kitchen Michael's bedroom felt cold. He quickly removed his clothes and dived under the bedclothes. It was great to be in his own bed again.

Wonderful to be spending this special holiday with the people he loved most.

He awoke towards six thirty because of the dawn chorus. Completely alert he looked round the room in the half-light expecting to see Hawkins or Deegan in a camp bed nearby.

Instead, he was in Oaklands, in his own bed. He was on Christmas leave. There would be no fatigues. It was all right to go back to sleep.

An hour later he heard a kettle boiling. It was Deirdre making a cup of tea before leaving to sing at the later masses. He finally rose about ten-thirty. Weak winter sunshine flooded his room, highlighting the harvesting scenes on the pastel wallpaper. He put on shirt, pullover and trousers and went to the kitchen. His parents were there eating boiled eggs, toast, and porridge.

—Are eggs, toast and porridge enough for you? asked his mother.

—Yes, perfect Mother.

—Did Deirdre wake you Michael? asked his father.

—Yes, I heard her boil the kettle. I was only half awake.

—It's good she ate something. She has a long morning ahead of her.

His father passed him the *Independent* for Christmas Eve. Hostilities on the Flanders Front seemed to have slowed down. This is probably because of the weather, thought Michael, or perhaps the message of the Prince of Peace has been heeded by both sides.

—Things seem to be quieter in Flanders, Father.

—Yes Michael. Perhaps there's some kind of an unofficial truce. Many of the Germans are Catholics, and the remainder are staunch Protestants.

—Wouldn't that kind of inaction be something, Father?

—The Kaiser and his generals won't like it. Neither will Kitchener or French.

—They're not in the Front Lines.

—Exactly, let's hope no one on either side dies in the next few days.

—That was what Father Fogerty prayed for last night.

—Perhaps it'll happen, said Dr. Sullivan wistfully.

—Rosemary and Brian seem to be very quiet. Where are they? asked Michael.

—They're in the dining room opening the last of their presents Michael, said his mother. Most of the presents we've given them are practical or educational. At least they'll be occupied for the next hour or so 'til the fascination wears off.

Just then Rosemary rushed in, a box camera in her hands.

—Thank you very much for the camera, Mother, Father, she said excitedly. Now could the three of you look towards me. This will be my first photo.

—Are you sure there's enough light, love? asked Dr. Sullivan.

—Call Brian, love. He should be in the picture too.

—Oh. I suppose he should. Brian, come and have your photo taken.

Brian came in, his hair dishevelled. He scrunched in behind his parents.

—Taking the box camera from Rosemary, her Dad said, right now, Rosemary, go beside your mother. It's only right that you should be in the next photo. Smile again, Michael.

–Right, Father.

–Now I'd like everyone to go into the dining room and take their ease, as most of you can smell our turkey is now well cooked, and our plum pudding is simmering nicely.

–I have a few more things to do. I'd rather do these things myself. I'll let you all know when I need help. So all of you go to the dining room and amuse yourselves, said Mrs. Sullivan.

Brian and Rosemary were still immersed in their new presents. Dr. Sullivan picked up the most recent edition of *The British Medical Journal.*

–There's an article here by a Doctor Rivers about stress disorders that soldiers on active service develop. It seems like a whole new field of medicine Michael. Rivers is attached to Craiglockhart, a hospital for Nervous Disorders just outside Edinburgh. It seems like cutting-edge knowledge.

–Perhaps you could pass it on to me later if it's not too technical, Father.

–By all means, son. The language so far is quite simple.

Michael read a little more of the *Independent*. There were Christmas greetings from Archbishop Walsh of Dublin, and from John Redmond. Hopefully the winter wheat crop would be above average.

As much of it was already pre-sold to the army, farmers would benefit from higher incomes.

The aroma from the kitchen was becoming stronger and more enticing by the minute.

–Tom, Michael, come in here now, shouted Mrs. Sullivan.

She'd just opened the oven. The turkey stood in its chafing dish surrounded by bubbling stock and golden roast potatoes.

–Tom, could you lift the dish and place it on top of the range, she said giving her husband two thick dish towels.

–Yes, of course dear, said Dr. Sullivan bending his knees and gingerly picking up the dish.

–Now, Michael, I've made a mushroom soup as a contrast to what we ate last night. It's in that large copper pot there. Could you pour it into that silver bowl there? We'll have it right away.

–You've checked the table, haven't you?

–Yes Mother, it's all set – I checked everything. What about Deirdre?

–She should be along any minute. It's already gone one forty- five. The last mass ended about twenty minutes ago. If I keep the turkey too long on the stove, it'll begin to dry out.

As Michael and his father went towards the dining room his mother quickly washed her hands and followed them.

—Tom, perhaps you could say a formal grace given the day and the feast, she said.

—Of course Annie.

Bless us O Lord, and these thy gifts,
Which of thy bounty, we have received,
Through Christ our Lord, Amen.

—I'd like to say again how happy we are that Michael is sharing this Christmas with us. Jack and Mary are spending this feast with Mary's family in Portsmouth. Chris is with his sweetheart in Kinsale.

—So all our family is well and in God's care.

—This is lovely, Mother, as great as the oxtail soup was last night, said Michael.

—Yes, it's better than anything they give us in Castleknock, said Brian.

—Right, eat it while it's hot. We have many more good things to sample.

They heard the front door opening. Deirdre came in, her face flushed.

—Sit down, Deirdre. You must be famished, said Dr. Sullivan. Michael, give her a double helping of soup.

—Yes, thank you Father. The road was a bit icy on the bicycle, but I had the wind at my back. That helped.

—This is lovely, Mother, said Deirdre.

Michael picked up the empty soup plates. Then he, Deirdre, and his mother returned to the kitchen.

—Place the turkey roast potatoes and giblets on this large dish, Michael. Your Father will carve as usual.

Michael did as instructed, then proceeded to the dining room, followed by his mother and Deirdre carrying the vegetables.

—This is like the Shelbourne Hotel in Dublin, isn't it, children? said Dr. Sullivan.

—It's better, father, said Brian. Last time we ate there the food was cold.

—You'll do the honours, Tom, said Mrs. Sullivan.

—Of course love. You'll have white meat as usual?
Sit now, you've done Trojan work, hasn't she children?

—Yes Mother. Relax now, you've been working since yesterday evening, said Deirdre.

—Thanks for saying that, dear, but I wouldn't have it any other way.

—Some red wine Mother? It's a vintage Bordeaux, said Michael.

—If you say so Michael. I expect you'll become an expert once you get to France.

—Perhaps Mother. The war won't continue much longer.

—That's what we pray for, son.

They ate in the warm glow of a coal fire and one oil lamp. Michael wondered if coming holidays would be as happy. *Thank you dear Lord, for this holiday and for my family, he prayed silently.*

—If you and Rosemary are really good, you can have a small glass of wine with your second helping of turkey Brian, said Dr. Sullivan.

—Is this wise Tom? asked Mrs. Sullivan.

—Of course Annie. Children in France have their first glass of wine at age ten.

—Thank you Father, said Brian and Rosemary as one.

—Yes, but we'll add a little water. It takes a little time to develop the taste. We don't want either of you getting drunk.

—We'll be careful, father.

—It's a little bittersweet, said Brian.

—It's an acquired taste, Brian. You'll like it more next time. ...as long as you don't get to like it too much.

—Eat up everyone, but leave a little space for dessert. Michael, please clear the table. Deirdre, come with me.

Mrs. Sullivan and Deirdre returned minutes later carrying a large plum pudding, brandy butter and a bottle of Hennessy's brandy.

—Do the honours again Tom, said Mrs. Sullivan placing a package of Swan matches, the plum pudding, and the brandy on the table.

—With pleasure love.

Dr. Sullivan poured the brandy liberally. Rosemary and Brian stared in wonderment as blue flame enveloped the pudding.

—The first portions are for Rosemary and Brian. Be careful children, said Dr. Sullivan cutting into the dessert.

—It's still on fire, said Rosemary.

—That'll go away in a second, love. Deirdre, give Rose some brandy butter.

—It's lovely Mother, even better than I remember, said Brian.

—I'm glad you like it Brian.

They lingered over the dessert, savouring its flavour.

—Would anyone like a liqueur now, or should we wait? asked Dr. Sullivan some fifteen minutes later.

—Perhaps we should wait for now, said Michael.

—May I be excused, father? asked Rosemary finishing the last of her pudding.

—Why, dear? asked her mother.

—I just want to read the latest *Katie* book by the light of the fire.

—Yes, of course.

Rosemary sat on a hand knotted floor rug, *What Katie Did Next* held lightly in her hands, her shoulder-length blond hair highlighted by the embers.

—You'll have to hire extra help to keep suitors at bay in a year or so father, whispered Michael as he pulled out his rolling paper and tobacco. His father nodded agreement.

—You'll have a cigarette Father? This is Turkish tobacco.

—Oh, yes Michael. Where on earth did you find it?

—In a little shop on Patrick's Street in Cork. It was the last couple of ounces they had. There won't be any more until after hostilities end. We'll just have to content ourselves with Wills or Players for the duration. Good Virginia tobaccos, but not in the same class as Balkan Sobranie.

They both savoured their cigarettes, the exotic aroma filling the room.

—Well, perhaps Deirdre and I should prepare coffee now? said Mrs. Sullivan, some minutes later.

—Take your time Annie, there's no rush.

—We'll repair to the kitchen for now Tom. I find it's become a little stuffy here. There's more air there. Enjoy your cigarettes. We won't be long.

They returned some twenty minutes later with two large coffee pots and six mugs.

—The perfect ending to a lovely meal. Thank you both, said Dr. Sullivan.

—This is lovely Father, said Michael savouring the strong coffee and a glass of Hennessy Cognac. His mother and Deirdre drank Grand Marnier, Brian and Rosemary, glasses of Cantrell & Corcoran's lemonade, his father a Bushmills single malt.

—Do we have anything planned for tomorrow? asked Michael.

—No, perhaps we could all sleep late, then go for a long brisk walk.

—Yes, that'd be great. I'm already tired of army hours, so the sleep-in will be great.

—We may have an invitation for supper. I'm on several committees with Colonel Cosbie of Rosnua Hall. He mentioned something of an Open House on the 26th.

Many local people will be there. However, we'll have to be formally invited. You know the quality.

—Indeed I do father. It would be a lot of fun.

His mother went to the piano and played *Dreaming* and several other short pieces by Schumann. She then signalled her husband and children. Together they sang *O Little Town of Bethlehem* before retiring for the night.

The sound of snow chimes woke him next morning. For a minute he thought he was in a foreign country, then realized it was local mummers celebrating St. Stephen's Day.

Going to the bedroom window he saw them. They wore hats of woven straw, old baggie trousers, had blackened faces, and carried sheaves of straw containing wren's nests.

Dr. Sullivan greeted them by name.

—Here's a half-sovereign, Tom Gibney. Compliments of the season to you all. Spend at least a little of this on food for the wrens before you slake your thirst.

—Of course we will doctor. Best to you and your family for the New Year. We're off to visit Miss Fisher and her brother now.

The rest of the morning passed quickly.

They were just finishing a lunch when Michael heard the gravel crunch and there was a ring of the door-bell. Brian found Colonel Cosbie's aide at the door, asked him to come inside, while he took the gilded envelope to his father.

—It's from Colonel Cosbie, said Dr. Sullivan opening it. He's invited all of us to an open house this evening at seven. It's semi-formal. Shall we accept Annie?

—Of course Tom. It's very generous of them.

Michael's Father went to the doorway.

—Right, Devlin. Thank Colonel and Mrs. Cosbie very much for their invitation. We'll be very happy to attend. There will actually be six of us. See you later and thank the Colonel again.

Dr. Sullivan gave Colonel Cosbie's aide two shillings.

Devlin, dressed formally in bow tie and tails, greeted them later as Dr. Sullivan parked his model T in front of the Cosbie Manor. Rain mixed with sleet hit them as they mounted the formal lime-stone steps, Devlin a few feet ahead of them. Resplendent in his formal red military uniform, Colonel Cosbie, bald with a fringe of steel-grey hair, greeted them as they entered.

–Thank you for coming Doctor Sullivan. Season's Greetings to you Mrs. Sullivan, and your family. Michael, when do you expect to go to Flanders?

–We're just completing our basic training Sir, but should be travelling in a matter of weeks.

–Good. Excellent. Your old playmate, my son John, is now a junior officer with the Fusiliers. He's been through that whole Marne business.

Devlin took their coats and gave them to a pretty girl of about sixteen.

–It's good to be out of the cold isn't it Annie? said Mr. Sullivan.

Her auburn hair piled high, Mrs. Sullivan wore a velvet lilac dress, Deirdre and Rosemary, taffeta dresses of apple-green and ivory, Brian a navy-blue suit and silk tie, Michael his new officer's uniform.

–This way doctor, please. I'm sure you'd like something to slake your thirst, said Devlin.

There were two silver punch bowls on an oval table in the alcove.

–The larger bowl is alcoholic. The smaller one a mixture of various tropical juices for non-drinkers, said Devlin.

The table fronted a large Victorian Christmas Tree complete with candles and a golden star. The oak-panelled room was lit by brackets of candles and a large chandelier; to the right a log fire blazed in an ornate fireplace. Almost obscured by large palm trees, a piano trio was playing.

–Devlin, give my younger daughter and son a little fruit punch first. Then Mrs. Sullivan, Deirdre, my son Michael and myself will have the good stuff.

–Right you are, Doctor.

Michael felt the navy rum in the punch hit the back of his throat. It took his breath away.

–Excuse me, Devlin. Could you give me a little of the non-alcoholic mix, and you might add a little more juice to the regular punch.
It's a tad strong said Michael.

–What are you saying, Michael. We need something with a bit of a bite to get the blood flowing, said his father.

–Yes father, but there are a lot of ladies here. If they have more than two or three glasses of this they'll be flying.

–Perhaps you're right son. Devlin, I expect you'll have to check this with Colonel Cosbie.

–I'll have to indeed, Doctor. Twas he told me to make a strong punch. 'Make it the usual way, Devlin' says he. 'We want lots of song and hilarity at this party.'

–Yes, but you don't want people with sick heads in the morning either. Tomorrow's a working day.

–You're right o' course, Doctor, said Devlin moving towards the kitchen.

Moments later he returned with a large jug of orange juice. He quickly emptied this into the punch bowl.

–Yes, that's a good deal weaker and you can still taste the rum, said Michael refilling his glass.

–Enjoying yourselves? asked Miss Fisher, their next-door neighbour.

In her mid-fifties, she had the slim elegant body of a much younger woman. The owner of a horse stable, she and her brother Maurice competed at point-to-point races and at the Dublin Horse Show.

–Yes, very much. Happy Christmas. Good to see you again Miss Fisher, said Michael. Do you have any news of Maurice?

–Well, as you know he's First Mate on a merchant ship. Since the beginning of hostilities, he's been working on convoys from New York and Boston. A little on the dangerous side, but important work. I do worry about him.

–And well you might, Miss Irene. The enemy will do everything possible to stop these convoys.

–We're beginning a New Year in a few days. Hopefully a year that will bring peace, Michael.

–My thoughts too, Miss Irene. I'm afraid our enemies have a lot of arms and ammunition yet. However, here's to peace.

–To peace, Michael. A day after the feast of The Prince of Peace.

She drank her small glass in one draft.

–Michael this is strong. It takes my breath away.

–Devlin already added extra orange juice about ten minutes ago. He says Colonel Cosbie told him to make it on the strong side.

–Well, we can't argue with our host. I hope there aren't too many people with sore heads tomorrow morning.

–That's my wish too. Still most people have soda water and aspirin in their homes.

–They have indeed.

–Michael, I see you've joined the colours. We didn't have much chance to talk on Christmas Eve, said Father Fogerty taking him to one side.

—No we didn't, Father. As you can see, I'm a junior officer now.

—Yes, and how do you like officer's training?

—Well, there's a lot to learn and we have written tests every two weeks or so. Still, I'm on top of things. There's so much enthusiasm. Both my fellow cadets and the enlisted men are chafing at the bit. They want to have their go at the Hun.

—I'm sure they do, Michael, but the better trained they are the more chance they have of surviving. I've some small experience in the matter. I was a chaplain in the Boer War.

—I wasn't aware of that, father.

—No, it's not something I like to talk about. We lost as many men from enteric fever and other tropical diseases as we did in battle. I still have nightmares.

—Oh, I'm sorry to hear that.

—Not to worry, Michael, they're less frequent than they used to be. Just take care of yourself and your men when you get there. Don't be foolhardy. Remember to keep your head down. Do anything to survive. Now let's talk of happier things. Do you get a chance to follow Cork's hurling fortunes?

—Not that closely, Father. They seem to have a good team this year.

—Quite good, especially since so many men have enlisted. Let's move over towards those large doors at the end of the room, they'll be opening them any moment.
That's where they're serving supper.

—Good idea.

Devlin opened the double doors a few minutes later. The long oak panelled room had an oval linen clad buffet table in the centre. A tall ice sculpture in the shape of a swan stood behind two enormous shells containing, shrimps, fresh oysters, and other seafood. To the right a chef, in full regalia stood behind a crown roast of prime beef. Roast potatoes and vegetables were arranged a little further to the right. Assorted desserts including mince meat pies, adorned an adjoining table. To the left, ten tables, each with a small Christmas tree and red candle, awaited guests. A baby grand piano filled the far corner of the room. The musicians took their places there.

—Eat as much as you'd like everyone. We'll have music and dance later, said a beaming Colonel Cosbie.

—Gosh, this is really wonderful, said Dr. Sullivan. The colonel must have a new cook, the variety and amount of food is greater than I remember it. Annie, we must remember to say this to the Colonel.

A little over an hour later lights were dimmed; the trio struck up the overture to *Die Fledermaus.*

—They're playing a piece by Offenbach, Father, whispered Michael. Is that a patriotic gesture?

—Was he not French, Michael? It's great music anyway, isn't it?

—And great fun too. I saw the operetta in the Gaiety in autumn of last year.

The trio continued with music from *The Chocolate Soldier*, *The lily of Killarney* and pieces by the Strauss family.

—It's now time for everyone to participate. I hope you have your party pieces ready, said Colonel Cosbie moving to the centre of the room.

—First I'd like to call Miss Fisher to the stage. She'll sing *After the Ball Was Over.*

Miss Fisher moved quickly to the stage and sang the classic in a relaxed soprano voice.

—Now I'd like to call a fine party pianist to the stage she said, pointing to Michael. I believe he'll give us the Percy French song *Abdul Abulbul Amir* and then grace us with some ragtime music.

Michael had sung the comic song many times before. He followed it with *Will Ye Go, Lassie, Go?* and ended with a full-handed piano version of *Maple Leaf Rag.*

—I didn't know you played ragtime, Michael, said his mother when he returned to their table.

—It takes a lot of practice, Mother. I like it a lot. Of course, the beautiful music you play takes a lot of practice also.

—Now Mrs. Sullivan will play several classical pieces on the piano, said Colonel Cosbie. Mrs. Sullivan.

—I've nothing really prepared, said Michael's mother shyly. If my daughter Deirdre will join me I'll play *Plaisir d'amour.*

Deirdre sang the classic with deep feeling and followed it with *Down by the Salley Gardens*. Michael's mother then played three short pieces by Schumann.

—Gosh, your voice has really matured Deirdre, and you were wonderful as always Mother, said Michael as they sat down.

—Well, Sister Columba has taught me everything she knows, Deirdre replied.

—I hope Father and Mother can get you professional teachers in Dublin.

The evening then took a lighter turn with Colonel Cosbie singing *The Foggy Foggy Dew.*

It was after midnight and Rosemary and Brian looked quiet tired. Michael began to feel groggy.

—Perhaps we should take our leave, Mother, he said. I'm feeling tired and as you can see Rosemary and Brian look very sleepy.

—Perhaps we should. I'll have a word with your father.

The following days were full of musical evenings, at Miss Fisher's, Father Fogerty's, and the Mercy Convent. On New Year's Day, with a mixture of apprehension and elation, Michael returned to Fermoy.

On the morning of the 26th January the battalion moved to Camp Kilworth in battle order. Listening to the uileann pipes Michael felt proud of his twenty recruits, proud of the battalion, proud of his regiment.

—God, what a desolate place, said Deegan as they settled into their quarters.

—Well at least it gives us some experience of mountainous terrain.

—Ye can say that again.

The Blue Dragon, an old fashioned hotel and bar was the only pub in the area. Colonel Crawford, their Commanding Officer, decided that only officers could frequent it.

—Goddamn. Blast it, and may the Colonel die for the want of it, Michael overhead a veteran say in a Cork accent as he read the notice in orders of the day. Here we are stuck in the middle of a mountain with Michelstown four miles away and Fermoy even further. It's inhuman, that's what it is.

—Ah, sure we'll survive, because we have to. When we get to France we'll have to put up with more than this, said John Cunningham, one of Michael's platoon.

Rifle-range practice and Lewis light machine gun training continued over the winter. Michael's platoon now averaged twenty rounds a minute. They kept their Lee Enfield rifles well-oiled and in good shape. Michael himself averaged twenty-five rounds a minute. Colonel Murphy, adjutant to the CO, called an informal meeting of his junior officers on the 15th of February.

—At ease, Gentlemen. At ease. Smoke if you wish. As many of you know the main reason our offensive at the Marne was successful was because veteran soldiers in our regular army were such good marksmen. I realize your platoons are also familiarising themselves with Lewis light machine guns. One machine gun has the fire power of a platoon of marksmen. It's a savage truth, but this seems the future of infantry warfare. Would you officers agree?

—I'm sorry Colonel Murphy, but I disagree, said Michael feeling his cheeks redden.

—Continue, Sullivan, continue, said the officer genially.

–My platoon now average fifteen rounds a minute. That's a round every four seconds. I'm proud of them. They're as good as any French or German platoon.

–Aimed shots, bulls-eyes every time?

–Yes Sir.

–I cannot credit that Lieutenant Sullivan, said Jamie Deegan. Your lads fired fifteen rounds a minute, but at the landscape.

–God be my witness, Deegan. Have I ever lied to you?

–Ach no Sulli, but you're embellishing the truth.

–Be that as it may gentlemen, said Murphy in a calm voice. I'm proud of your platoon Sullivan, especially since they're shaping up so well. However, I spoke with Sergeant Major Dixon a couple of weeks ago. He was previously an instructor in the musketry school in Hythe. He told me that trained riflemen can get up to twenty rounds on a target in a minute. So if any of your platoons are in the fifteen-to-twenty shot average they're doing quite well.

–If they'd give us the bullets to practice with, we might get up to that standard, Sir. But they dole out five rounds a man per practice and they're gone before the lads have mastered the business of sighting.

–Give us the ammo, Sir, said Deegan evenly.

–Yes, I'll look into that Lieutenant Deegan, said Murphy writing down the Northerner's views in a notepad.

–My advice is to keep training the men in marksmanship, but to concentrate equally on Maxim and Lewis machine-gun training. I'm sorry I have to conclude now.
Thank you gentlemen.

The weather became an enemy, changing constantly from rain to sleet and snow. Because of the lack of heat throughout the camp nearly everyone developed severe chilblains.

–The old man is coming, the old man is coming, his fellow cadet Frank Hawkins said one morning.

–Which one? asked Michael.

All the senior officers seemed elderly and were veterans of the Boer War.

–Parsons, you dolt. He's reviewing the whole 47th Brigade tomorrow at 9 a.m.

It was the 10th of March, 1915.

Much of the afternoon was spent in preparation, putting the recruits through their paces one more time. Then Michael, Deegan, and Hawkins supervised the oiling and cleaning of rifles and the polishing and shining of boots and regimental emblems. Packs were washed and hung over the table by the billet fire, web-belts were cleaned, every speck of mud and grease removed.

The packs were loaded with overcoats, mess-tins, razors, towels. These packs were packed tightly and squarely, showing no crease at the side or bulge at the corner. Ground sheets were neatly rolled and fastened on top: no overlapping was allowed. Sergeant Malone supervised the grooming and currying of horses for the senior officers. These preparations finally ended towards midnight.

–I don't know about you Frank, but I'm all in, said Michael as he finally went to bed.

–We'd best get as much sleep as possible Mick. Reveille is at six, said Hawkins.

At 07.00 hrs. next morning the battalion left Kilworth for the seven-mile march to Fermoy. At the racecourse they were joined by three battalions of the Munster Fusiliers, also members of the 47th Brigade. The men stood easy, awaiting the arrival of the veteran general, platoons sized from flanks to centres, the tallest men standing at the flanks, the khaki lines dwindling in stature towards the small men in the middle. Michael, Deegan, Hawkins and fellow junior officers quickly checked that everything was correct: no lace ends showing from under puttees, laces were not crossing over boots, each soldier with a recent haircut and freshly shaved, his hat set straight on his head, the regimental badge in proper position over the idle chinstrap, pocket flaps and tunics buttoned, water bottles and haversacks hung straight, the tops of the latter in line with bayonet rings, entrenching tools and handles scrubbed clean. This done Michael and his colleagues took their places at the rear of the group.

Colonel Murphy then stood front and centre and quietly addressed the men.

–Men, not a movement of any kind while I conduct General Parsons through your ranks. I mean this. Every eyelash must be still. If the general asks me your name and I make a mistake and say you're Brady instead of Walsh, you're not to say a word. You are Brady for the time being. If he speaks to you, you're to answer 'Sir' to every question. If you're asked what your age was on your last birthday, your age and 'Sir' is to be the complete answer. Is that clear to every man?

It was indeed. Abundantly clear.

Sir Lawrence Parsons arrived at precisely 9 a.m., a tall, thin, dapper man with stern eyebrows and a grey moustache. He was attended by a slim brigade major in horn-rimmed glasses. The major made several entries in his notebook. As guided by Murphy, he followed on the heels of his superior.

The Brigade stood statue-like and immovable, fingers glued to rifles and feet firm on the earth at an angle of forty-five degrees. From the rear Michael could see the still platoons in front, not a hat moved, not a boot shifted. The general broke the spell.

—What's your name private? he asked a red-haired soldier.

—Casey, Sir, said the soldier, with his colour rising.

—Turning to the major, the General said, another unbuttoned pocket. So far, there are only a few, he said.

The man with glasses made an entry. Through an oversight, Casey had lowered the prestige of the Leinsters: a pocket flap of his tunic was unbuttoned.

Kit inspection was something quite separate. General Parsons picked out several soldiers haphazardly and ordered them to open their packs - spoons, shirts, underclothes, socks, and the several necessities which infantry in marching order must carry on their persons were inspected carefully. One soldier was unlucky: he'd forgotten to pack a toothbrush and comb.

—What's this soldier's name, Colonel Murphy? asked the general.

—Private Cosgrave, Sir.

—He's forgotten two necessary objects Captain. He's brought down the general reputation of the Leinsters. I recommend two hours of fatigue duty.

—Yes Sir, immediately upon return to camp.

—All things taken into consideration, I'm happy with the fitness and military preparedness of the 16th Division, and with your training to date, said Parsons at the conclusion of his inspection.

Warfare is a constantly changing science. Since the Marne offensive our forces seem to have become less mobile. Because of conditions at the front and probably also because of the weather, we and our Allies have assumed defensive positions. This is especially true in the area of the strategic city of Ypres. Officers and junior officers, I want you to redouble your efforts in the training of the men.

The men cheered lustily. General Parsons shook hands with senior officers. The combined bands of the Leinsters and Munsters struck up *Let Erin Remember*. Led by Colonel Murphy on his mare Matilda, the men, by company, wheeled right, saluting the Divisional Commander as they marched by. Exiting the racecourse, the Battalion quickly traversed Fermoy's business centre as a small crowd of townsfolk applauded. Reaching the outskirts, Murphy signalled a halt, dismounted, and addressed the men.

—At ease, men. You may smoke. I think we've a lot to be proud of. To be frank, I was quite concerned as to our level of preparedness and fitness. This is why I was so thorough in everything my junior officers and I put you through over the last week. I've organized a beef dinner and an extra pint of Smithwicks for

each man this evening. We'll continue our march in five minutes. Bye the way, Cosgrave, you'll still have to do two hours of kitchen duty.
No hard feelings Private.

—No offence taken, Sir. Sorry I let down the side. I won't make that mistake again.

—You'd better, or I'll have your guts for garters, said Murphy smiling. Thank you men.

Over the next ten days close-order drill, squad drill, section drill, and platoon drill exercises were redoubled. Route marches of eight miles or more became the norm.

The men grumbled occasionally

—Listen lads, I know you're getting fed up of all this drilling. The honour of the battalion and the Leinsters is at stake, said Michael to his platoon. The men seemed to be in fine fettle.

Full-scale brigade exercises were being held in the bogs and mountains near Mallow in mid-April. Michael noted in his diary:

> *The battalion would be better out of Ireland. The men are fretful at being kept here so long.*

Chapter Five

The Lusitania and aftermath, Cork, May 1915

Virginia was having a busy morning at the North Infirmary. There had been five new admissions overnight. All suffered from breathing disorders. One woman in her early forties was in severe distress. A curtain had been drawn around her bed, an oxygen mask placed on her face.

—Put some extra blankets on her bed Nurse Martin, said Dr. Muldowney.

The grey-haired consultant was accompanied by five medical students from the nearby university.

—Make sure she doesn't throw them off, she has pneumonia. We have to break the fever, The next six hours are critical. Give her plenty of fluids.

—Of course Dr. Muldowney. Do you have any instructions regarding the other eight patients here?

—No, just keep them warm. Follow the instructions on their charts. There seems to be an epidemic of late winter colds. Everyone's resistance seems to be down and the heating and ventilation in the houses in this end of the city is poor. I must leave now. My students are anxious to see some surgical cases.

—Thank you Dr. Muldowney.

It was almost 11.00a.m, time for a fifteen-minute tea break. After checking the remainder of her patients Virginia left the ward and walked the short distance to the nurse's station.

—I've just made some strong tea, said her colleague, Norah McCarthy. It's Barry's Irish Breakfast Blend.

—Great tea Nurse McCarthy. It's better than Lyons's English Blend.

—We have to support our own businesses, don't we Nurse Martin?

—May I ask you something Nurse McCarthy? We've worked together for three months now. None of the sisters are about. Could we not use our first names in this instance?

—Of course. Call me Norah and I'll call you Virginia or Virgie if you wish.

—I'd prefer Virginia - it's what my parents call me. How was your day up to now?

—Busy enough. There was an accident down on Patrick's Street, a horse bolted. I think there was a loud bang of a carbide bomb or something that panicked him. The driver did his best to rein him in. He pulled on the reins with all his might. He wasn't successful. He fell off the cart and was pulled more than a hundred yards. Then the horse fell between the shafts and broke one of his

hind legs. They had to put him down. The driver had multiple fractures and cuts on his face. We have him in splints and Dr. Muldowney is setting his right arm in plaster of Paris.
They might keep him for a couple of hours just in case he has a concussion.

–So he banged his head?

–Yes, when he fell off the cart. You can't be too careful with head injuries. Oh! have a Goldgrain or a Nice Biscuit.

–I'll have a Goldgrain, Norah. Those other biscuits are too sweet for me.

The strong tea caught the back of her throat. The roughage in the biscuit felt good.

From the large windows Virginia looked down on flowering cherry blossoms both white and pink. Several Mayflowers were also in bloom. To the right was Shandon Church, whose bells were famous throughout the country. Further below lay the city, it's busy port and the azure sea.

–I wish they'd allow us to smoke Virginia. I only began six months ago, but I already smoke ten a day; I think I'm hooked.

–You might be Norah. Still ten a day isn't that much. I smoke more than that if I'm really busy. Sure it's one of the few comforts we have.
I wouldn't worry Norah.

Norah laughed a deep throaty laugh.

–Well, we'd best get back to the grind. Less than four hours to go; I can't wait to get out into that sunshine.

–Neither can I, said Virginia, finishing the last of her tea and rinsing her enamel cup with warm water.

The patient with pneumonia appeared to be breathing with great difficulty. Virginia rushed to her bedside. She pressed the bell on her table. Then put an extra pillow under her head and shoulders to raise her up.

Her breathing was still laboured, but seemed a little easier. Dr. Muldowney answered the bell and saw what she'd done.

–You did well, Nurse Martin, he said taking the woman's pulse and checking her respiration. I'm afraid it'll be another couple of hours before her fever breaks.
It's touch and go 'til then.

–Sad, doctor. She's a lady with a young family.

–We've done what we can, nurse. We'll have to wait and see.

The rest of Virginia's shift was without incident. She filled her replacement in on the patient's status and went to the changing room.

She had just changed into her street clothes when there was an urgent knock on the door.

–All off duty staff are to report to Sr. Columba's Office. There appears to be some kind of emergency and Sr. Columba needs us, said a small nun in her mid-forties.

–I'll be there immediately Sr. Patricia, said Virginia, putting her beret and windbreaker back in her locker.

Twelve anxious nurses and two Sisters of Charity crowded Sr. Columba's large office.

–Thank you all for coming, said the genial nun, I've just had a telegram from the Cunard Company in Queenstown. There's been an emergency.

–At two fifteen this afternoon the luxury liner Lusitania en route from New York to Liverpool, was hit by two torpedoes off the Old Head of Kinsale.

–It sank very quickly, in less than forty minutes. Because of this, most of the lifeboats couldn't be launched. Up to twelve hundred are feared dead.

–The Cunard Company have asked that as many of us as possible give medical and psychological assistant to the survivors. We have two emergency ambulances ready to make the journey to Queenstown. Dr. Muldowney and Dr. O'Hara will head our contingent. Now, would all of you change back into your uniforms? I'll be coming with you myself, as will Sr. Patricia and Sr. Conleth. As this is a medical emergency, I really can't say how long you'll have to remain on duty. I understand that a group of St. John's Ambulance workers, and a contingent from Victoria Barracks are already underway.

–I expect to see you all in uniform at the emergency ambulance entry in ten minutes. The coming hours won't be easy. Nurse McCarthy has been in situations like this in the past and will bear me out. May God help us in this difficult time.

With a hush, all filed out of the superior's office.

–So you've been in this kind of emergency before Norah? asked Virginia.

–Yes, there was a terrible fire in a tenement house about a mile from here six years ago. There were no fire escapes. Three people died from the smoke. Seven people had very bad burns. I'm afraid what we're going to witness will be far worse. So remain calm Virginia. If I can be of any help to you, I will. I'm sorry, I have to have a quick puff now. It calms me down. See you in three minutes.

–Grand, Norah.

They arrived in Queenstown some fifty minutes later. The well paved road hugged a cliff slightly above the port area. The Commodore, an art deco first class hotel, was to their left.

5 - The Lusitania and aftermath, Cork, May 1915

Smoke billowed from Queenstown station, arriving goods trains filled with food for the survivors created a cacophony of sound. A Royal Irish Constabulary officer ordered them to halt, and they paused briefly while Dr. Muldowney advised them of their mission. The sergeant told their driver the quickest route to the Cunard dock. Looking through the ambulance window on their left, Virginia noted the massive gothic cathedral of St. Coleman. To her left, Sr. Columba and Dr. Muldowney conferred with a company official. They were joined by Sr. Patricia and Sr. Conleth, Dr. O'Hara, and the nurses in the second ambulance.

—Sisters and nurses, said Dr. Muldowney. The Honourable Mr. Duggan and members of the St. John's Ambulance Brigade are already here and have seconded two large baggage storage areas as makeshift triage areas. Our duty is to work with them and give every assistance possible to the survivors.
Not only are we to give emergency medical assistance, but we're to try and calm them and take emergency telegraph messages to the Cunard offices for transmission to their families. Sisters Columba, Patricia and Conleth and of course myself and Dr. O'Hara have the right to administer opiates and other tranquillizers to the injured.
Those of you that have worked in emergency in the hospital may also do this. Those of you still in training will fill a vital service by cleaning and bandaging wounds. Now I'd like you to divide yourselves into three groups and go to these sheds. They're just below us to the right. I'll talk with you again in about three hours.

—Virginia, have you been in this type of situation before? whispered Norah McCarthy.

—Yes Norah, just once, following the Bachelors Walk shootings last year.

—Stick with me anyway. It's best we work together.

The air in the large baggage room was fetid, smelling of pus, methylated spirits, and iodine. Virginia felt she was gagging and reached for a glass of water. Most of the patients were suffering from shock, their faces white as sheets, their hair matted with salt, many with one or both arms in splints; though covered in grey woolen blankets they trembled continuously.

Dr. Moore of the St John Ambulance Brigade has given nearly all of them sedatives.

—I can't give them any more for now, said Dr. O'Hara.
For the present simply give them tea, juices, or water, as Dr. Muldowney said.
Take down their instructions if they want telegrams sent.
If they want simply to talk, just listen to them. They've been through a horrendous ordeal. Nearly all of them don't know where other members of

their families are. Now there are fifteen empty cots here. We can expect more patients.

—Nurse, have you seen my mom? a small voice from the front of the shed asked.

Virginia looked towards a small girl with sunken eyes and salt encrusted hair. She couldn't have been more than seven. She held a small china doll to her chin.

—No love, I haven't, Virginia replied in as soft a tone as possible. Come with me now dear, we'll get you something to drink, and we'll do our best to find your Mommy.

Leaving the baggage room Virginia saw more survivors, beckoned to them, and led them to the second baggage room, where several local women were serving mugs of hot soup and ham sandwiches. Behind a woollen curtain at the rear they had a supply of towels and dry warm clothes. She entrusted the child to them and returned to the nursing station.

A tall woman with a deep gash on her forehead stumbled into the hall. Norah McCarthy caught her in her large arms and led her to a vacant cot.

—Oh God. I'm so happy I've survived, she mumbled.

—Let's get you some brandy and some warm clothes Ma'am, said Nurse McCarthy. Virginia, could you pour her a glass?

Immediately Virginia reached for the Hennessy bottle and poured a measure.

—Drink this Ma'am, 'twill do you good, said Nurse McCarthy.

The lady sipped slowly. Colour began to return to her face. Meanwhile Norah McCarthy held her firm and slowly removed her torn sodden clothes.

Virginia had a bath towel and vigorously rubbed her backside and entire body.

—Thank you both, the woman mumbled.

Now they had her clothed in a loose-fitting gown and wrapped in blankets.

—A little more brandy Ma'am? asked Virginia.

—Yes please. Oh, could you inquire if a Mr. Friend has been brought ashore. We were on the same deck on the liner and are good friends.

—Of course Ma'am. May I have your name please?

—Yes, I'm Miss Theodate Pope. I was on B deck of the ship.

Virginia noted this down and went to the telegraph office. Sadly, they had no news of Mr. Friend.

—I'll keep my eyes and ears open nurse, said the information officer.

Returning to the converted baggage room, Virginia found Miss Pope in a deep sleep, and that three more cots were full.

A handsome officer of the Munster Fusiliers brought a woman in her late sixties to the door of the treatment centre, and beckoned Virginia.

—Nurse, this is Mrs. Hutchins. She's just lost her husband. They were en route to London to celebrate their wedding anniversary. She's very distressed. Try and comfort her.

I must leave. A merchant ship is docking. It's towing about six lifeboats. I know I'll be bringing others here.

—Mrs. Hutchins, come with me said Virginia. You must be very tired.

—I am, nurse, she sobbed. Harold died about forty minutes ago. I've only just realized it, Sunday would have been our fortieth wedding anniversary. We'd hoped to spend it at the Savoy. Now Harold is gone I don't know what to do. Oh God! Why did you take Harold and leave me here?
Couldn't you have given us this last vacation together? Why did you leave me here alone, Lord?

Roused from sleep, several survivors looked at Virginia quizzically. She put her index finger to her lips and tried desperately to think of something to say. The still beautiful Mrs. Hutchins looked her directly in her eyes.

—God's ways are not ours Mrs. Hutchins, she whispered haltingly. This terrible war affects us all, especially the innocent. I wish there was something else I could say.

—You see, Harold was quite ill, nurse, and would probably have died before year's end. It's just that it's so sudden. Why couldn't we both have died?

—Again, God's ways are not ours, Ma'am. I pray he gives you peace in the coming days. Now lie down there while I get you a bowl of Oxtail soup.

Sr. Conleth, large, strong, in her mid-fifties, helped her.

—Time you took a break, Nurse Martin, said the sister fifteen minutes later.

—Thank you Sister.

Virginia looked at her watch. It was seven forty-five. She, Norah, and their contingent had been working for almost four hours. Brilliant evening sunshine highlighted the azure sea which was calm as a lake. She walked the short distance to the first aid station. A kindly woman wearing a full flowered apron offered her a chicken sandwich, a bowl of potato soup, and a mug of strong tea.

—God, you must be famished nurse. This will revive you.

—Thank you Ma'am, you're a godsend.

She sat back in a rough kitchen chair, closed her eyes and breathed deeply for several minutes; then attacked her food. The chicken sandwich was spread thickly with butter, the soup hearty.

The strong tea revived her. She drank it quickly, then approached the middle-aged lady for a second cup.

—It's great tea, Missis. It really revives one.

—Yes it's Lyons's the shops here ran out of Barry's. Lyons's is a good brand too. Anyway, we kept it on a gas heater. I think if got stronger as time passed.
Let me know if you want more.

—I will indeed.

Sipping the last of her tea Virginia again sat back in her chair and closed her eyes.

—So this is where you've been hiding Nurse Martin, said Norah McCarthy a mischievous tone in her voice.

—Sorry Norah, Sr. Conleth insisted I take a break.

—Arrah, that's all right Virginia. She said the same thing to me just now.

Well I'd better get back Norah. We shouldn't both be here at the same time. There'll be more survivors arriving soon.

—There will indeed. Here, have a cigarette, 'twill do ye good.

Virginia coughed as she took the first few puffs of the Players Norah offered. Then she inhaled and began to feel the effects of the nicotine.

—This is quite nice Norah. It does calm one down. I'd best be away. I'll see you in a tick. Enjoy the food.

—I will. See you.

Dressed in an ill-fitting suit a bespectacled balding man approached Virginia. Both his hands were covered in bandages.

—Nurse, can you direct me to the St John's Ambulance Depot? He asked.
I'm Samuel Abramowitz from Paris. I was in New York to buy medicine for my ambulance services. Sadly, the crates containing them have sunk. I have some medical training and may be able to help.

—You're a survivor?

—Yes, that's how I blistered my hands. He made a weak attempt at a smile.
After the torpedo struck there was an explosion, everything seemed to turn black.
Huge spouts of very black water came up all round us and then washed over the decks. There was a lady standing by the rail just above where the shell struck. A

huge water-spout rose up beside her, then fell on her knocking her down. She got up again though, so she can't have been seriously injured.

—What happened after that first shock doctor? asked Virginia.

—Well, I realized what had happened and wondered whether the ship would sink. I can't say that there was panic, but there was certainly great confusion. The first thing I noticed was that an order was issued that women and children should go at once to the boat deck. Another thing I saw was that when a large number of passengers were going up the stairs, followed by seamen and stokers, some children fell. They were carefully picked up and set on their feet again. Then I decided that the ship would certainly sink. I felt I'd be safer in the water.

The liner was still moving forward, however, probably from force of mass. I realized that if I jumped immediately, I'd soon be left far behind and out of sight. There wasn't a sail or smoke to be seen on the horizon. Then I had to decide whether to drop into the sea by the bow where she was sinking or by the stern. I decided on the stern. I needed a lifebelt. I found one in my cabin. I removed my clothes in the effort to attach it I returned to the upper deck and made for the stern. The vessel lurched knocking a lot of passengers down. Time was getting very short.

I was never a high diver. The drop was over thirty yards. Then I noticed a long rope and decided to risk going down that. I climbed over and lowered myself hand over hand, using my bare feet to steady myself. The rope trailed off into a wire rope and when I looked up I saw that several stokers were right above me and that I needed to hurry. I slid the last few yards. That's why my fingers are bandaged.

On reaching the water I immediately struck out in hope of getting as far as possible from the sinking ship. I treaded water for a few minutes. Presently I saw a lifeboat. I swam after her, came in back of her stern and climbed in. The other passengers were panicking thinking there wasn't a plug in the bottom of it. There was! I relaxed a little, turned round and looked towards the Lusitania. She was sinking by the bow and her stern was rising higher out of the water. There were boats here and there and a number of people clinging to wreckage.

Then the liner simply lurched and went under. The water turned into froth over where she'd been. Large air bubbles came bursting up. Then flotsam came up and floated round: deck chairs, tables, suitcases. Incredible to think that just minutes earlier there had been a great liner there.

Suddenly Mr. Abramowitz seemed to realize how long he'd been telling his story.

–Oh! forgive me, he said. Even though my hands are covered with Elastoplast I believe I might be of assistance.

–Certainly Dr. Abramowitz. I'm sorry to have delayed you. If you follow me, I'll introduce you to Sr. Columba and Dr. Muldowney of our group.
I know they'll be very glad of your help.

In the half-light, groups of survivors hung about the harbour and rushed each lifeboat as it arrived, or tugboat as it docked. The operation was no longer a search and rescue one, simply the grim task of retrieving and identifying bodies.

The officers and men of the Munster Fusiliers were kind, but firm, telling them that the bodies were being brought to the local town and that by milling round them they were impeding them in their duties. Most of the survivors wore ill-fitting clothes supplied by the St John's Ambulance Brigade. Virginia had little time to look seaward.

–Nurse Martin, have you assisted at a birth during your time at Vincent's? enquired Sr. Conleth.

–I have, Sister, it was a normal delivery.

–Well, this is a premature delivery. The mother, Mrs. Cunningham of Brooklyn, is in her eight month. Dr. O'Hara is very experienced in these matters. Follow me.

–You've assisted before, Nurse Martin? asked a smiling Dr. O'Hara.

–I have, doctor.

–Well this should be relatively easy. The contractions are coming every six minutes. The baby is arriving early because of the stress Mrs. Cunningham's been through.

–Relax as much as you can Mrs. Cunningham. When I say push lean forward and bear down as much as you can. Very shortly you'll have a new boy or girl.

–If it's a girl, I'll call her Lucy. She'll be one great gift after all this trouble, gasped Mrs. Cunningham.
Jesus H. Christ. The pain is really fucking awful, Sorry Sister.

–Not to worry, love, I've heard worse. Just bear down now. Nurse Martin, hold her right shoulder, said Sr. Conleth. I'll be holding her left one. Breathe easy now, girl.

–Keep your feet well apart love, said O'Hara. You're doing great. Great! Two or three more pushes and you'll be a new Mom, Take it easy now.

–I will doctor, gasped Mrs. Cunningham. Ow! Ow! Ow! Jesus, Mary and Joseph, the fucking pain, cried Mrs. Cunningham minutes later.

–You're doing great Mrs. Cunningham. I can see the head. The colour is good. Just one more push and the baby will come out Sr. Conleth and Nurse Martin are holding you. When you feel the contractions just push.

–Right doctor. Please call me Christina.

–Christina it is. Breathe easy again. Take your ease for a minute or two.

–Fine Dr. O'Hara. May I ask your Christian name?

–Brendan.

–Brendan it is ...Oh God!

–Right I have the head now. Just one more really big push. I have the shoulders now. Oh, it's a boy. The afterbirth is coming away.
Just a moment now.

Dr. O'Hara gave the newborn a slap on its buttock. It cried.

–Just suction the nose a little Sr. Conleth. I'll cut the cord in a moment and place him in a nappy. Right, there you are, Christina, your new son.
You've done a wonderful job.

–So have you, doctor. His name is going to be Brendan. Is Conleth a man's name Sister?

–Yes, I believe it is. He was a Celtic saint.

–So I'll call him Brendan Conleth. Thank you also nurse. Your name is?

–Virginia. Virginia Martin.

–Now I'll take the lad for a minute or two, Christina. I'll bring him back to you, said Dr. O'Hara.

–That'd be really lovely doctor, sighed Christina.

Virginia gently washed the newborn in a basin, wrapped it in a small nappy, covered its head with a small cloth cap, wrapped it in a baby blanket, and returned it to Dr. O'Hara.

She had a feeling of profound peace as she completed these tasks. For all the pain and tragedy of the day at least one good thing had happened. A new child was born.

–Well this calls for a small celebration, said Dr. O'Hara. Both mother and child are sleeping now. Both you Sr. Conleth, and you Nurse Martin, behaved perfectly. Here's to Brendan Conleth Cunningham. He proffered a small bottle of Paddy Whiskey.

–Ye'll have a small drop, both o' ye. Ye've earned it.

–If you insist, Dr. O'Hara.

–I do. *Beatha slan agus saor Brendan agus a sa mathar. Slainte.*

–*Slainte Mor* replied Sr. Conleth and Virginia.

–Nurse Martin, Sr. Columba has found a boarding house at the far end of the town. The house is called Clematis Lodge. I want you, Nurse McCarthy and four others to go there.

–We'll expect you back at 7.30a.m.tomorrow morning.
Sr. Patricia, Sr. Columba and two nurses will cover the night shift.
Sleep well, said Sr. Conleth some thirty minutes later.

–Thank you Sister, I'll try, replied Virginia.

The house was on a 300 foot incline almost directly behind the new cathedral. Looking down, Virginia saw that small craft were still entering the harbour. Perhaps there were still survivors, but realistically, more than ten hours after the tragedy, could there be?

–Time for bed, Virginia said to Norah McCarthy, as they entered the small kitchen of their lodging. Make some tea. I've something we can use as a nightcap.

She produced two whiskey snifters from her knapsack. She lit a Gold Flake while Virginia put a kettle on the coal cooker. Virginia rinsed out a teapot, then added two spoons of tea and boiling water.

–It's been a very difficult day Virginia, the worst of my career so far. We're really in the war now. I simply can't understand why the Germans, a very civilised race o' people would sink a ship with more than two thousand people on it.

–I don't either, Norah, but didn't that elegant lady Miss Pope say that there was a notice or advertisement in a New York paper saying that all shipping going to England was considered hostile and a target.

–Yes she did, Virginia. There have been rumours for some time that guns and other arms have been shipped to Liverpool on ships docking here. President Wilson doesn't want England to lose this war Norah, but from what I've read, most Americans don't want their country to fight.

–It's clear that they don't Virginia, but the fact that nearly all those who drowned today were Americans will mean that the President will have to take very strong action.

–Yes, he probably will, but isn't it strange that there wasn't a patrol boat of any kind in the area after what Mr. Churchill said recently about keeping the sea lanes safe.

–I'd say there's more to that than meets the eye. It might be made clear later.

—I doubt that Norah, not for a long time. The Navy are very tight lipped about these things. Anyway, thank you Norah, and your very good health. I'll sleep better for this.

The whiskey didn't help. Virginia simply couldn't sleep. Images from earlier that day crowded her consciousness. Perhaps if she recalled a happy event it might help. She remembered the first time she met Michael's family the previous August. The banter between Michael and his younger brother Chris, their evening spent at the small lake at the bottom of his father's farm, the mournful cry of the water hen, the swans with their half-grown cygnet, the threshing of the wheat and barley the next day. Then the trip they made through counties Clare, Galway and Mayo as they traveled to Sligo. It was sad that she couldn't have shown Michael her hometown and Rosses Point, but she'd made the right decision in returning to Vincent's.

The glowing reference Sr. Dymphna gave her on transferring to the North Infirmary attested to this. It also increased Michael's love and affection. More recently there were the two days they'd spent at Acton's Hotel Kinsale at Halloween. The masked ball which continued well past midnight was unforgettable,

She'd let Michael spend two hours alone with her in her room that evening.

—I love you with all my heart, Virginia, he said hoarsely, I can't wait 'til we marry.

He kissed her longingly on her cheeks and mouth then released the buttons of her blouse and caressed and kissed her breasts.

Then he placed his hand gently between her legs and massaged then kissed her sex. She's raised her buttocks and begun to moan. She was moaning now as she remembered everything, sighing *Michael, Michael, Michael* She continued caressing herself feeling her body tremble.

Perhaps she was committing sin, but was it really sin? Wasn't the body good? She was in a committed friendship with an understanding of marriage.

The sexual act was the greatest part of marriage. Jesus himself had blessed it at the wedding at Cana.

Her juices began to flow, she trembled several more times, then cleaned herself with a new handkerchief. Minutes later she fell into a deep sleep.

After a light breakfast at six forty-five next morning all six nurses returned to the triage area.

—Sisters, nurses, I've just had this note from Mr. Murphy of the Cunard Company, said Sr. Columba. He's advised me that as of today it's unlikely there will be more survivors and that things are more of a recovery of bodies mission. Our duties here remain and are to give practical help and care to all our patients and to send telegrams and other messages for them. Oh! I've had a special request. There's been a telegram from the American Embassy in London. It appears that there were a number of important people on the liner. Their families have requested that their remains be coffined and sent to New York for burial. This means that as far as possible the bodies at Lynch's Quay, and in the Market Hall be identified and photographed, I take it all of you have seen undamaged bodies. Would those of you who feel they'd be able to help do this difficult task raise their hands?

Virginia, Norah, and Nurse Lombard volunteered. Sr. Columba gave all three surgical masks.

–You'll probably need these. The smell can be quite bad. I've a couple more for the Cunard people. Right, there's a Lieutenant McGuinness of the Munster's down at the entrance who'll give you further instructions and bring you to Lynch's Quay. Thank you all in advance.

The smell in the warehouse of rotten eggs, of death, was pervasive, invading Virginia's nostrils as she and Nurse Lombard entered the morgue area. It stayed in the back of her mouth and made her want to retch.

Shafts of sunlight filled the room, contrasting with the scene to the rear. Large bluebottles and horseflies had discovered the bodies and buzzed incessantly. A Mr. Nichols of the Cunard Company had a copy of the passenger manifest and referred to it as they went from body to body.

Virginia, Norah, and Nurse Lombard had indelible pencils and small labels which they attached to the fingers of those identified. Those identified were to be sealed in oak coffins for shipment. Those Americans not immediately identified were to be photographed coffined and shipped home. The photographer had a medium sized camera and did his work efficiently. Virginia found the job difficult. She could see the strain in Nurse Lombard's and Norah's faces. She reasoned they all felt the same. By four that afternoon the task was completed.

–Well, we'd better return to the hospital area and Sr. Columba, said Norah McCarthy.

–Girls, thank you all. Mr. Nichols thinks very highly of you. I wish I could give you some time off, but we're short staffed and you're needed. Have a cup of strong tea before you begin again. I wish I had something stronger to offer.

–Don't worry Sister, we'll be all right, said Norah McCarthy.

Virginia wanted some good news and went to check on Christine Cunningham. She was nursing her new-born.

—He's a hungry little man, Nurse Martin. I nursed him the first time, around eleven o'clock. He suckled just a little. Now he seems to have got the hang of it. Both of us slept well last night and most of the day.

—You needed it Mrs. Cunningham, after the day you had and the great work you did in bringing him into the world.

—Well he came a little early, but I wouldn't have it any other way. Dr. O'Hara gave him a full check-up at noon. He says I have nothing to worry about. He showed me how to burp him and told me to always support his head. Sr. Patricia had already instructed me in these things, but I didn't tell Dr. O'Hara.

—Can I put him in his cot, Christine? He seems to be nodding off.

—Yes, of course Nurse Martin. Just wipe his little face and my breast.

Virginia gently placed the baby in his basinet.

—Have you had any word of your husband, Christine?

—Yes there was a telegram. He's travelling from London to Liverpool and will be in Cork late tomorrow. I think I'm being transferred to your hospital early so we'll meet there.

—That's wonderful Christine. I'll look in on you later.

Much of the day was spent in making the hospitalized survivors comfortable. Then, towards seven in the evening, Sr. Columba spoke to Virginia.

—Nurse Martin, we're transferring Mrs. Cunningham, her son, and two critical patients to our hospital by ambulance. Dr. O'Hara will be going. I'd like you to assist, especially with Mrs. Cunningham. You'll have time to pick up a change of uniform, and perhaps a cup of tea. I expect you back here by nine thirty.

—Certainly Sr. Columba.

Virginia returned to Christine Cunningham's camp bed. There she found Dr. O'Hara and an ambulance attendant.

—So Christine, we're transferring you and your son Brendan, by ambulance to the maternity ward of our hospital. Christine. Johnny Lynch, our attendant here, and myself will just transfer you to a stretcher right now. We'll leave the little fellow in his basinet. So Jonny, you've got the under-sheet?

—One two three. There you are Ma'am.

—Christine please, doctor.

—Christine.

Jonny Lynch and the doctor quickly carried the stretcher to the entrance of the makeshift hospital, moving a little slower up an incline to the ambulance. Virginia followed with baby Brendan. Two survivors with compound arm fractures were already seated in the rear of the ambulance. The stretcher was placed on a broad wooden shelf some ten inches above the floor. Johnny Lynch asked for Dr. O'Hara's help with the starting crank. It caught quickly, and Dr. O'Hara moved to the back of the ambulance, locked himself in, and knocked on the dividing panel. They moved quickly away.

Again, they made good time to the hospital, Lynch and Dr. O'Hara unloaded their precious cargo and directed the injured to the emergency section.

–We've only a little over ten minutes before we return to Queenstown, Nurse Martin, just enough time for you to change into a fresh uniform and for me to shave.
I'll see you then.

–Fine Dr. O'Hara.

They returned to Queenstown in good time. Then, at ten thirty, Sr. Columba gave Virginia, Norah McCarthy, and Nurse Lombard leave to return to their lodgings. They found three colleagues drinking tea in the small kitchen.

–Have a cuppa, said a tall thin nurse named Gaffney. It's strong. There's boiling water in the kettle if you want it weaker.

–Thank you Nurse Gaffney.

–I want to thank all of you for your wonderful very professional work, said Sr. Columba, as they began their shifts next morning.

–You're excused from the obligation of mass today. However, there will be a Requiem Mass tomorrow for all the victims of the sinking.

–Many of the survivors will need assistance, so I want nearly all of you to help. Today I'd like you to give meals and sit baths to the survivors here and to continue your great work. God Bless.

The day went quickly. Many of the survivors were still very traumatized. Miss Theodate Pope however, was composed.

–Nurse Martin, could you tell me if there's any news of Mr. Friend, my co-passenger? she asked.

–I haven't heard Miss Pope, I'll check with Sr. Columba.

–No there's been no news to date Nurse Martin, said the superior - Mr. Nichols of the Cunard Company has no news. Mr. Friend could be at the Commodore Hotel or any of the guest houses occupied by the survivors.

–Fine. I'll tell Miss Pope this, Sr. Columba.

Virginia went back to Miss Pope to tell her there was no news.

—I just hope he survived, Nurse Martin. We're very good friends. We donned lifebelts and jumped from the liner about the same time, but got separated in the water.
I did see him there, but got bumped in the head so many times and at one point felt I might die.
Well, I've survived. Thanks to a Loving God. However, I'd like to meet Mr. Friend again. We'd so much in common.

—It's only been three days Miss Pope. I'll keep checking for you with the St. John's Ambulance Brigade.

Virginia's thoughts kept returning to Michael. There had been no letter from him except a telegram of a week earlier saying that his regiment was about to cross the English Channel to Northern France. She understood there was to be further training before going to the front.

At eight the following morning, Sr. Columba addressed all her staff.

—Funeral services for the victims are at ten this morning. There will be a solemn High Mass at St Coleman's Cathedral celebrated by Most Reverend Dr. Browne, Bishop of Cloyne.

—At the same time, in the Church of Ireland, there will be a memorial service for the Anglican victims.

—I expect the majority of you will go to St Coleman's. Sr. Patricia and Sr. Conleth will accompany Miss Pope to the Anglican Service. We've been advised that there are to be just three formal funerals. The mass funerals were to have begun at nine, but have been delayed 'til noon.

—A special train with many relatives is arriving here at eleven. Nurse McCarthy, could you meet these relatives and help them in the location of their loved ones' remains?
The general funeral will now begin at noon, with a formal public funeral at three. In advance of Mass time, please go with our patients who walk with difficulty, or are in wheel-chairs, to the cathedral.

The newly built cathedral was crowded with representatives of church state and faithful, Magenta light from gothic windows highlighted frescos on the opposite walls depicting the lives of St. Patrick, St Brigid and St Coleman. The air was heavy with the scent of lily of the valley, lilac, roses, and wax candles. Mr. Murphy and Mr. Nichols represented the Cunard Company.

Virginia stood behind Mrs. Berrigan, a middle-aged woman in a wheelchair, at the third row right of the nave of the cathedral. Survivors in ill-fitting clothes filled the rest of the bench, and other benches to the rear.

Coffins draped in British, and American flags for the Catholic victims of those countries were in the sanctuary in front of the high altar.

As on past occasions, Virginia found the *Missa Pro Difunctis* with its *Dies Ire* chant very sad. The whole tenor of the chant seemed to be on God's justice, and not on the mercy and forgiveness preached by Jesus.

In his homily, the bishop of Cloyne referred to the horror of the tragedy, the great number of victims, and the steadfast courage of the survivors. Taking as his text the gospel passage, *I am the resurrection and the life. He that believeth in Me, although he be dead shall live. and everyone that liveth and believeth in me shall not die forever,* he emphasised the promise of resurrection.

Well at least there's hope in this gospel passage, hope that all those innocents and their families were at peace, thought Virginia.

Following the singing of the Credo, twelve survivors left their seats and moved to the entrance of the cathedral. Then they advanced towards the altar carrying bread and wine.

The choir departed from the formal mass and sang:

Eternal Father, strong to save
Who's arm hath bound the restless wave
Who bidd'st the mighty ocean deep
Its own appointed limits keep
O hear us when we cry to thee
For those in peril on the sea
O Christ, who's voice the waters heard,
And hushed the raging at Thy Word,
Who walkedst on the foaming deep,
And calm amid the storm did sleep
O hear us when we call to Thee
For those in peril on the sea

Most of the congregation in the third and fourth rows of the aisle wept at the conclusion of this hymn. Virginia felt the hymn comprised the hope that this horrendous tragedy might be the last at sea and that the sacrifice of so many lives might hasten peace. Mrs. Berrigan, Virginia's charge, sobbed uncontrollably. Virginia, holding a handkerchief, knelt before her, holding first her hands, then hugging her upper body.

–There, there, Mrs. Berrigan, my heart goes out to you in your great loss.
Perhaps your husband and son will be found. They could have been brought to Kinsale or another small port.

–No, Nurse Martin. In my heart I know They're gone. I'll never see them again. Why, why, did God allow this?

Virginia tried to think of an answer, but couldn't. Close to tears herself, she knew she had to remain strong.

–God didn't commit this act, Mrs. Berrigan, it was the enemy. Those in charge of their army and navy are consumed by hate.

–How can they approve the killing of innocent people? Yet they'll face God immediately they die; He probably won't be merciful to them.

–He won't Nurse Martin.

–*That they may rot in hell,* she whispered.

The widow continued to sob, then, with a sigh, righted herself. With most of the congregation, Virginia and Mrs. Berrigan received communion. She felt peace, and prayed that Christ would give comfort to the survivors and courage to continue their lives.

Following the final blessings Virginia went towards the main door, but it was impassable for her with the wheelchair. Naval and army contingents crowded the doorway. *Where were the Naval patrol boats two day earlier?* she thought again.

Mrs. Berrigan seemed weak, and was slumped in her wheelchair.

–I'll find another way out, Mrs. Berrigan, and get us back to the hospital area as soon as I can.

Re-entering the cathedral, she found a side door which led to a small lane. Taking several side streets she managed to get to the port area avoiding the military contingent and massive crowd.

Sr. Columba was already at the makeshift hospital entrance. She welcomed Mrs. Berrigan and led them towards the back of the baggage shed.

–This should hold you for an hour or so Ma'am, she said, offering a bowl of oxtail soup and a chicken sandwich. I've made further enquiries regarding your husband and son. There's no word as yet.
Be strong. I'm having you transferred to our hospital in the city later. We'll take good care of you there 'til you're stronger. Have courage, Mrs. Berrigan.

–I'll try Sister.

Throughout the afternoon they heard Chopin's *Funeral March* and the *Dead March* from Handel's 'Saul' played by various military bands. Then the strains became fainter as the funeral procession moved towards the New Cemetery some distance from Queenstown.

Virginia, Nora McCarthy, Nurse Lombard and the contingent continued with their duties. Towards six, several extra ambulances, both from their hospital and other hospitals in Cork City, arrived. Then at seven o'clock they departed from Queenstown with casualties for the North Infirmary and other hospitals.

At nine o'clock Sr. Columba addressed all her nurses.

—Thank you all again for going well beyond the call of duty over the last three days. You've worked in the very beat traditions of the Sisters of Charity, and of our hospital. I've devised a little lottery here, sadly with only two prizes. Sr. Conleth will give you tickets. Sr. Patricia will draw two from this large bowler hat. Put your initials on the back of your ticket.

—The prize is five days in Killarney at The Lake Hotel. I wish I could give you all some time off, but I can't - our hospital is full to the rafters. Let's move ahead now. Sr. Patricia, shake up the tickets in the hat, then draw two.

—Right! Sr. Patricia?

—The first ticket is number 35. The initials at the back are N McC.

—That's me, that's me, shouted Norah.

—The second ticket is number 50, The initials at the back are V.M.

—That's me, said Virginia feeling relief and peace.

—I'll give both of you your vouchers right now. Enjoy Killarney and the lakes. As to the rest of the team get to bed right away and I'll see you all at 7.30 a.m. tomorrow.
God bless you all and renewed thanks.

Virginia returned from Killarney to the North Infirmary the following Monday, refreshed and renewed.

—Did that seem to help Nurse Martin? asked Sister Conleth.

—Indeed it did, Sister. We saw the upper and lower lakes, Muckross House, and even the rooms that Queen Victoria and Prince Albert had in their visit of fifty years ago.

—That must have been interesting. It's nice to see how the quality live. Now to work. The only person from the original group of veterans is Lieutenant Brown. His physical wounds are healing, but he's still very frail mentally, and has temperamental outbursts that are very hard to handle. As you witnessed a couple of weeks ago, he was so distraught that we had to restrain him physically. That can't have been easy, Nurse Martin.

—No it wasn't, Sister. It was sad to see him in so much pain and not to be really able to help him.

—Yes, the only thing that seems to help is to give him a sedative. Yet even in his sleep he seems to cry out a lot. Sister Columba has been in touch with the co-ordinator of a hospital a little north of Edinburg called Craiglockhart. There's a psychiatrist that she's trying to contact to give two days of lectures on the treatment of these types of patients. It's probable that he'll visit here in about ten days.

—I'm sure we'll all learn a lot Sister.

—We will. Oh! by the way there are new patients coming from Belgium in a day or so. Keep your energy level up.

—I'll try to do that, Sister.

The veterans from Flanders, nearly fifty in number, arrived two days later. Ten had respiration problems because of gas inhalation, six had second degree burns on their legs and arms; a blond-haired man of twenty-five had severe stomach wounds and was carried in by stretcher. The remainder had either an arm or leg in plaster of Paris because of breakage.

—Get this man to bed immediately, Nurse Martin, said Sr. Conleth looking at his chart. Also, could you place a tent over his stomach and don't attach the blankets too tightly.

—Certainly, Sister.

—Don't rush too much, nurse, said the young man with a broad smile. Sure, the man who made time, made plenty of it, and right now I'm rich in time.

—Indeed you are. We just want you to get well, Sergeant Findlay. You should be fit as a fiddle in six weeks or so.

—Fit for what, nurse? I've done my bit, seen things I never thought I'd see. Ypres was a beautiful market town once, I'm told. It's mostly in ruins now. I don't want to go back there.

His voice was becoming shrill.

—Well perhaps you won't, sergeant. There's always home service. Your duties will certainly be light to begin with.

—I hope you're right, nurse. I'd like to sleep now. The twenty hour journey by sea has left me really tired.

—Right Sergeant Findlay, I just need to adjust your blanket a little. It's not too tight, is it?

—No nurse, it isn't.

He closed his eyes breathed deeply and was instantly asleep.

Dr. Muldowney checked on Findlay about several hours later.

—Well, they seem to have done the necessary surgery on you in Flanders, Sergeant. However, there was some shrapnel they weren't able to remove. We'll keep an eye on it through x-rays. If it stays put, we'll leave it where it is, but if it starts to move it may mean other operations. I'll keep you up to date on things.

The following morning, Sr. Columba called a meeting.

–I'll be brief. Firstly, I want to thank all of you for the excellent work you're doing. I've actually had communication from authorities at Victoria Barracks regarding this.

There's one piece of news I have: it's that the Vincent de Paul Society at the nearest parish want to send volunteers here on Tuesdays and Thursdays with small gifts and to read parts of the New Testament with the veterans. Now, as you know, not all of them are Catholic, and I have some reservations about this. However, I couldn't find a way to refuse, as the Society does a lot of good work in poorer parts of the city. I expect we'll have to play things by ear. Have a good day, nurses.

The volunteers, six ladies in late middle age, duly arrived at two that afternoon. They advanced on the nearby beds where the severely injured patients were, and after giving them a cigarette, spoke to them of the gospels, regardless of whether the soldier wanted to talk of this or not. Many of the walking wounded made excuses of having to go to the toilet and didn't return. The ladies looked knowingly at each other, but didn't halt from their mission. One of them suggested they say the rosary. There was a tepid response which she seemed not to notice.

–In the name of The Father, and of the Son and of the Holy Ghost, she began.

Several of the veterans made the responses and the prayer was completed in fifteen minutes.

Throughout all this, Sergeant Findlay feigned sleep. One of the women approached him and held his hand which he'd left outside of his blanket. Findlay still feigned sleep.

Then he appeared to be partly awake, and holding the middle-aged lady's hand slowly drew it deeply under the blanket. After a moment she gave a little shriek and ran straight to the ward Sister's office. A little later Sister Conleth approached Sergeant Findlay. A half smile hovered about her lips.

–You must have heard me scream, Sister, I was lying here half asleep when suddenly I found a hand being very intimate under the bedclothes.

–Really, Sergeant Findlay, and leprechauns have a crock of gold with them if we can catch them. Go on back to sleep now. Be good and if you can't be good, you know the rest, she giggled.

The mood in the ward remained relaxed for the rest of the day.

Though he'd been through hell Findlay, apart from bags under his eyes, had a baby face. As he began to recover he noticed that soldiers and staff who passed his bed smiled, laughed and often made cooing sounds.

–Nurse Martin, tell me this and tell me no more: why is it that my comrades giggle or laugh as they pass my bed?

–I really wouldn't want to say, Sergeant, it's something of a secret.

–How can it be a secret nurse, if everyone seems to know it?

–Well it's because of something a tad medical written on your chart.

–I can't see my chart because of this tent, and also, I'm not supposed to get out of bed except to go to the lavatory with an orderly. Ah, Nurse Martin, be a dear and show me the chart.

–Fine, but you'll have to promise me not to laugh too much. You might break the stitches round your surgical wounds.

–I'll risk that, nurse. I promise to be good.

With a flourish Virginia took the chart from the hook at the end of the bed and read it to Findlay.

–It's nothing sergeant, she said, between giggles. Just a notice asking visitors not to feed the infant.

Under protest she showed Findlay the chart. Someone had drawn a baby's bottle full of milk, and a small blue potty. Findlay, obliged to answer to the name Babe for the remainder of his stay, was convinced that Tom Madigan, a less injured sergeant in his battalion, had perpetrated the prank.

–Mum's the word Kevin, said Madigan. All I'm saying is that one of those holy ladies is involved.

–Who is it Tom, who?

–Well, all I'm saying is that she's a little stout and has a jolly face a bit like Santa Clause. I can't say more than that.

–Does she wear a veil and a blue serge uniform?

–She does.

–It's Sister Conleth then.

–It might be her or another of the good sisters.

Findlay put up with the gentle ribbing until he was mobile. Then he destroyed the cartoon.

–What's commonly known as shell shock is not a sign of cowardice, said a tall heavy-jowled, bespectacled man in his late fifties, with a thick mustache and thinning brown hair.

His gentle voice was a mixture of British and Australian accent. It appeared he'd spent part of the 1890s in the South Sea Islands.

–Now all of you know most of the symptoms of shell shock; attacks of hysteria, quite often very sudden; extreme nervousness at any sudden sound; violent shivering and shaking like an epileptic; stammering and at night, bedwetting.

–The expression 'war is hell' is very true, and the victims of this illness have really been through hell. All have been, for months at a time, in the front lines, or less than five hundred yards behind lines. They've faced the Hun every day and also suffered from lack of sleep late rations and perpetual fear that the next shell hitting the front lines would have their name on it. Personally, I'm in awe of their great courage. Even though shells have exploded yards from them none have shirked their duty. To quote Tennyson, they have "*Gone into the jaws of death*" as their forebears did at Waterloo. Colleagues of mine and I have developed a cure, a talking cure which seems to allay some of the symptoms of this malaise. The first line of this cure is your patience and loving care.

He paused for a glass of water.

–The actual cure may take several months, but as I've said the first care-giver in the cure is you, as caring nurses and sisters. There are certain medicines which may alleviate the symptoms of nervous disorders; however, they must only be taken as prescribed, and under the guidance of a psychiatrist. Now, perhaps you Sr. Conleth and Dr. Muldowney could bring me to the ward where some of the most affected patients are?

–Of course Dr. Rivers. Come with me, Sister Conleth. Those nurses who are not immediately needed come with us also.

The assembly, numbering almost twenty, moved as a group to the locked ward one floor above.

The doors opened on a ward with thirty patients. Sitting by the entrance, was a patient in a cane chair, who seemed almost catatonic.

–How are you today Lieutenant Brown?, asked Dr. Muldowney

–What medicine do you have him on Dr. Muldowney? asked Dr. Rivers.

–We've been using a small dose of *Valerian*, Dr. Rivers.

–Well, perhaps you might make the dosage even lower doctor.

–Certainly, Dr. Rivers. There are times he's so distressed we have to use restraints. Most of our staff haven't gotten really proper training in the treatment of these disorders. We often fear for their safety.

–Yes, that's sometimes the case, doctor. We simply have to keep in mind that they're very ill and act with kindness. Reduce his medication by half.

–Of course Dr. Rivers.

The other patients were hyperactive jumping from one foot to another, crying out from time to time.

—There are other treatments for these ailments. Dr. Muldowney. A colleague, has developed a type of electric shock therapy which appears to achieve very quick results.
One of the side effects is partial memory loss. Of course, from the view of the War Office, it's in many ways more effective than the therapies I've developed. It allows damaged men to return to combat more quickly. However, my therapy returns a whole person to the army and most importantly his family and friends. I stand by it.

Dr. Rivers broke down the hospital staff into groups of ten and gave them further instruction over the next four days.

—Do you think we learned something, Virginia? asked Norah McCarthy as they ate lunch on the last day of Dr. Rivers' visit.

—Well, his instruction has confirmed many things I already knew Norah, that kindness and real patience can go a very long way in healing these troubled brave men.

Because of her changing schedule Sister Columba recommended that Virginia find lodgings a little closer to her workplace. After a brief search Virginia found a large room with a working fireplace on a secluded lane off Wellington Road. Her landlords were an elderly couple whose grown son was with the Munster Fusiliers in Flanders.

—So your sweetheart, Lieutenant Sullivan, is in The Leinsters in southern Belgium Nurse Martin? Perhaps they know each other? I remember our Joe saying that they trained with the Leinsters at Kilworth Camp.

—Yes, I believe both regiments trained together, Mrs. Dillon. Could you excuse me, I'm quite tired. I need to rest up a little.

Virginia mounted the stairs, shut the door to her room and went immediately to bed. She quite liked this couple, but felt it was prudent to keep her distance. She could see that Mrs. Dillon and her husband Jim were kind, but felt that some of Mrs. Dillon's questions were intrusive. It was better to keep her own counsel.

The fact was that she only felt really at home at the hospital. It was her milieu as no other place in her life had been. She knew without being told that she was doing a good job. Srs. Columba and Conleth respected her, as did Drs. Muldowney and O'Hara. Norah McCarthy had become like a sister. But even when she and Norah were in Killarney some weeks earlier, she itched to be back in the swim of things and chafed at being away from things that really mattered.

A new batch of veterans had arrived from Flanders. Many had been blinded in gas attacks, or had bad lung problems which weren't really curable. A Newfoundland regimental officer was among them. When Virginia first heard his voice she thought he was from Co. Galway.

—Do you have a name, sweetheart?

Virginia rinsed a bloodstained facecloth in a stainless-steel pan filled with hot water.

—Of course, it's Nurse Martin.

She met the officer's eyes for a second giving him a small smile. She ran the cloth down his arm to clean his infected wound, trying not to put pressure on it.

—Are you in the Connaught Rangers? You have a bit of a Galway accent.

—No, nurse, no, I'm from a fishing village called Carbonear on the east coast of Newfoundland. A lot of Irish settled in our part ages ago. It's why I have the accent you hear.

—Oh I expect it would Lieutenant Milligan. You know the Irish name for your country is *tir na eisc*, the country of fish.

—It's that all right. The cod and herring fisheries are the lifeblood of our nation. There's little or no topsoil on most of the island, so agriculture isn't that strong. I've spent most o' me life on small craft.

—And yet you joined the army, not the navy, Lieutenant?

—Well they were recruiting in our town in 1914, All the lads joined the Royal Newfoundland Regiment. It was kind of a 'pals brigade'. We thought the war would be over by Christmas then. No bloody luck! Sorry for the profanity Ma'am. But it hasn't been easy.

—We're aware o' that here, Lieutenant. We've seen all kinds of casualties. We're here to try and make you well again.

—Don't do it too quickly nurse. The grub here is great and I'm sleeping well for the first time in months. But tell me your first name. Nurse Martin is too formal for someone who's just washed most of my body. I might go any time?

He was trying to hold her left hand with his free arm.

—Go where? To the next life? Ah go on, you'll probably live to be ninety.

Virginia applied pressure to one of his wounds. He withdrew his hand.

—Sorry Lieutenant, the motto is 'first do no harm', but some pain is unavoidable.

—I know you mean no harm, Nurse Martin. But what's your Christian name?

–That's for me to know and you to find out. But seriously, Sr. Columba, that friendly sister of Charity you met on arriving here, insists we follow this protocol Lieutenant. It's a black mark if I tell you.

–I'll find out by hook or by crook, Nurse Martin. We Newfoundlanders are persistent.

–You've already shown that, Lieutenant. Forgive me, we're now getting to the really hard part.

The young officer's sciatic nerve had been completely severed in his right leg by shrapnel. When he'd arrived at the hospital sixty hours earlier, he was close to death. His face was deeply grey, his eyes deep in their sockets. His right leg seemed useless. It looked like another amputation. But Dr. Muldowney on examining him said there was a chance of repairing the nerve and saving the leg, and while that chance existed he was really damned if he was going to saw it off. Virginia was on theatre duty and witnessed everything.

–Prep him, Dr. O'Hara, there's no time to lose.

He indicated the chloroform mask.

–Use a few extra drops. I want the man deeply asleep throughout the operation. I've seen this before during the Boer War. I'll do my best, God willing.

Muldowney actually located the two ends of the nerve. They had sprung apart like a broken thread and were embedded in a mass of tissue and clotted blood. Virginia saw them all torn and shredded by the shell fragments. The surgeon trimmed them and had sewn them together with neat small stiches. Then in the deep dark bloody hole he wrapped animal fibrin round the joint to strengthen it before closing the wound with more neat stiches. It had been the most awe-inspiring operation she'd witnessed in her career so far, and she set great emphasis on thoroughness. Dr. Muldowney had helped her dry the instruments in the basin following the operation, because it was very late. He talked in matter-of-fact language about the operation, hoping it might 'do the trick'. He thanked Virginia for 'her invaluable assistance'. She replied that it was only her job, but it was nice to be thanked, and by such an unassuming man. Dr. O'Hara had had to rush away as another casualty was hemorrhaging.

The massage sister was under instruction to move the leg just a little, every day. It would be a miracle if the Newfoundlander walked away from the hospital on his own feet.

However, at this point Virginia wasn't sure about miracles except for surgical interventions.

Lieutenant Milligan was making a remarkable recovery following strictly the exercise set down by the massage sister. He walked first with a folding wooden frame, and later with a hand crutch, the length of the ward and to the exercise room at the end, where he stood between the exercise bars and walked over and back twenty times. He also worked with dumb bells and weights "to strengthen me right arm."

–Why the right arm, Lieutenant? asked Virginia.

–'Cause that's the one I uses for slinging Mills Bombs (hand grenades) if we're on a raid or in close combat, Virginia.

–Quietly, quietly John, she whispered. Otherwise, Sister Conleth or Sister Columba will be after me. You're making great progress.

–That I am, Virginia. Perhaps I'd better slow down a bit or I'll be back in hell again soon.

–Don't you miss the lads?

–I do, a lot, but I figure I'll see them soon enough. Doctors Muldowney and O'Hara are giving me a complete physical in a week. If they pass me, I'll be going back.

–Aren't you a bit afraid, John?

–Not really, Virginia, I was in the beginning. I was scared to death. But now in a sense I'm used to it. Jimmy Cheevers, Michael Smith, and the others from Carbonear who joined at the same time as me are boys I've known me whole life. We're more like brothers than friends now.

–Yes, I know the feeling in a smaller way. Nurse McCarthy and I, and even Sister Conleth and Dr. O'Hara and all of us who helped during the Lusitania disaster became very close at the time. We worked sixteen hours at a stretch over the three and a half days, and bonded.

–Yes, you would have. It was a real crime wasn't it? One that cries out to God for vengeance.

–I agree with you there. According to the people I nursed, there was absolutely no warning. The survivors said there were two explosions. It's not clear if the Germans fired two shells or just one. The ship went down in twenty minutes. There was a very heavy loss of life. I know you've seen much worse John, but it really took me many weeks to come to some kind of peace with it. When I go to church, I ask Christ to help me deal with it. I still have nightmares, but they're a little less vivid now than they were in June and July.

–It gets easier, Virginia, but it will never go away completely.

—I'm sorry, John, I have to look out for other patients. Let me know how your physical goes and be sure and say goodbye if you're returning to Flanders.

—I'll be sure to do that, Virginia. Mind yourself.

—I will, John.

She kissed him lightly on the cheek.

Chapter Six

Boulogne-sur-Mer, France
and Intensive Training at Étaples, Pas-de-Calais, May 1915

The soldiers awoke in broad sunshine under white breezy tents. Women moved between the men stretched out in their cots, offering small baskets of choke cherries. Michael bought some.

They were hard and bitter.

Mesmerized by the landscape, Michael reflected on the events of the last forty eight hours. Behind them Boulogne-sur-Mer stood silent in the clear morning air, the sea beyond a vast, silver calm.

Staring out at the quiet French farmland and sea, Michael could hardly believe he'd left Ireland not two days ago. The regiment's departure by train at Fermoy had been a series of jubilant fêtes. At the train station near Camp Kilworth, and at Thurles, Ballybrophy, and Portarlington, crowds on platforms threw flowers and thrust bottles of whiskey indiscriminately through compartment windows.

—...shouting For me darlin' Jimmy who's going to the war.

Mothers cried into handkerchiefs and onto shoulders, stout fathers nodded, boys jumped into horse-carts, waving their hats wildly, and when the final whistle blew, red-eyed girls rushed to the windows screaming and hugging. As the train started to move, people walked with it, unwilling to let go, crying and kissing through the window frames until the platform dropped off, giving way to hedges and short streets, then trees and the green stretch of fields and the sound of forced-back sobs and tears from young men leaving home for only the second or third time in their whole lives.

At Kingsbridge station Dublin, as the soldiers loaded packs and took formation, children stuck small flags and pennants into the muzzles of their rifles. Then the whole regiment marched to the port in jaunty step, the band playing *The Girl I Left Behind Me*. Michael's parents had motored from Rosnua to the North Wall to see him off. He had given his mother a kiss and a lingering hug and handed his ceremonial sword to his father. His father saluted.

Then the men boarded the converted cattle vessel that was their transport, and the ship weighed anchor. Below decks, when he reached his cabin, a converted stall for bulls, Michael gagged. As he bent over to throw up, the reek of cow dung watering his eyes.

6 - Boulogne-sur-Mer, France; Intensive Training at Étaples, Pas-de-Calais, May 1915

The Irish Sea was choppy and the cattle boat pitched a great deal. At Holyhead, Lieutenant Colonel Murphy gave each soldier a printed message from Lord Kitchener.

> You are ordered abroad as a soldier of the King, to help our French comrades against the invasion of a common enemy… Never do anything to destroy property, and always look upon looting as a disgraceful act… You may find temptations both in wine and women. While treating all women with perfect courtesy, you should avoid any intimacy. Do your Duty, Fear God, Honour the King.
> Kitchener

Some men chuckled contemptuously, crumpled the paper and dropped it on the roadway. As an officer, Michael conspicuously folded Kitchener's note into his Active Service Pay Book.

As he was beginning to understand, the men had many reasons for going to war, not least grinding poverty, courtesy of several centuries of landed English gentry. In the struggle between anger and patriotism, anger often took the day. Michael turned away from the cattle ship. They would be boarding a train shortly, on their way to boarding a ship to France, and battle with the Germans. Soon nothing else would matter.

There were no direct rail links to their embarkation port, Southampton, so they were obliged to travel to London. The battalion reached London by 9.00am, and Southampton by noon. Michael took the opportunity to send a quick telegram to Virginia while they awaited the arrival of their troop carrier to carry them to France.

When the troop ship they awaited docked, it had to unload its cargo of wounded soldiers. First came the boys on stretchers, carried by the lightly wounded, many with head bandages, descending the gangplank. They wore maple-leaf insignias and held onto each other's sleeves and appeared to be newly blinded. Their breathing was loud and laboured. The word went around: chlorine gas, two weeks ago in Ypres.

Michael, taken aback by watching the wounded descend, walked up to the group of Canadian officers at the foot of the gangplank.

–This gives me and my officers an awful sense of what we'll soon be facing.

–Most of these lads will be dead by month's end, said a Canadian voice quietly.

Then at 19.00 hours they finally began embarkation.

Rifle in hand, field glasses and compass swinging around his neck, Michael struggled up the gangplank with his 40-pound pack and 120 rounds of ammunition. Suddenly his new hobnail boots shot out from under him on the slick metal.

–Come on you fucking Mick! came a shout from the boarding warden. Naw damn well move, blast ye!

Only his rifle catching on the handrail in the dark had stopped him smashing his nose to pieces.

They crossed the Channel, in increasing darkness, all lights were extinguished, smoking strictly forbidden on deck; the men were packed into the lower decks like sardines. Flanked by two Royal Navy destroyers, the string of troop ships followed a zigzag pattern to avoid submarines. The diesel fumes below deck were overpowering. As the ship rocked and jerked, men started to vomit into canvas bags and pass out. The stench was nauseating, in the smoky half-light the men coughed and retched, and looks of near panic were etched into every second face.

The carrier reached Boulogne-sur-Mer past midnight. French port authorities quickly placed gangplanks at every ship exit. The men had gone up to the main deck in an orderly fashion as soon as they realized they were nearing dock. Lieutenant Colonel Murphy was first to exit, and quickly finding a port streetlight, he pulled out and studies a map of the area while the troops disembarked.

–Officers and men of the second Battalion, our designated encampment is about two miles southeast of the town. I'll lead you there on foot, said Murphy to the assembled battalion.

For some reason, the regimental band decided to start playing again - this time La Marseillaise, horns and Celtic bagpipes at full blast, as they marched from the port into the town square at two in the morning. Windows burst open from the old stone buildings, and night-capped heads thrust forth, cursing a long strings of French curses. Then stray dogs took up the tune, howling and barking, and the cries of babies began to echo in the cacophonous pauses.

The men tramped out of town and the ground began to tilt into a hill. Gasping and slipping, the band stopped mid-bar with wailing aftersound. The hill steepened. A soldier fainted and was dragged off the footpath, left to recover on his own. An hour after disembarking, in the moonless dark, the men reached their camp overlooking the port and tumbled into the tents they found.

And here Michael stood, spitting choke cherries into the beautiful sea air.

At 1200 hrs Lieutenant Colonel Murphy called a meeting of the Battalion.

—Men I trust you've slept relatively well. I've just had a telegram from General Parsons. We're to travel tomorrow to Étaple, a training area in le Pas-de-Calais, for further combat training before moving to the front lines of Ypres. This further training has been sanctioned by General French and High Command. Personally, I will warn you that this will be extremely challenging to both officers and men, but all must undergo it. We'll travel by train at 10.00hrs tomorrow. Dismiss.

The train journey next morning was relatively fast as this region of France was mostly unaffected by the conflict. Built mostly on land reclaimed from the sea and with a pine forest towards the rear Étaples-sur-Mer hosted a large military hospital comprised of several wooden buildings, and large canvas hospital tents all marked with clear Red Cross emblems. The hospital tents could be seen from the troop train as they approached. On detraining at 1700hrs Michael, Hawkins, and Malone were met by the pungent smell of pine, mixed with that of fish and sea. Consulting another map Lieutenant Colonel Murphy again addressed the Battalion.

—Men, our designated barracks area is a mile from this station, a short distance before the hospital. Tomorrow morning at 8.00 hours you're to assemble by company at an area known as The Bull Ring. It's part of that headland a little to the southeast. I'll be with you at the handing over, but then have to go to Ypres for a strategic officers meeting. Try and get a good night's sleep as the coming days will be very demanding. Dismiss.

For the next ten days, Michael's company dug trenches and learned to fight with boots, fists, teeth, and shovels.

—Why don't we have our guns? asked a private.

—Because, you milquetoast excuse for a soldier, you dropped it in the mud when you soiled your drawers, that's why, explained training officer McGrindle, a muscle bound man of six feet. Now shut up and keep digging.

Sergeant Major McGrindle seemed to wake up angry. He was particularly fond of a wide tidal beach south of town where the sand was sodden and heavy.

—Gentlemen. Do you see that long spit of sand where the water has oh so recently receded? he barked at them.

—Yes sir, they shouted.

—You know the drill, smirked McGrindle.

Michael blanched as Casey and Donohue shot him and his fellow lieutenant a furious look. It was Sunday morning at 7:00. For some reason the company believed they would be released from trench duty because it was Sunday. McGrindle did not share their belief.

As they worked, McGrindle swore at the men with trilingual relish. French, English, and Mandarin - a Hong Kong battalion had just passed through Trench shovels, presently were his weapons of choice as he barked random insults at whoever wasn't shovelling hard enough.

—Johnson! Stokes mortars come in two sizes. Drop it in the firing tube, press the trigger! *Woo-tin-fa!*

—What does that mean, sir?

—It means *sissy-girl – weakling*, in Mandarin, you mouse.

Other times, McGrindle taught them armaments.

—Gentlemen. The Lewis gun is light and has no recoil. Watkins, pay attention or I will smack the tears right out of your eyes. Squeeze once; the Lewis will keep firing until the magazine empties.

Forty-seven shots. Slip in another magazine, like this ...peachy.

After what felt like an entire day, exhausted beyond the point of hunger or reason, the men had a deep, straight trench in which to have their lunch.

—Not bad. Not bad at all, said McGrindle jumping the five-foot incline.

Too exhausted to speak, his charges said nothing.

After a short break, during which most of the men had eaten and instantly fallen asleep, McGrindle stood up.

—Alright worms, wake up. Sleepy time is over. Do you see that trench the Royal Hussars have dug?

In the distance, maybe eighty yards or more, a thin line of dark sand lay across the beach.

—I want you lot to crawl on your elbows and knees—no hands, no feet—to that installation. Be quick about it. The tide is coming in.

McGrindle enjoyed his work.

6 - Boulogne-sur-Mer, France;
Intensive Training at Étaples, Pas-de-Calais, May 1915

After three hours of crawling back and forth between trenches, and over to a small mountain of barbed wire for wire-cutting practice, McGrindle dismissed them for the day.

French fishermen on the pier, sorting their catch into boxes, stopped to watch the bedraggled host of mud-men staggering past them along the beach.

After ten days of unmitigated drudgery and pain, at 17hours McGrindle spoke to the assembled company.

—Men, you're now in relatively fine fettle. I feel I've done my work and you're ready for front line duty. Dismiss.

At 21.00 hrs the next evening the Leinsters struck camp. Authorities at Étaples had furnished them three pack mules to carry camp gear and other equipment, The projected march was scheduled to take at least twenty-four-hours, with a rest period of five hours. With sixty pound packs on their backs, they marched through the night to Ypres. At 1.00hrs they stopped and unloading the mules, they set up tents in a ruined village. They resumed their march at 07.00 hrs, arriving finally near 20.00 the next night. Exhausted, they made camp, ate, and fell into their bedrolls. Lieutenant Colonel Murphy joined them during the night from brigade HQ.

As dawn broke, they heard the bombardment begin. High above them, in the distance, the sky shone vermilion and red. With intervals of two hundred yards between companies, the men crossed the Yser Canal northwest of Ypres, giving the city a wide berth.

Pools of wet splatter started to appear beside the road, and as Michael found himself gagging and retching, he realized why. At one of the hourly halts, Sergeant Malone asked Michael if he was ill.

—No, no, Tommy, it's just the smell of decay and manure. It catches me by the throat every so often.

Malone nodded sympathetically.

—One more curse to bear, sir. We'll all get used to that too.

They marched on past noon. The well-kept buildings and neat hedgerows of Flanders reminded Michael of home: farmers and herders in slow-moving, frugal husbandry with the land, a place of wayside shrines reflecting a deep faith. But when Michael's company reached a small mount overlooking the front, the tidy grey farmsteads ended abruptly, giving way to a landscape of pockmarked hollows. Beyond was only burnt out shells of buildings, charred hedges, and seemingly empty villages.

—Men, welcome to hell. This is Ypres, said Lieutenant Colonel Murphy. Your orders are to relieve an Irish Battalion near the ruined village of La Brique. You'll be in support lines to begin with. I know you'll do the battalion proud.

The smell of chlorine gas clung to the discoloured grass and drifted into the nostrils when the wind stilled. The Leinsters were relieving the 1st Battalion Royal Irish Fusiliers. By midnight, blank eyed and exhausted, the men were ensconced in their new trench homes. The Ypres Salient, a six-mile defensive semi-circle, began at Boesinge in the north and ended at St Éloi in the south.

As the men soon discovered, it was near impossible to fortify. Digging just eighteen inches brought one immediately to water, and rain was incessant from October through April. Thousands had already died in defence of the ancient strategic city.

A bright star appeared just ahead of their line: a flare. It lit up a whole section of sky with its cream-like halo, outshining the Milky Way / Moon, before descending gracefully behind German lines.

Then a quick flash to the north, and a British shell fell in No Man's Land. Then another, and another, each explosion planting a pillar of violet tinted smoke and light beside the one before.

—Keep your head down, Lieutenant, said a Royal Fusilier as Michael craned forward. If you need to see, look through this.

He passed Michael a box periscope. As he took it, Michael saw the indifference on the man's face. He realized the sergeant no longer needed to see No Man's Land to know what was happening there. Sound alone was enough. Michael peered into the box: a few denuded willow trees, the blown-out remains of a farmhouse, mounds of mud, and splintered artillery, and the sight of decaying bodies.

—Seen enough? asked the sergeant as he took back the viewfinder. Get some sleep. While you still can.

In a large wood and galvanized steel structure the Royal Fusiliers called a dug-out, Michael finally drifted off just before dawn. At 0900, his batman Gilligan woke him for oatmeal, eggs, bacon that seemed to have been rolled in sand, and tea tasting of paraffin.

The tower of Ypres Cathedral, amazingly intact, stood in the distance near a half-bombed structure the men called the Cloth Hall.

A runner, carrying a message down the line, stopped to casually inform some of the men that enemy aircraft would be dropping bombs on their lines at dusk.

—What about the anti-aircraft guns? asked Hawkins.

—They fire alright. Doesn't stop Jerry, said the runner, displaying great calm for his age.

After the boy had left, Michael quietly ordered his men to inspect and reinforce the dug outs. Soon, the men were looting beams and doors from the nearest farmhouses.

Back from foraging, a breathless Delaney approached Michael.

—Sir, we found a body, he said.

He turned aside and began to vomit.

Nearby, Malone let a heavy metal pole slip off his shoulder.

—Oh. What did you do? asked Michael.

—We covered its face with a cloth, said Delaney.

—His face, corrected Michael.

—Yes. Sorry Lieutenant Sullivan, said the private.

There was a pause.

—Is that all? asked Michael.

He was growing appalled. Delaney stared at Michael and said nothing.

—Didn't you at least try to find his identity disk? asked Michael.

A pleading look came over Delaney's face.

—Sir, rats got the eyes.

Michael realized he had to set an example. Bodies must be treated with the utmost respect. How could his men go into battle, knowing desecration, not dignity, awaited them if they were killed?

—How about the number of his regiment, then?

—There was nothing there, sir. His pay-book was wet pulp.

—Private, the brass on his collar. What did it say?

—It said 22, sir.

—Alright, the Van Doos. A Canadian Regiment I'll report that.

—But sir, if you report it, we have to go back and collect the remains.

Michael looked at him.

—That's correct, Delaney.

—But his uniform, it was just maggots.

Delaney was starting to shake and cry.

—We can't leave him there, Michael said. You'll have to go back and bury the man.

Michael looked around. The men were standing, listening closely and silently.

—Malone, you're in charge, said Michael. Cunningham, Casey, go with them.

Delaney turned his face to the trench wall and threw up with a loud barking sound. No one moved. After a long pause to wipe his mouth on his sleeve, Delaney stood straight.

—Yes sir, he said.

Michael said nothing.

Some time later, Sergeant Malone reported to Michael that under the Canadian, the men had found three more rotting corpses from the same regiment, which they buried in a single grave.

That evening, after the cutting down of a still standing hedge in No Man's Land to improve sight lines, the bodies of several more dead Canadians were dug up from the soil, their limbs rotted and dismembered. As Michael considered what to do, the heavens opened, and a torrential rain came down. Michael said a quiet prayer. Thank you—no more decisions about the dead. Thank you—for the iron sheet Gilligan installed on the dug-out earlier that day. But the torrent created a small river in the trench, and one by one, in the roaring dark, the sleeping men's dug outs caved in, burying them in blood, mud and dirt and washing their rations down the slope towards No Man's Land.

The trenches they had worked so hard to shore up the previous day were now shapeless and completely flooded.

—We might as well be on beaches at Étaples, grumbled a voice in the dark.

The men pulled back to better fortified dugouts in and around La Brique.

At 03.30 hrs. a long planned British attack began. The enemy quickly counter-shelled. In the woods behind their encampment ordinance began to whistle and thud in the sharp crack of trees, the sky lit up with charged smoke and distant screaming voices. A direct hit on a gun crew killed five men.

A British plane crash-landed northeast of La Brique. Slanting across the sky, bright flames grabbing at the wings, Michael watched as the pilot and observer spilled from the cockpit. Michael ordered a platoon to pick them up. Returning on stretchers, both flyers were terribly burnt, groaning and writhing in agony.

At the dressing station, the doctor injected them each with a full vial of morphine. Within seconds, their cries stopped. An orderly sawed through their heavy canvas pants with a scalpel.

6 - Boulogne-sur-Mer, France; Intensive Training at Étaples, Pas-de-Calais, May 1915

—Goddamn it, these lads' legs are full of holes, said the doctor on duty. Creegan, give me that long bandage. Hold up the leg. We'll make a tourniquet above the knee, that's the only way to stop the flow.

—Will they lose their legs? asked Michael.

The doctor said nothing.

The attending nurse repeated the lieutenant's question.

—Don't be stupid, nurse. Of course, they'll lose their legs.

The sister grimaced and said nothing.

—Sullivan, don't look so downcast. You've probably saved two lives. I'll see you and your men are mentioned in my report.

The British ground attack up the line had been successful. The surrounding lines began reacting, cheering and carefully moving forward where possible. The men retrieved more lumber from the outlying ruins of Ypres and looted wine from an abandoned cellar. German shelling toppled the stone wall of an ancient mill house soon after they exited. It was a good evening.

The next day they learned that a working party of Royal Fusiliers, pilfering supplies like them, had been under a wall when it collapsed. None survived.

By dawn the German counterattack had retaken most of the ground gained. British casualties were heavy, especially in places where the barbed wire had not been properly cut and men, their advance slowed, had died in crossfire by the dozens. Runners carrying messages spread the bitter yet truthful word that it wasn't the field gunners' fault—there had, as usual, been a severe shortage of shells.

A brief truce was declared so ambulance workers could collect the dead from No Man's Land. For the first time in days, a sorrowful and angry silence filled the lines.

Chapter Seven

North Infirmary, Cork, May - June 1915

Most nights Virginia startled awake from the same dream.

The pale faces of the drowned, lying on the warehouse floor in Queenstown, would open their eyes, and motionless, stare up at her in silent reproach. In the latest version she was conveyed as if paralyzed down the line of bloated bodies. She felt queasy and kept gagging on a strong smell of rotten eggs and a musty rancid odor, the whiff of death. And she woke up, as usual, when she came to the child, barely two years old—just as it began to open its eyes. A measure of whiskey, a few deep breaths, a towel for the sweats, and the grey of dawn outside her rooming house window would return her to sad sober reality.

She had received a cryptic letter from Michael in France. Some words had been inked over, but not his strange phrasing: We are in an area where people eat apples. After work at the Cork City hospital, she'd got hold of an atlas with detailed close-ups of northern France. Where people eat apples. And there it was, a seaside village. Étaples. She felt sure that must be it.

Michael you clever imp, she said to herself.

She would write back, but not burden him with her troubles. The chipper tone did not come naturally to her. Positive, but not false, she told herself. How lovely to sleep outside in summertime. Of course, sleeping under canvas must be a bit unpleasant when it rains.

Michael wrote often and at length.

> *Sweetheart, today is the centenary of the Battle of Waterloo, and we're having a do... a few firkins of Murphy's stout and the local tac. One can really taste the hops in this Belgian beer...*
> *Still can't say exactly where I am, but it's a fortified city of great commerce. The heresy of Jansenism may have originated hereabouts...*
> *Hawkins and Deegan are such good company, the other day we shared a flask of rum...*
> *Our routine now is six days at the front, six days on fatigue (humping supplies), and six days of "rest" (marksmanship, mock trenches, night raids) ...*
> *I want to hear about my Ginny, and how life is treating her... Oceans of love and kisses... but oh, for a real one!*

As she read Michael's letters Virginia kissed them and said a silent prayer for his safety. But he gave out few sweet nothings, sometimes nothing more than

Love, Michael. And there was no naughty conversation at all. He wrote as if someone was reading over his shoulder.

Weren't they engaged to be married? Couldn't they share their most private thoughts? Virginia realized she had been quietly anticipating a greater intimacy. Perhaps he felt embarrassed. Maybe he didn't know how to initiate things. But surely he did not expect her to take the lead?

Then she realized why he was so tight-lipped: the government is reading our letters - a censor, a moralist, an unknown man in a room. Just imagining it made her tense. Michael was clearly limiting what he said. Damn them, thought Virginia.

Sister Columba called a general meeting.

—I've just had a letter from Victoria Barracks. We've been designated a veteran's hospital. In addition to our regular duties, we'll tend to forty new beds for badly injured soldiers.

—What kind of injuries? came a voice from the assembled nurses.

—Bad enough to require surgery, said the sister evenly.

—Jesus, who'd they think I am, Florence Nightingale? said Nurse McCarthy under her breath.

—Further, continued the sister, we're to establish a special ward for soldiers with facial injuries. This will be in Wing C, isolated from the rest of the hospital.

The nurses and staff grew silent.

—All reflecting surfaces should be removed from this ward. On no account are hand mirrors to be given out. Not even while shaving a soldier.

—What kind of facial injuries? asked McCarthy.

She was imagining the worst.

—You'll see soon enough, said Columba after a pause. Many men will be suffering from neurasthenia.

—What's that? said a voice.

—It means they're crazy, said another quietly.

—Ladies, please. It means many things. Some patients will exhibit obsessive behaviour, such as repeating the same word all day and night. Others will tremble and burst into tears at loud or sudden noises. Many will be angry, and some will be violent. Watch yourselves. Be professional and caring, but not intimate. These are tortured, damaged men.

Virginia began to tremble, fearing for Michael. Would he become afflicted with shell-shock? How would she cope with the suffering she was seeing? Her nightmares since Queenstown were getting worse.

—But we're not alone, continued Sister Columba. Dr. Tyrell here is a specialist in the treatment of neurasthenia. He joins the staff as of today. You are to give him every possible deference, and be directed by him in your approach to these injured men. Doctor, I cede the floor.

Tyrell, a short man in his late fifties, stepped forward.

—Thank you sister. Good morning everyone. Well, where to start? Neurasthenia is an illness that has always existed. It's shock to the brain. Many events can trigger shock, not just a shell attack, although that will be the common cause among our patients. When a shell explodes near a man, and he survives, his body may heal. But he may still be carrying invisible wounds inside—wounds of the mind that haven't healed. The mechanics of this injury still mystifies, but we specialists believe the shell's impact physically shakes the brain inside the protective case of the skull. We call these scars to the psyche.

Tyrell stopped talking and adjusted his pince-nez.

—So how do you treat them? asked a nurse.

—Mostly rest. Quiet. The talking cure pioneered by Dr. Freud has shown excellent results in some patients.

—The talking cure? said McCarthy. We haven't been training in—

—Don't interrupt, McCarthy, said Sister Columba.

Tyrell looked around the gathered staff.

—The talking cure is based on the most advanced medical science we have. It takes advantage of the human need to speak and be understood. None of you have been trained in this new medical science.

But you do know how to listen and lend an ear. So, for now that will have to do.

There was a skeptical silence.

—What about the crazy ones? said McCarthy.

Sister Columba glared at her.

—Be a comforting presence with or without words. If the men talk of their experiences, don't react, don't pull back. Simply listen. Let them talk of their fears.

—Will the soldiers be returning to the front when they get better? asked another nurse.

—Some may sleep for several days and be ready to go back to their regiments. For others sleep is just the beginning of treatment. For others no treatment may be effective.

—What other duties will we be expected to perform on the... special cases?

—Bathe them, said Tyrell. Help them dress. Be patient. Speak quietly. If they lash out or attack get help, but try not to scream, as it may disturb the other patients.

A chill passed through the gathered.

—When do they get here?

—A hospital ship is on its way already, said the sister.

—Where from? asked Virginia breathlessly.

—The Ottoman front. Somewhere called Gallipoli.

The first contingent of soldiers arrived from the Mediterranean a week later. The men's faces were darkly tanned, their forearms peeling, their bowels dysfunctional and infected. Within a few hours both the special and regular wards smelled horrific. Over the next days, ample food and well-balanced meals made the situation worse.

Virginia and the other nurses helped their patients struggle to the bathroom and cleaned up accidents in transit. Changing bedding became so frequent that a nurse was assigned to that single activity.

—For Chrissake, what got into these fellas? said McCarthy after cleaning out yet another bedpan.

—I'm helpless as a toddler, said one man in a singsong Cork accent.

—Don't worry, Corporal Kenny, accidents happen. We'll get you fit and strong again in no time.

—Not too quickly, nurse, if you please, he said weeping. I like it here.

Virginia stroked the man's head softly.

—I can't fight the Turk. They're devils.

—There, there, said Virginia.

She imagined she was touching Michael.

—Do you think I'm a coward? Kenny asked Virginia.

She smiled, and shook her head to reassure him.

—You're home now. You've fought bravely for your country.

This seemed to help. Kenny breathed deeply. Virginia smiled.

—I'll look in on you later.

The corporal looked at her dreamily, as if he were already in love.

—Thank you Nurse Martin.

In the following weeks more injured soldiers arrived, some from Gallipoli, some from Flanders. Soldiers from the Turkish campaign often suffered from strange skin ailments that no one had ever seen before, which become infected, leading to rapid sepsis and emergency amputations. The men from Flanders all had foot ailments, which they called trench foot.

As Virginia nursed the men, she thought constantly of Michael, and treated each soldier in some small way as if he were Michael. She became very popular.

One of the more curious cases was Captain Cole, a tall, gentle officer with brown eyes. He was so emaciated that bones protruded from his waxy, yellow-green skin, and his eyes were hollow with horror. He was quietly and completely insane. The nurses liked him and treated his stories of visiting the King and Queen as the gospel truth.

—Both their Majesties were especially kind to me today, he told Virginia one afternoon as she washed him in a galvanized tub. His majesty commented in a most positive manner upon my medals.

He gently pulling at the frayed lapel of his hospital gown.

—Her majesty said I have been so brave.

—Yes, you have, said Virginia.

She was smiling, tears in her eyes.

In mid-July, shortly after the arrival of the Gallipoli veterans, Virginia was on the nightshift. It was a quiet time, mostly boring and sleepy, but good for catching up on gossip and news of the war. As she read the paper for reports from the front, a distant shriek came down the stairwell from the third floor. From the locked ward, most likely. Then Nurse McCarthy, Virginia's shift partner, swung through the doors.

—Hey Ginny, call Dr. O'Hara. It's Kenny. He's sobbing and screaming uncontrollably. I'm going back up.

When Virginia and the doctor got there, Kenny was brandishing a metal lamp and screaming at McCarthy to leave him alone. His shirt was ripped apart and he stood aggressively in his drawers. O'Hara took off his glasses and white coat.

—We'll have to restrain him. Brace yourselves, girls. Virginia, get the needle ready. If things go badly shout out for the guard and telephone Dr. Thornton at home.

His eyes wild with terror, Kenny had retreated behind his bed.

—Corporal, you're in a hospital in Ireland, said the doctor. The war is 2000 miles away. You're with friends.

The other men in the ward, the ones who weren't heavily drugged, were sitting up in their beds, crying, or quietly imploring Kenny.

—Come on lad, calm down, someone said in the moonlit dark.

—You're alright, mate, said another.

Kenny stared straight ahead and seemed to be in a haze of memory.

—Get down, Dixon, get down, he said weakly. No, Walker's gone. Run, goddammit, run. Dixon, what are you saying—stop bleeding, for fuck's sake.

—Okay now, said O'Hara.

He was holding Kenny's arms from behind and guiding him face-down onto the bed. Kenny began to thrash.

—Now, McCarthy, he said between clenched teeth. The bands, the bands.

The nurse threw the restraints across Kenny's prostrate kicking form, then ran around the bed quickly to secure them.

—Oh! she shouted.

—Norah! shouted Virginia.

McCarthy was on the floor.

—Come on, nurse, said O'Hara.

He was fighting off blows from Kenny, who was getting purchase on the frame and fighting back hard.

Virginia dropped the needle. Pulling hard on the two bands, she doubled them into quick knots and went for the third.

—He caught me in the head, said McCarthy, on her knees.

Kenny began to sob loudly. He seemed to have given up.

—Ginny, the needle, said the doctor.

As the other veterans whimpered and cried, Kenny passed out abruptly. Nurses and doctor stood, gathering themselves.

—Go back to sleep, men, said O'Hara. We'll make sure Kenny is taken care of.

They silently obeyed.

Nurses and doctor wheeled Kenny's bed into a small room and locked the door.

Back at the nurses' station the doctor examined McCarthy's bloody lip.

–This'll make a good story someday, he said.

–McCarthy winced. I can't see that one ever getting better.

McCarthy left for home soon after with a throbbing migraine. O'Hara stayed on with Virginia.

–What did you give him, doctor? asked Virginia.

–A morphia solution. He should sleep for about six hours. Make sure to tell the relieving nurse to check the bands aren't too tight. Loosen them if necessary.

–Of course.

–Great work, Virginia. Grace under pressure.

–Thank you doctor.

Later that morning Dr. Thornton passed Virginia as she was leaving.

–I hear it was a difficult night. Are you all right yourself?

–Fine, Dr. Thornton. Wish I could say the same for Nurse McCarthy.

–Yes I heard, Thornton chuckled. A black eye for her trouble.

He squeezed her arm.

–Get some rest Nurse Martin. There are more men arriving tomorrow.

–I will doctor.

As she cycled over the hill, back to her boarding house, the last of the fishing boats had already left the harbour. The town felt deserted. It was as if the war had swept through Cork and whisked every able-bodied soul away to some far-off purgatory. Only the elderly and children were still here, somewhere, invisible, and the war was within them, all around, everywhere and nowhere.

–Hey!

Someone had stepped out suddenly from behind a cart. Virginia swerved at the last second, barely avoiding a crash.

–Watch out! she heard an old woman shout.

Get some rest, Virginia told herself. That's an order.

Chapter Eight

Vlamertinghe, R&R, June 1915

After ten days on the front, the Leinsters received orders to rest. Their camp was in the wooded area of Vlamertinghe.

Leaving the front was a shock: the men had forgotten the world could be green. Marching to Vlamertinghe a man would break into spontaneous tears just looking at the unblemished trees in full foliage.

They remained stooped and jumpy, reacting sharply if a change in the wind made a whistling shell at the front sound closer than it was. But the wooded camp was a form of medicine. No sentries were posted.

The wind in the wood, and the gentle surrounding hills, smothered all sounds of war. The men slept as if the war had been a bad dream. The next morning a full breakfast on clean plates gave them all an unaccountable happiness.

After some lackadaisical bayonet practice, and a long lunch, Michael and Hawkins marched their platoons to Poperinghe for refreshments. The local farmers, it turned out, liked boisterous, rowdy singing as much as the Leinsters.

In the late afternoon, marching in drunken formation back to camp, the men singing a dirty rendition of *The Rose of Tralee*. A bicycle courier ticked slowly past, saluting the officers from his saddle.

As soon as they reached camp, Michael and Hawkins were called into the captain's hut.

–They're planning a major offensive, said Colonel Murphy.

–Who? said Hawkins, blurry-eyed.

The colonel stared at the flush-cheeked lieutenant.

–Sober up, Hawkins.

–Yes sir. Sorry, sir.

The colonel continued.

–Hooge. Three miles east of Ypres. Hell Fire Corner.

–When do we leave? asked Michael.

–In forty-eight hours.

–Shall I tell the men?

–Not yet. Let them enjoy their R&R.

–What's our role? asked Michael.

–We're in support. The 17th Brigade is the tip of the spear.

Michael and Hawkins looked visibly disappointed.

—Yes, I know, I'm sorry, said the colonel. There was a coin toss and we lost. There's nothing to be done about it. We'll just have to wait our turn.

—When do they attack? asked Michael.

—Dawn on the ninth. We leave at dusk on the eighth.

Two days later the battalion took the road to Potijze, east of Ypres. Marching quietly by gold-green hedges and ripening wheat fields, they heard the whistle and thump of shells grow and grow until the sky began to flash unnaturally.

Soon after dawn the attack began. The rip and thump of British shelling filled the air with smoke and noise. Then a mighty roaring, and the explosions began: that was the men charging the German lines.

Gathered at headquarters, sitting on their packs, the men ate their rations in silence.

At 09.00 they heard the good news: the attack by the 17th had been a success. A cheer swept through the lines. The Second Yorkshire and Lancashire Regiment had linked up with the King's Own, on the far side of a newly established mine crater and were holding their ground.

The Leinsters were ordered to Hooge to support the sappers as they began tunnelling under the line. But some miscommunication kept them waiting beside the road for the entire day, listening to the crack and whoosh of assault and counterassault. Approaching dusk, the Leinsters were directed to their new billets.

Another day passed. Stewing with frustration, the men played cards with a surly edge and gathered in circles as the occasional fight broke out. Michael gave strict orders that anyone found drinking alcohol would be given a reprimand. Discipline was essential. Finally, after three days, the Leinsters were sent to Hooge.

The route they had recently taken to leave the front was utterly changed. Roadside trees had turned to shattered stumps. Telegraph poles stood drunkenly at all angles. As they turned toward the new front, the ridges were covered with men who had been killed in the final assault of the German position: blackened and bloated from several days' exposure to the elements, their bodies were unrecognizable.

Haversacks, webbing, and splintered rifles lay everywhere amid stakes and stretches of barbed wire. Here and there, a mangled heap of khaki on a crater rim told of a direct hit. The Leinster column snaked past a terrible sight: two stretcher bearers lay dead across a body on the stretcher, the supporting slings still on their shoulders. All killed, presumably, by the same shell.

At Hell Fire Corner, an important rail junction that the Germans shelled perpetually, the Leinsters dug in under constant fire. In their newly occupied trench were the remains of the enemy, the Wurtenberger regiment: some killed by concussion or massive bleeding, others suffocated by earth in collapsed dug-outs. Their faces wore agonized expressions. Here and there, where portions of the trench had been blown in, legs and arms in grey uniforms stuck up between piles of sandbags. Thousands of rounds of fire and unexpended cartridges lay about the parapets and the trench floor. In depressions, the trench became slippery, near-impassible pools of mud and blood. Buzzing flies, human groaning and the convulsed sounds of vomiting were constant.

—Looks like they got our message, sir, said Cunningham.

—Bloody right said Deegan.

—What do we do with these body parts? asked Johnson.

—Ah, collect them in a pile, there'll be a reckoning soon, said Deegan.

—I believe that's already happened, said Cunningham.

—Right, spat Johnson. Angel of fecking death.

As the morning heat increased, bluebottles and flies of every description began to swarm like a great plague. Attracted by sweat, they tried to land on the men's hands, foreheads, any exposed skin.

The humming noise drowned out any talk below a shout. There was no protection from them. Smoke from a cigarette might help—but now was not a time to smoke.

All that day, the Leinsters secured Hell Fire Corner, then regrouped at midnight and marched back to their new dug-outs near the Menin Gate. Exhausted, beyond shock, the men lay down to brief, wordless dreams.

The following morning Brigadier General Harper addressed the officers.

—Our orders are to consolidate our new position around Hooge. You must dig in, put down barbed wire until evening. A major German counterattack is certain. For God's sake, tell the men what they're up against. Now get to it.

In the still-growing heat the Leinsters returned in silent single file to a new position on the front, east of Hell Fire Corner. The same unburied bodies lay everywhere, now more swollen and grey after another day suppurating in the August sun. They lay about in hundreds: flopped across the parapets, face down in the trenches, in scattered pieces in No Man's Land. The British dead belonged to the 2nd Yorkshire Battalion, and the dug-outs were full of more dead Wurtenbergers. With every other step Michael felt he was walking on a body part or slipping into a shell-hole.

—Feck it! cursed Deegan under his breathe.

Lord, help me be strong, prayed Michael.

By twilight, after twelve hours shoring up the line in the steaming heat, the plague of flies had doubled and was now partially blackening out the sun. The smell was unimaginable. Small-arms fire continued to whizz around and over their heads. Field gun shells fell nearby.

—They haven't found their range, said Cunningham.

No one answered: everyone knew it would only be a matter of time before they did.

As the sun set, a shiver of relief and apprehension came over the Leinsters. They were glad to be relieved of the flies and the sun, and they knew what was coming, but they welcomed it: fighting a real enemy, even to the death, had to be an improvement over the present nightmare. In the grey and brown world of No Man's Land the pale debarked trunks stood out like ghostly sentries.

The enemy front line snaked through Chateau Wood just fifty yards away. Behind it, Lake Hooge shone with the creamy glow of British flares. Suddenly they were under attack. Only a single barricade separated the Leinsters' left flank from the enemy. Feeling his vulnerability, the hair rose on the back of Michael's neck. He grimaced and bent down, resisting a powerful urge to stand up and run, turning his fear into anger and hate.

The Leinsters were ready: Deegan had sent the sappers and bombers to wire up a few surprises earlier in the day. At a signal, the men covered their ears. The explosion tore through the ground.

Mud, blood and dirt rained down on them, and then the screaming began. In the mayhem, Deegan and his bombers outflanked the enemy, entered the far end of the trench, and drove back thirty Germans. Hand grenades and small arms silenced whatever unlucky opposition was trapped between. Two of Deegan's men received flesh wounds. They refused to go to a dressing station.

But this was just a rogue assault, not the counterattack. The Germans were still shelling, snipers still firing. Word came down the line that the counterattack would likely come at first light.

Michael grabbed a shovel.

—Come on, men, we've got a reprieve.

—What do you mean?

–C'mon–shovels and picks, said Michael.

–We're pinned down, sir. We can barely move.

–We're deepening this trench, goddammit. Dig.

At dawn, single shells fell all along their line. Then all was silent. Michael and Deegan realized that these were ranging shots for a fresh bombardment. Within fifteen minutes they were proven right.

The enemy gunners fired groups of five shells in quick succession, all within areas of twelve yards, and followed these with shrapnel bombs. Three out of every five shells hit the trenches that had so recently been rebuilt, obliterating them.

As the parapets fell on the men, exposing them to hails of deadly shrapnel, casualties mounted. A direct hit knocked out a machine gun section, killing three Leinsters instantly. As there was no communication trench established yet, some of the walking wounded decided to take their chances and rush back over the ridge to get help. A few made it, most did not: their bodies lay unmoving a few metres above the line. After that, Michael and Hawkins ordered the badly wounded to stay put. Bandaged and bleeding, they lay all day at the bottom of the trench, waiting for dusk, trying not to die or think about the expanding pools of fresh blood around them.

The trench no longer existed as a trench. Despite the brown darkness of the air–the dirt and earth flung up by the shells stayed aloft for long seconds–the men were badly exposed, and enemy shrapnel was ripping apart the line.

–Jesus fucking Christ!

Private O'Shea was looking down at his shattered right arm. Blood spurted in a fountain from a hole just below his elbow.

Michael remembered his father applying a tourniquet to a workman injured in a farming accident. He had to do something.

–O'Shea, take these.

He shouted at the blanched, shaking soldier, waving some pills in his face. Then, realizing the private was in shock, he shoved the morphine tablets into O'Shea's open mouth.

Tearing a field dressing into strips, he cut away the remains of O'Shea's right sleeve and slipped the narrow dressing into his ravaged armpit.

–Keep your arm away from your body, said Michael.

Looping the dressing through a short piece of wood, he then began twisting the loop until it grew tight. Gradually the flow of blood slackened.

–Take hold of this.

He put the wooden handle of the tourniquet into O'Shea's opposite hand. The private was falling into a dreamy haze.

—Every twenty minutes or so loosen it a little. This way some blood will flow back into the rest of your arm, and hopefully the doctor will be able to reset and save it.

—Alright, said O'Shea.

—Stretcher bearers will be here soon.

Michael was lying. O'Shea was drifting in and out of consciousness.

—Oh Christ! Johnson, stay with him.

—I'll do my best sir, said Johnson.

Michael ran half-bent down the trench to see how Hawkins was faring. Suddenly he was lifted by a strong blast and was surprised to find himself smashing into a bend in the trench wall.

He heard muffled shouts.

—Dig quickly, lads.

—Here.

A hand pulled Michael down. His nose throbbed and his mouth was full of sand. He was being pulled down into the earth. He fought against it. Then the earth parted and light stabbed his eyes. He gasped, realizing he was not breathing.

—He's alive.

Michael felt slaps on his back, then hands tussling his hair and slapping his cheeks. He coughed and pushed the hands away. Slowly he pulled a handkerchief out of his breast pocket and wiped his mouth.

Faces smiled.

—Good to have you back Mick, said Hawkins.

There was an unusual new smell and Michael realized that he'd soiled his underpants and trousers. For the next ten minutes, as he regained his strength and hearing, he watched his platoon frantically free four more men from the earth.

Privates Coughlan and Leonard brought him a cup of tea. The enamel cup was chipped round the edges and greyed by smoke, but the tea was strong and reviving. Michael felt he could go on.

At the sun fell into the German's eyes, stretcher-bearers ventured forward. As they did, the Germans fired into the sinking sun, knowing what was happening across the line. Several ambulance workers were hit and fell, and some wounded soldiers, hit a second time, died quickly. Every few minutes a shell exploded and uncovered body parts that had been previously buried, sending them flying into the trenches.

–Sir, are you feeling your oats again? asked Cunningham.

–Alright, thank you, said Michael.

His ears were still ringing, but he felt safe among the men. He did not want to part from them. Past midnight the shelling eased. Michael and his fellows readied themselves for the ground attack still to come.

–Fix bayonets! came the screamed order from Hawkins.

A new wakefulness and adrenaline filled the men. Michael looked down the line: their faces were grimy and blackened, yet there was a light in their eyes. After almost 24 hours of solid shelling, they were spoiling for a fight. A single strand of badly smashed wire stood between their trench and the German line.

But the ground attack never came. Instead, the British large guns behind Ypres started firing. Swish, swish, bang, bang. Close over their heads flew the shells, slamming into the enemy parapets.

Everyone lowered their heads in fear the shells would land short. They didn't, but they were so close the noise left them deafened. Michael felt quite dazed. He hoped he wouldn't be deaf permanently.

Then the British howitzers went to work. Trees from the wood behind the enemy line flew into the air, landing in the German trenches, and great columns of earth erupted into the purple-grey sky.

In the distance, Lake Hooge periodically exploded into spouted geysers, like a Paris fountain.

Then a battery of French 75s discharged, and Michael felt the air sucked out of his cheeks as they pounded the German lines, covering everything in a haze of green fumes from the British munitions. The enemy was showing signs of panic: amid the smoke and fire, Michael saw SOS rockets shoot up all along the German front. Evidently the enemy expected an attack. Michael laughed: the Leinsters' attack?

Out of his 48 men on the line, they'd had 18 casualties.

There was a whooshing thump, and a massive explosion nearby. Men and equipment flew into the air like confetti. In crouched position, Michael staggered down the line: Company Headquarters had taken a direct hit. When he arrived, stretcher bearers were already there on hands and knees trying to bandage writhing forms. Private Dooley ran into the blackness of a smoking crater nearby, carrying a Red Cross kit. Privates Healy and Rattigan, who had been injured earlier in the day, lay blackened from head to foot.

Healy was in a terrible state. He'd been hit in the stomach.

—Water, water, he whispered.

Deegan said nothing.

Healy looked over and saw Michael.

—Sully, for the love of ... give me a drink, he said.

Michael too said nothing. Water was bad with any stomach wound. It would be fatal to say yes. Then Ryan, a stretcher bearer, leaned down with his canteen and rinsed out Healy's mouth.

—Be quiet for a few minutes. I'll bring ye to the dressing station any second now.

But Healy couldn't stay quiet.

—Oh God have mercy! he screamed.

Then came the singular whoosh of a shell heading straight for them. Michael, Deegan and Ryan dove for cover. There was a tremendous crash as a shrapnel shell burst directly above them.

Lieutenant Deegan turned red-faced in the blackened space, gulping uselessly for air.

—Winded... Small breaths... There you are, sir, said Ryan.

He doubled Deegan into a fetal position.

—And wounded, he added, nodding at Deegan's legs.

Deegan had been hit by shrapnel in the thigh and calves. With stretchers nowhere in sight they slung Deegan onto Private Morrissey's back and roped his bloody boots, which had been blown off in the explosion, around his neck.

—Got a wound here that will send me home Mick.
Hold the fort till I'm back, will ye? Deegan joked painfully, his breath regained, his legs swathed in blood.

—Goddamn it, I'll do my best Jamie, said Michael.

He was moved by Deegan's bravado. Afraid that his emotions might get the better of him, he moved off to look at the rest of the injured.

Ryan knelt beside Healy, who lay entirely quiet.

—Tis as well, sir, said Ryan. He'd a piece of metal, big as your fist, in his stomach.

As dawn rose over Hooge, the mutual bombardments ceased. A lone British Sopwith Camel droned high above the lines, observing the damage.

The Leinsters stayed at the ready, but the enemy did not leave their lines. It seemed the Germans were playing chicken, hoping the Leinsters would evacuate first and relinquish the ground they'd fought so hard to hold. But retreat was far from the men's mind. Among the Leinsters who remained, their minds were filled with one thought: attack. But without orders, without covering fire, it would be a massacre. Bloodied, but unbroken, they stewed in their holes.

The men were extremely thirsty, but not hungry. The sickening smell of burnt human flesh had driven away all appetite. Michael ordered the platoon to stay busy: attend to the wounded, deepen the trench, build up the parapets—anything to stop thirst and fatigue overtaking will and reason.

Michael headed out with thirty men to bury the dead. It was a difficult job. The Durham Light Infantry had taken heartbreaking losses earlier in the previous week, and their bodies had been churned up by shellfire. As they descended into craters, the ghastly stench filled the sinus and throat, rendering soldiers almost helpless with nausea. Michael halted all work until every last man had tied a handkerchief over his mouth and nose. An antiseptic balm was passed around. Smeared on the inside of the linen, it cut the stench enough to work. The object was to find identity disks, Army Books or any personal effects for next of kin. All the dead, even those badly dismembered, were treated with care.

Near one of the corpses, Michael spotted a small copybook splattered in blood. He put it in a pocket of his uniform.

The dead were buried in threes and fours. To each burial a shovel of chloride of lime was added to cover the stench and speed decomposition. Rifles and other equipment were salvaged.

After fourteen burials, Michael led the group back to the front lines and issued rum. One veteran sergeant took a double ration and fired several rounds at the enemy. The Germans didn't reply.

In late afternoon an official order came down the line to withdraw to the rear. The men cheered. When the men got to the rear trench, they settled in and tried to relax. They pulled out their trophies of war, stashed for safekeeping in holes and trench walls, and began to examine them and offer exchanges. Cunningham produced an enemy helmet with a single pristine bullet hole in the middle of the forehead. Malone pulled out a heavy German rifle with a saw for a bayonet.

Then word spread that the Brigadier General and Commanding Officer were coming down the line on inspection. The men put away their souvenirs, wiped their faces, and stood at attention.

Walking unafraid at full height, the Brigadier appeared in the distance at Hell Fire Corner. He saluted Michael and Hawkins and, striding toward them, took in the hellish scene while pulling on his lit pipe.

–Tremendous, men, simply tremendous, he said.

–Thank you sir, said Michael.

–The battalion has performed wonderfully. I notice the work you've done consolidating the trenches. Excellently done, lieutenant.

–Thank you sir. It's been a tough fight, but the men are ready for more.

–That's the spirit.

–There's only one thing wrong, Lieutenant Sullivan.

The Brigadier pointed with his pipe.

–There's a leg in grey trousers sticking out from the parapet. Have it removed and buried immediately.

–Yes sir. Right away.

Michael called over Cunningham and told him to remove the limb.

–Sir! Cunningham shouted, then took a step closer to Michael and whispered.

–Half the wall is resting on it, sir.

–Make a show of it, Michael whispered back.

At 22:00 the Leinsters were relieved by the 1st North Stafford Regiment. In the dark, the platoons fell back two hundred yards behind the line. But they did not return to their billets—they were to form carrying parties for the Royal Engineers to bring material forward to shore up the line.

In the dark it began to rain heavily. Fallen trees every ten yards had to be negotiated and numerous shell holes, full of water and deadly mud, could drown a man in minutes. The enemy was also sending up star shells to expose any work parties moving between the lines. Each time a flare illuminated, Michael and the men had to crouch and wait long minutes for it to extinguish.

Michael did not remember the end of the journey. He woke to find himself underneath a fire step at headquarters. They had been shelled, he had passed out, apparently, and the men had put him there to rest. He had been asleep for six hours. It was now past dawn, still raining.

The men had eaten already. Completely famished, Michael managed to find a meal of beef broth, iron rations - the tinned boiled beef - and tea.

–Are you all right, Mick? asked Hawkins.

Objects swam before Michael's eyes. His teacup began to slip from his hand as he slumped over. Everything throbbed.

–What I'd give for a couple of aspirin, he whispered.

–Rest, said Hawkins. For once we have time.

Chapter Nine

Cork, a birth, June 1915

–Nurse Martin, how much longer do you have left on your shift? asked Doctor O'Hara.

–About two hours, doctor, Virginia replied.

–Right. Ask Nurse McCarthy to cover for you. I've got to make a house call. An overdue birth on Wellington Road.

–Oh? I live not far from there. Who is it?

–A Mrs. Donohue. Contractions every four minutes. We must leave now.

O'Hara's tone was warm and commanding.

Virginia fetched her coat and O'Hara opened the ambulance door and guided her up the step, his hand on the small of her back. They made the two-mile journey in under three minutes, the driver sounding the claxon the whole way. Virginia wondered how to make it clear to O'Hara she was spoken for. He probably already knew. But she liked him.

Why say anything until there was a need?

–Thank you Donal, said the doctor when they reached the flat. Stay here. I may need a stretcher.

The driver helped Dr. O'Hara up three flights of stairs with one of his surgical bags.

–Right you are. Good luck to ye both.

–Nuala's in the bedroom, said Mr. Donahue, meeting them at the door.

Mrs. Donohue was a tall woman in her twenties. She lay on a large bed, her knees raised, the sheet underneath her stained with blood and urine. Her face was a lather of sweat.

She was breathing in rapid gasps.

–Breath deep Nuala, said O'Hara. Wait for the next contraction. Work with it.

While Nuala Donohue concentrated, the doctor looked around the room and addressed Tom Donohue, who was standing behind them looking mildly panicked.

–Tom, I've got a job for you. Put the kettle on. Nurse Martin can then wash and sterilize our surgical instruments.

–Thank you, yes, sorry, he said in a jumble.

–That's all right, Tom. Just bring the water to a boil and keep any other kettles you have piping. We're going to need a lot of hot water.

Tom left. O'Hara chuckled softly.

—Poor lad. Scared to death.

Me too, Virginia wanted to say, but stayed silent.

O'Hara placed his hands on Nuala's stomach. He moved them around quickly, frowning.

—The child is in a breech position.

Virginia knew this was not good.

Nuala started huffing. Then she screamed. The contraction came and went.

—Can I help, doctor? said Virginia.

O'Hara didn't seem to hear her.

—I'll try to turn it. Deep breath, Nuala. Now.

She cried out in pain, whether from the doctor pressing or another contraction was unclear.

—No luck. Let's try again.

The baby wouldn't shift.

—Ginny, go behind Nuala and support her lower back. We'll try another technique.

O'Hara got down between Nuala's legs and applied pressure to the left and right of her vagina. As he strained with the effort he began to smile slightly and explained the situation to Virginia.

—It's moved a little, into a frank breech position. Knees crossed in front of the face. We may have to use the forceps.

—Should I get Donal to transport her to the hospital? said Virginia before O'Hara cut her off.

—Shush... no, we're doing fine here.

Then he mouthed the words 'no time'.

—When the contractions come, Nuala, get ready to push. All right?

Nuala groaned, and nodded.

—Tom, where's that water? shouted O'Hara.

Contractions were coming every two minutes now. In the intervals, Nuala lay back on her pillows and trembled. The water arrived, and after doctor and nurse had washed their hands in separate basins, O'Hara plunged his instruments into a third and left them there, steam rising.

Nuala huffed. Another contraction. More screams.

Virginia realized she was sweating and trembling herself. The room felt like a sauna.

O'Hara took the forceps from the steaming basin and let them cool for a moment.

—Alright, here it comes, Nuala. Push hard.

She shouted and gasped.

—That's it, you're doing well, I can see the baby's little bottom, O'Hara said.

O'Hara took the forceps and wedged them along either side of what looked to Virginia like a small piece of pork.

—Alright, here it comes. That's it. Push!

The groans turned to screams as the doctor pulled hard on the forceps.

—Jesus fucking Christ! shouted Nuala Donohue.

The baby's lower back was out, its legs slightly crossed.

O'Hara checked the umbilical cord wasn't wrapped around the baby's head.

—You're doing great, Nuala. Here it comes. Push!

Taking a deep breath, she cried and gasped and screamed.

The baby was half out, its limbs dangling and floppy, while its head remained inside.

O'Hara adjusted the forceps gently over its skull.

—Alright, one more push. Here we go. Push push push...

On the verge of passing out, Nuala groaned deeply and pushed.

After a slow hesitation, the baby's head popped out in one slick motion. O'Hara caught it by the chest with one hand, still holding the forceps by the other, then passed the bloody flopping child to Virginia like a warm loaf. Virginia wrapped it in a towel and started rubbing it vigorously.

Virginia cut the cord with surgical scissors and knotted it expertly.

—You have a little girl, she said.

She handed the baby to Dr. O'Hara, who placed the tiny bundle on her mother's chest.

Exhausted, Nuala Donohue barely opened her eyes to look, then started to cry.

—Twas all you, Nuala, said Virginia.

—In perfect health, it would appear, said O'Hara. All ten fingers and toes.

Tom came in and knelt beside his wife.

–She's beautiful, doctor, he said. Thank you.

Outside the doctor leaned against the ambulance smoking while Donal brought out the remaining medical equipment.

–You did well in there, Virginia, he said. Thank you. I'll call on you again next time.

Virginia felt a blush at the use of her Christian name.

–Thank you doctor. I learned an awful lot today just being by your side.

O'Hara smiled and nodded.

–You've had a lot of experience delivering babies? asked Virginia.

–Yes, at the Coomb in Dublin. Every day, often several a day.

–My goodness, said Virginia.

For the most part she had only watched, but she was exhausted. O'Hara smiled, and sensing her fatigue put his hand on her arm.

–Take the rest of the afternoon off, Nurse Martin. I'll take the news to the Registrar's Office.

He and Donal got into the ambulance and drove off.

As the sun shone down fiercely on the silent road, Tom Donohue opened a window above. Small, clear cries drifted down.

CHAPTER TEN

Poperinghe, August 1915

It had been weeks since Hooge. What bodies as could be found had been retrieved, buried, and mourned. The decimated company had yet to be replenished. The men knew today's and the previous days' activities were meant to keep them busy—make-work assignments to help them walk off their anger on patrol, dig into their sadness, with a shovel in both hands, instead of a bottle in one and a closed fist hammering the face of another soldier. But even drinking and fighting were preferable to thinking too much about why they were here.

Today they were on patrol, moving idly though fields of wheat, far from the front lines. They had walked for hours already, through dozens of fields, meadow after meadow of unharvested crops undulating in the afternoon sun: clover, hops, barley, hay, maize, all growing overripe on the stalk. The farmers had fled the violence of the front and there was no one to harvest it.

What a waste, thought Michael, grabbing another stalk and pulling it through his teeth.

A sign ahead from the scout Delaney froze Michael and the men in their tracks. A quick flick of Delaney's wrist and they dropped to their knees. No one moved or breathed. Was he just having them on, to ward off boredom and keep them on their toes? The thought made Michael angry. The distant sound of shelling and gunfire drifted west from the front. Then in the lazy silence between thumps they heard what Delaney must have heard: a pressurized rumble, something strange beyond the trees, in the direction of Poperinghe.

While Malone and Delaney moved forward in a crouch, Michael and the rest of the men waited, pulling ears of ripe maize off the stalk and eating them ravenously.

Malone and Delaney returned.

—It's an engine, sir, said Malone. Farm machinery.

The patrol stood up cautiously and moved into the trees. On the other side, a building loomed – a large stone farmhouse, brawny, grey, common to Flanders. At odd intervals, metal vents in its side released a short burst of steam and clattered loudly.

—It's a brewery, sergeant, said Michael.

—How do you know that, sir? said Malone.

Michael pointed up. On the main wall in large capitals were the words *Brasserie Douverigne et fils.*

Malone frowned and nodded. The thought occurred to Michael: Malone can't read.

Walking around the building to the courtyard, a small handmade sign could be seen tied to a chair: BATHS AND REST STATION, BRITISH EXPEDITIONARY FORCES. The men looked at each other, then at Michael, keeping their rifles high and ready.

Michael knocked loudly on an ornate wooden door. The door opened and a large man in an undershirt, carrying a hand towel, stepped out and sighed.

—Allo you lot. I 'spected you two hours ago.

—Are you joking? asked Michael.

The man's face changed.

—What's your regiment? he asked.

—The Leinsters.

—Oh. I was 'spectin the Canadians.

No one said anything.

—They're late, the fellow spat. I 'spect you'll be wantin' to take their place?

The soldiers stood around, not knowing what to do.

—Well, what's it gonna be? You want a bath or not?

The men looked at Michael. Their patrol was half over. No one would miss them for hours. Reading Michael's thoughts, Malone nodded.

—Alright, said Michael.

—Peachy, said the man. Jenkins is me name, at your service.

Saluting Michael casually and slinging the towel over his shoulder he showed them into a changing room with benches on one side and a rolling metal conveyor on the other.

—Place uniforms and soft sundries in the fumigator engine. Then into the vats for a well-earned wash.

The men began to strip.

—Everything, boys, shouted Jenkins. Yes, nickers too.

As they dropped their clothes into the fumigator the bath master shoved a bar of red carbolic soap and a white towel towards each naked soldier. The men looked alien to themselves: twelve shockingly pink bodies with brown faces and black hands. Growing boisterous in the chill, the men whooped and hollered down a long corridor that led into a cavernous main room. Eight huge wooden barrels loomed before them, a narrow staircase leading up to the lip of each. There was no beer brewing inside them, only steaming water.

—Four men to each bath, no more, shouted Jenkins. And watch those steps.

Scalding at first, the water temperature quickly became blissful. For well over five minutes there was silence, broken only by the occasional soft splash and a deep sigh: the sound of men finding something they had not known they'd lost since coming to France. Dust, mud, sweat, dried blood, artillery powder—weeks of war were coming off in layers, leaving the wrinkles of their necks and armpits, and the valleys of their bellybuttons and buttocks. So much dirt, thought Michael, dunking his head, so much more than I thought. The steam rose languidly to the glass ceiling.

Eventually Corporal Cunningham broke the silence with a song.

Oh she washed me all over, I remember
and powdered and puffed me, you see
Then she lay me in a cradle by the fireside
In the little shirt my mother made for me

—The men laughed and took up the chorus and frolicked and washed themselves as they went through the verses. Then it was Malone's turn, striking up an old Dublin street song.

Oh the herald angels sing, ling-a-ling-ling!
They've got the goods for me.
Oh Death, where is thy sting-a-ling-ling?
O grave, thy victory?
The bells of hell ring-a-ling-a-ling,
For you, but not for me.

Each barrelled quartet sang lustily in turn until the sharp peel of Jenkins' whistle brought them back to earth. With a groan and a final quick rinse, the men rose dripping from the cisterns. Down the rickety stairs towels waited on a long table. Through another door clean shirts and socks were issued to each man, along with their own uniforms, steamed and pristine.

Leaving the bathhouse, the men formed up without a word and marched back to their billets, whistling quietly into the twilight.

The next morning, after a lazy breakfast of bacon, canned tomatoes, bread, and strong tea, Michael opened the notebook he had found in the crater. It was in fact the diary of a German soldier, Frederich Kressis of the 132nd

Wurtenbergers Regiment. Michael had not read or spoken German since secondary school, but understood the words well enough.

> *August 6 – What a feeling, to ask oneself, every second–when. When shall I die? For four hours since 8a.m. the fire and bombs haven't stopped. The earth shakes and we with it. Another comrade in our platoon, Hauerman, died this morning. Will God save me from this hell? I have said the Lord's Prayer. I am resigned.*

From your pen to my lips, thought Michael, then recoiled at the intimacy of his own thought. These damn Wurtenbergers had killed or wounded seventy officers and 1700 men from the Leinster 3rd Battalion. Michael hated them. And yet this man's thoughts and hopes seemed so close to his own. An image of the German soldier lying peacefully in a crater, alongside several good men of Leinster, filled and calmed Michael's mind. They were all with their Creator now.

Stuck to the inside cover of the diary was a photograph of a pretty brunette holding a small boy, and another photo showing Kressis himself with the woman in wedding dress. To grow up fatherless, thought Michael, looking at the smiling toddler. Poor soul.

Perhaps there was a way to get this diary to Kressis's wife. Lieutenant McCartney had interrogated some prisoners from the Wurtenbergers. Michael would try to give it to one of them. But not yet.

There was a cough outside the billet door.

—Enter, said Michael.

It was a courier delivering a note from Colonel Murphy - a summons. Michael donned his great coat and strode down the line, bringing Hawkins with him.

—Good morning sir, said Michael, saluting and entering the officer's tent.

—At ease, gentlemen. I'll be with you in a jiffy, said Colonel Murphy.

The colonel finished studying a contour map on his field desk, and looked up.

—Well thank you for coming. Your platoon proved themselves damn well in defence of Hooge.

—Thank you Sir, said Michael. The losses testify to that.

The colonel smiled grimly.

—Indeed, he said. Indeed.

–But we want to prove themselves further, sir, said Hawkins. We want to go over the top.

–I know, Lieutenant, I know, sighed Colonel Murphy, and I'm sorry; all in good time. The battle for Hooge isn't over.

–Yes sir.

–I want your men to rest and recuperate while the company is reconstituted. I'm moving you out of Ypres for the time being. There's a strategic canal to the north, near Noordhofwijk, that needs defending.

Michael was disappointed, but tried not to show it. He and the others saluted briskly and left to give the men their orders.

The colonel saluted absentmindedly and returned to his contour maps.

Later that evening, in torrential rain, the company reached the canal outside Ypres. The Shropshire Light Infantry, glad to be relieved, came out of their funk holes in rain-slickers and cheered the arriving Irishmen. The Leinsters' gumboots slithered in the muddy funk-holes and there was much cursing and slipping, but the men quickly found shelter. In the larger officers' dug-out, Gilligan and Cooney were already slinging hammocks for Michael, Hawkins and Malone.

From his kit Hawkins pulled a half-bottle of Black & White Scotch Whisky.

–Time for a nightcap, he said. Present cups!

–Hawk, you're a wizard and a wonder, said Michael as the strong whiskey hit the back of his throat, then warmed his stomach.

–What did you promise the quartermaster to get this? chuckled Malone.

–I'll be marrying his sister, said Hawkins.

The next morning after line inspection Michael and his colleagues took in the terrain. They were on the east side of the high-banked Yser Canal, fifty wide yards of black malodorous bog-water stretching from Ypres to Dixmude in the north. Several pontoon bridges crossed the canal, with the Leinsters stationed beside the largest, Number 4 Bridge, opposite the village of Noordhofwijk. With a line of bushy poplar trees running along either side the canal made a tidy contrast to the mud ditches, grim dykes, rotting fields, and burnt-out farmhouses all around.

But it was a beautiful early autumn day, and now the rains had passed summer refused to leave. As the day progressed and temperatures rose, men began to strip and swim in the soupy mess.

In shirt sleeves and open collar, Michael mopped his brow and watched them.

—The germs in that water, he said to Hawkins, while watching the men.

—O Christ. Something's latched onna me leg, shouted Corporal Cunningham.

He swam to the bank and hopped out, his leg bleeding. Malone called for iodine.

—Sir, look here, shouted a voice.

From the bilgy water a soldier carefully held aloft a coiled springy mess of barbed wire.

—Alright, dredge that section of the canal, said Michael. No swimming till that's done.

Loud groans arose from the men.

—Outta there you lazy shits. Clear that wire, screamed Malone.

Shelling was light on the canal, but enemy aircraft paid the occasional visit.

Four machine guns set like double-breasted buttons were the canal's only defence. As enemy planes droned down upon them from a great height, the Leinsters gunners sent up tracer fire to find the range, but to little effect: the planes dipped and dove with the evasive intuition of dragonflies. The German fliers repeatedly tried to drop bombs on the canal bridges. Yet only multiple direct hits seemed to do any real damage to the bridges, and the German flyers rarely brought their crafts within range of the big guns, preferring to drop flares and phosphorous bombs on nearby Turco Farms instead.

As the enemy sorties became infrequent the men relaxed. In the warm weather the muddy towpath turned bone-dry. Swimming was no longer verboten and the men made much of two ancient pirogues tied to the bank. Launching each with a mock ceremony of royal speechifying, fake admiralty hats, and an unbreakable green bottle that cracked the gunwale of one during its christening, the men set off on comic odysseys across the black water, using trench shovels as paddles, returning to shore after a few dozen strokes, bailing water, while men on the banks threw clods of dry earth at Ulysses and the Leinster-nauts, as they came to be called.

—Repeat the 'heavy artillery' shouted Michael, laughing.

The air filled with thick clods. Overloaded, a pirogue flipped and six men floundered in the grubby canal.

—Beautiful registering Sullivan, shouted Sweeney going under.

—Bloody fantastic Donal. If only our Mills Bombs did the same.

—Faith and a greasy prayer, sir.

The days passed. The healing rest continued.

The following week Michael's unit began working in reserve with D and C Companies at a farm east of the canal, reinforcing a communication trench. They were near the front now, behind the 1st Royal Fusiliers. During one of the long breaks in fighting the Germans opposite—not forty metres away across no-man's land—started shouting across the lines in English.

There were ironic compliments about near misses, grim promises about the fate of certain snipers, and some genuine shared laughs.

Then a soldier yelled.

—Hey Tommy, your London is on fire. So sorry. Anybody there from Gravesend?

There was some confusion in the ranks. The censorship ban meant that rank and file soldiers had not heard what the Germans already knew: London had been massively bombed in early September. The Royal Fusiliers were a Cockney regiment from East London. The air grew tense as new cartridges were loaded.

—You goddamned murderers, shouted the Fusiliers.

—It is for the Dardanelles, schweinhund, shouted the German.

Mounting the fire-steps, the Fusiliers unloaded into the German lines, who replied with shrapnel shells. The barrage continued for ten minutes. Light casualties ensued.

A few days later copies of the Daily Mail reached the front. The massive bombing raid had stretched from east London to Peterborough in the north. But amazingly only four civilians had been killed—and the Shutte-Lanz, a German airship, had been shot down by a British biplane. Morale lifted at the news.

The morning after the Fusilier's angry barrage Michael was called to the Adjutant's dug-out close to the Ypres Ramparts. Colonel Murphy met him outside the tent.

—Lieutenant Sullivan, the men in the battalion haven't been paid in five weeks.

—No, sir, Michael nodded.

The easier days at the canal had eased the men's worries, but the grumbling and sly remarks about the lack of funds had been increasing.

—With your experience as a banker, you're well equipped to act as paymaster, said Murphy.

—Here's a voucher for 40,000 francs, he said to Sullivan. You can remit it with the Field Cashier at General Headquarters in Lavoie.

—Yes sir, said Michael.

—Oh, and Sullivan, GHQ has moved to Lavoie Château, east of Proven. You can jump a transport.

On the Poperinghe road outside Ypres, Michael hailed a lorry, which dropped him at B Company's makeshift stables. There he commandeered a horse and rode cross-country to Lavoie.

Leaping sod embankments and stone fences on horseback Michael felt completely alive. Every bluster of sweet country wind filled his heart with a fresh burst of happiness. After an hour the afternoon turned gold and grey. He crossed onto the chateau road. As he approached the main house the road grew wider and the treed vistas more majestic until, around a corner, the chateau rose in stark grey contrast to the green trees and fields all around.

At the gate he was directed to a small side courtyard and a door marked Cashier. The transaction was impersonal: after the briefest of glances at his voucher, the uniformed figure retreated, returning quickly with a large panier filled with crisply wrapped bundles of brand-new French francs. A quick salute and the cashier's window snapped shut. Only then did Michael note the half-dozen marksmen idling on the surrounding roofs. Michael transferred the bundles of francs to his haversack.

Haversack heavy with battalion pay, his horse stabled for the night, Michael walked back to the house at the top of the road to spend the night. There he had a chicken dinner with Holland, the lieutenant in charge, whom he knew slightly from training days at Kilworth. Tired from his travels and in such peaceful surroundings, Michael forgot about war that night and slept deeply for the first time in days.

By the next afternoon Michael was back at the canal with the men, who seemed to know his purpose already and gathered outside his lodgings. Setting up a long table, he placed green felt on it and paid the men, company by company. The singing continued long into the night.

Malone recounted an unusual incident that had occurred while Michael was away. One of the battalion's local guides, standing out in the open the previous day, no gunfire or shelling sounding anywhere near, had been hit in the arm by a seemingly random stray shot.

—Where did the bullet come from? asked Michael.

—May have travelled from the front, said Malone.

—But that's miles away, said Michael.

—Yes sir, nodded Malone. And what's worse, 'twas an explosive bullet. Completely shattered the fellow's shoulder bone and got the artery. Blood everywhere. Garrison rode in the ambulance with him to Vlamertinghe. Doctor shot 'im with morphine for all the splinters in his face and chest.

—Christ almighty, said Michael. Will he make it?

Malone only tilted his head and shrugged.

The following days were passed in drills and route marches. While Michael and his men had been on R&R, there had been a major offensive launched up the line at Loos. Land had been taken in fierce fighting, then given back unwillingly to the enemy.

The next day, the weather still brilliantly warm, Michael, Hawkins and Malone went for a row in the canal in the company dinghy. Their nominal purpose was to inspect the embankments from water level, but they aimed to have fun doing so.

As they paddled along splashing and laughing a Fokker E1 suddenly flew out of nowhere, low along the right bank of the canal. Aiming straight at the dinghy, it bore down, twin guns pointing directly at the men. Then it pulled up and launched tracer bullets over their heads.

—Shite. Guns, guns, shouted Hawkins almost tipping the boat as he stood in it.

All four gunners along the bank opened up simultaneously in a deafening volley, swivelling furiously forward to catch up with the disappearing aircraft. But too late: several heavy bombs fell from the Fokker. The plane popped skyward, then dipped sharply east behind the poplars.

There was a tremendous explosion behind them. Wood planks, metal bars, and concrete blew into the air with an ear-popping rush. As Michael and the others turned, shielding themselves, the central section of Number 4 Bridge collapsed like a guillotine into the water, and a massive wall of grey-white water swallowed the dinghy. Michael felt himself tumble and spin into darkness. Elbow and face scraping the stony bottom, he tried to hold his breath, but couldn't. As the deafening water entered his lungs the dinghy surged beneath him and he popped up, coughing and retching—and was thrown rudely back into the drink as it came crashing down on his head. Shouting men dove in and pulled the half-drowned officers to the bank.

Number 4 Bridge had been cut in half. The plane had come out of nowhere and the lone lucky strike had done more damage than a week of attempts by a dozen aircraft. But this would be repaired in two days.

That evening in the dug-out, over strong whiskey, Michael relived the moment with Hawkins and Malone. How had everyone missed the Fokker? Why hadn't the pilot killed them?

—We were dead ducks. He had us in his sights, said Michael.

He was sipping his fourth or fifth whiskey, well dry, but still wrapped in blankets.

—He could have sunk us alright, said Hawkins. He pulled up at the last second.

—Maybe he was following orders, said Malone. Take out the bridge. No more, no less.

—They say the German flying corps is mostly landed gentry, said Hawkins.

—If that's the case, here's to gentlemen, said Malone.

Face flushed, he raised his glass. All toasted in silence.

The next night the men were loaded on transports: London buses painted dark brown, their former stops—Hammersmith, Earl's Court, Piccadilly—still visible above the military drivers. It made Michael intensely nostalgic for home.

At Poperinghe, Colonel Murphy addressed the regiment: the offensive at Loos had been a failure. Casualties were high.

—This is the day you've been waiting for, to prove your mettle, he said. We're going up the line to relieve the King's Royal Rifles.

The men cheered.

—You are bravery's very own battalion, men. Show the world what Leinsters are made of. Give them bloody hell.

The men cheered louder.

Chapter Eleven

Trench foot, November 1915

Heavy frost at night was followed by weak sunshine. It took a toll on the men. Sandbags bulged outwards and collapsed. Trenches became open drains. Even with duckboards everyone sank inches with every step; after less than thirty minutes in the line water had seeped through their leather boots. High waders weren't much better. Rubber didn't breathe. The men's feet became hot and tender. They changed socks every day, keeping a clean and dry pair in the inside pocket of their uniforms. Despite all this the instance of trench foot was rampant. Touring the front lines at stand-to, Michael found the men so cold and benumbed they were unable to pull back the bolts of their rifles.

Rum worked miracles. Most veterans drank their portion in one gulp.

—*Begorra*, tis tickling yet.

This was Kelly, who had served fifteen years in India. All in turn would lick their lips, stamp their feet, and life would smile on them again.

Sir John French, accompanied by Colonel Murphy, toured the line late one morning towards the beginning of November and was pleased with the Battalion's work and the great spirit of the men.

Because of weather changes and continual stress, infractions of military discipline were becoming more frequent. Military Courts were now weekly fixtures; Michael attended most of these, in the position of Soldier's Friend.

—These two men Sir, said the subaltern, are a disgrace to the army.

He was red in the face and seemed thoroughly in earnest. They must have done something to upset him to this extent - clearly this wasn't just a routine court-martial.

Men were as scarce as hen's teeth and had been for months. Michael had come to H.Q. to beg for some for his platoon and here were two rangy lads, Cork-men, being thrown away like trash.

Tough, too. Cool under fire. Quite unimpressed by the proceedings. Perhaps they'd been there before. They had made up their minds.

Their crime sheet carried the grim charge:

PVT MULLINS – PVT O'RIORDAN
REFUSAL TO OBEY ORDERS IN ACTION.

—Well, what do you have to say for yourself Private Mullins? asked the Colonel quietly.

—The forward post was unprotected Sir. Seven other fools obeyed and went out there. They're still out there, said Mullins, through gritted teeth.

—What do you think we enlisted for Sir, the second lad cut in, to throw away our lives?

He stopped short. But the court got his meaning. The Colonel frowned and rustled a sheaf of papers. But the court understood. After almost eighteen months of war, the situation was familiar.

—These men are lying Sir, the lieutenant shouted.

A very familiar note. What was the word of a private against an officer? Even a second lieutenant, and with their record?

They would clearly spend months in detention.

Michael cleared his throat and caught the attention of the court.

—I beg your pardon Sir, if the court please.

—What's the matter Sullivan? The colonel's face had a sort of hopeful look.

—I think Sir, that all these men need a break from front line duty, he said quietly.

—That's what you think, the junior officer shouted.
Let me tell you I don't want these two upstarts, and no other decent officer will want them!

—Exactly. said Michael quietly. Then addressing the court, he continued.

—I'm ready to take them, Sir.

The colonel's mustache twitched. He understood.

—Not so fast, Sullivan. Are you willing to be responsible for these men?

—I am Sir.

—Very well. Carry on, and God help you.

He took his first good look at the two trouble makers and felt a cold tingle run up his back. Two more men. They looked as if they'd been cut from granite.

And these two would show him something unless he managed to show them something first. He'd have to get the advantage on them and keep it.

—You can have these two reprobates, the young officer jeered—and welcome.

—Just parcel them up and I'll take them now 'said Michael - and by the way maybe they'll be soldiers before you will.

The colonel had raised a sheet of paper now so that he could just peer over it, but it didn't hide his shaking shoulders. The orderly worked to restrain his own laughter.

God! they were easily amused. There had been little to laugh at for several months and men made the most of what there was. Ypres had taken its toll on everyone. The 24th Division was like a man with his legs cut off, who laughs rather than blow out his brains.

This was in part why Michael had been so curt with the young untried officer. The man was just young and untested. He was obviously proud of the officer's stripes on his arm. He hadn't paid for them in blood and sweat; that wasn't his fault; he'd pay his dues before things were over. The Hun would make sure of that.

—March right in front of me and take it easy, said Michael.

They were in a communication trench.

—Afraid we'll do a bunk? asked O'Riordan in a surly voice.

—You'd have deserted long ago if you were going to! Now duck!

They had ducked already.

The trench floor rose a bit at that point and there was a set enemy rifle skimming the sandbags where a careless head might stick up. The gun fired once a minute taking an irregular toll.

—I wasn't born yesterday, said Mullins. The bullet cracked on the minute.

Mullins and O'Riordan started to straighten up. Michael lunged forward knocking both down with himself on top. Crack! Crack! Crack! Three bullets zipped through the space where their heads would have been.

—It wasn't all clear Mullins. That sniper read your mind. Now move along and keep your head down for ten paces said Michael.

—And what business is it of yours whether they snipe us or not? said O'Riordan sullenly.

—I've had too many casualties - I can't afford to lose more men.

They went ahead two paces.

—You have been at Ypres? Michael asked.

—Oh yes, O'Riordan said.

The uncharged way that O'Riordan replied was evidence to Michael that he hadn't been. But Mullins HAD been there. The string of curses he uttered was proof.

—And what he knows, I bloody well know, O'Riordan finished, adding a few curses of his own.

—You're mates?

—What he says, I say. Where he goes, I go, said O'Riordan emphatically.

Good there was something human left in them to work on.

—Tommy, give them discipline, but not too much. They seem like they've been through a lot already. Mullins fought at Mons, he advised Malone.

Mullins and O'Riordan adapted quickly to life in their new platoon and turned out well. The word got out, and in quick time, so called bad eggs were being sent from everywhere.

Soon Michael had an almost full platoon, forty-five men.

The arrangement was satisfactory, but it didn't stop there. H.Q., not wishing to build the platoon further, began to snatch the remaining good eggs in Michael's platoon and replace four of them with bad eggs. Then things went a little too far in Michael's view, when a notice arrived that Sergeant Thomas Malone must report to H.Q.

—You're on the mat Tommy, said Michael - what have you done?

—Absolutely nothing, said Malone, sewing a button back on his tunic – that is, nothing you could put your finger on. Maybe it's because of some missing spirits. To the best of my memory that theft was attributed to a civilian, said Malone.

True, some spirits had been reported missing from the officer's mess, but the theft was attributed to someone in civilian dress. It must have been a small case of whiskey. Malone wasn't one to bother with anything less. Michael was in the habit of giving the men a tot of whiskey in the cold or wet weather. Usually he bought the spirits in the quartermaster stores in Poperinghe. When this wasn't possible other, measures were necessary.

A lot of things had happened since the theft and they decided H.Q. wasn't interested in such a petty thing, and there was nothing else suspect in Malone's recent activities, so he and Michael had to appear without any real defense, not knowing where the attack would come from.

There was an officer with Lt. Colonel Murphy at H.Q. He looked Malone over with greedy shining eyes, as if he were looking at a large, undercooked steak, A cheery-looking private with a torn uniform stood next to the officer. A medium hard-chaw with disciplinary problems Michael judged, but quite trainable.

Murphy seemed a little uneasy and avoided Michael's eyes, instead fidgeting with a pencil. Michael knew something delicate was afoot.

—Lieutenant Sullivan, this is Lieutenant Quigley.

—He's brought me a recruit Sir, I take it?, sad Michael.

The private took a step forward a broad grin on his face, He was packed and ready.

—He's a bloody good soldier that one, said Quigley.

—Why don't you keep him then, Quigley? asked Michael, gently.

—I know the lad, said Malone, stepping forward. He'll do,

He saluted smartly and began to march off, the soldier ahead of him.

—Hey, there! Wait a moment! The Lieutenant yelled.

—Right. Not so fast Sergeant, said Murphy.
I have an order here requesting your transfer.

Malone about faced and looked at Lieutenant Quigley.

—Is it to him, Sir? he asked.

Murphy nodded.

Malone began to walk slowly towards the officer. His eyes were shiny and closed to narrow slits, the right side of his face twitched visibly, his left fist closed and lifted. Lieutenant Quigley jumped back.

—Sergeant Malone! shouted Michael.

—Yes Sir.

He turned towards the lieutenant and relaxed, quiet as a lamb.

—Take that man to the line. Quick and lively now.

He marched out. Michael took a quick audible breath.

—Excuse me, gentlemen, he said, I had to act, that was a close call you know.

He tapped his forehead in a sinister way.

—You must forgive him Sir, he said to Quigley, he hasn't been himself lately. Too much time in the front lines probably. No one can handle him but me for some reason. We may have to send him down the line if—

Michael shook his head dejectedly.

—That's very sad, very sad indeed, sighed Colonel Murphy. Well I leave it to you, Sullivan, he added with an impressive cough, carry on.

Michael clenched his jaw tightly shut, let out another sigh, and tried to look depressed.

—Well gentlemen, I'd best be getting along, said Lieutenant Quigley. I hope, Colonel Murphy, that the sergeant will be taken care of before he endangers a whole battalion.

—You lying scoundrel, you, said Murphy, choking with laughter.

—Yes Sir?

–Did you two bastards rehearse that charade in advance?

–No Sir. It was impromptu. We don't need words to understand each other Sir.

–And you expect to pull off a stunt like that?

–Yes Sir.

Murphy looked carefully at Michael, and at the request to transfer Malone to the other company.

–I'm going to cancel this transfer.

–Yes Sir.

–Well maybe that wasn't such a good idea of the colonel's after all, to put all his bad eggs in one platoon, said Malone to Michael later, inhaling a cigarette in their dugout .

–The colonel must have seen that too, It seems a good idea. And by the way, Tommy, you weren't going to follow through and break Quigley's jaw?

–I don't know Mick, said Malone– for half a second I was ready to kill him.

–Gentlemen, we're moving to the strategic St Éloi Sector in the coming days, said Colonel Murphy at his briefing next morning. Palin, McCartney, I want you, Hawkins, Sullivan and Lavelle to reconnoitre the area this afternoon. It's been a hot spot for the last six months. Understood?

–Yes Sir, they replied in unison.

St Éloi, at the neck of the Ypres Salient, was strategic. The British and German lines were close together: often only fifty yards separated them. The village itself was a cluster of ruins on high ground at the junction of a crossroads southeast of Ypres. Whichever army controlled St Éloi controlled access to Ypres. Constant shellfire had reduced the area to a state of nakedness. As Michael and his colleagues looked through periscopes from the front lines they saw hundreds of yards of wire entanglements stretching along the front, and behind them the jagged silhouette of the ruins of St Éloi Monastery stark against the sky. Slightly to the left, a little southeast of the village, stood a large shale promontory known as the Mound of Death.

The area had been the site of numerous battles. It had been occupied alternately by both British and Germans. The previous February, the 1st Battalion of the Leinsters and the Princess Patricia's Canadian Light

Infantry had distinguished themselves there. Behind the lines were graves of fallen comrades of both regiments.

Now the 2nd Battalion were about to take over this sector, not in a major offensive, but tenuously holding down an exposed section of frontline under deplorable conditions. A ruin of a house three hundred yards behind allied lines had to be safeguarded for its strategic position.

Late on the evening of their first day in the line, Michael and Hawkins were hailed by an Irish Lance Corporal in charge of mining parties directly behind their company.

–So you've been here since the first offensive, Corporal Enright? asked Michael.

–Yes Sir, I was alongside your other battalion here in March. They left me here, me being in charge of all the mines, do ye see, when they went off to the Sanctuary Wood, and I've been here ever since. One week I blows 'em, and faith, the next they blows us, and in the meantime I takes a promenade to Voormezeele for a meal and some local beer.
We and the Germans have gone back and forth, installing mines all around this area.

–Is this true, Enright? said Michael. Have a slug o' this. You need it for your type o' work.

He passed him a flask of Powers.

–Don't mind if I do, Sir. Your very good health.

He took a deep draft, saluted and turned on his heels.

–There goes a very brave man Frank, said Michael to Hawkins.

Late the following morning Michael led his platoon to further reinforce the wiring at the crater nearest their front line. He found Private Breen, a bombing expert from Cork, fraternizing with a German who spoke a little English. He wore the ribbon of the Iron Cross from the second buttonhole of his tunic. The conversation was filled with many gestures.

–What's your rank? asked Breen.

–I'm a corporal, the German replied, indicating the stripes on his collar. What rank are you?

–I'm a soldier like you, said Breen - a dead shot with either rifle or machine gun.

Work on the wiring of the crater continued until late afternoon. For their part the enemy continued wiring another edge of the same crater.

That evening the Battalion arrived in billets, tired and covered in mud. There wasn't much to look forward to except a few days rest in the cold draughty wooden huts of A Camp, and endless fatigues to the front lines.

They were fighting a new enemy: frostbite. Military discipline completely forbade the removal of boots while on front line duty, even while in dug-outs. At A Camp Michael had trouble removing his boots. When he did he saw that his feet were blue and cold to the touch. He washed them in warm water and Epsom salts. They remained swollen and cold. He had the classic symptoms of trench foot, he realized with shock. Flinging himself on a cot he pulled out Conrad's *Under Western Eyes* and was immediately lost in Geneva's world of cowardice and bravery. He read for an hour then went to sleep.

—You'd better see Doctor Morley right away, said Hawkins the next morning. I think you're going for a bit of a rest, Mick.

—Lieutenant Sullivan, your feet are in a bad way. A week in our base hospital at Poperinghe will do you a power o' good, said Dr. Morley, signing Michael's sick leave chit. Let me have a look at your hands as well. They're swollen. Two large chilblains. How can you clean a weapon, pull the pin from a Mills bomb, or write a report with hands as inflamed as these? Here's a small tube of ointment. Rub it right into the skin. It should help. Now if you rush a little you'll be able to hop a transport to the hospital.

When they arrived at the hospital they met the administrator, Sister Mumford.

—We've had a telegram about you Lieutenant, she said as she examined the chit from Morley. You're just in time for a late lunch. Then you can have a nice hot bath. Change into hospital garb and read or rest for the rest of the day. A number of your comrades are here. All seem to have the same ailment as you.

Later, freshly bathed and clad in hospital garb, Michael sat on a deck chair in a closed heated veranda and looked out at the grey sodden landscape. It was good to be out of danger. Away from the trenches, if only briefly. He'd follow Morley's advice and make the most of this time.

Ash-blond Lieutenant Nolan who'd joined the battalion only six weeks earlier, and Privates Lawlor and McGing joined him on the terrace.

—How about a few hands, lads, asked Nolan, pulling out a deck of cards.

—Don't mind if I do, said Michael.

—Twenty-one?

—Great. Should we add a little wager to spice things up? asked Nolan.

—We'd better not Lieutenant, said McGing. It's more than a week since we were paid. Speaking for myself and Lawlor we've spent most of our money and need the rest for beer and Woodbines.

—Fair enough McGing. By the way, we don't stand on rank here. Just call me Nolan.

He shuffled the cards expertly.

—Christ Eddy, if you learn a little more French you're a shoo-in for a job in Monte Carlo when hostilities are over, said Michael.

—We'll see when the time comes, said Nolan smiling. Right, five cards each to begin with.

They happily played until their call to supper—a mixed grill of bacon, sausages, black pudding, and lamb chops.

Their ward consisted of twelve beds separated by curtains. Michael had chosen a bed near a window. As he lay in it he could hear the muffled sound of battle in the distance.

He realized he was exhausted, and slept soundly.

Dr. McGuinness saw him following breakfast the next morning.

—You know we've had men lose toes and even parts of their legs because of this ailment, Sullivan. At all events you're in relatively good shape. We're worried about the middle toe of your right leg and the smallest toe of your left. Keep the weight off your feet for now. Have foot baths in warm water and Epsom salts morning and evening. Apply the powders and whale oil that Sister Mumford and the nurses give you. Eat what's placed before you, catch up on rest, and consider the whole experience a bit of a break.

—I already do that, Doctor. Can you say how many days I'll be here?

—About a week Lieutenant. Keep well.

The following days had a strict routine. Wake up at 07:00hrs. Considerably later than in reserve. Morning toilet 07to 07:30. Full English Breakfast including oatmeal, scrambled eggs and bacon at 08:00hrs. Then foot baths in Epsom salts followed by a massage of whale oil and foot powder.

—I want all of you to spend twenty minutes on a stationary bicycle. Then lift ten-pound weights for five minutes. After that you're to shower and then you can have your elevenses. All right men? said Sister Mumford following their massage.

—Yes Sister Mumford, they replied as one.

The days merged into each other. Michael developed a further routine of reading for an hour each afternoon, then writing letters to his parents or Virginia, then playing canasta or 21 with Nolan, Lawlor and McGing.

—You're looking a good deal better, Sullivan, said Dr. McGuinness as he examined him on the morning of his fourth day. The circulation in your feet seems improved. The lesions are healing up nicely. I'll have to pass you as fit for duty in a day or two. You know the routine. Try and keep your feet as dry as possible. Apply goose fat and foot powder to them immediately you wash them.

Always keep a fresh clean pair of socks somewhere on your person. change your socks as often as possible, ideally twice a day. I don't have to tell you that these rules apply to the men even more than junior officers. Keep well. I don't want to see you back here for many months. Your blood pressure is still a little high. This is normal considering the constant stress you're under. Right. Take care of yourself, Sullivan. Don't take any unnecessary risks. Dismissed.

Michael was in the draughty wooden huts of A Camp when the battalion received orders to move up the line. The communication trench was impossible to find; Michael, Hawkins and their companies were forced to go overland by a path known as Suicide Road. Eventually they reached the junction of two trenches. They were only one hundred and fifty yards from the enemy.

If they made one unguarded movement they'd be bombarded.

Michael motioned for complete silence. A star-shell went up. Everyone froze. As the flare faded they hurried ahead. Stray machine gun bullets whizzed by. Thankfully the enemy hadn't got their range. Finally arriving at the front line they all heaved a sigh of relief. At least they had the protection of thick, well-vetted trench walls to keep stray shells away. They passed a quiet night bothered only by sleet and rain.

Visiting sentry posts at stand-to Michael was surprised to see a human skull at eye level. It still had some hair on its scalp. A shell must have unearthed it.

—Maloney, when you have a second would you rebury that skull? Goddamn it! you must be sick looking at it.

—Not really Sir. I've been busy with other things. I'll do that right away, Sir.

—Say a prayer for the poor wretch. I'd say he was killed instantly.

—I'll do that too, Sir.

Corporal Cunningham reported that he'd discovered a large enemy working party repairing their front trenches.

—When was that, John? said Michael.

–About thirty minutes ago Sir.

–What action did you take?

–We fired a few rifle rounds their way. It didn't bother them one bit.

–Right, we'll see about that.

Michael rushed to the nearest dug-out, picked up the field telephone and called the coordinates in. Seconds later a hurricane round of shrapnel was fired in the enemy's midst.

This was followed by sharp cries of pain.

–Serves them right they were so fucking brazen, sniffed Cunningham.

Next day, Sunday 29th of November, dressed in dun vestments Father Maloney said Mass for the men just behind the support trenches. Michael allowed half his 11th Platoon to attend.

They returned to their posts serene, yet ready for action.

Five members of Hawkins's 10th Platoon were transporting boxes of ammunition in the support trenches. The first two rounded a bend when an enemy mortar shell came down, bursting in the midst of the last three, killing them instantly, but miraculously, not detonating the ammunition box.

The enemy had become shameless. Under cover of a white flag several stood up on their parapets and started talking in broken English to members of C Company. Michael's company respected the white flag, and no one fired on them.

Late that evening they were relieved by the 31st Battalion of the Canadian Army, without incident. The night was starless, the weather misty. Practically everyone fell into a ditch or shell hole returning to Kemmel.

Though some four miles behind the lines, Kemmel was in the shell zone. Most of the buildings were either ruins or badly damaged. Guard duties were routine, halting everyone at night and seeing that all transport were separated by at least twenty yards to cut down on casualties. All sentries had been given whistles which they were to blow immediately if they saw an enemy aircraft approach the village. Three blasts for an enemy plane, five if they were uncertain, one sharp loud blast when the coast was clear. The idea was to warn everyone to get under cover. If a hostile plane noticed new movement it communicated with enemy artillery, with potentially disastrous results.

As he was returning to barracks that evening Michael saw three cyclists come out of the gloom. He challenged them and was surprised to hear strongly accented English. His suspicions were aroused. There had been a memo in the Guard Room about enemy spies. Could these be they? He saw they were going in the direction of De Klijte. He turned heel and walked towards Kemmel with them. Arriving in the village square, he tried to persuade them to go to the guard room to show their identity cards. They didn't seem to understand and were growing irritated. Luckily Corporal Cunningham was about to go off duty.

—John, would you accompany these men to the Guard Room for passport control? asked Michael.

—Yes Sir.

Cunningham guided them up the stairs.

The next morning Michael heard the conclusion of the story. The sergeant on guard could make nothing of them and called in the Military Police. They in turn were suspicious and called Belgian gendarmes, who were also distrustful, but finally let them go. Closer to Christmas Michael saw one of the three in a small bistro near Locre. He asked him had he reached his destination that night. He was still quite angry, but did not blame the Irish troops.

—*Le gendarmerie Belge ont été des imbéciles.* Our papers were in order, signed by a captain.

Later Michael heard him singing happily in both Flemish and French.

Privates Lawlor and McGing rejoined the battalion. They carried warm, dry socks tied by a string around their necks.

—Don't get either of us wrong Lieutenant, said Lawlor. We liked everything about that hospital in Poperinghe, especially the nurses. But we volunteered to fight. We're glad to be back.

—Glad to have you back, lads. This sector is as sticky as Ypres. We lose good men every day. Try to keep your heads down.

—You can count on that Sir.

They were moving up the line via Suicide Road. The rain was continuous and hard. As they passed the deserted Ration Farm they were heavily shelled. As a company they threw themselves face forward in the mud. Michael tried to cover his face, but ended up with some up his nose. He blew his nose to clear it. Arriving at the rear trenches they waded through mud up to their ankles for 500 yards.

Finally reaching the front lines they realized the trench was about to collapse. For more than an hour they shovelled back the earth from the top of the trench. Michael joined in, It's tough work, adding to their troubles they were under fire. Every ten seconds a bullet goes pinging past. All are in a lather of sweat. Now their senses are assailed by the smell of decomposing flesh.

—Jesus McGing, you've dug up a fucking Kraut, whispered Lawlor.

—It's not my fault, Liam. He's been here for months.

—Well cover him up for Christ's sake.

Later they unearthed the remains of several horses killed in the first months of the offensive. Even funk holes and dug-outs were flooded. They spent a miserable night, their feet and hands frozen.

After forty-eight hours holding this section, they received orders to move. Deep impenetrable mud made moving even a couple of hundred yards extremely difficult.

—We'd best take our chances, lads, said Michael going over the back of the trench.

Enemy bullets whizzed past his head. He simply dove into the support trench. This wasn't the life for anyone with weak nerves, he thought. Gasping for breath he checked on Malone, Cunningham, and the men, then lit a Gold Flake. Later that evening they moved to reserve at Lorche.

CHAPTER TWELVE

Christmas spiritual and social, December 20, 1915 - January 7, 1916

There was quite a lot of mail: a small package containing a letter, a mystery novel and fruitcake from Virginia and a larger parcel containing cake, stilton cheese, port, and Findlater's whiskey from his parents. Michael read accompanying letters silently.

Dearest Michael,
We're busy at the hospital with seasonal ailments at present. Patients with lung illnesses fill several wards. Many live in damp tenement houses. When we send them home they're well for a couple of weeks and then are back with us again. For me the worst are the children. They have no resistance to pleurisy and similar ailments. Run very high temperatures before their fever breaks, and sometimes die. A little girl from Patrick's Lane died two days ago. She was just eight. Her parents were heartbroken. She's in God's Hands now. The little angel.
I'm free at Christmas and spending it with my parents. Take care of yourself my dearest one. I look forward to seeing you in the New Year.
Your Virginia

God willing he'd see her soon.

His parents' letter told of Rosemary and Brian's progress in boarding school, of events in Rosnua, and of his father's practice.

Chris has managed to get a few days off from Tim Hickman and Brother and will be with us, as will Deirdre, Rosemary and Brian. We had a letter from Jack. He's now part of the surgical team in a naval hospital in the islands near Gallipoli. He's busy and sends his love.
Happy Christmas, Michael. Hope these items remain fresh and add to your cheer. Share them with your comrades.
Love Mother and Father

Christmas Is coming,
The geese are getting fat
Please put a penny in the old man's hat,
If ye haven't a penny a ha'penny will do,
If ye haven't a ha'penny.

–God bless you, Malone kept repeating. I hope we can get through this holiday without any casualties Michael.

–You and me both Tommy. Make sure the lads take every precaution. The brass have already sent strict orders that there's to be absolutely no fraternizing. Hostilities are to continue as usual.

–So there'll be no peace on the birthday of The Prince of Peace.

–No, not according to the higher ups. I expect they're deadly afraid that what happened last Christmas might occur again. Ours not to ask the reason why, Tommy, said Michael.

–Yes. Ours but to do or die, Sir. I know the poem.

Following Mass the next Sunday they were again in reserve.

There was the soft plop of a shell twenty yards to their right. Their eyes began to smart. Michael urgently signalled they should put on their goggles to cover their eyes and noses.

The men seemed uncomfortable, but continued with the task in hand, transporting ammunition to the front lines, firing machine guns as enemy planes hovered over them.

Whiz-bangs barrelled past. Bent over in a communication trench, Michael felt hot air from a shell glance by him. Instinctively he collapsed in a heap. The shell burst near Cunningham and two privates. They were unharmed.

They were back in reserve in Kemmel. Gilligan came with a large parcel for Michael on the 22nd. It bore army markings. Opening it he discovered a bottle of Greek Brandy, two bottles of white wine, six hundred Turkish cigarettes and a note:

Dearest Michael,
Hope this package will arrive in time for Christmas. For security reasons I can't really say exactly where I am. Suffice it to say that I'm still in the eastern theatre as part of the surgical staff in a large military hospital. Compton Mackenzie the, Scottish writer has been here, he's part of intelligence now. He's a down to earth jovial man. We shared some roast lamb and a couple of bottles of wine together. He's been transferred to Cairo now as he speaks Arabic fluently. We promised to meet up when hostilities end.
Mary joins me in wishing you a Very Happy Christmas,
Best for 1916,
Jack

Michael kept two hundred cigarettes, and gave the remainder to Malone to divide among the men.

–Tommy, I'm sorry it's only four hundred. They're much stronger than Woodbines. Perhaps the lads will only smoke half a fag at a time.

–They'll be well appreciated Mick. You know that.

–Why wouldn't I, Tommy? The cigarette is the soldier's friend. Two hundred are more than enough for me to share with my colleagues. I'm going to have to cut back a bit myself, as I've a lingering cold.

Preparations for Christmas were continuing. Every single turkey within twenty miles of St Éloi or Kemmel had been bought by other regiments. But there were lots of geese and ducks and other fare.

–Geese is lovely if it's roasted slowly and the fat drains off, said Michael to Hawkins later that evening.

They were in a small bistro in Kemmel drinking blonde de Bruges.

–This is really quite a good beer, Mick. One of the better Belgian brews.

–Yes. I'm almost tempted to give up Smithwicks.

–That'll be the day. I know you, Sullivan. Asking you to abandon your Kilkenny brew is like asking a Dublin man to give up his Guinness.

–I suppose you're right Frank. By the way, we're going to have to pace ourselves in the coming days.

–How do you mean? We're not going up the line 'til after Christmas.

–True, but when we do, remember, post-Christmas, we'll be visiting other platoons in adjoining trenches, and there's tradition that we have, an obligation to drink whatever we're offered by each platoon - and we'll be carrying our own offering. It could be port, red or white wine; it could also be army issue rum, any variety of whiskey, or even some illicit trench *poitin* distilled a week ago.
If we can't walk a straight line after we've paid our respects to the men we'll be letting down the corps.
Sooner than all that, we have company inspection to get through.

–When did you learn this, Mick?

–It was posted in the guardroom this morning. Captain Palin has signed off on it.

–Thanks for the warning Mick. One lives and learns.

The schedule of services for Christmas was posted on the 24th. Services for Church of Ireland servicemen were to be at 11a.m. on the 25th, while Midnight Mass on the 24th was to be celebrated in the Convent of Mercy in Locre.

At 10 that evening Michael, Lieutenant Lavelle, Malone, and Corporal Cunningham marshalled men from several companies into army transport for the five mile journey to Locre.

The men were in good spirits, but subdued.

The convent chapel was large, as before hostilities several hundred orphans had been resident. Folding doors to a refectory had been opened, doubling the available space.

A wise decision, as several Canadian Regiments in the area had allowed their Catholic members to attend. By 10.30 every available inch of space was filled. Some soldiers had to remain in the convent courtyard. Fortunately it was a clear starry night.

As Father Maloney mounted the altar the choir sang *Il est né le Divine Enfant.* It was a French Canadian carol new to Michael. Most of the Canadian troops quietly joined in.

Maloney began:

–Members of The Leinsters Regiment and our Canadian allies, thank you for celebrating the central truth of our faith this midnight: the doctrine that through the cooperation of the Virgin Mary, Christ, the second person of the Blessed Trinity became man almost two thousand years ago. It's sad that as we're celebrating the birth of the Prince of Peace, war continues its deadly ravages just miles away. It's even more poignant when we consider that practically all the soldiers facing us are Christians, many of them fellow Catholics. Yet we've been in a state of war over this Flemish city for almost two years. How far have our heads of state and military leaders on both sides strayed from the message of Christmas?
With you I pray that this New Year 1916 will bring a cessation of hostilities and a just peace. May Jesus, Prince of Peace, keep you safe and well as we celebrate His birthday. Happy Christmas one and all. *Joyeux Noel au Congregation de Réligieuse de Sacre Cœur, et à nos camarades Canadien.*

Members of the children's choir, two soldiers from the Leinsters, and the 22nd Regiment of the Canadian Army presented the bread and wine to Father Maloney at the offertory. At the consecration, members of both armies stood at attention. Michael prayed for Virginia, his parents, sisters and brothers; he prayed also that he would continue to act with courage, for an end to hostilities, and a just peace. He knew that his parents, Deirdre, Brian and Rosemary were probably in the parish church in Rosnua at that very moment. He mind strayed to Christmas 1914 and all the celebrations of just a year earlier. With an effort he focused on the present.

The choir sang *Panis Angelicus* during communion which was received by the whole congregation. Then all sang *Adesté Fideles*, Following the last gospel the congregation silently filed out of the chapel. Father Maloney stood at the front door wishing as many as possible a happy Christmas.

–See you at the Regimental Dinner tomorrow, Lieutenant Sullivan, he said, shaking Michael's hand.

–You will indeed Father. I'll be thinking about getting my platoon through company inspections all right, and tomorrow, I'll be visiting some of my troops and exchanging drink. It can be a bit of an ordeal.

–I understand Lieutenant. Well, all I can say is, get your men well prepared - and watch what you're drinking. Safe home now.

–You too, Father.

Looking quickly at his watch Michael saw that it was already 1.30a.m. He felt a great sense of peace. Yes, he was almost a thousand miles from all those he loved. Yet he appeared to be where God wanted him to be. A close misty rain was falling. Feeling suddenly cold, he closed the top button of his trench coat and quickly boarded the transport to Kemmel. Malone, Cunningham, and the others in his platoon were subdued on the journey, each alone with their thoughts.

Arriving at his billets he had a quick drink of Powers and went directly to bed.

He arose at 08:00hrs and had two boiled eggs, oatmeal and strong tea. He consciously lined his stomach in preparation for visits to his listening posts. Fortunately there were only three. Malone with a stick of five men manned one.

–Compliments of the season and your very good health, Lieutenant, he said handing Michael a mug of aged whiskey.

–Yours too, Tommy. And may the New Year bring an end to this war. What is this, Tommy? It's quite mild.

–It's old Paddy. A relative from East Cork sent it.

–Good stuff, Tommy.

–Only the best, Sir.

Arriving at Cunningham's listening post he was offered a mug of what he thought was white wine, His nose warned him in time that it was whiskey or *poitin* distilled just days ago. He had to show leadership! He managed to down it without a cough or splutter.

—Jesus, that's good stuff John. Well, all the best. Will you be at the dinner this evening?

—It's been relatively quiet so far Sir. Perhaps the Krauts are having a little good cheer themselves.

—I wouldn't be surprised John. After all they're Christians. See you at the dinner then.

—You will.

McGing and Lawlor were part of the final listening post he visited. They offered him a red liquid which looked like wine. He drank it at one gulp, then gagged.

—Damn you Private McGing, what have you cut this wine with?

—Oh, it's something called *mar du pays*; Lawlor and me picked it up last week in an underground shop in Pop, I think it's some kind of a brew from grapes and boiling water.

It's got a bite hasn't it?

—It has indeed. Damn it, you might have warned me McGing.

—Yes Sir. We need it to keep the dampness out.

—I'm sure this grog does - it's as strong as the stand-to rum.

—Just about. Will you be playing at the friendly soccer game tomorrow afternoon Sir?

—Probably, Private.

—Lawlor and me will see you there, Sir.

—Good. Carry on, Private McGing.

A close misty rain had begun. Michael welcomed it on the tight skin of his face as he slithered towards the relief trenches. He felt prematurely tired and needed a brief nap before the evening, and the regimental dinner. He removed his boots and leggings and threw himself on the cot in his billet.

He woke at 16:30hrs., washed, and shaved. He then donned the newest of his uniforms and made his way to the main building of A Camp. Sherry and light refreshments were at 17:30hrs. with dinner scheduled for 18:00hrs. A coal fire burned brightly in the cut stone fireplace of the barracks refectory. Charcoal braziers placed at the corners of the hall kept dampness at bay.

The dinner was an affair of Companies. Colonel Murphy, Captain Palin, Captain McCartney, Dr. McGuinness, Father Maloney, and two ranking officers of the French Army, in blue—one heavy set with a brass hunting horn round his shoulder, the other slim, obviously his aide-de-camp—comprised the head table. Hawkins, Nolan, Lavelle, and Michael sat at the head of the their company tables. Given the difficulties in finding either turkey or goose the menu was sumptuous: *Hors d'oeuvre*; *Consommé a la Royal, Rognons sauté. Oie Rotie* (Roast Goose), *Sorbet au citron*, Pudding Noël, Orange, *Noix* etc;

Café cognac, *digestif.* Litre flagons of both red and white wine and flagons of water were placed strategically at various points on each table.

The fried kidneys were lamb and melted in the mouth; the goose had been cooked slowly and was quite tender. The army is certainly taking care of us, but then we've earned it, thought Michael.

Because of the number of dignitaries the men were well behaved. McGing and Lawlor drank a little too much and began digging each other in the ribs. Malone gave them a severe look. After his second glass of wine Michael felt the skin of his face began to tighten. He reached for the water flagon and added almost a glass of water to his red wine.

The *sorbet* cleared both his pallet and his head. It tasted of lime and lemons. Everyone clapped as the flaming Christmas puddings were brought in on silver salvers. Michael tentatively ate a bite. It was as tasty as his mother's.

Red in the face, Hawkins rose from his table, bowed to Colonel Murphy and quickly left the refectory. Poor Hawk. Must have had to drink more instant trench brew and *mar du pays* than I did, thought Michael. I have to pace my consumption of wine for another hour, then perhaps I'll be able to leave.

The staff serving the head table were more generous in serving wine and spirits there than to the rank and file. Soon the table was exploding in laughter and humour. The older French officer removed his cap. His bald head was pale, but his big round face was rosy and very happy. The old man laughed, then hummed and pulled on his moustache with his lower teeth.

—Colonel Murphy. *Joyeux Noel.* Thank you and the Regiment for your hospitality. I'm so happy to be here, Michael overheard.

The younger officer kept his head down and smiled slightly when spoken to. He ate his meal as if he had to. Duty was duty. Relations with members of the Allied Armies had to be maintained.

The senior officer was a different type.

—*Mais votre vin est des très bons gouts* Colonel Murphy. *Laissez moi regarder la bouteille*, he said reaching quickly for the bottle, almost upending it.

—It's Château Haut-Brion, Colonel Biron. I think the original owner of the chateau was an Irish soldier named O'Brian, said Murphy. Vintage 1900.

–*Oui, c'est un grand cru, mon Colonel*, said the plump officer taking another sip and rolling it on his tongue.

After another burst of laughter the jovial officer rose, put a foot on his chair and blew his hunting horn. The mellow tone filled the refectory. His aide-de-camp didn't react.

He'd seen this behaviour before. Perhaps this was the custom of the country, an ancient right won in battle. It was proper for the colonel to blow his horn. It maintained a link with military history.

Clearing his throat, Colonel Murphy rose.

–*Monsieur le maire*, Colonel Biron, Father Maloney, members of the Leinsters Regiment. Thank you for being part of our Christmas celebrations. In spite of the war raging round us, it's good that we take time to remember the events of almost two thousand years ago, and the dogma that Christ took on human form. The teachings of forbearance and peace are central to His message. It seems to have fallen on deaf ears at present, but we pray that the New Year we're about to begin will bring an end to hostilities and the advent of peace. Again, thanks to everyone for being here. *Merci à tout le monde d'être parmi nous.* Coffee cognac for officers including junior officers will be served in the small annex to the left. We'll close with *God Save Ireland* and *God Save the King.*

The annex was lit by oil lamps. To the right two batsmen stood behind a bar decorated in green felt complete with coffee service, vintage cognacs, Cointreau, Grand Marnier, and single malt whiskeys including Bushmills and Glenfiddich. They're certainly doing us proud thought Michael. He opted for black coffee and Remy Martin V.S.O.P.

Now red in the face, Colonel Biron had a double measure of single malt.

– *Mais c'est merveilleux*, Colonel Murphy. *Le meilleur whiskey au monde*, he said rolling the Bushmills on his tongue.

He was certainly enjoying himself, and hummed a couple of bars of the popular song *Fammes*. Later he became sentimental, speaking of his dear wife in Pas-de-Calais.

Yes, he would show why France would fight, till not one Boche was this side of the Rhine. That or death. He became even more serious.

–Gentlemen, observe this.

He put his hand inside his tunic and tugged at what looked like a pack of cards. The pack was too tight, and he'd tugged too hard: the cards shot across the front of the makeshift bar.

The gathering became hushed, a tad embarrassed; these were photographs of nude women. Some completely nude, others in various stages of décolletage, comprised the pack of cards.

Was the Colonel intimidated? Not a bit, It was the sort of thing that might happen to any good man, if he were careless with his address book. He began to sort the pictures in a specific order.

...perhaps looking for a specific maiden? Fascinating!.

Then for the first time that evening his aide-de-camp showed interest in his master's doings. He stood behind the Colonel, intently scrutinizing the collection of nude ladies. His interest was genuine. Suddenly he pointed fiercely at a photograph.

—*Mais celle-ci est ma femme!* he shouted.

He punched the elderly officer in the eye. The large man fell backwards, colliding with a chair. Over it went and so did he, with a frightful banging of steel on the stone floor.

Murphy was horrified. So was everyone present. Michael looked at Captain Palin and fellow subalterns Lavelle, Hawkins, and Nolan. All looked shocked and confused. What happened when a French officer punched his superior in the eye? What ought members of the British Army do when they were official guests? Michael could recall nothing in King's Regulations dealing specifically with this type of delicate situation.

Burly Lavelle was assisting the colonel to his feet, but he sprung up, shook with laughter as he straightened his tunic, placed his peaked hat on his head, and went into the courtyard.

Outside he played another fanfare on his horn. A ceremonial voluntary, perhaps. He soon returned. As he entered he was met by his aide. They embraced each other and kissed.

Colonel Murphy gave an embarrassed laugh. The entente cordial was intact.

Following Sunday mass in a church in Kemmel the next day, they had lunch and repaired to a local football field for a friendly match against members of the 7th Battalion. Lieutenant Vincent Holland and several junior officers of the 7th had been in basic training with Michael. Playing on the wing Michael tried for a quick goal. He missed badly.

Then hell and confusion broke forth. The enemy sent over a long-range shell which burst in the middle of the teams, injuring three. Cursing to high heaven, Michael rushed to their aid. His stomach was a tight knot. Members of both teams bandaged the injured and had them transferred to hospital in Poperinghe. Then the ball was kicked off once more. The game continued as if nothing had happened. The enemy must have admired the cool courage of both teams, as they did not fire again. The 2nd Battalion won two goals to one. That evening the weather changed, becoming blustery. Towards two the following afternoon, they marched on flooded roads to St. Éloi, They were in a slightly different sector.

The distance from the enemy trenches was less than a hundred yards. To their right in the centre of No Man's Land was a half demolished barn.

At 07:00hrs the following morning a runner brought a note from Captain Palin. It spoke of a special task to be carried out that evening, weather permitting. The note read:

> The man bringing your rations tonight will bring you four pairs of heavy wire cutters. If you are short of anything or want further information, let me know and I will do what I can to help.
> C. Palin, Adjutant

The special task was defined in a secret order delivered towards 17:00hrs. It read:

> A patrol under Lt. Sullivan, consisting of one officer and five men, supported by a bombing party of one NCO and ten men, will undertake the capture of a certain shack controlling a forward position in front of the German lines opposite trench L4 with the idea of seizing anything that shack may contain and afterwards blow it up.

That evening two patrols set out to reconnoitre, one of them under Michael's command. On returning, it was decided that the operation would be carried out on the night of January 2nd.

This allowed time for a small celebration of the New Year on the 31st, with a toast in Colonel Murphy's dug-out to "a glorious peace and a happy homecoming".

From the way baby-faced Corporal John Cunningham and the privates in his platoon looked at him, Michael could see that the men were fired up and eager to attack on Sunday 2nd January. He hoped the weather would be favourable. Nervously he walked up and down the line asking if everything was all right.

–You're up for this Tommy? he asked Sergeant Malone.

–Certainly, Mick, whispered the veteran sergeant. It's the first real mission since that action in Ypres six weeks ago. The men are itching to go.

–God I hope so. We're counting on them.

20:00hrs. Wind, rain, heavy darkness–ideal for a strategic operation.

22:00hrs. Received word that it was a go.

01.35hrs. Orders received to leave trenches; the patrol climbed up over the parapet. Michael was accompanied by Sergeant Malone and Corporal Cunningham.

Veteran Lance Corporal Enright acted as guide. Private McGing carried the fifteen pounds of gun cotton, and Private Lawlor the charge wire, which he unrolled behind him. They easily crossed their three lines of barbed wire, sometimes crawling on their stomachs, and sometimes on hands and knees. The saturated mud clung to their hands, the dampness seeped through their uniforms. They then ran in crouched position towards the enemy line. The intention was to get to the right side of the shack. Malone and Michael were ahead of the pack, who were slowed by the weight of the gun cotton and the unwinding of the electric wire. The German barbed wire was new, four feet thick and three and a half feet high. The darkness was illuminated by frequent flares. The wire clippers could only be used for minutes at a time, when there was quiet, more gloom.

In the darkness as he cut close to a steel post Michael gashed his right hand. *Jesus H Christ* he muttered. With pressure and a cotton pad, he stopped the flow. It was necessary to cut the barbed wire in over thirty places to get through. The white hut was illuminated against a dark background. Bullets whistled on both sides of them. Michael felt somehow outside events.

He seemed to be watching himself as they manoeuvred through. His breath came in short gasps. Now they were thirty feet from the hut - was it occupied? In a few seconds they crossed the barbed wire and were there in the hut. There wasn't a soul. There was almost a foot of stagnant water on the floor and in a shallow trench, connecting it with enemy front lines. Formerly it was perhaps a forward machine gun emplacement. After placing the gun cotton in the roof and joining the wires to the explosives box, and then to the plunger, they took that device with them and left.

02.25hrs. The patrol returned without incident. At 05.30hrs. the field telephone rang.

–It's time Sullivan, barked Colonel Murphy. Push the plunger.

A minute later the spark did its work: a dull explosion, a bright flash, a cloud of black smoke. Michael quivered with excitement and a strange exultation, as if his team had just won the rugby triple crown. He wanted to tell Hawkins and Nolan all about the operation. He wanted to shout to high heaven.

Daylight showed a smoking hole where the hut had stood.

–We've done a fine night's work Mick, said Malone, sipping his syrupy tea.

The field telephone rang.

–Sullivan, excellent work. I'll see that you and your squad are mentioned in dispatches, said a tired sounding Colonel Murphy. Now get some rest, you've earned it.

–Thank you Sir.

There was an immediate increase in enemy air activity. A German plane swooped over their lines. Within minutes anti-aircraft guns opened up on it. Their aim was very inaccurate, shells bursting hundreds of yards away. Then their gun battery opened up right behind their trenches. These shells were more accurate. The aircraft took swift evasive action. A British plane cautiously chased the aircraft. The enemy again took evasive action, banging a burst of fire from its rear guns and sending the allied plane to ground in a pall of smoke at Locre. The British plane was the latest model, though at this point German aircraft were faster and more manoeuvrable.

The reason for the persistent hostile aircraft activity was the light railway construction behind allied lines. The enemy were trying to sabotage it. De Klijte, a small village near Locre, was heavily shelled.

Days later the entire regiment assembled in a park near Locre to hear the recommendation of a V.C. for Private Johnson, a member of Hawkins's 10th Platoon. The Right Honourable Bonar Law, General Sir Lawrence Parsons, commander of the 16th Irish Division, and Colonel Murphy were present. It rained persistently: after fifteen minutes standing at attention, Michael's clothes were soaked through. He began to shiver. Looking to his right he saw Nolan and Lavelle grimacing. When the hell will this be over, we all appear to have caught something, he thought.

The speeches were mercifully short. Touching Nolan and Lavelle on their shoulders Michael pointed them in the direction of the company mess. He produced a flask of Powers, got a kettle of water and made three hot toddies.

–God that hits the spot Michael, said Nolan with his colour rising.

–Your good health Michael. You're the soul of kindness, said Lavelle.

–We need something to keep the circulation going lads. We have at least another six weeks left 'til spring.

The following day they received orders to take over a new camp near Poperinghe. The advance party had left on the 6th January.

The next morning, rising at 5.30, the Battalion prepared to decamp, had their breakfast, and left Kemmel to advance to Poperinghe. The Battalion reached Poperinghe at 9.30hrs.

Their new quarters were indescribably muddy, the wooden huts cold and untidy.

–Tommy, I know it's over and above routine duties, but could you put together a stick to tidy our huts up? Michael asked Malone.

–Of course Mick. I'll try and find some dry kindling for the stoves as well.

They were in reserve for the next few days. Standing orders stated that they were to be ready to move up the line at ninety minutes notice.

On Friday 14th January they marched by company at ten-minute intervals to Belgian Château, southwest of Ypres. Owing to a shortage of accommodation, three platoons from D Company stayed in quarters.

Arriving at the Château, the Battalion Grenadiers and four Lewis Machine Gun teams left directly for trenches at Hooge to relieve the North Staffordshire Battalion. While on route to Hooge the next day, each company stopped at Ypres Asylum to exchange their leather ankle-length boots for rubber waders.

–Here to put on your eternity slippers Sir? said the quartermaster taking Michael's boots.

–Damn it Sergeant, don't even whisper those words said Michael, laughing in mock horror.

Under sustained fire they occupied trenches on the Menin Road, at Hooge stables, and surrounding the massive Hooge Crater.

Towards eight next morning an enemy reconnaissance plane flew the full length of their defences. It's probably from their photographic section thought Michael, pulling out his pistol and aiming a futile shot. Allied anti-aircraft opened up, but their aim was inaccurate. The aircraft was headed northeast.

Hooge was so strategic that much of the next few days were spent looking through box periscopes observing activity on the east side of the Crater.

On the 19th they were relieved by 9th Battalion Northamptonshire Regiment and returned to the Zillebeke Lake dug-outs. For the first time in months, they'd had no casualties.

They followed normal training routine for the next three days: Mills bomb exercises, rifle range practice, short-route marches. General Parsons congratulated the Regiment "on the fine spirit displayed by all ranks under heavy strain." They returned to the Menin Road-Hooge area on the 25th. Towards 1.00a.m. the enemy bombarded them with light artillery. Michael hugged the side of the forward trench, then gave a sigh as he saw that their own artillery hidden in Ypres woods retaliated with vengeance.

Late the following evening Lavelle and Hawkins carefully patrolled No Man's Land.

At 12.30hrs. Michael led a squad similar in personnel to the group of ten days earlier. Arriving at the enemy's front he lay flat, his right ear close to the ground. He strained to catch a word, a cough, or the sound of a boot squelching in the sodden earth. There was no sound. He wondered if the enemy hadn't abandoned this section of trench.

There was an unnerving silence in this section. Everything was still. There was no moon. But the sky was not dark it was a strange blue colour. If possible, they were to capture at least one prisoner. A man had been seen earlier peering over the top of this trench.

Michael ceased to think. His body became rigid. He fondled his pistol. With the pistol in his right hand, he slowly pushed his body forward moving on his left side. He listened intently.

Like a snail he moved inches at a time. Then he stopped suddenly. He had heard something. It was the sound of teeth gnawing on a crust of stale bread or an army biscuit. Was it simply a rat, or was it the enemy?

There was a German in front just five yards away. He turned gently on his stomach bringing his pistol to his front. Then he touched his pockets to see that he had the required number of Mills bombs. He settled his helmet a little further forward on his head so that it shielded his face. Then he raised his back so that he was on his elbows and knees.

He crawled forward as slowly as before, breathing through his open mouth. He reached the forward post and lay still behind a little hillock that formed part of the parapet. The enemy was within a yard of him. The enemy coughed as he chewed the army biscuit.

Michael slowly raised his right knee. He put his right foot to the ground beneath him. He held his pistol in his right hand. He put his left hand on the ground. Then he jumped. He landed right on top of the soldier. In falling his foot struck something hard. He tumbled over the man. His head struck the side of the trench leaving him slightly dazed. Almost immediately he rose and held out his hands groping for the enemy.

Michael's hands dropped. In a glance he saw that the German was much bigger and stronger than him and that he was almost at full height. Now the enemy was incapable of movement through the paralysis of fear. If Michael were to touch him, he would struggle like a madman. He consciously imitated the enemy's face. He opened his mouth and dilated his eyes.

They remained motionless, watching each other, like very young children. The German's rifle lay at the side of the trench. Michael could feel his pistol under him. He hoped the muzzle was still clear. They were both unarmed, so close together they could hear one another breathing.

In the half-light Michael could just see the soldier's face. He was a big-boned boy of less than eighteen. His cheeks were red and soft, his loose-limbed body covered in baby fat. Michael's face now bore some of the ravages of the last six months. He had deep bags beneath his eyes.

Although his mouth remained open as if in terror Michael's mind remained calm, determinedly watching for an opportunity to capture the enemy. If he could only reach his pistol or reach the jack-knife in his right uniform pocket. The object of the raid was to take the soldier alive and deliver him to Captain Palin or one of his superiors for interrogation. Anxiously he wondered where the rest of his platoon were.

The youth then did a curious thing. At first his face broke into a smile. Then he laughed a low gurgling laugh. His eyes still remained dilated and full of terror. Slowly he raised the hand that held the crust of bread until it was right in front of Michael's face. Then his expression changed becoming serious again. The look of fear left his eyes. His lips trembled. Then his whole body shook. Gesticulating with his hands and shoulders he offered the crust to Michael. He moved his lips saying words Michael didn't understand.

Michael became confused. Was the boy trying to poison him or was he simply generous? No, the boy had been eating the crust himself. He took the bread. Fumbled with it for a second then put it in the upper pocket of his tunic. The boy became delighted, gabbling continually. Then the enemy became hostile again, his hands jerked up and down uneasily. He looked at Michael intently.

Michael took off his steel helmet. There was a crumpled cigarette behind his right ear. He gave the Gold Flake to the enemy. The boy relaxed again. He took the cigarette, then kissed Michael's hand. Michael was overcome by emotion. He surrendered completely to this new feeling of kinship and kindness. Were it not for his natural reserve he would have returned the boy's kiss. Instead, he smiled like a happy two-year-old. His head spun with confused emotion. He took the boy's hand and held it to his forehead muttering *'lieb,lieb'* again and again.

He loved the boy as he loved his three brothers. He felt carried up from that cold muddy battlefield into a dream state where life reaches the secret of heavenly beauty.

They were startled from their reverie by the boom of a single cannon, quite near, to their rear. They felt the whizzing of the shell just inches above their heads.

The boy soldier jumped. His face grew stern. He sat on his haunches and took Michael's hand. He began making guttural sounds, pressing Michael's hand fervently.

Michael also came to, but more slowly. Like a sick man awaking from a heavy sleep, he scanned the boy's face, seeking the meaning of the change caused by the passing shell.

He became aware of the boom. Then his caution and cunning returned. Was the shell a signal?

Still uttering friendly guttural sounds, the boy crawled to the bottom of the trench and picked up his rifle. Michael struggled with the desire to knife the boy soldier while his back was turned and an identical desire to throw his arms around the youth and ask him to stay. The homicidal desire subsided, and he felt very lonely, as if he were on the point of losing someone he'd loved his whole life. He remained motionless, watching the enemy with soft eyes. Yet he felt very angry at not being able to hate the soldier and kill him.

Having picked up his rifle the enemy paused and looked at the crumpled cigarette still in his hand. Then he smiled, his face aglow with joy and friendship. He made curious soft sounds, pointed to Michael's helmet, then took off his own helmet.

Immediately Michael jumped violently. Then he became rigid. The lust for blood overwhelmed him. The enemy's bare skull acted on his senses like a maddening drug. It had whitish hairs on it. The sight of it added to his bloodlust. A singing sound started in his head, just to the rear of his forehead. He again felt invincible, gripped by the fury of despair.

The skull disappeared. The boy put his helmet back, looked over the trench in both directions. Then he struck his chest a mighty blow. Murmured something and crawled towards the support trench. Michael was just able to control his anger. He couldn't let this boy get away. His mission was to take a prisoner.

Michael quickly found his pistol in the mud, He made sure there was no mud in the bore. The enemy was already several yards away in crouch position - *Kommen Sie her!*, he shouted.

Quickly taking aim he fired, The bullet caught the soldier at the top of his shoulder blade. He turned towards Michael.

—*Kamerad, Kamerad*, he whispered. *Ich dachte du wärst mein freund. Ich komme mit dir.* The boy's face still seemed friendly. Pistol in hand Michael got behind him and prodding the boy in the back from time to time marched him to the forward section of the enemy's front trench.

With his pistol still in the boy soldier's ribs he forced him to climb out of the enemy's trench. Ten minutes later he gave the correct password and regained his own trench. He marched the boy to a support trench and passed him over to Malone and Cunningham. They brought him to Captain Palin.

Sipping a whiskey later that morning he recalled all the emotions he'd felt. He'd already been coarsened by war. He wondered if the junior officer who coldly took aim at a departing youth in enemy uniform was still the same Michael Sullivan who had volunteered just fifteen months earlier. No, he wasn't, he was now a cold killing machine. At least he'd managed to control his bloodlust and taken the boy prisoner. How on earth could he have killed someone who'd given him food? Saying a quick prayer, he tried in vain to sleep. The kind childlike face of the youth kept swimming before his eyes. *Lord please end this war very soon before I become a monster* he prayed silently.

–Sir, there are very strange sounds coming from the north-eastern section of our front line, said John Cunningham late the following evening.

Michael remembered that just days earlier the enemy had blown several mines in this sector. This could be hostile mining.

–Right, Corporal, we can't be too careful. Clear our trench for a distance of thirty yards and establish extra bombing posts. I'll call H.Q. and have them send a mining expert.

As long as the enemy don't find out that this is a weak point. We should be all right.

–Yes Sir, right away, Cunningham saluted.

The mining expert, a member of a bantam battalion, arrived early the following morning. Armed with several sticks of TNT, blasting caps and entrenching tools he dug several bore holes in the cordoned-off area.

–Naw Sir. T'aint enemy miners in any case. 'Tis a family o' young rats. Your lads can reoccupy the section.

–Fine, Corporal Tennant. Here's an extra nip o' rum, said Michael.

–Don't mind if I do Sir. Your good health.

–And yours Corporal.

The weather continued misty and damp. There was little sign of spring. In mid-February battalion headquarters was moved to an advanced position in the trenches. Two platoons moved forward to support the front lines, and the garrison at Ypres Ramparts was reduced to one company.

They experienced heavy shelling of the roads near their front and second trenches, but little real damage was done.

That night a hostile patrol of one officer and six men were spotted on the far side of a crater to their left.

–Take that ye bastards, said Malone throwing several Mills bombs.

The enemies quickly returned to their lines, then opened up with light shells in the vicinity of Hellfire Corner. Nine men from Nolan's 9th Platoon were wounded; a corporal was killed.

They were shelled continually the following morning and early afternoon.

–Gas! Gas! shouted John Cunningham hitting a gong.

The cloud was moving from their left across their front line in a south-westerly direction. Everyone quickly donned cumbersome masks. To their left, Hawkins's 10th Platoon experienced heavy rifle and machine gun fire and replied in kind.

–Man the parapets, Michael ordered his platoon.

The enemy bombed a nearby small crater. Some Germans appeared to be climbing out of their front lines. Michael directed machine-gun and rifle fire in their direction. They disappeared.

Gas alert was cancelled as it was learned that the cloud was not gas, but a smoke screen released by the enemy as they combined two diversions.

–Stand firm, Michael commanded.

The men hadn't eaten in fifteen hours. Then, at 02.30hrs, rations finally arrived.

The respite was only temporary. A very heavy bombardment of their trenches began at 07.00hrs and continued all that day until five. Every single calibre of shell was thrown at them.

Crouching as low as possible in the front- line Michael felt that his ears would burst. There was nothing to be done, but to stay put. Any exposure would mean instant death.

British retaliation began tardily, and was ineffectual. Why were the big guns so late? Were they somehow short of ammunition?

That evening they were relieved and returned to Camp E just east of Vlamertinghe.

The following morning Dr. Morley accompanied Michael, Hawkins, Lavelle, and Nolan at foot inspection. Ten men in all were sent to hospital. The rest of the day was spent in short rushes, marksmanship, and a route march of five miles.

The morning of the following day was free. Michael decided to explore the area immediately behind the camp. He found an almost frozen stream just behind the horse lines. Under some briars near the low banks were both fowl and animal tracks. Could these mallard ducks be returning from the south he wondered. The animal tracks looked like those of an otter. There had to be fish whether perch or trout in the stream. With his bayonet he dug up a few earthworms, cut a thin briar branch, found some string, bent a safety pin, threaded the worm onto it, and set the rod into the bank. If he caught something it would make a real change from company food.

He hoped to come back to this rod that afternoon, but the battalion were ordered to Belgian Château at 18:00hrs that evening. They arrived at 20:00 p.m. and remained in support. The reason for their rapid return was that the enemy had exploded a large mine. Command was taking no chances! The crater was quickly occupied by the 9th Sussex. At 22.30hrs. they were ordered back to Camp E.

Finally, they spent some quiet time in the front lines. The weather changed suddenly, going well below freezing. Michael's hands became swollen again. The ointment Dr. Morley had given him helped. Despite charcoal fires Camp E was like an open barn. They were issued sheepskin inner jackets which at least kept their upper bodies warm. At the end of the month, High Command sent reliefs of four hundred men to the south of Ypres to reinforce the canal line defences south of the city.

–At least the work will keep us warm, said Malone.

As the reinforcement work was nearing completion, the Battalion was released to go north to the coast for a rest. Rest - what that word used to mean! It was mid-March now and finally warm. Even Flanders looked spring-like.

They marched by the banks of the Yser canal, north out of Ypres, between budding trees and flowering almond and cherry blossoms, heading towards Boezinge, and Yser where the canal joined the Yser River, and continuing along the river to Dixmude.

They camped on the outskirts of Dixmude and completed their march next day, arriving in the small town of Nieuport towards 14.00hrs. on Wednesday 15th March.

They were again under canvas. Michael shared a tent with Hawkins, Lavelle, and Nolan. The camp was on a hillock about two miles from the sea. The spring sunshine seemed to atomize the very air of the area. The air was rich, maritime, salubrious. It was as if you could grab a handful of seafood from it. Seagulls seemed maniacal as they cried and quarrelled continually. There must be a spring running of mackerel or herring thought Michael.

–St. Patrick's Day is just a day and a half away. Do you think High Command have anything planned Mick? asked the cherubic Nolan.

–You can bet the bank on it Ed. We've been doing our bit these last eight months. Colonel Murphy has sent back many strong reports. The Seventh Battalion has just joined the fight. As a matter of fact I wouldn't be surprised if the commander, General Hickie, isn't part of our celebrations.

–It'll be fun in any case, said Hawkins.

The following morning was sunny and bright. At 6.45a.m, the Catholic members of the battalion assembled by company in the central area of their camp. Then, to the strains of *Let Eireann Remember*, *The Minstrel Boy*, and *The Brian Boru's March*, played by the Battalion Piper in saffron tartan, they marched the three-mile distance to the local church.

Colonel Murphy met them there and distributed shamrocks to everyone.

–Happy St. Patrick's Day men. We'd better not keep Fr. Maloney waiting. Remember me in your prayers.

–Don't worry, we will Sir, said Sergeant Malone.

The men seemed happy to be alive, to be finally away from the sounds of battle.

–God, isn't it great to be here, Sir? To be out or it for a while, whispered Corporal John Cunningham.

–You've said it John, said Michael.

Dressed in white vestments, Fr. Maloney said mass.

–Today we remember St. Patrick and the special gift he brought when he returned to our island in 432; the gift of our faith. As soldiers you live your faith each day as you endure the hardships of front-line combat and the rigours of the winter we've just come through. From my many conversations with all of you I know that you're all proud sons of Ireland and St Patrick. So, have a wonderful celebration and enjoy this spring weather and our upcoming beach races.

Following the consecration, the congregation sang *Hail Glorious St. Patrick* and *Faith of our Fathers* as the mass concluded.

Colonel Murphy had arranged a traditional breakfast of oatmeal, rashers and eggs, brown bread, honey and strong tea in Le Lion de Flandres, a restaurant near the church.

—Eat as much as you want, men. No beer or whiskey right now. Some of you are riding in the races. You'll need clear heads for that, said Murphy.

—Happy St Patrick's Day and your very good health Sir, said Captain Palin. Hip, hip, hooray.

—Hip, hip, hooray, shouted the men.

Horses from both the 2nd and 7th Battalions had been transferred by rail to Nieuport overnight. A two-mile section of beach had been marked off with small flags on white sticks for the regimental races.

Colonel Murphy met them at the entrance to the roped-off area.

—Right men, as you can see, company horses are in the area to our left. Horses belonging to the 7th Battalion are to our right. I want at least ten men from each of our two battalions to participate.

I'm sorry I can't allow any betting. We've found that it's bad for morale. I'm riding myself. Gina's the horse for me.

—That's not fair to the rest of us Colonel, said Lieutenant Plowman. Gina's going to win everything.

—Rank has its privileges, Captain. It's all in fun. Isn't it?

—Of course Sir, said Plowman.

Two dun-coloured ambulances distinguished only by their large red crosses arrived from nearby hospitals. They disgorged almost twenty nurses: English in grey and scarlet, Canadians in scarlet and blue, French and Belgians in white. There was a naval officer doing liaison with the Battalion Artillery; and last but not least, a grey-whiskered lord, possibly Lord Midleton, who, having insisted on coming to France with the 7th Battalion, had been appointed Salvage Officer.

Michael chose Matilda, a chestnut mare, for the two-mile flat race. As he tightened the cinch, she whinnied a little.

—There, there Matilda. No need to panic. We're just going for a little canter. It'll be fun. You'll see, girl, he said softly into her ear.

The horse quieted down. He mounted her and rode the short distance to the improvised starting gate.

Five horses from each regiment, ten in all, lined up behind a long thick rope. Michael had to rein Matilda in.

With the report of Palin's pistol, they were off.

Michael had a plan. He felt that if he reined Matilda in for the first mile and a half of the two -mile course and then gave her a little of the whip he might either win or place.

He followed his strategy. Several riders from the 7th Battalion made the early pace. Then about two minutes into the race Michael gave Matilda her pace. Murphy had followed the same plan.

Suddenly horses from the 7th fell behind. It became a two-horse race. Oh my God - Colonel Murphy is my commanding officer. I'm going to have to let him win! He pulled tautly on the reins. Matilda whinnied, but slowed down. Murphy won by a head.

—I won. I won, Sullivan, Murphy said.

—Yes you did Sir. It was really no contest, said Michael.

—I'm not so sure Sullivan. You certainly ran a strategic race. I thought I saw you reining in Matilda in the last fifty yards.

—Really, Sir? said Michael innocently.

Wearing his dress uniform, General Hickie placed a laurel garland round Gina's neck and gave Murphy a red rosette. As second, Michael earned a yellow rosette, riding Matilda.

Hawkins came first in steeplechase. Nolan, with his light weight, won two point to points on George, a white-faced Connemara pony.

They returned to Le Lion de Flandres, now festooned with green buntings and flags, saying *Eireann go Breagh.*

The Divisional Dinner was attended by the nursing staff of area hospitals and was less formal than Christmas festivities.

Speaking a mixture of Flemish and French, Colonel Murphy thanked the local Mayor and the owners of Le Leon de Flandres for their hospitality.

—Now I'd like to welcome the true Roses of Flanders here, the fair members of the Medical Services: *Bienvenue à tous nos collègues médicale et les belles infirmiers qui sont venu célèbre notre fête nationale. Que la fête commence!*

He raised his hand; the regimental band adjusted their instruments. Captain Palin found a megaphone and invited everyone to dance.

—We'll sing Irish songs later men. For now, I want everyone on their feet. I'm sure these beautiful nursing sisters are great dancers.

Michael thought lovingly of Virginia. How light she was in his arms. Perhaps he was wrong to insist that she work in a veteran's hospital in Cork.

The band began with a relatively good rendering of the Overture to *Die Fledermaus*, then played *Sweetheart* from Victor Herbert's Maytime and continued with *Wait 'til the Sun Shines Nelly*, *Beautiful Isle of Somewhere*, *I'm Falling in Love with Someone* and *Alexander's Ragtime Band.*

—Only six couples on the floor. What's happened to our gallantry, men? asked Palin in mock indignation. The band are now going to play a very popular song from the summer of 1914. I want everyone on their feet for the next song and if you know the words join in with *Play a Simple Little Melody*.

Michael's pulse raced as he remembered dancing with Virginia to that same song in August 1914.

—Lieutenant Sullivan. Still seated? asked a middle-aged nurse.

—Sister Mumford! As I live and breathe! What are you doing here?

—Well we've been caring for you for eighteen months. General Hickie invited us here. We're very happy to celebrate with the Irish Division.

—You've got your dancing shoes on?

—Of course. Let's take a turn.

Light as a feather in his arms, Sister Mumford glided with Michael across the floor.

—Lord you're as great as Irene Castle, Sister, whispered Michael.

—It's Marion, Lieutenant Sullivan. Flattery will get you everywhere.

She held him closer.

Michael's mind was racing. Was this woman attracted to him? She was perhaps fifty. Her steel-grey hair apart, she seemed athletic and younger than her years. Yet he'd better be careful. As Matron of an army hospital Sister Mumford had the same status as a Major or even a Colonel. She probably followed King's Regulations to the very letter. Caution was the word. He would be friendly, but nothing more.

—That was lovely Marion, said Michael as the dance ended.

—Yes, it was fun Lieutenant. Won't you join us? There's a new arrival from Ireland I'd like you to meet.

—Certainly Marion.

Four nurses, all in their mid-twenties, were seated at an alcove table.

—Girls, I'd like you to meet Lieutenant Michael Sullivan of the Leinsters 2nd Battalion. He was a patient of ours in late November. Nothing serious, just trench foot and fatigue. He's light on his feet. So be good to him. Michael, these are nurses Louise Madden, Mary Ivers, Peggy Carney, and Bernadette Harrington.

—Very pleased to meet you, ladies. May I freshen your drinks?

—No, I think we're all right for now. Sit down, Michael, sit down, said Marion Mumford.

—How many of you have been here since the beginning? asked Michael.

—We all have, but in base hospitals at Rouen and Étaples. We've only been with Sister Mumford in Pop since January, said a redhead.

—You're in the thick of it now.

—Yes we are - let's not talk of it. It's Ireland's Day. Let's celebrate, said an auburn haired girl.

—You said it Peggy. Let's.

The orchestra played a tango then continued with *Peg O' My Heart*.

—They're playing your song Peggy. Let's take a spin round the floor.

—Fine Michael. It'll be fun.

Peggy was an excellent dancer. She followed his every step. The orchestra changed to *the Waltz from The Merry Widow* and followed this with *Moonlight Bay* and *Me and My Girl*.

—Do you have a sweetheart Michael?

Michael felt a certain reserve.

—I do, back in Ireland. Her name is Virginia. She's a nurse in the North Infirmary in Cork. I'm fond of her.

—Too bad. We could have been great friends.

—We still can. But Virginia is special.

—I understand that. However, I'm here, you're here. Could we not meet from time to time?

—Yes, as much as our duties allow. Perhaps we should get back to Sister Mumford and the girls?

—We should. I don't want to monopolize you.

—You're not doing that, Peggy.

Hawkins joined them and asked Louise Madden to dance.

Members of the orchestra took a break at midnight. Palin again bounded on stage.

—I wonder if there's anyone here who's a good pianist. Anyone at all? We'd like to keep the music going while the band relax.

—Captain, Sullivan here is a very good pianist. Aren't you Lieutenant? said Hawkins.

—I'm a bit out of practice Lieutenant Hawkins, but I like the instrument, said Michael, feeling his face colour.

—You're elected, Sullivan. Get up here. The stage is yours, said Palin.

—Right, Sir. I'll start with *Maple Leaf Rag* and continue with up-tempo pieces. For as long as my fingers hold up.

—Great Sullivan, great.

Michael played *12th Street Rag*, *Tin Roof Blues* and *St Louis Blues*. Then, getting into his stride, he sang and played *Wait 'til the Sun Shines Nelly* and *Me and My Girl*.

His fingers began to hurt so he switched to slower pieces. *Darling I am Growing Old*, *Silver threads among the Gold* he sang, then *A little bit of Heaven*, *Mother Machree*, *Sweetheart, sweetheart, sweetheart* and feeling his fingers get even sorer Jerome Kern's *They Didn't Believe Me*. The men had invented different lyrics to this song. He opted for the original words.

The members of the orchestra slowly re-entered the stage. Their leader Captain Campbell touched Michael on the shoulder and took his place at the piano.

The evening continued happily for another hour and a half. Then Colonel Murphy bounded on stage.

—I'd like to thank each and every one of you for being here. It's been a very happy day. A perfect celebration of our Patron Saint. We'll close with *God Save the King* and *God Save Ireland*.

Michael and Hawkins bade farewell to Sister Mumford and the nurses. Swaying a little, they walked the two miles to camp.

Morning began far too early with reveille at 06.30 hrs. Soon the neighing of horses filled the camp area, rattling Michael's sore head.

—Up and at 'em, Mick, said Hawkins, punching his shoulder.

—God damn you Hawk, have a heart, said Michael scrunching deeper into his sleeping bag.

—You're in the army Mick. Like it or not. Our first exercise is at 07.30. Get up.

Gilligan had brewed a large pot of strong tea.

—Have a slug Sir. It'll hit the spot.

It did. The fog in Michael's brain began to clear.

The weather continued to be spring-like, close to freezing in the morning giving way to bright sunshine at noon.

The permanent base staff, known as canaries because of their yellow armbands, took charge of renewed basic training. Straw dummies had been installed at the far end of the municipal beach. In full battle gear carrying a rifle, fixed bayonet, six Mills bombs, ammunition, full pack, and wearing their tin helmets, they rushed these dummies, letting out raucous yells.

They jumped down eight-foot trenches, scrambling out as quickly as possible to avoid the bayonets of the following wave of men. They chucked their dummy Mills bombs out of the trenches as quickly as possible and re-learned how to fire rifle grenades and other weapons. A gas chamber stood to their right at the far end of the beach. Wearing their cumbersome masks, they ran as quickly as possible through it.

Later, still in full equipment, they went through the final assault course. The straps of Michael's shoulder bag cut deeply into his back. The pain was sharp and excruciating. He wondered if washing the blistered skin with salt and warm water would be enough to keep it from becoming infected. The series of rushes was tricky, full of barbed wire, shoulder-high wire and shell holes. From hidden trenches, trainers continually threw large fir cones representing Mills bombs. Michael found he was getting quite angry. This mock war was as bad as being under fire at Hells Fire Corner. Why had they to endure all this supplemental training? What had the top brass in store for them? He remembered the old saying: Sufficient for the day is the evil there of.

He'd get through this training one way or another.

By lunchtime he Hawkins, Lavelle and Nolan were exhausted.

—What's the matter, men, out of shape? said Captain Palin. One late night and you're like a bunch of women. Veterans like Malone and Corporal Cunningham are putting you to shame.

You're letting down the corp. Enjoy lunch. You've got another two hours.

His tone was light. They knew he was joking.

Refreshed, they returned to the beach. The trenches they'd occupied earlier now contained three feet of water and were on the point of collapse.

Michael felt his anger rise again. He dug faster and faster. His rubber boots squelched in the glue-like sand. Each movement was an effort. The mixture of sand and mud felt heavier and heavier. He took a quick look at his watch: 15.30 hrs. Finally, half an hour later, Sergeant Major McGrindle blew a sharp blast on this whistle.

—That's it for today men. I'll see you lot tomorrow morning at 08.00hrs.

—But it's Sunday Sergeant Major, ventured Nolan.

—So it is Lieutenant. You may attend church either before or after our exercises. Hostilities continue every day of the week. Be here at 08.00 hrs. Understood?

Chapter Thirteen

Easter Rebellion, Dublin, April 1916

Early on Wednesday 19th April 1916 Colonel Murphy called Michael to H.Q. Noting that he'd lost weight and hadn't had leave in over three months, the colonel gave him a travel chit for a ten day furlough.

Michael found a transport truck leaving Nieuport, and two hours later he stood in Ypres station. It was full of soldiers on leave, hoping to find a place on one of the ambulance trains leaving for Hazebrouck, and on to Boulogne-sur-mer, and a troop transport returning to England. There was confusion and a lot of milling about. The train left the station at 12.00 p.m. Michael had found a seat beside an auburn haired officer.

—Well look on the bright side, we've been lucky finding transport this quickly, the man said in a sing-song Welsh accent. By the way I'm Graves. I'm trying to get to North Wales for Easter with my family.

—Sullivan. I'm with the 2nd Leinsters. I'm meeting my fiancée and parents in Ireland.

—So we both have long journeys ahead of us. Still it's good to be out of it. If only for a few days.

—It is indeed. Have your lot had it rough in recent months?

—It hasn't been too bad. We've been based mostly round Bethune and Cambrai. It's a relatively quiet sector. By the way, what did you do before all this?

—I worked in one of Ireland's leading banks. When I volunteered they promised to hold our positions for the duration. I quite enjoyed my work. And you?

—Well I studied in Charterhouse, a public school. I have mixed feelings about that. I'd just been accepted at Oxford when this mess began. I've had both prose and poetry published and hope to teach. That's if I can get through this.

—Graves. Graves. Your name has a very familiar ring to it.

—Well my father grew up in Ireland. He wrote poetry as a young man and added words to several ballads.

—Yes, now I remember. The most famous of these is *Father O' Flynn.*

—My father's a poet and academic, but not a businessman. He sold the rights to that song and many others outright to Charles Stanford. Then when the ballad became famous Stanford and the publisher got all the royalties, not my father. It's a bit of a sore point with him.

—I'd expect so.

–Sullivan, I wonder if you'd excuse me, I'm on the last chapter of Maugham's latest novel, *Of Human Bondage*. My parents sent it to me two weeks ago. I haven't been able to put it down.

–I saw his comedy *The Noble Spaniard* in Dublin a couple of years ago. It was great fun. He's more of a playwright than a novelist isn't he?

–Well he's had great success on the West End. This new novel will establish him as a serious writer. It's about a doctor working in East London. Maugham studied medicine, you know.

–There are rumours that he's in an ambulance unit attached to the French Army. He's about forty now so he needn't have enlisted.

–I expect he wanted to do his bit. His medical training must also be an asset.

–I'm sure it is. So again, excuse me Sullivan. We'll talk later.

Michael's edition of *The Daily Mail* was two days old. It told of French casualties in the continuing offensive at Verdun, and in an editorial suggested that England should do more to help its ally.

The train swayed a lot on the worn tracks, especially at switching points, but they made good time and arrived in Boulogne-sur-mer towards 16.30hrs.

–We don't have time for a proper meal, Sullivan. We'd best have a fry or fish and chips in a tearoom near the docks.

–Good idea, Graves.

The Black Swan, an English style restaurant a hundred yards from the harbour, served an excellent mixed grill.

–Gosh these lamb chops are really fresh, and the sausages and black pudding as great as in Ireland, said Michael.

–Yes this hits the spot. It's a good deal fresher than officer's fare. Eat up, Sullivan. We'll need to board ship by 17.20 at the latest.

Michael didn't need urging. He ate with zest.

Their transport was a civilian boat, now armed with four light guns. It was crowded with soldiers and nurses travelling home on leave. All the cabin space was occupied. Michael and Graves found space in a former ballroom where they left their rucksacks beside an oak-panelled wall.

–They should be reasonably safe here, said Graves. Apart from shirts and underclothes there's nothing of value in my valise.

–That goes for me too, Graves. Let's go on deck, get some fresh air and watch the coastline.

–Great idea.

The harbour was dominated by a large hospital ship, painted completely white with a large red cross emblazoned dead centre on both sides. It stood high in the water.

—I expect there are fewer casualties than usual, said Michael.

—Fewer British casualties, Sullivan. The French are still suffering terribly at Verdun.

—Yes, there were new reports in the newspaper I was reading. They're our Allies. I expect there'll be some moves to help them.

—Yes, the brass will certainly do something to help them and quite soon.

—Heard anything definite?

—No, but there are rumours of another big push soon. Time will tell. That hospital ship will probably depart tonight. The sooner our lads get expert care the better.

The sea air filled Michael's lungs, temporarily removing his fatigue and leaving him exhilarated. In the twilight to his left Boulogne and the French coast loomed indigo and dark green; to his right the English Channel was a washed out grey.

In accordance with military regulations the Midleton was accompanied by a destroyer. All lights were extinguished on board and smoking on deck was forbidden. Moving in a zig-zag pattern, both ships appeared to be making good time.

—We'd better try and get a little shut-eye, Sullivan. We should arrive in Folkestone at about eight o'clock and at St. Pancras Station a little after ten-thirty this evening.

The throbbing engine action and calm sea relaxed both Michael and Graves. They fell quickly asleep in the vaulted oak ballroom.

The troop train to London from Folkestone was only one-third full. They both stretched out across unoccupied seats.

St. Pancras was a hive of activity, yet only partly lit when their train arrived at ten-thirty. They found an army-operated foreign exchange office, changed their remaining francs for sterling, and with a quick farewell made their separate ways across the city, Michael Kings Cross and on to Euston and Graves to visit a friend in the City.

Euston was gradually coming to life as Michael arrived. Finding a telegraph office, he asked for a form and quickly wrote a message to his parents.

—I'd like to send this telegram to Kingstown, Co. Dublin, Ireland, said Michael.

He had written:

```
TO DR & MRS SULLIVAN, C/O ROYAL MARINE HOTEL
KINGSTOWN, CO DUBLIN.
ARRIVING KINGSTOWN TOWARDS 1.30 PM THURSDAY
AFTERNOON ON MAIL BOAT LOOKING FORWARD TO
SEEING YOU BOTH, AND VIRGINIA, LOVE MICHAEL.
```

–Could you ever send this right away?

He passed the clerk his message.

–Yes Sir, our Kingstown office will have this in ten minutes. Let's see. Thirty-two words. That would be one shilling.

–Thank you. By the way, I understand the Holyhead train bypasses Liverpool?

–The train branches off at Crewe and goes via Chester. Arriving at Holyhead, it goes directly to the docks. You'll miss the night boat, but will be there for the morning boat.

–Thanks again.

The train for the west coast was scheduled for 1.15am. Michael knew there would be several announcements prior to departure, so finding an empty bench, he placed his bag behind his head and closed his eyes.

–This is a final announcement. The through-train for Holyhead will depart from platform five in ten minutes, said a voice through a megaphone.

Michael rubbed his eyes, rose quickly and ran the three hundred yards to the platform.

–Slow down, Lieutenant. Take a deep breath, said the ticket agent in a kindly Liverpool accent. Third class is almost full, but there's lots of room in first. Move on now.

The pristine compartment smelled of lily of the valley. Michael placed his kit bag on the overhead rack, and placing a handkerchief between his head and the lace headrest, settled back to sleep.

He awoke some five hours later to views of rugged countryside in the dawn light. It reminded him greatly of Virginia's home county Sligo. Clusters of beech and oak trees radiant in light green, crab-apple, wild-cherry, and mayflower blossoms interspersed with purple heather covered the hills. It was great to be alive. Great to be so close to Ireland and those he loved. Michael reckoned he was about a ninety minute journey from Holyhead as they came away from Chester.

The train reached the docks area towards seven-thirty. The ship departed at 9.30. He felt ravenous with hunger. He found the bar and tea room and had a ham and cheese sandwich and strong tea. It was scalding English Breakfast tea. He drank it slowly, savouring its flavour. He then went on deck and watched the Welsh coastline. To his left a tall red sandstone spit of rock jutted threateningly from the sea floor, home to South Stack Lighthouse. Several hundred puffins had colonies there. They screamed raucously as the Mail Boat steamed past.

It was a brilliant late spring day, a harbinger of the weekend to come. He was alive and in relatively good health. Yes, he'd lost weight, suffered from chronic bronchitis, and had survived a dank cold Belgian winter pretty well living in drains. A winter full of shellfire, sniping, bombs, vermin, and unbelievable continual stress. Why had he survived when so many of his comrades had died?

Was it simply the randomness of the front lines or was there another reason? He wasn't foolhardy, took normal battle precautions. So had his missing comrades. Yet he'd survived while Deegan and so many others hadn't. He prayed silently. With Easter observances he'd have the opportunity to pray more formally. He'd also have the joy of being reunited with Virginia and his family. He lit a Gold Flake and drew the smoke deeply into his lungs.

–Christ!

What a damned mistake! He began to cough and couldn't stop for two minutes. Finally regaining his breath, he tossed the half-consumed cigarette into the brine. How right the men were in calling both Woodbines and Gold Flake cigarettes coffin-nails. He breathed in the sea air deeply. He'd really have to try and get over his bronchitis. Perhaps his father could recommend some potion that might help. He resolved to cut out all fags for the immediate future.

Lulled by the motion of the ship he began to feel calm and relaxed. Turning to his right he found a deck chair and fell into a light sleep.

He awoke to the persistent sound of a small bell. Opening one eye he saw that it was atop a buoy. This probably marked the channel for Dublin Bay. To his left stood the ruined Celtic church and solid Martello Tower of Dalkey Island, to his right the broad arm of Howth Head, and beyond it Ireland's Eye and Lambay Island. He scrambled to his feet, then went to the toilet and splashed cold water in his face.

The Mail Boat docked some twenty minutes later. He retrieved his rucksack and made his way to the gangplank. Michael's parents had told Virginia of Michael's expected arrival, and she and his family were waiting for him on the dock.

–Welcome home my darling Michael, said Virginia, throwing herself into his outstretched arms.

He kissed her and held her a long moment.

–You're thinner, she said.

–Perhaps. You're more beautiful than ever. Let me look at you.

Strands of blond hair fell over her forehead and shone a deep gold in the afternoon sunlight. Her blue-grey eyes sparkled. Her long light-blue dress accented her athletic figure.

—You take my breath away. But then again you always have.

—Michael, Michael, we're so glad you're here, said his mother who was close to tears.

—Yes, you're thinner, so, said his father holding him at arm's length. We'll try to fatten you up, but we have to fast for another two days because of Holy Week. We'll have a real feast Easter Sunday and on Monday.

—Don't worry Father. Just being here with all of you leaves me in the pink. Where are Deirdre, Rosemary, and Brian?

—Brian is at the hotel. He took up chess recently and was engrossed in a game. Deirdre began her nurses training at the Mater in March. She's on duty this weekend. Rosemary has had to stay in the convent in Rathfarnham. The nuns wouldn't let them home for Easter this year. They said it was too close to exam time and that last year most of the students returned late.
Those Loreto nuns are strict.

—Now Tom, it's not that bad, Michael's mother said pointedly. We'll see her on Sunday. She has a routine there and quite likes it. I won't hear another word against the sisters. I'm sure the pupils WERE late in returning last year.

—Let's move. You've just the one bag, Michael?

—Just my haversack. It's all I need, Father.

The fortress-like hotel was on a low hillock adjoining the harbour. Though built in the 1890s it had awnings, battlements, manicured lawns, a formal garden and four grass tennis courts.

—This is really beautiful Father. Can we afford it?

—Don't worry your head, son. They have a promotion for Easter. Besides, tourism is a little less than usual because of hostilities. They're glad to have us. Your room is on the third floor, room 38. You're sharing with Brian. I hope that's all right.

—Of course Father, it will give us a chance to catch up. Will I have time to take a bath? I haven't had one for several days.

—Yes son. As long as you don't spend too long. Supper is at eight.

Room 38 was bright, with two large wrought iron beds, white bedspreads, lace curtains, sky-blue wallpaper and a large picture window with a complete view of the harbour and Dublin Bay. What a view thought Michael. He quickly removed his uniform and made his way to the bathroom. There were lavender crystals. He threw a handful in the bottom of the large bath and tested the water before stepping in. The hotter the better. What luxury to have a hot bath.

Actually, he'd lied to his father. It had been more than a week since he'd had a bath. That was in a canvas bath while in reserve. The hotel soap was goat's milk and very mild. He'd have to be careful not to linger, supper was at eight o'clock sharp. He was particularly thorough in washing his hair.

—Are you ready Michael? It's almost eight, said Brian opening the bathroom door.

—Yes, I just need to run the comb through my hair. Come in. Let's have a look at you. How do you like Castleknock? I hope you can handle those third-year bullies.

—I can take care of myself, Michael. I've only had one real fight, with a lad from Cork. I gave him a bloody nose.

—Good on you, Brian.

Brian had grown several inches since Michael's last visit. He'd lost weight. His jaw was firm, with a slight fuzz of red hair at his cheeks and above his lip.

The large dining room was half full. There were several naval officers in uniform with their wives. Other couples were in semi-formal wear, the men in business suits, their wives in taffeta dresses. Both Virginia and Mrs. Sullivan wore long linen dresses, Virginia's beige, his mother's lavender.

—You're even more handsome, Michael, now you've bathed, said his mother.

—So are both of you.

—Shall we choose? said his mother, scanning the menu. There's a Dublin Bay Chowder as soup, and plaice as main course. We can't have meat as we're moving into Good Friday. If we have the same thing it will be easier on the kitchen.

They ordered clam chowder and Dublin Bay plaice for five.

—You play chess, don't you Michael? asked Brian as they finished supper.

—Yes, I played it a fair bit while studying in 'Knock. I'm a bit rusty now though.

—That doesn't matter Michael, I've only just learned the game and don't know any of those moves where you can win in three minutes.

The library bar had book-lined walls, deep leather chairs, and low drinks tables. *I'm on holiday, it's my first break in three months* thought Michael as he signalled the barman.

—A Redbreast for me and a lemonade for my brother please.

The whiskey was mellow and full-bodied, a great deal better than the scotch issued at the front. Michael slowly sipped it then turned to the chessboard.

–Pick a hand Michael? said Brian, taking a castle from each side and holding them behind his back.

Brian held out both hands, the black rook hidden in his right hand, white rook in his left. Michael slapped his right hand.

–I got you, Brian said smiling. I play white.

They were quite well matched. Brian won the first game in a little over twenty minutes. As he studied the board after the second set up, Michael remembered a skilled opening from his secondary school days. Brian countered and the game went on for forty minutes, ending in stalemate.

Michael realized his glass was empty and ordered another whiskey.

–More lemonade Brian? he asked.

–No, mineral water please. This late at night, lemonade makes me too lively.

They played two more games, each lasting forty-five minutes.

Outside, it had become pitch black except for the beam of the Baily Lighthouse from across the bay. Michael glanced at his wrist-watch.

–Brian, it's eleven o'clock, time to call it a day. It's been quite a long day for me. We'll play again tomorrow.

–Sorry Michael, I forgot that altogether. I get so involved in the game I lose track of time.

–That's the great thing about chess. It completely absorbs you. The really great players can see about eight moves ahead. I wouldn't put myself at all in that league, but if you continue to play you'll reach that level.

–Ye think so?

–I do indeed. Now let's to bed. I'm dead on my feet.

–Brian, do you mind if I draw the heavy blinds? Michael asked as they reached the room.

–Of course not.

Even with the blinds closed there were glimmers of light every thirty seconds or so from the Baily Lighthouse. A lot better than the blinding flash of high explosives, or even the star shells that Michael was accustomed to. He sunk into the deep mattress and pulled spotless linen sheets around his chest. It was the first time he'd slept in a clean bed in months, since his last visit home.

–You settled in all right, Brian? he enquired.

–Fine, Michael.

–Right, I'm turning off the bedside lamp now. Sleep well.

He awoke to birdsong and bright sunshine. Brian had raised the blinds and was looking towards Howth Head across the bay.

—Sorry, I didn't mean to disturb you Michael, he said hearing him move.

—What time is it Brian? Michael asked sleepily.

—Nine thirty. They stop serving breakfast in an hour. We'll have to move if we want anything.

They ate very lightly because of Lenten observance, a meal of boiled eggs, toast and strong tea.

—Virginia, will we have time for a game or two of tennis before we have to go to St. Michael's? asked Michael as he drank the last of his tea.

—Yes I'm sure we have, Michael. We only have to leave for church about two o'clock. That gives us time for at least one game.

—We don't really have to change, do we? I'll just take off my tie and the top of my uniform. I expect you'll find a way to shorten your dress, Virginia.

—Yes, but I have to warn you I've been practicing, Michael. There's a court behind the hospital in Cork City. We play there as much as possible.

They played two sets. Virginia won most games. Michael found himself watching her face, earnest in concentration as she went up on her toes while serving. Her short sleeve fell back to the shoulder of a fit arm. *She was more beautiful than ever. She would soon be his wife. Perhaps even later that year. As soon as hostilities ended.* He missed several shots watching the sun at her back send blinding rays through her blonde halo.

—Game set and match, Michael, she said. You're in another place. You shouldn't have missed that last ball.

—Sorry love, my game is rusty. I find it difficult to give attention to tennis. I'm just so happy to be here, and that we're going to be engaged.

He heard his voice crack and tried to remain in control.

—That's true for me also my darling. I've looked forward to your visit for so long. We're together now. This war will end soon. We'll be married before long. We've our whole lives ahead of us.

—God willing sweetheart, God willing.

—It's almost two o'clock, Virginia and Michael, said his mother from a nearby lawn.

Father wants us to be in good time. We'll have to be at the church by at least two thirty to find space. You have less than fifteen minutes to freshen up.

—Fine Mother, said Michael taking Virginia's arm and walking quickly towards the hotel.

The interior of the gothic church was stark, the marble high altar bereft of normal covering, the large crucifix behind it and the statues at the entrance and at points through-out, covered in mourning purple. Though they arrived in good time they found seating together with difficulty.

Michael always found the mourning of Good Friday trying. He knew that in obedience to His Father, Christ had died for him and for all men. But hadn't he risen again? Wasn't this the true message of Easter? He took a deep breath. Lord help me get through this and teach me the true message of your sacrifice, he prayed silently.

Monsignor Byrne, a tall man in his thirties, was imposing in his black vestments. He seemed conscious of the impatience of the congregation and kept the ceremonies moving at a fast pace. Following the dramatic recitation of St. John's Passion narrative, the celebrant drew a parallel between Christ's sacrifice and the privations of the men in the front lines.

—Many of our men have made the supreme sacrifice at Suvla Bay and in both Battles at Ypres. May God continue to protect them and return them soon to our shores, he said in conclusion.

—Monsignor Byrne seems a very kind man, said Michael softly as they left the church.

—Indeed he does, Michael. All those prayers, ceremonies, and his homily took a little over an hour and a half. It's the fastest Good Friday celebrations I've ever been to, said his father.

—Perhaps he just wants us to enjoy the late spring weather, said Michael.

—Yes, I think he does. Why don't we motor to Dalkey and Killiney. There's still lots of sunshine.

—Great idea father.

His father parked the Model-T at the entrance to Killiney Park and they walked up the hill to the monument. His mother spread a rug on the grass. She and Virginia sat there while Michael, Brian, and their father looked southwards. At their feet the bay stretched, bordered by golden sands, to Bray Head. The sea shimmered in the spring sunlight. Several small craft with spotless sails glided silently over its surface. Near the sea at Ballybrack was an apple and cherry orchard replete with pink and white blossoms.

—You know they call this bay the Naples of Ireland, Michael, said his father. I've seen the Bay of Naples. If anything, this is more beautiful.

—When did you see Naples, Father? asked Michael and Brian.

—Years ago, Michael. When I worked on the East India Line. Long before I met your mother. It was another life.

—Hey you three, have some hot tea, said his mother opening a flask and producing five enamel cups.

—The very drink for a warm afternoon Annie, said his father.

—This is lovely, Mother, said Michael and Brian together.

—It's good that you brought this Mrs. Sullivan, said Virginia.

—Yes, it's a pity we can't eat treats, but it's Good Friday. We must surrender small things. Easter's almost here.

—Yes, and it'll be a holy one, Mrs. Sullivan.

—Yes and the last one of this war, Virginia.

—Amen to that Annie, amen to that, said his father.

Michael knew that hostilities would continue for at least another year. The German offensive at Verdun was greatly weakening the French army. Yet the fortress was sacred to them.

They would fight to the last man. There were rumours that Britain as an ally had a strategic plan to help. This was all in the future. There was no point in mentioning any of it to his family.

As a serving junior officer he was bound by military secrecy.

—Yes let's hope this is the last year of war, he said with a sigh. Virginia, why don't we explore this park a little.

—Of course Michael, she said rising and draining the last of her tea.

—Be careful you two, said his father. There are a lot of nooks and crannies in the hills just behind us. Some of the shale isn't that firm.

—We'll be careful father, said Michael, holding Virginia's hand and striding towards a copse of fir trees. Sphagnum moss with clusters of purple heather carpeted the ground beneath them. Gorse in full bloom filled the air with fragrance. Ahead lay the vastness of the bay, with Howth Head in a slight haze. Below and to their right lay the granite breadth of Dalkey Convent, the railway tracks and a little further Dalkey Island.

—I never tire of looking at that island, Michael, said Virginia as they reached the trees.

—Yes, it's very beautiful, but so are you.

He kissed her on the lips.

—I've been wanting to do this all afternoon love, he said.

—And I've wanted to be alone with you, Michael. Your parents are nice to be around, but we need time together.

—There's a shady spot here, he said undoing the Sam Brown belt and the top of his uniform.

He spread it on the ground at the base of a flowering chestnut tree.

—It'll get a little soiled, said Virginia laughing.

—It's only dust. It'll come out.

They lay in each other's arms kissing tenderly.

—I was beginning to think we'd never be together again, my love, said Michael.

His voice was breaking.

—What is it, Michael? said Virginia with panic in her voice.

—Nothing really. Sorry to alarm you. Deegan and so many friends died in the last few months, our regiment's been involved in no major battles yet every day someone I know is either killed or gravely injured. You know they came out with some facts a few weeks ago. The average lifespan of an officer of my rank is six months. I've been at the front nine months. So, I've beaten the odds.

He laughed.

—It doesn't matter, Michael. It doesn't matter. You'll survive. We'll marry soon. On Easter Monday if you wish.

—No, my love. No. The odds of my being killed are too great. It would be unwise to marry now.

—I don't think so, Michael. I really don't.

—Patience is a virtue too, love. We'll bide our time.

—Right, my brave archangel. Your parents did well when they named you Michael.

She punched him playfully in the ribs.

—Maybe they did and maybe they didn't. I'm certainly no angel. Give us another kiss.

—God you're irredeemable. What am I going to do with you at all?

—You love me because of my good looks and my charm. Go on now, admit it. I'm not going anywhere. So you'd better hold onto me.

—All right, I will. I will, you devil. Will you just stop tickling me, said Virginia, laughing hilariously and gasping for breath.

A large figure blocked their view of the bay. Michael realized it was Brian.

—What are you doing here, Brian? Spying? he asked.

—No, Michael. No. Father asked me to tell you that we'll be leaving in about five minutes.

Brian's face was scarlet. He shifted his weight from one foot to the other in embarrassment.

–That's fine, Brian. We'll be right along, won't we Michael? said Virginia.

–Yes, we will. Sorry I spoke like that, Brian, said Michael, standing up and shaking the dust off his jacket.

–Oh that's all right Michael. See you at the motor.

Brian walked back up the incline.

The evening passed quickly. They all played several games of canasta before retiring early. Only Michael's parents rose early enough for Holy Saturday Services at St. Michael's. Virginia, Michael, and Brian were just finishing breakfast as they returned a little before ten.

–Martina, can we still have breakfast? they asked a young waitress.

–Yes, of course Dr. and Mrs. Sullivan. What would you like?

–Porridge with cream, then poached eggs, sausages, and toast for two, and a pot of strong Earl Grey tea. All right Annie?

–Of course Tom.

–How were the ceremonies, Mother? asked Michael after they'd sat down.

–Beautiful, but long, replied his mother. Monsignor Boylan gave a sermon on the meaning of Christ's three days in the tomb. There had already been all those readings about the Exodus and Passover. It's a good thing we were sitting down at that point. I thought I was going to faint.

–Yes, but you got through it with flying colours Annie. It's all over now for another year, eat up now, said the doctor patting his wife's shoulder. Oh I forgot to mention that Deirdre is coming out by tram at around noon. We'll meet her at the Pavillion in Kingstown and then go to Bray in the motor. There's a band concert there this afternoon. It'll be fun.

Deirdre was in great spirits when they met her off the tram.

–You seem in great health love. Isn't she, Annie? said her father after they'd embraced.

–Yes, I love nursing, Father. The hours are long and I find night shifts difficult, especially if I'm only on nights for one or two nights at a time.

–That's normal, love. It takes several days for the body to adjust. How do you like taking care of sick children?

–That's what I like best of all. Many have high temperatures, but once the fever breaks, they recover quickly. Soon their spirit returns, and they play pranks on us all the time.

—It takes a special person to nurse sick children. I think you may have the gift, said Mrs. Sullivan.

—She inherited it from you Annie. She's your daughter! Now Deirdre, put your bag in the boot. We're going to Bray for the afternoon. Sit in the back with Virginia, you've a lot to talk about, said the doctor.

The Model-T made good time and they arrived in Bray towards one o'clock. The resort was quite crowded. A carousel, flying chairs, swings, and other amusements had been set up at the foot of Bray Head. Easter bunnies, mime artists, and clowns in floppy shoes and greasepaint circulated among a throng of children of various ages. The Easter bunnies had baskets of small chocolate eggs and gave freely. To the right and back were several makeshift tea rooms and pancake shops.

—We can have something light to eat here, said Dr. Sullivan moving gingerly through the crowd. The concert isn't 'til four. The bandstand is on the promenade just on the left. We've plenty of time. So will we all have pancakes and caster sugar and lemon?

—Yes, that'd be perfect Father, said Deirdre, Michael, and Brian together.

—So it's pancakes for six. All right Annie and Virginia?

—It's Pancake Tuesday all over again, said Brian as he poured caster sugar on two pancakes.

—These are lovely, Father. But not as good as Mother's.

—No not by a long way, Annie. Yours are thinner and much lighter, said his father smiling broadly.

The weather was sunny, with cool breezes from the sea. Egged on by Virginia, Deirdre continued to tell of her student nursing experiences.

—It'll get easier as the months go by, Deirdre. You'll have to follow the old motto. Never stand when you can sit, never sit when you can lie down.

—How can I follow that with Mother Attracta, Matron, and sisters of the Mercy nuns always behind me, Virginia?

—You'll find a way, Deirdre. I had my own troubles with Sister Dymphna at Vincent's. She has a great love for me now. It'll be the same for you, just continue to do your best.

—I do, Virginia. It's just that I get so tired at times.

—Try to get to bed at an early hour when you're not on night duty, girl, said Dr. Sullivan. Continue to take those iron tablets I prescribed for you. Eat as well as you can and take a spoonful of cod liver oil from time to time. I know it tastes awful, but it's full of nourishment. You've got the next two days free. Make the most of it. Sleep as late as you like tomorrow and Monday. You deserve a rest.

—Thank you Father. I'll do my best to relax.

—You always do, girl. We're both proud of you.

They made their way quietly to their left to the area in front of the bandstand. Several rows of folding chairs had been set up. They took seats towards the back.

—It's best not to be too close to the band, said Dr. Sullivan. Sometimes the trumpets play so loudly that it hurts the ears. Isn't that true Michael?

—Yes, very true Father.

The musicians took their places in groups of two or three. Then the bandmaster, dressed formally in scarlet, took his place before them. He tapped his baton on the music stand then raised it.

The band played selections of Moore's, melodies including *The Harp that Once*, *The Meeting of the Waters*, and *The Last Rose of Summer*. They included several selections from Dubliner Victor Herbert's Irish Rhapsody and Sweethearts, concluding with *The Mountains of Mourne* and other Percy French airs.

—What a lovely programme. Did you like it, Michael? asked his father.

—Yes, it's a bit different from what we hear in concerts when we're in the rear lines. Our bands there aren't as good, and the programmes have more of a military nature. You know, *Hearts of Oak*, *Keep the Home Fires Burning* and tunes of that type. It's lovely to hear real Irish music.

—Yes, if you only had more time, we could go to a variety programme at the Theatre Royal or The Queen's. Well, on your next visit.

—Hopefully, Father. But I'd really just like to do more simple things.

—Of course Michael. If we hurry now we'll avoid traffic on our way back to Kingstown.

They ate lightly that evening. Afterwards Michael, Virginia and his parents played bridge while Brian instructed Deirdre in the rudiments of chess.

—We should motor to Rathfarnham to see Rosemary, said Dr. Sullivan as they left St. Michael's following Easter Sunday Mass. If we travel by way of Stillorgan and Dundrum we should reach the Loreto Convent Motherhouse in a little over half an hour.

Set a little back from the main road and with a short avenue, the three-story convent sparkled in the spring sunlight. Dr. Sullivan parked the Model-T near the main entrance, walked the few feet to the oak door and knocked. A black clad nun in her late thirties responded.

—Happy Easter Mother. Dr. Sullivan and his family here to see his daughter Rosemary.

—Just follow me doctor, said the nun leading him towards the interior.

—May I call the rest of the family, Mother. I'll only be a moment, said the doctor.

—Of course.

Dressed in her navy-blue school uniform, her honey-blond hair shoulder length, Rosemary joined them minutes later.

—Happy Easter girl. You're really quite a lady now. Isn't she Annie? said Dr. Sullivan kissing Rosemary on the forehead.

—Yes indeed Tom. You're smart in your uniform Rosemary, and have grown at least an inch since January, said Mrs. Sullivan kissing her daughter several times.
Have you had a nice Easter so far?

—We prayed a lot, Mother. Mass this morning was very beautiful. You would have loved the music, Deirdre. All the postulants and novices formed part of the choir. In addition to Gregorian Chant they did several pieces by Palestrina. I thought I was in heaven. Of course I missed being with Mother, Father, and all of you, but this was lovely. Oh, Michael, Virginia, it's so great that you're here.

She rushed forward and kissed them both.

—Look at you Rosemary, you're more beautiful than I remember, Rathfarnham agrees with you, said Michael holding his sister.

He felt his voice break. He was just able to control his emotion.

—You're becoming more ladylike every time I see you, Rosemary, said Virginia.

—Thank you Virginia. You look beautiful in your summer dress. Light colours suit you.

—Rosemary, you've grown up a lot, said Brian.

—So have you, Brian.

With a knock the young nun reappeared pushing a tea trolley complete with white china cups and an assortment of sandwiches.

—With Reverend Mother's good wishes, Doctor, said the sister pouring two cups.

—Thank you Mother. You're very kind. Please tell Reverend Mother that we're taking Rosemary for afternoon tea in the Dublin Mountains. We'll have the tea, but please take away the sandwiches. Oh, and what time should we bring my daughter back?

—Bring her back at about seven o'clock, Doctor. Evening prayers are at eight. Bedtime is a little later.

—We'll have her back in good time Mother. Thank you again.

The nun left carrying the sandwich plates.

Lamb Doyle's Inn at Sandyford was a ten-minute drive from the convent. They were still in good time for Sunday lunch. Dr. Sullivan ordered spring lamb for all seven of them and then continued talking to his youngest daughter.

—So you like Rathfarnham, Rosemary?

—Yes, very much. Apart from our regular subjects we have French conversation, needlework, and art. We go for walks in the mountains each Wednesday. I've filled a sketchbook already with drawings and have painted several watercolours of views from there.

—That's wonderful girl. Isn't it Michael?

—Indeed it is father. Rose, I wish I had your talent.

—*Oui, mais tu as d'autre dons*, Michael, *comme la sagesse et courage. Tout la famille te admire surtout moi.*

—*Merci, chère Rose. Je fais mon devoir c'est tout...Tu sais, tu parles avec un très bonne accent.*

—Our teacher Mother Columba is part French and completed secondary school in Paris. She tries to give us the real sound of the language before teaching any irregular verbs.

—That's the best way to learn. The way children do. You can worry about grammar later.

Conversation flowed freely as they ate. Aware that there were subjects that he could not speak of because of army discipline, Michael tried to steer topics away from himself.

He was with Virginia in the bosom of his family; he lived in the moment. Both Rosemary and Brian were becoming great young adults. They had their whole future ahead of them.

That was sufficient.

—We need some exercise after such a lovely lunch, said Dr. Sullivan as he drove to the base of the Three Rock Mountain near the inn. All those that are willing join me. You'll stay here and continue reading *Mansfield Park*, Annie. Virginia, Rosemary, Brian and Michael, are you game? It's an easy climb, the view gets better with every step you take. Let's go. Each one at his own pace.

There had been several days of sunshine. They kept to well-trodden paths, the shale under their feet was firm and dry.

–Look at the view, isn't it a little bit of heaven? asked Dr. Sullivan as they reached the summit.

It was heavenly, thought Michael, especially after the destruction he'd seen in Flanders. Dublin on the left; Kingsbridge Station, the Four Courts, the General Post Office and the Customs House sparkling in the afternoon sunshine, the Liffey a silver thread. Howth Head, its purple heather clearly visible across from them, with Ireland's Eye and Lambay beyond.

On the right Kingstown, Dalkey, and Bray Head. The scent of heather, gorse and thyme filled his nostrils. It was great to be alive.

–I wish I could freeze this view, Virginia. It's more spectacular than the view from Killiney. So different from everything I've seen in Flanders.

–Yes Michael, your father's right. Paradise must be a lot like this.

–Let me sketch you, said Rosemary. Father, Brian, Deirdre, join Michael and Virginia here.

She motioned them to the right. Working quickly with lead pencil and her sketchpad she filled in the faint outline of Dublin, then their forms in the foreground.

–I'll fill in some colour tomorrow, she said showing her drawing to her father.

–You're a wonder, Rosemary, said Dr. Sullivan. Look at this, Michael, Rose has made tremendous progress, hasn't she?

–She has, Father. This is really professional, Rose.

Virginia, Deirdre and Brian admired the sketch in turn.

–Rose, may I have this once you've completed it? It'll bring back memories of a very happy day, said Michael.

–Yes, of course. That's why I pulled out my pencil and sketchpad.

They spent the next hour exploring the area further. As the light began to fade Dr. Sullivan looked at his watch.

–Goodness it's after six. Mother must be wondering where we've got to. I'm sure she's finished *Mansfield Park* since we left her. It's almost time we were bringing you back to the nuns, Rose.

–Do you have to, Father?

–You know that I do, love, those are the regulations the sisters laid down this Easter. We can't always have things our own way. Chin up now. You know I don't like sad faces.

–Of course Father.

She smiled broadly.

—That's my younger daughter.

Mrs. Sullivan lay dozing in the back of the Model T, her book open on her lap.

—It was so warm and peaceful I fell asleep; she said, hearing their feet on the shale.

—Well you might dear, you've had several early mornings because of Easter ceremonies, said her husband.

They reached the convent in good time and with a promise to revisit Rosemary before their departure to Rosnua. They quickly returned to the hotel. Following a light supper, they played bridge late into the evening.

—There are races in Fairyhouse all day tomorrow. Michael, would you like to attend? asked Dr. Sullivan as he and his wife departed the game-room for bed.

—No, Father. Thank you very much. It'll take well over ninety minutes to get to the racecourse from here. The roads will be crowded. I'd rather have an unplanned day like we had on Saturday.

—That's fine, son. We'll find a lot to do in Kingstown. Goodnight all. See you in the morning.

Michael, Virginia, Deirdre, and Brian retired minutes later.

Easter Monday was another bright clear late spring day. Michael wore casual clothes.

—Michael, what would you say to a day of golf at Greystones? Green fees there are reasonable and we can also rent clubs, said Dr. Sullivan as they ate a late breakfast.

—That would be wonderful, Father. My game is rusty though. There are very few golf courses in North France and Belgium.

—Don't worry, son. I've only played once this year. My handicap is eighteen. The trip will be a lovely outing for all of us.

They left at 9.30 and reached the clubhouse about forty minutes later. The weather continued sunny with a southeasterly wind. They rented four sets of clubs and played a mixed four ball, Michael and his father against Virginia and Mrs. Sullivan.

—We'll give the girls two strokes, Michael. It mightn't be necessary as your mother's a strong player. Still, noblesse oblige.

Brian and Deirdre carried the ladies' clubs and they set out.

Giving the ladies extra strokes proved a folly. Michael and his father were soundly beaten at the seventeenth hole. Two up and one to go.

—I need to phone Mother Attracta to tell her exactly when I'll be back at the hospital, Father, said Deirdre as they drank coffee towards three o'clock.

—That's fine, girl. I'm sure they'll let us use the phone here in the clubhouse.

—This is strange, Dr. Sullivan was told by the club manager inside. The operator keeps saying he can't get through to town. There's some kind of an emergency in the city.

The Sinn Feiners are out on some kind of manoeuvres. The phone lines are down, Westland Row and Harcourt Street Stations are occupied, and there have been skirmishes on the rail-line between Kingstown and the city.

—This is difficult, Tim. My older son Michael is a junior officer on leave and the two young ladies in our party are hospital nurses. I expect that they all will have to resume their duties. Say nothing directly though. It might cause alarm. I'll break the news gently.

—Mum's the word, doctor. Don't you worry.

—What's the trouble, Tom? Why the strained face? asked Mrs. Sullivan as her husband returned.

—It's probably nothing, Annie. Or something that'll be over in a matter of hours. Elements of Sinn Fein or Professor John McNeill's group have seized Westland Row and Harcourt Street Stations and there are reports of disruptions on the train line from Kingstown.

Michael felt his stomach tighten. Damn it, he'd left Belgium to get away from violence. Now it had caught up with him. Virginia, his mother, and Deirdre were quite pale.

Brian laughed nervously.

—There have been rumours of this for weeks, said Brian. At least in North Dublin. No one knew the actual date. Professor Pearse of St. Enda's School is involved. The other leaders are shadowy. England's difficulties have always been Ireland's opportunity.

—Is that so Brian? said Michael feeling his skin tighten and hands become moist. And what of all the fine soldiers from both the South and North of this island who've been laying their lives on the line for the last eighteen months? What of them?

—Things have changed greatly here in the past few months, Michael. Ask Father. People are behind Professor Pearse and John McNeill.

—Now, boys, now! said Dr. Sullivan. Michael, Brian is partly right. Public opinion has changed a lot here. The Irish Volunteers have a lot of support.

He signalled the waitress.

—Could we have another pot of coffee and five brandies, dear.

—Right, we have to decide on a plan of action now, he continued.

—My duty is clear, Father, said Michael breathing deeply. Military Regulations state that in times of civil emergency a serving member of His Majesty's Forces must report to the nearest military facility. Beggar's Bush is too hard to reach. The nearest barracks is Portobello.

—Virginia, while I realize that you'd really like to return to your position at the North Infirmary in Cork, it's probable that city has been sealed off and that there are no trains leaving Kingsbridge. Do you wish to remain here with us or do you think you might be needed as an extra emergency nurse at Vincent's?

—Dr. Sullivan, I think I'd better get to Vincent's, talk to Mother Dymphna or the Mother in charge, and volunteer there.

—We'll get you there, Virginia. We should be able to drop you as close to Vincent's as possible. Michael, we'll get you to Portobello.

—Deirdre, we'll have to somehow get a message to Mother Attracta. It'll be very difficult to get across the city. You'd better stay with us at least tonight. Things might be more settled tomorrow. Right, drink up, we've a long evening ahead of us.

—We'll try to get as near as possible to the nurses residence, Virginia, said Dr. Sullivan as they drove past the Royal Dublin Society Grounds in Ballsbridge.

The weather remained sunny, the avenues near the show-grounds a riot of pink cherry blossoms. As they came closer to the city Michael recognized the sound of sustained small arms fire. Soldiers had set up a flimsy barricade on a nearby bridge and were being fired on from several occupied houses. There was no oncoming traffic.

—Be careful, Father.

Dr. Sullivan increased speed and turned up by Herbert Park towards Morehampton Road. There he turned right, continuing by Leeson Street towards Stephen's Green. At Michael's request, he stopped at the right-hand corner of Lower Leeson Street.

—I'm sorry we couldn't get you directly to the residence, but at least Father managed to get you as close as possible, said Michael as he kissed Virginia goodbye on the front steps of the hospital. I don't know when I'll be able to see you. This disturbance may last a few days or even longer. Be careful, love.

—You be careful too, Michael, said Virginia, turning towards the front doors.

Michael ran towards the Model T. He heard sporadic gunfire from The College of Surgeon's directly across Stephen's Green. With Iveigh House,

University Church, and Wesley College on his left, Dr. Sullivan continued towards the southwest corner of the green. He made a sharp turn at the Russell Hotel and sped up Harcourt Street to Portobello Bridge.

—This is the closest I can get to the barracks, Michael, he said minutes later stopping on Portobello bridge. Be careful you don't do anything foolish in the coming days. Your mother and I are proud of you. Don't take any unnecessary risks. God bless you, son.

—I'll do my best Father, said Michael, retrieving his soft bag and sprinting towards the front gates of army quarters.

The sentry on duty seemed nervous. He referred Michael to the Adjutant Major Rosborough of the Irish Rifles.

—Thank you for complying with Kings Regulations so promptly, Lieutenant, said the stocky middle-aged officer. Please report to the quartermaster Captain Forster and aid him in any way you can. Dismiss.

Forster, a slight man in his late thirties, was busy with preparations for the expected arrival of men from all the Irish regiments.

—We expect men from all regiments, Sullivan. Housing and feeding them will be quite a chore. We'll probably run out of food by Thursday. Unusual times, Lieutenant. But then again you're used to that.

—Indeed Captain, said Michael as he placed clean uniforms, shirts, underclothes, sheets and blankets for fifty on a large table.

—We're told that the General Post Office, Jacobs Biscuit Factory, and St. Stephen's Green have been seized by rebels, Sullivan. There's no confirmation of this, of course.

—The College of Surgeons and the Green are definitely occupied, Captain. There was sporadic gunfire as my father drove past at speed to get me here.

—Many of the garrison here went to the races at Fairyhouse. They'll have trouble crossing the city.

—I expect so Captain, but if they're in mufti it may not be a problem.

—Many of them are, so perhaps you're right, Lieutenant.

Late in the evening several officers in civilian dress returned to the barracks. They told of a breakdown in public transport and sporadic looting on Moore and Middle Abbey Streets.

—It took more than an hour just to cross the city, said a young officer. The majority of people seem to be against these rebels, but the ruffian elements are using events to their advantage, pillaging and looting.

—It seems to happen everywhere there's a breakdown of order, Lieutenant Cosgrave. There's a lot of it in Belgium, said Michael.

Towards nine, a Sergeant McAdam of the garrison returned to barracks dressed as a woman. He seemed very shaken and was white as a sheet.

—I was in a pub on Cuffe Street just behind the College of Surgeons. I had two or three drinks in the nook with Marie, a waitress at the Shelbourne, then, around seven o'clock, six men in slouch hats and green uniforms came in armed to the teeth. Luckily we were in a shady area. If any one of them had seen me, I'd a been dead on the spot. Somehow Marie spirited me to a room at the back where she found a shawl and a skirt. She saved my life.

—Indeed she did, Sergeant. I'd hold on to her if I were you. Here's a fresh uniform. From the looks of you, you could do with a stiff drink. I'm sorry I've nothing to offer you. Try and get some sleep. It looks like tomorrow will be a heavy day.

—Yes, we'll be fighting fellow Irishmen. Not a very nice thing, Lieutenant.

—No it isn't.

—Sullivan, Major Rosborough has ordered that rifles, bayonets and a hundred rounds of ammunition be issued to every man here. Would you see to it, said Forster some minutes later.

Michael carried out this order with the help of Sergeant MacAdam. Then, feeling quite fatigued, he retrieved his soft bag and retired. He shared a room with Milligan, a Sandhurst cadet.

—I'm sorry Milligan. I'm all in. It's been an eventful day. Forgive me if I retire right now.

—Oh that's fine, Sullivan. I'm doing the same. We'll need to be alert tomorrow.

Michael awoke to the sound of sustained rapid fire. It came from the canal side of the barracks. Both he and Milligan dressed quickly and ran downstairs to the darkened mess hall. It was crowded with officers of several regiments. Some drank tea. Others simply rolled out their sleeping bags and returned to sleep.

—Some ninety minutes later, Rosborough turned on every bulb in the mess hall to get all their attention. Gentlemen, I need a volunteer to replace the Officer of the Guard on the Main Gate. Now completely awake, Michael came forward.

At the front gates Michael replaced a junior officer named Duggan. Duggan's eyes were leaden. He looked as if he could sleep for a week.

Lionel Davies, an elderly civilian, had taken refuge in the barracks. Unable to sleep, he approached Michael and his men at the front gate.

—Lieutenant. Connolly's crowd, the Citizen Army, have taken over Davys pub on the Rathmines side of the canal. They've pinned down a column of men just down from us. The soldiers are returning fire, but can't break out. They need help.

—I'll see what we can do, Mr. Davies. Perhaps we can send a patrol in fifteen minutes or so. I'll do my best.

Minutes later a machine gun detachment joined the beleaguered column. They riddled the pub with fire. There was no return fire. The foot soldiers waited several minutes, then they charged the pub in force. The enemy was nowhere in sight. They'd fled by back lanes towards Rathmines Town Hall.

The remainder of Michael's watch was relatively calm, with sounds of sporadic gunfire coming from the Green and College of Surgeons.

Towards seven thirty a distinguished officer approached Michael and his platoon. His cap at a rakish angle, he sported an auburn moustache and short cleft of beard on his lower lip.

—Good morning Lieutenant, I'm Vane, he said cheerily.

—Morning Major, said Michael, noticing Vane's red braid and the insignia of the Munster Fusiliers.

—Right, we don't stand on ceremony in situations like this. I'm here to assist Rosborough in any way I can. Anything to report, Lieutenant?

Michael told of the Davy's pub engagement.

—The rebels seemed to have vanished into thin air, Sir.

—Yes, that often happens in situations of urban war. I'm sure you've seen it in Ypres.

—Very often, Sir.

—Don't let me interrupt you, Lieutenant. I'm just trying to see how we can strengthen these defences. Do you think we could place an extra machine gun here? There's a gap in the defensive wall and in the sandbags.

—Of course Sir. It should make the barracks much more secure.

—Right. Fine. Place the tripod and the gun here lads.

He indicated the position to two privates who accompanied him.

—There's a building with a flat roof about thirty yards to our left, Lieutenant. See it?

—Yes Sir, I think it's a public house, said Michael.

–We'll have to secure it. If we don't it will be a perfect vantage point for the insurgents. Send two squads out now.

–Right away Sir. Sergeant MacAdam, let's go.

The pub was in bad repair, with flaking grey paint. The front door of the business section was padlocked. Michael, MacAdam, and the squads were able to reach the flat roof without going through this area. Built at least ninety years earlier, the small building was directly in the line of fire from Davy's.

–This little shop is probably very popular with the locals, MacAdam. It's too bad we have to occupy it, but you can see how strategic it could be to the enemy.

–Yes, if they were to take it they could attack the barracks directly. That's if they had some Mills bombs and a couple of machine guns, Lieutenant.

–We're not sure of their fire power, Sergeant. I think all they have is rifles and perhaps some German stick grenades. My father drove so quickly past the Green yesterday there was only time to make out that it was occupied.

MacAdam posted two machine guns on the flat roof and soldiers at the front and rear of the premises.

–Everything's secure now Sir, he said.

–Right, Sergeant. I'd best report back to Major Vane. Carry on.

–Who's the Commanding Officer here Lieutenant? asked a gaunt officer who approached the barrack gates at about the same time as Michael returned.

–Major Rosborough, Captain. There are officers and men from several regiments here, but Rosborough is in command. His office is on the second floor to your right.

–Thank you Lieutenant. I'm Bowen-Coldhurst. As you can see I'm with the Irish Rifles. It took the best part of six hours to get here from County Meath. It's good to be among friends.
I don't understand these Shinners. Taking up arms when volunteers from the whole of Ireland are in the front lines.

–Nor do I Sir, said Michael indicating the stairway to the CO's office.

He remembered hearing of a Captain Bowen-Coldhurst's bravery at the Battle of Mons, but couldn't recall any details. He'd had less than two hours sleep in the last twenty-four.

He desperately needed rest, if only for an hour. Making his way to the Mess Hall he found his sleeping bag. He then went upstairs to the room he'd been assigned the previous evening, lay down and was immediately asleep.

The crack of rifle fire and a cry of pain awoke him some two hours later. One of the platoon guarding the main gate had been hit in his shoulder by sniper fire. Lieutenant Dobbyn arranged for two soldiers to help him to the infirmary.

Michael rejoined his platoon. To their left, parts of the College of Surgeons appeared to be in flames. Further to the left and north, a cloud of black smoke billowed above Sackville Street.

Damn it! Michael thought to himself, *it's as bad or worse than Ypres.*

The main guard were jumpy. The enemy, invisible, fired off a sniper round every eight to ten minutes. The weather was bright with occasional sun-showers. Michael thought he saw a glimmer of silver atop the red-sandstone of Rathmines Town Hall.

—Madigan, give me your rifle, he said to a crouching soldier.

He waited for what seemed like an eternity, then seeing the rifle barrel again, took aim and slowly squeezed the trigger.

—That fellow won't bother us again for a while Madigan, he said, handing back the rifle.

To their left a group of about twenty people gathered at the corner of Camden Street and Portobello Harbour. A bearded man in plus fours and a tweed jacket addressed them. Under the circumstances all gatherings were illegal. Michael called Madigan, Brady and three other privates and went to investigate.

Francis Sheehy Skeffington was the man in tweed. He wore a VOTES FOR WOMAN badge on his lapel, suggesting a seasoned street orator.

Michael knew the pacifist journalist by repute. He vividly remembered the counter demonstration Skeffington had led the night of Prime Minister Asquith's visit in September 1914 and recalled that this nationalist journalist had been imprisoned briefly under the Defence of the Realm Act. Released after only one week, Skeffington, as joint editor of *The National Democrat*, had written an open letter to Professor MacDonagh of the Volunteer Movement, objecting to all forms of violence.

—I'm trying to organize a committee of local persons to prevent looting, Lieutenant, he said to Michael.

—Be that as it may, Sir. These are difficult times. Would you and two other members of your committee be willing to come to the barracks so that we make take some details?

—Certainly, Lieutenant.

At the barracks Michael turned Sheehy-Skeffington over to the Adjutant Colonel Rosborough.

—We won't detain you for very long Sir, he said leaving Rosborough's office.

Michael was proven wrong in this. The two members of Skeffington's committee were released, but perhaps because of his previous incarceration the activist was held longer.

That night towards ten o'clock Captain Bowen-Colthurst gave orders that Sheehy- Skeffington be taken from his cell.

—I want twelve volunteers for a sortie in the suburb of Rathmines. We're taking Mr. Sheehy-Skeffington as protection in case of a Sinn Fein attack. Right then, let's go.

Because of earlier actions there, Rathmines Road was quiet as a morgue. Then out of the gloom two youths came towards the platoon.

—Wasn't Marie Maguire wonderful in the solo part of *Panis Angelicus*, Tom? asked one.

—Yes, she sings like an angel. To think that she's only a year older than us.

—Stand and identify yourselves, said Bowen-Colthurst in a cold officious voice.

—I'm Tom Coade. This is my friend Jim Clyne.

—Don't you ruffians know there's a war on? You should have been home an hour ago.

—We weren't aware of this, Sir, said Coade, a lad of thirteen. We were at choir practice at Our Lady of Refuge Church. Rehearsal was supposed to end at ten o'clock, but we ran late.

—I put it to you that you're part of the youth wing of the rebel movement and that you're carrying messages from here to the armed men in the College of Surgeons, said Bowen-Colthurst.

—No, Sir. No. We're going home from choir practice. Call on Father O'Boyle at the church presbytery if you want to check, said Coade anxiously.

—Damn it. You goddamned liar. You're runners for the rebels. I'll teach you how to talk to an officer in His Majesties Forces.

He hit Coade ferociously on the side of his head. Coade fell to his knees.

—We've nothing to do with the rebels, Sir. Nothing! I hope they beat the shit out of you. You've no right to treat us like this.

—Right, we'll see about that, you stupid insolent bastard, said Bowen-Colthurst removing his pistol from its holster. Take that you fucking Sinn Fein rebel.

He shot the youth in the back of his head at point-blank range.

Blood and brain tissue covered the sidewalk as Coade slowly fell forward. In the confusion Clyne broke away from his captors and ran up Rathmines Road at breakneck speed.

—Shoot him. Goddamn it. Shoot him. I want no witnesses, said Bowen-Colthurst.

The platoon fired a rifle volley into the shadows bringing down Clyne.

—Now pick up the body and bring it to the barrack morgue. Our official report will state that this rebel youth was shot while resisting arrest. Is that clear, men?

—Yes Captain, they replied.

—I can't condone this Captain, said Sheehy-Skeffington. You shot the youth in cold blood without provocation. I'm making a report to your commanding officer on our return to barracks.

—That's if you live that long, you goddamned traitor, said Bowen-Colthurst moving threateningly towards the handcuffed journalist.

—Now Sir, please, said Sergeant MacAdam forming a protective shield round the prisoner with three of his comrades.

Maintaining this shield around Sheehy-Skeffington, and marching well behind Captain Bowen-Colthurst, Sergeant MacAdam returned to barracks and conducted the journalist to his cell.

—Is the commanding officer available? asked Skeffington.

—No, Sir, he's on a sortie. I'll make sure he knows of your request immediately he returns, said MacAdam.

A shaken MacAdam rejoined Michael and the main guard towards midnight.

—What's the matter MacAdam? You look like you've seen a ghost, said Michael.

—In a way I have, Lieutenant. I'm not sure if I should tell you this. I have to tell someone.

He recounted Coade's murder in graphic detail.

—There's something terribly wrong with this officer, Lieutenant. He shot the youth in cold blood. Now he'll try to kill Sheehy-Skeffington. Mark my words.

—We have to report this to the Adjutant, MacAdam. Bowen-Colthurst is suffering from battle fatigue or something worse. At all events he's unfit to command. Follow me, Michael said with a steady certainty in his voice.

—Major Rosborough has been called to Dublin Castle for a strategy meeting. Major Vane is on a sortie in the Rathgar area, said Rosborough's aide de camp.

—So Captain Bowen-Colthurst is effectively in command, Lieutenant? said Michael.

—Yes, until Major Vane's return. Is anything wrong, Lieutenant Sullivan?

—No, nothing I can discuss right now, Lieutenant.

He quickly left the CO's office, followed by MacAdam.

—Sergeant, it's best if you return to the main guard. I want to keep Bowen-Colthurst in sight as much as possible. At least until Major Vane returns. I agree with you that Mr. Sheehy-Skeffington is in grave danger. I'll find some excuse to remain near the orderly room where he is being detained. Thank you for your report and your confidence in me.

Michael soon learned that Captain Foster was responsible for the care of Sheehy-Skeffington and two other prisoners.

—May I be of assistance Captain? asked Michael.

—Yes you may, Lieutenant Sullivan. We'll be bringing breakfast to the prisoners in about two hours. Perhaps you could help me with that?

—Yes, certainly Captain.

Michael crept silently towards the orderly room. Bowen-Colthurst was already there. Michael saw no need to confront him. He hid behind a pillar and observed. Tall with a slight stoop at the shoulders, a grave expression, and deep black circles round his eyes, the officer seemed to Michael to be carrying the whole weight of the insurrection on his shoulders.

He marched incessantly in front of the entrance to the cells. He appeared to have a small bible in his hands and stopped occasionally to read a passage.

Intrigued, Michael watched for several minutes, then recalled that he should be available to Captain Foster.

—There are three prisoners in the cells, Sullivan. Skeffington has the small cell and two middle aged men we detained at Kelly's tobacco shop are in the larger cell. We'll serve them breakfast first. All right?

—We'll bring them the standard army breakfast, Sullivan. They haven't eaten since we detained them. I'm sure they're hungry.

A kitchen orderly had just cooked a large pot of oatmeal. Michael ladled three large portions into each cereal bowl. Then he made sufficient toast for three and added butter, marmalade, milk and sugar. The orderly brewed him a large pot of tea.

—I'm ready now Captain, Michael reported to Foster.

—Right then, said Foster taking down the keys to the cells.

One of the detainees in the cell adjacent to Skeffington, Dixon, was a dwarf of a man, a little over four feet. Dressed in a frock coat with deep shadows under his steel-grey eyes he reminded Michael of a harlequin.

–Why have we been detained, Captain Foster? MacIntire and I have done nothing wrong. We're both journalists. We both support Redmond and the Irish Party. We've had no truck with Connolly or John McNeill.

–Captain, I've come out strongly in favour of Redmond and our soldiers in Belgium and France in all my editorials in Searchlight, said MacIntire, a burly black-haired man.

–Listen men, I'll report all this to either Major Rosborough or his assistant Major Vane. I'm sure you'll be released later this morning. This food will keep you in form 'til then. Eat it while it's hot.

–We will, and thank you Captain, said MacIntire.

The next cell was a great deal smaller. Skeffington had his hands handcuffed behind his back. He stood up and bowed to both Foster and Michael. Michael wondered how the journalist could have slept at all with his hands like that. Both he and Foster were impressed by Skeffington's dignity.

–Forgive me Mr. Skeffington, I wasn't aware that you were still handcuffed, said Foster. I'll get the keys and remove them immediately.

Foster turned and walked quickly towards his desk.

–Is there anything I can do for you Sir? asked Michael.

–Yes, could I have a clean handkerchief? I need it to wipe my mouth.

–Of course Sir.

Michael gave him one from his uniform.

–Also could you tell my wife that I'm here and in safe-keeping. She has very little money for provisions. When I was detained I had eight pounds in my pocket. Could this money be sent to her?

–Yes, of course Mr. Skeffington. I'll see to it personally. I'm really surprised you're still here. I meant what I said late last evening.

–Here we are Mr. Skeffington, said Foster removing his handcuffs. Enjoy your breakfast.

–Thanks for all your kindness Captain Foster, said Skeffington a warm smile enveloping his face.

–I can't believe that this kind, gentle man could have anything to do with revolution or violence, said Foster as he and Michael returned to his office.

–Nor can I Sir. By the way, where are his effects? He's asked that the eight pounds he had with him when detained be sent to his wife. I said I'd see to it personally.

–I'm not sure where his effects are, Lieutenant. Perhaps Colonel Rosborough has kept them in his office. At all events I'm recommending that all three journalists be released this morning.

–Captain Bowen-Colthurst won't be in agreement with you, said Michael.

–Yes, I know. I feel uneasy about that man. Thank God he's only in command until Majors Rosborough or Vane return.

–That's sometime later this morning, Sir.

–Yes, depending on how difficult it is to cross the city at the moment.

Michael did several routine duties and returned to the Quartermaster's office towards ten thirty. Bowen-Colthurst was having an angry disagreement with Captain Foster.

–I'm the ranking officer here, Foster. I have urgent business with Skeffington, Dixon and MacIntire. I demand access to the cells.

–I have no instructions regarding this, Captain Colthurst. Lieutenant Dobbin is actually in charge of the cell guard. His instructions are the same as mine, said Foster evenly. Besides, Majors Rosborough and Vane should be back here presently.

–Don't frustrate me, Foster. These are times of war. Those three men in cells are enemies of the Crown.

Bowen-Colthurst's voice was rising even higher. He turned on his heels and rushed directly to the guard room. If anything, his face was even darker than that morning.

–Out of my way, Lieutenant, he said almost knocking down Michael in the process of passing him.

Michael thought he heard Colthurst mutter a quotation from the bible.

–Get me Major Rosborough now. I must speak with him. It's extremely urgent, Foster said on the telephone, as Michael entered his office. He's no longer at the Castle?

–He's en-route to us here. Please God he'll arrive within the next ten minutes. We have a crisis here. I must hang up now.

Foster's voice cracked.

–We have to stop that officer, Sullivan. He's going to shoot all three prisoners. It's nothing but blood lust. We have to intervene. You've your Webley pistol haven't you?

Foster rushed from behind his desk, his pistol drawn. En-route to the guardroom they were joined by Lieutenant Hayward, an elderly officer.

–Colthurst's gone barmy. He'll kill all three.

Fresh-faced Lieutenant Dobbin refused Colthurst entry to the cells. The Captain, his pistol drawn and cocked already, had duplicate keys. He was accompanied by veteran Sergeant Aldridge.

—Lieutenant, I'm taking these prisoners out and I'm going to shoot them because I think it is the right thing to do, he said as he opened the cell doors.

Bowen-Colthurst then told the three prisoners to stand against the far wall of the ammunition store. The standing guard then loaded and fired before any detainee realized what was happening.

Michael, Hayward, and Foster were still en-route to the guardroom when they heard two volleys being fired. As they reached the room they heard a third volley.

They arrived to see three stretchers being carried out. Two of the bodies were roughly covered by blankets. The third, also covered, had a bowler hat over the face. Limp arms covered in blood hung down from this third stretcher. Given its general size and a *claddagh* ring on its left hand Michael recognized this body as Sheehy-Skeffington's.

Alternate emotions of horror, revulsion, and anger filled Michael's being. The hair on his head seemed to stand up. His breath came in short gasps. He could hear his heart race. He wanted to punch Bowen-Coldhurst full in the face, to break his jaw, to beat him within an inch of his life. How could a career officer in the British Army commit such a horrendous act? This was blood lust, nothing else. He'd been living among shots, counter-shots and gunfire for months. This was cold premeditated butchery. Michael's stomach heaved. He felt he'd be violently ill.

Both Foster and the elderly Hayward were white as sheets.

—To my office gentlemen, please, said Foster turning on his heels.

—First things first, said Foster reaching into a cabinet behind his desk. It's only early morning, but we need this.

He poured three large measures of whiskey.

—I'm making a complete written report of this heinous act right now. The phone logs will confirm that I phoned authorities in the Castle just before we ran to the guardroom. I want you both to confirm what we saw on arrival there and to jointly sign my report.

—That goes without saying Sir, said Hayward.

—Yes, of course Captain Foster, said Michael. Is there anything we can do right now to restrain Captain Bowen-Colthurst?

—No, he's in a blood rage and he's armed. Also he's still the ranking officer. At any enquiry he'd claim we were insubordinate and hadn't the authority to arrest him. Where the hell are Rosborough and Vane?

—I think I hear a platoon coming through the front gates right now, perhaps it's Major Vane, said Michael.

—Right, just sign this. I think it's a true description of events, Lieutenant.

Foster passed Michael a yellow foolscap pad.

—Yes it is Captain, said Michael scanning the scribbled writing.

He signed and passed the pad and fountain pen to Hayward.

Major Vane had learned something of Bowen-Colthurst's actions of the previous night as he returned from Rathgar, when several members of a semi-hostile crowd had shouted Murderer! Murderer!

On returning to barracks Vane made careful enquiries of his junior officers and of Sergeant MacAdam.

—This is our report of what we witnessed, said Captain Foster handing Vane the pad with three signatures. Phone records will show that I called the Castle, first to reach Major Rosborough and then for instructions once I realized the gravity of the situation.

—Yes I don't doubt that you did, Foster, Major Vane replied evenly. Bowen-Colthurst's actions are against all the rules of war. At least as I understand them, and I've been a serving officer for twenty years.

From his face he was clearly extremely upset.

—I served in the Boer War and witnessed repressive acts there. Bowen-Colthurst's actions are worse than anything I've witnessed. I'll see that Major Rosborough is fully informed.
Dismiss, gentlemen. And thank you.

Towards one thirty in the afternoon Major Rosborough returned to barracks. He granted Major Vane's request for an urgent meeting.

—With all due respect Major Rosborough, soldiers and junior officers heard Vane say. This written report is the testimony of eyewitnesses. Captain Bowen-Colthurst has committed conduct unbecoming of an officer. I demand that he be confined to the cells pending a full enquiry. If these norms are not followed I regret to inform you that I can't hold myself responsible for the defence of this barracks.

—Easy Vane, easy. Your experience of martial law is greater than mine, given your time as a military magistrate in the Boer war. May I suggest that you instruct all the officers and NCOs here on their duties regarding prisoners under these emergency circumstances? I'll arrange that you give this lecture immediately. Are you agreeable?

—Yes I am, Major.

Supplemental Orders of The Day and a loud bell announced Major Vane's address. Seated behind a long table covered in green felt Major Rosborough called the gathering to order.

—Major Fletcher Vane needs no introduction to most of you here. He joined us on Monday because of the emergency. He's at present attached to the Munster Fusiliers. Like many here he was on a brief furlough over Easter. He's studied at the Military College in Oxford and has served in the Scots Guards and the Middlesex Regiment. Before the present war he served with distinction in South Africa where he acted as military magistrate. He is very knowledgeable as to the application of both civil and martial law. This is the subject of this guidance he's going to provide. Major Vane.

Vane rose to polite acknowledgement from the more than one hundred and fifty present.

—Gentlemen, what he says about my service as a military magistrate is true, and I'm very familiar with the application of law in time of war. Last evening and earlier today a fellow officer, acted in a reckless and callous manner completely without respect for the rights of military prisoners or the rule of law. High Command at the Castle have been informed and I'm sure a court-martial will follow. The rights of prisoners of war must be respected. They should be housed and properly fed in accordance with the norms expressed in King's Regulations and the Articles of War. They should not be subjected to physical or mental abuse. The flagrant abuse of military authority both last evening and this morning has resulted in four deaths. All these victims were unarmed. Their deaths cry out for justice. Any further deviation from the norms I referred to will result in the immediate suspension and detention of the officers and men involved and their court-martial at the earliest possible date. I fully appreciate that these are difficult times and that we're all under great stress. However, we're professional soldiers in service to the King. We must behave professionally and impartially if we're to keep the respect of the population of this city. Thank you for your attention gentlemen we have work to do.

Michael returned to duty as part of the main guard. Towards dusk Vane approached him.

—Sullivan, come with me. There's an important strategic target we have to raid. Take ten men and follow me. I have orders that Alderman Kelly is to be taken into custody for his own protection. He owns a tobacco shop at the junction of Rathmines Road and Portobello Harbour Bridge. Chances are that he's there. Know where it is?

—Yes, of course Major. It's where Skeffington spoke before his arrest.

The section marched quickly towards the house and halted in front of it. Not taking any chances, Michael and three soldiers entered the shop and raced up the stairs in search of Kelly.

They found the Alderman in hiding in the cellar. His wife, a woman in her late fifties, became distraught.

—Please, Lieutenant. My husband is a Justice of the Peace. He hasn't broken any law. He's respected by everyone in the neighbourhood. If he's detained I have no way of protecting the shop against looters.

—I'm sorry Ma'am, my orders are to bring the Alderman to barracks for questioning and his own protection, said Michael feeling his face flush.

Vane had quietly entered the cellar.

—Mrs. Kelly, I'm Major Fletcher-Vane, Assistant Commanding Officer at Portobello. I give you my word as an officer and a gentleman that no harm will come to your husband.

The section, with Kelly as a willing participant, marched cautiously towards Portobello barracks. They hugged the corners of houses closely and ran in short spurts, coming under sustained rifle fire from Jacob's Biscuit Factory some five hundred yards south east.

—Christ. That was close Lieutenant, said Major Vane, as they entered the front gates. Sergeant MacAdam, please conduct Alderman Kelly to the orderly room for further questioning, and set up a camp bed for him in the guardroom. Lieutenant Sullivan, you may dismiss. You've had a very full day.

—Thank you Sir, said Michael saluting.

He returned to his bedroom. It was ten o'clock and he'd had four hours sleep in the last day and a half.

A corporal woke him close to three in the morning with new orders. He was to take three transport wagons to the captured Davy's pub at Portobello bridge and remove all liquor, firkins of beer, and beer bottles. There was quite a large stock. Michael couldn't help thinking of the party patrons of the pub would have had if they knew the pub was unoccupied. Time was of the essence.

He and his platoon moved wooden boxes containing bottles of Guinness and Smithwicks. They worked steadily, completing this chore by six o'clock. Michael then had some weak tea and again retired.

He awoke a little after eight, washed and shaved, and had oatmeal and boiled eggs.

Major Vane called him to his office shortly after nine thirty.

–Sullivan, with all the soldiers from other regiments present in the barracks we're running desperately short of provisions. I'm leading a convoy of eight wagons to go to Kingsbridge Station to remedy the situation. Apart from yourself there will be two other junior officers and fifty men. Bring as many provisions as you can, Sullivan. Don't do anything reckless. Try and be as inconspicuous as possible both on your way to Kingsbridge and especially on the way back. Also, for reasons of security, I want you in the leading wagon. Right. Dismiss. The best of luck to us. I'll head the group in thirty minutes.

Led by Vane on foot, the convoy left by the side gate of the barracks and followed the road by the Grand Canal. They moved in an arc made by the South Circular Road as it curved towards Kilmainham.

Moving between canal bridges, in effect following the tow path, Michael caught glimpses of the Dublin mountains, the ruins of the Hell Fire Club, and places where he'd walked with Virginia and his family just days earlier. Trees grew along the tow path, giving them lots of cover. The mules in the convoy pulled on their reins, wanting to feed on the deep green grass beneath the trees. Still greener were the stalks of wild iris growing half in canal water. Sounds of muffled gunfire came from the city. The convoy travelled unmolested.

They passed within yards of the South Dublin Union. Michael was aware that this strategic building had been occupied by the rebels since Monday. Vane motioned for extra silence. The building, a nursing home and mental hospital, was just fifty yards away. A high wall surmounted by broken glass shielded them from view.

Vane signalled Michael to continue on to the Station, while he guarded their departure.

Michael's eyes began to smart as he entered the concourse of Kingsbridge Station. Two steam engines under full power shunted wagons towards back tracks, belching out black smoke. He asked directions to the officer of the day and presented his written orders.

–Lieutenant Sullivan, your written orders are not quite in order. As they are I can't execute them. See Major Walsh. Perhaps he'll give you authority. He's just over there, said a Captain Weldon.

–Been under fire. Running out of nosh? asked Major Walsh glancing at Michael's orders with a wry smile. Yes, I'll approve this.

He signed with a fountain pen.

–Go to that section there. Weldon will take care of you now.

Exhausted soldiers were everywhere. They lay on the less-used platforms and atop large boxes throughout the station.

Loading and double-checking of supplies and provisions took almost two hours. At the same time Michael unhooked the mules from the transports and had Corporal Maloney give them oats and water.

Forty of the company of fifty-five were occupied in the task. The remaining men used the time to rest or buy light refreshments at the station tea room. Major Walsh had wisely closed all station bars.

Michael's troop rejoined Major Vane, and on Vane's instructions, MacAdam blew three sharp peals on his whistle. The company re-formed and began to move off. Major Vane again walked ahead of the line with Michael now in the fourth wagon. They were just about to pass near the South Dublin Union when Vane brought the march to a complete halt and motioned for utter silence. Members of the Notts and Derby regiment a little ahead of them had taken up defensive positions. Sustained rifle or possibly machine gun fire appeared to be coming from the upper floors of the hospital/poorhouse complex. Michael's notes on this conflict, written that evening read as follows:

> *We are posted all along the road. I place my men in gardens at various points along the road and near a convent, and some across a field at its back. It's 14.30 . I decide it would be better if we command the area to our right and begin posting men in the backs of houses, asking the occupants first if they have any objections. I cross a turnip field and take Sergeant MacAdam and five men down to the canal bank.*
>
> *We climb a railing and a barbed wire fence and take over a small house nearby. I take MacAdams with me to a tiny room on the top floor and look out towards the far side of the canal. In the near distance I see a man crouching under a low wall. I draw MacAdam's attention to this and he immediately fires. The man disappears. Shots are coming from a red brick house across the canal. I fire ten rounds there.*
>
> *Now my ears are ringing. I can't hear. MacAdam and I keep low behind the window in case there's return fire. After five minutes in this position the coast seem to be clear so we go cautiously downstairs to a corner shop where I'd posted some men. A man there is extremely upset as his elderly father was last seen on a hill across from the canal. Jesus Christ! I may have been firing at him, I think. The anxious man has field glasses. I borrow them, but can see nothing. I return to the row houses. Some Notts and Derby men are crossing a field and are fired on mistakenly by our men. I withdraw my men from the row houses.*
>
> *A man and his daughter cross the small lawn in front of their house*

> *with tea and cake! Things aren't very clear except that an attack is being made on us from somewhere across the canal.*
> *Crouching, I cross a field with my platoon and go down a low path and over the canal lock gate. In a granary nearby I find an officer and a hundred men. I continue on to a second bridge to scout. We come under fire from our own troops. It unnerves us. We retreat to the granary. I take an NCO and one man with me, go back to the road and report to Major Vane at the entrance to the South Dublin Union. He sends us to the canal bridge.*

—If I get my hundred back along the canal will you and your platoon storm the brewery? asks an elderly colonel.

—Sir, before we storm anything, I must have your word that you won't fire on us, I reply.

I return to Major Vane with my troop and twelve Notts and Derby men. He's attacking the South Dublin Union where the enemy are in strength. Well at least we finally know their main base!

Vane is very calm. He's been directing the engagement standing upright carrying just his ceremonial cane. The union is being attacked across a field. My group are in support. We lie on the long grass to the rear. The advance party, a group of about twenty, are making short runs just ahead of us. They signal us up and we dash and crouch in the long grass between the trees. We smell the scent of the apple and pear trees. We use all cover available, but there's very little. The rebels are flailing us with rapid fire from the windows of the Dublin Union. I see something quite unusual, a green, white, and orange flag flutters from one of the windows. I know nothing of the symbolism involved. Several Notts and Derby curse mightily and aim at the flag post. The flag continues to fly. The rest of us fire at the windows trying to silence enemy fire. At times we succeed.

—Lieutenant, have you any water?, shouted an officer in front of us over the din. One of my men is badly hit. The water may help.

I got a water flask from one of the men and crawled up with it. The injured man was in fact a policeman. He was lying on his face, but looked grey. In fact he was dead, as the officer quickly discovered. Several minutes later his corpse was completely destroyed by a direct hit. His head shattered like a smashed melon, bone and brain matter hit me on the face and chest. I'm consumed by revulsion and anger. My heart races. My breath comes in short gasps. I burrow deeper into the long grass. I can't help wondering if these murderers are in fact Irishmen. Where were these amateur soldiers dragged up? I wonder.

I fired off five rounds in quick succession to no avail. Ammunition was running short. We sent a messenger back asking for more. He returned saying my platoon was needed in the rear. We're to move on.

I discovered that I was three men short. I returned to the attacking party and found one of them. MacAdam stepped from my left to my right, so that if we were fired on, he'd be first in line. The convoy reformed and began to move off. I glanced at my wrist watch. It was after seven o'clock. I was covered in filth from head to foot and completely deaf. Someone gave me a drink of water from his canteen. I felt slightly less thirsty.

We continued towards the barracks via the South Circular Road. We passed a party of prisoners. Some of our company began to sing.

The convoy finally returned to Portobello towards nine. Michael supervised the unloading of the transports. This took another forty minutes. He then went to the orderly room to make his report. He was almost deaf and began his report, not realizing that others were speaking.

—Be silent Lieutenant Sullivan. Other officers are giving their reports of today's action. You'll have your turn in a moment. At ease, said Major Rosborough.

Several minutes later he turned to Michael and spoke sharply.

—Perhaps it would have been better if the convoy had continued on and if you personally hadn't joined in the action, Rosborough said.

Something was rotten in the chain of command. While Major Vane was absent that afternoon, an elderly colonel based at Dublin Castle had arrived at Portobello. Without consulting Major Rosborough, he took Colthurst and twenty men to raid Sheehy-Skeffington's home, hoping to secure evidence against him. Since Sheehy-Skeffington was truly a pacifist they found nothing except a picture of the Kaiser and a drawing of an encounter between a Zeppelin and British aircraft, painted by Owen Skeffington, aged seven. All the journalist's manuscripts and correspondence, including love letters to his wife, were confiscated as subversive.

Michael had read only one pamphlet by the journalist. He remembered that it reminded him a little of Jonathan Swift with its irony and sarcasm. However, it wasn't seditious, and was completely anti-violent. His curiosity got the better of him.

—May I have the key of the document storage area Captain Foster, he asked towards eleven o'clock.

—For what purpose Lieutenant Sullivan? personal or professional? Foster asked.

—I'm sorry, Sir. It's more personal than professional. Like you, I quite liked Mr. Sheehy-Skeffington. I understand that much of his journalism has been seized. I'd be fascinated to have a look at it.

—Very well Sullivan. But be prudent.

—Oh, Mum's the word Captain, Mum's the word.

The seized documents covered a large table. They comprised manuscripts, typescripts, manuscript proofs, and rejection letters. A bunch of letters tied with a blue ribbon fascinated Michael.

He glanced at one.

> *My dearest Hannah, I'm trapped here in London on my latest assignment. There is much activity at Westminster, Dillon and Redmond may have mustered enough votes for passage of the Home Rule Bill. We'll see. Weather here is more like the South of France. Very hot with little air. Oh how I long to see you and little Owen again. I should manage to get away by next weekend.*
> *Your loving Francis.*

The letter was undated. Michael guessed that it was written in June of 1914, a time of great hope. He felt a pang of deep guilt. He was invading Mrs. Skeffington's privacy. He quickly put the letter back in the pile and retied the blue ribbon.

Another letter, postmarked London S.W.1, drew Michael's attention. It was a letter of apology from George Bernard Shaw for having to cancel a scheduled interview. God! Skeffington knew everybody.

Michael noticed that a strange cold anger now pervaded all soldiers in the barracks, from officers to NCOs and privates. The audacity that these Shinners or rebels should take up arms against Britain at such a critical time in her history! It simply was not playing the game. But whose game? Was it really in nationalist Ireland's interest to wait until England had triumphed over the Axis powers and then take her on, or to strike now when her resources were strained? Pearse, Plunkett, and Connolly would have said that he was not being disloyal to England, but loyal to Ireland. He understood their views, but felt they were mistaken.

The rebels were being shunned by Dubliners whereas men in uniform were being befriended. Michael had witnessed this just hours earlier. He's heard several Dublin women shout.

—What are these Sinn Feiners doin? And me poor Tommy fightin' out there in France.

From a regular soldier's point of view, the rebels were hard to recognize, as their uniforms consisted of a belt with a holster for a revolver, equipment very easy to dispose of. One could be a soldier at one second and a citizen the next. This made homeland British troops nervous and suspicious of everyone.

Michael was helping to suppress an insurgence. He was nervous and uneasy about it. However, it was his duty. He bore no hatred. He'd known of Pearse's views since 1914. His brother Chris supported Pearse and McNeill. Their views differed from his. He respected them, nonetheless.

A youth of fifteen was hustled through the front gates, his hands above his head. As he passed he was prodded by several soldier's bayonets.

—We found a green uniform in one of the bedrooms of your house. Who does it belong to? Tell us, tell us! a junior officer shouted menacingly.

—I don't know Sir, I don't know, the boy replied, bursting into tears. It could be me Dad's or me brother Tom's - both were in Redmond's volunteers. They wore green. Me brother was fightin' in France with the Dublin Fusiliers. He was home at Easter.

—What's his name and rank, boy?

—Private Tom Clancy, Sir.

—Right, let me check this list — he's with us here son. He's out on patrol at present. Be a good lad now and go home to your mother. Don't go outside after eight o'clock at night any evenin', otherwise you'll be arrested again. Right, go on with you now.

The youth rushed to the front gates at breakneck speed.

Light had faded now to the afterglow of twilight. To the north, the sky was red from burning houses on Sackville and North Earl Streets. Michael prayed that only rebels and regular soldiers were suffering through these horrors.

As he went past the orderly room towards his sleeping quarters, he overheard Colthurst priming a sergeant who had participated in either the murder of the youth Coade or of Sheehy-Skeffington as to what to say to Rosborough at an official enquiry.

—The prisoner was trying to escape, Sergeant, said Colthurst in a clipped voice.

Both the sergeant and Michael knew that this was a bare-faced lie. The prisoner had done nothing of the sort. He'd been shot on the Captain's direct order. Colthurst, sensing he was being overheard, moved several yards so as to be out of earshot.

As he stretched out in his sleeping bag Michael wished he'd a flask of whiskey. Visions of the exploding corpse from that afternoon crowded in on his imagination. His face still smarted from where the bone and brain matter had hit him. He prayed that God would have mercy on the fallen policeman.

A very elderly Colonel had come to the barracks and wanted to be helpful. He was a small plump man with white hair and drooping moustache who'd last seen action in the Boer War. He was not a partisan warmonger. To Michael, the man seemed to take a boy scout's joy in being useful. He had an infectious sense of humour and was a friend of Major Vane.

Hearing that the Colonel wanted to convert a lorry into an armoured car, Michael approached him and offered his services as a driver. He didn't tell the old gentlemen that the only vehicle he'd driven to date was his father's Model T.

—Excellent, Sullivan. Excellent. Now there are two other drivers, a Military Transport Corporal and a cadet. You can get in some practice on that lorry there, just drive it round the barrack square to get the feel of it. All right?

It was more than all right. Driving round allowed Michael to get the feel of the transport and to relieve tensions from the previous day. Later that day it was arranged to swap that lorry for a larger Guinness transport. That evening Orders were cancelled and rumour said the jig was up. Hostilities were less. Armouring the lorry comprised new techniques and would be expensive.

—Want to inspect defence positions with me, Sullivan? asked Major Vane.

He looked quite fatigued, but was in good form.

—Yes, certainly Major.

At that point, a youth in a strange uniform was brought through the gate by Sergeant Williams - khaki jacket, white collar and badge-less cap - had been stopped on his motorcycle by a patrol. He was explaining himself to Williams.

—I'm a member of the Officers Training Corps at Trinity. We've held the college against the rebels since Monday, he repeated again and again, his hair unkempt, his face flushed.
Will no one believe me?

—Right. Is this your story, young man? said Vane authoritatively.

—Yes Major.

—Goddamn it, man. Look at the cut of you. For a junior officer you don't set much of an example. Still it's been four very difficult days. We must take that into consideration.
Sergeant Williams. Can you fill me in?

—Yes Major, said Williams.

He was a tall professional in his late fifties.

The youth had been thoroughly searched, and among the objects in his possession were three objects wrapped in tissue paper, much more useful towards love than war.

—Disgusting Sergeant Williams, disgusting, said Vane in mock horror.

A call was made to the university and the young man's story verified.

Shortly afterwards, a lady of the evening and her john, who explained that they had been taking a walk together, but were now on the way home, were also questioned and let go.

—Mind how you go now, said Vane as they left. I thought that that profession was confined to Montgomery Street north of the river. Still, there's no one more enterprising than a whore, is there Sergeant Williams?

—That's the God's truth Sir, said Williams, with his colour rising.

—Right Sergeant. There doesn't seem to be much enemy activity here. Carry on, said Vane, saluting and turning towards barracks.

Muffled sounds of explosions from at least two miles away reached their ears as they carefully made their way back to Portobello. The guards on the main gates were alert and insisted on the password before granting entry.

—Care to join me for a drop of the hard stuff Lieutenant? said Vane as they crossed the quadrangle.

—Yes Sir. Thank you very much.

A thick envelope lay under the baseboard of the major's bedroom door. He read its contents quickly and with deep concentration. The quarters were devoid of personal belongings apart from a framed picture of Vane's wife on the night table.

—Sit down, Lieutenant Sullivan, take your ease, he said indicating one of two large leather chairs.

He moved to an oak desk and magically produced two tumblers and a bottle of Redbreast.

—I expect you'll have this neat Sullivan? Why dilute a great whiskey?

He smiled warmly.

—Why indeed Sir? Michael agreed.

The whiskey was smooth, but potent. It warmed Michael's throat and chest. He began to relax. It seemed extraordinary that this kindly, brave, and just man had taken an interest in him, a New Army Volunteer. However, it was clear that Vane could associate with any soldier he wanted to. Why him? Perhaps he'd read his war record to date ...but then his war record wasn't in Portobello, it was in Belgium. Whatever it was, he felt comfortable with this officer, and knew he could trust him. He told him briefly of the conversation he'd overhead between Captain Coldhurst and the sergeant.

—I'm not at all surprised, Sullivan, replied Vane. There will be an inquiry. I'll make sure the officer in charge knows this. You'll most probably be called. Are you prepared to testify?

–Most certainly, Major. To my mind Captain Bowen Coldhurst's conduct is conduct unbecoming of an officer.

–Quite so Sullivan, quite so. I have news of another matter. The South Dublin Union fell this evening after fierce room to room fighting, Vane said, pointing to the envelope he'd just read.

The rebels fought bravely especially an English-born sympathiser named Charles Burgess. He prefers to be known as Cathal Brugha. At all events this brave man barricaded himself in the hallway of the Union's Nurses Home just as our lads entered. He exchanged fire with ten of ours and was hit by several bullets. Almost surrounded, he nevertheless dragged himself through a kitchen to an open yard at the rear. From there he had a view of the back door and the door to the kitchen. He managed to set up another barricade and made sure our lads got nowhere near.

He was well armed and managed to hold our lot off for more than two hours. All the time there he sang *God save Ireland*. It seemed to sustain him. Edward Kent, Commandant of the rebel company, surrendered. Towards eight o'clock Burgess was found in a pool of his own blood. He's in Vincent's now. He's not expected to live. A very brave man, Sullivan. Here's a thing. How do you counter that kind of heroism and dedication to an ideal, Lieutenant? I'm damned if I know.

–Yes Sir. I've seen a little of that kind of idealism among captured Axis prisoners in Belgium and in a diary we found on a dead German. Very difficult to counteract.

–Repression and reprisal won't work, Sullivan. If my period in South Africa during and after the Boer war has taught me anything, it's taught me that. I fear it's going to happen here Lieutenant. The authorities don't read any history. If they act in the same manner as after the Wexford rising in 1798 they'll start a movement of tit for tat killings which will have no end.

They'll lose the support of the common people here and could ultimately lose the country.

There was a tremendous ear-shattering sound from the centre of the city. Vane drew the curtains and opened the windows. Night had turned to day. Flames leaped hundreds of feet high. Sparks soared like shooting stars crowding a full moon.

–Old Dublin's burning, Sullivan. Mark my words there'll be hell to pay, said Vane.

The cause of the conflagration was uncertain. Was it shelling by forces of the Crown or something highly flammable that had exploded?

–God I hope the St. John's ambulance service or Red Cross are in the Sackville Street area to aid the local people, Sir, said Michael.

–They probably are Sullivan. At all events, there's nothing to be gained by sending reinforcements from here to the area. This engagement will continue right through 'til morning. It's probably the rebels' last great effort. I hate to say this, but as soldiers I admire them.

–Yes Sir. So do I. Thank you Sir. I'll probably see you during my normal service tomorrow.

–Yes, that's certain. Good night Sullivan.

–Good night Sir.

To everyone's surprise the order for the outfitting of the armoured car had been approved by High Command. Michael and Sergeant MacAdam drove the Guinness lorry to the railway works at Inchicore. The army had been in charge there throughout the week. A junior officer found several skilled workmen.

–Men, this lorry must be made bullet proof immediately. It's necessary for operations. Work as quickly as you can, said the officer.

–Can you estimate when it will be ready, Lieutenant? asked Michael.

–Yes. By early evening. I've given it top priority.

Michael and MacAdam hitched a ride on a transport to barracks, and returned towards midday.

The rebellion was virtually over. Dublin Castle deemed that mopping up operations begin immediately. Orders of the day were that Sinn Fein offices on Harcourt Street be raided and incriminating documents seized. Michael, MacAdam, and ten soldiers went there early that afternoon. They proceeded by lorry, coming under scattered rifle fire. On arrival they encountered no resistance. They simply went from room to room removing anything of interest. A locked safe was eventually carried with difficulty to the street. In an upstairs room Michael found sheets of official stamps. They looked like postage stamps.

–MacAdam, do you have any use for these? he asked the veteran sergeant.

–No not really Sir. I can't use them for mail from the front.

–Nor can I Sergeant. My younger brother collects stamps. I'll take a sheet for him.

–Good idea, Lieutenant.

He kept one sheet for himself and two for the elderly colonel in charge of this operation. He left the remaining stamps where he'd found them.

–It's time we got back to the railway works Sergeant, he said to MacAdam, once they'd turned in the seized documents.

–Right you are Sir.

The armoured car was a cross between a submarine and a bakers van. It reminded Michael of a basking shark, but was a tad less sleek. The round cylinder of a train engine boiler had been mounted on the lorry; this would be protection against any rifle or machine gun bullets. Loopholes had been cut in the sides through which a gun could be fired. The front of the lorry was protected by steel plating.

–My God this is a miracle Lieutenant Gallagher, and that the work was completed so quickly, said Michael accepting the vehicle. Give my compliments to the workers.

–Christ it moves well MacAdam, in spite of all the extra weight, he said putting it in gear.

–We'd best put it to work Sir. It'll make operations easier.

The armoured car was a great help. They went out that evening searching for people late for curfew, herding them to the back of the transport. They came under fire at one point and quickly took refuge in the car. From the interior they could fire in any direction. They did so, but quickly stopped as the reverberations in such a confined space were deafening. Prisoners at the far end cowered together putting their fingers in their ears.

Returning to barracks, Michael noted that there was a proclamation not only on the regular notice board, but in many areas, from General Maxwell who had taken command of military operations.

All buildings occupied by rebels would be destroyed. Captured leaders would be treated as prisoners of war, but would be tried by military court and be subject to the full extent of military law.

A Colonel McCammond had taken over as commander of Portobello, replacing Major Rosborough.

Late that evening, Major Vane passed through the quadrangle. He acknowledged Michael's salute and motioned him to come closer.

–Many things are afoot Lieutenant. I've tried to meet with General Maxwell with no success. He was simply too busy. I did meet with Major Price, Chief of Intelligence. I briefed him on Bowen-Colthurst's actions. Price simply wouldn't believe me and had the impudence to say that he thought that men like Skeffington were just as well out of the way. I was furious Sullivan, and just managed to retain my self- control. My line of action is clear he said pointedly. My position here is becoming untenable Sullivan. I've asked for and been granted several days leave. I've one further option here; if it isn't successful I'll have to take the matter to the War Office. Mum's the word at this point Sullivan.

—Of course Sir, that goes without saying.

Next morning Michael, MacAdam, and company were given the task of transferring prisoners from Portobello to the larger Richmond Barracks. They used the armoured car for these runs, taking seven or eight prisoners at a time. At Richmond Barracks these unfortunates were processed in groups of four. Most had been held at Portobello simply because they'd been unable to explain why they were out after curfew. At Richmond Barracks, rebel soldiers wore several different types of uniforms; all were green uniforms: some wore rough tweed coats and slouch hats like the Australians; others were clearly staff officers, with yellow tabs on the lapels of their jackets, corresponding to the red tabs of senior British Army officers. On one of the runs Michael sat opposite a grey-haired, red faced, sad eyed, old man whose face seemed very familiar. Suddenly Michael remembered him.

—You're Ned Jordan the barman in Madigan's in Rathmines.

—I am indeed Sir, he replied dejectedly.

—Why were you detained, Ned?

—Soldiers found a blood-stained waistcoat in my lodgings during a raid the other evening. My lodgings are very near Davys pub. There was a lot of fighting there, as you know. One of the rebels fled through my lodgings and probably threw away the clothing while running.

—You didn't know him, Ned?

—In a fashion, yes. He'd come into Madigan's now and then of a Friday evening.

—He wasn't a friend, was he Ned?

—No, not even a regular customer.

—Stick to that story Ned. They've nothing really to hold you on. Between soldiers and prisoners this barracks is bursting at the seams. I'm sure many of those here will be released in a couple of days.

—I hope so Sir, he said.

A thin, raven-haired girl, with her arm in splints, was among the last of the prisoners Michael ferried. Instinctively he reached out to help her into the car. She drew away and glared at him, scorn and defiance in her face. That thin tightly closed mouth seemed to be saying 'Traitor, turncoat, I count it a privilege to be your enemy.' Yet he was Irish too. God how he hated acting as a jailor.

Patrick Pearse—teacher, poet, Commander of the rebel army—had formally surrendered to General Lowe at 3.45 that afternoon, Saturday, April 29th. Michael learned this that evening. Michael had overstayed his leave by two days. He was certain Colonel Murphy was aware of the situation. Nonetheless, he felt it was important to communicate with him directly by telegram and resolved to do this as early as possible.

He went to the cable centre at Portobello and wrote:

```
COLONEL MURPHY,
BECAUSE OF THE EMERGENCY HERE AND PURSUANT TO
KINGS REGULATIONS, I REPORTED TO PORTOBELLO
BARRACKS THE EVENING OF LAST MONDAY APRIL 24TH.
I'VE BEEN UNDER THE COMMAND OF MAJOR ROSBOROUGH
AND CARRIED OUT MY DUTIES AS DIRECTED. THE
LEADER OF REBEL FORCES FORMALLY SURRENDERED TO
GENERAL LOWE THIS AFTERNOON,EFFECTIVELY THE
EMERGENCY IS OVER
TOMORROW I'LL INFORM COLONEL ROSBOROUGH AND
EXPECT TO TRAVEL FROM THE NORTH WALL IN THE
EVENING AND RETURN TO THE FRONT ON WEDNESDAY
MAY 3RD THE EARLIEST
MICHAEL SULLIVAN, 2ND LIEUTENANT,
LEINSTER REGIMENT, 2ND BATTALION
```

–Could you send this right away Tommy? he asked the telegraph officer.

–Yes, of course Lieutenant. My God you look all in.

–It's been a busy day Tommy. But nothing compared to what the men in Sackville Street of both stripes have been through.

–Yes those fires last night looked like hell on earth.

–I'm sure they were Tommy. It's amazing anyone lived through them. Well goodnight now. I hope you manage some sleep. I'm away to bed myself. Tomorrow will be a long day.

He arose at six the next morning. After breakfast he and a platoon went to Dublin Castle on assignment. From there they went with wires and cables to a telephone exchange behind the G.P.O.

Sackville Street, and especially Moore and Henry Streets, were almost impassable, full of stonework, mortar, and rubble. It was hoped to repair the sub-station and establish better communications with the north of the city. The exchange itself wasn't too badly damaged, but the G.P.O. and buildings on Moore and Henry streets were simply smoking shells, their interiors completely collapsed, a jumble of half-burnt furniture, charred fixtures and wires, and charred registry records.

Several technicians stayed to repair the exchange while Michael and the rest of the group went to Islandbridge Barracks and the Royal Hospital Kilmainham for necessary equipment. In the afternoon he made a second trip to the Castle. At a narrow doorway to one side of the main yard a very tall officer, the

Assistant Provost Marshal, was handling out captured mementos to people milling round the doorway. To Michael these keepsakes seemed crude and badly made, looking more like objects from the 1798 rebellion than of modern manufacture. He was interested in two large objects with brass embossed harps which looked like animal harnesses. He then reported to Major Rosborough, now part of Head Quarters Staff.

—We're pleased with your service Lieutenant Sullivan. Here's my written commendation. It reads:

> 2nd Lieutenant M. Sullivan has served with this Battalion since the 24th of April 1916 and has done excellent work during the recent Sinn Fein rebellion.

—Feel free to present this and my compliments to your commanding officer, Colonel Murphy. Now, there's a sailing from the North Wall this evening at nine. If you take it you can re-join your regiment by the middle of the coming week. Dismiss.

Michael saluted smartly, turned on his heels and made directly for Portobello.

He had a little over two hours to pick up his haversack and get to the North Wall. He'd try to contact Virginia by phone at the hospital. There simply wasn't time for a meeting. She was possibly doing extra shifts because of the rebellion.

In a real sense he was glad to be away from any repressive action in the wake of this rebellion. Just transferring prisoners as he'd done for most of the previous day was galling enough. He was returning to a type of tension he knew, and to comrades in arms.

Chapter Fourteen

Back to the frontline, May 1916

He was exhausted when he finally arrived in Poperinghe. He'd been travelling for almost four days. The longest part was the journey from Boulogne. The crowded train seemed to be travelling at about ten miles an hour. At least twice an hour they were shunted to a siding so that a munitions train could pass. Corporal Daly of the 3rd Battalion Dublin Fusiliers was with him all the way from Dublin.

Like Michael he'd been on leave and had gone to the nearest barracks, in his case Beggar's Bush.

—I saw that dreamer Mr. Pearse read a document outside the G.P.O. on Easter Monday, Sir, he said as they settled down on the troop ship leaving the North Wall. He spoke about 'the dead generations from which Ireland received her tradition of nationhood.' All my friend Mick Mahon and myself were interested in was in getting to Fairyhouse as quickly as possible. The confusion caused a traffic blockage.

—Did you get to the races at all, Corporal?

—No. It appeared that the G.P.O. had been occupied by Pearse's comrades. Windows had been blocked up; shots were fired. A mob from Moore Street and Mountjoy Square was forming. They seemed to be intent on trouble. I made my excuses to my friend Mick and hurried down the quays to Beggars Bush.

—Did you see much action in the following days?

—Indeed I did Lieutenant. Some of it was crowd control. Most of it was house to house fighting with those God-damned Shinners. It sticks in my craw, Sir. I'd far rather take on fifty or more Germans than my own people. I'm glad to be going back.

—That goes for me too, Corporal Daly. I joined the battalion at Portabello Barracks. Most of the action I was involved in was in Rathmines, Rathgar, and at Islandbridge. Several really bad incidences occurred. One officer was relieved of command and will probably be subject to court-martial. I'm sorry I can't talk further about this, Corporal, as it's before the court.

—I understand, Lieutenant.

Daly was an attentive travel companion. He found space for them on trains and on the transport to Boulogne.

—Well Corporal, I think your regiment are north of here, said Michael as they stepped onto the damaged platform at Poperinghe. I think the Leinsters are south of here, somewhere near Messines Ridge. I expect we'll both connect with them one way or another. Take care of yourself. Keep your head down.

—Yes. Sir. You too Sir.

He saluted smartly.

—No need for that Daly. Take care.

He picked up his rucksack and walked to 43 Gasthuistratt, site of Talbot House, the club for all ranks. He knew he'd be able to contact his company from there, and arrange transport. A corporal sat at a small desk inside the front door.

—Let me see Lieutenant Sullivan, the corporal said, consulting a file to his right. Yes, the 2nd Leinsters are now in reserve at a camp named Kortepyp. A mile or so from Neuve-Eglise.
There's a munitions transport going that way in a half hour. You can sit in front with the driver.

—Will I be able to get on it here Corporal?

—Yes, I'll telephone them. Take your ease Lieutenant. There's no one in the smoking room across the hall. I'll call immediately once they arrive.

—Thank you Corporal.

Michael quickly found a large leather chair in the rest area. He lay back in it and was instantly asleep. The corporal roused him some forty minutes later.

—Corporal Evans has space for you, Lieutenant. He'll drop you as close as possible to your Battalion.

—Thank you Corporal.

Some tillage had been done in this area. Sitting with the driver in the army transport Michael saw acres of green shoots of two or so inches above the soil. Perhaps there would be less fighting here by summer. Or at least the chance of a harvest. Presently they arrived at a well-fitted camp of wooden huts.

—Camp Kortepyp, Lieutenant, said the driver. My destination is a bit further ahead.

—Thank you corporal, said Michael picking up his haversack.

Hawkins, Lavelle, and Nolan were housed in a hut about 40ft square. Dappled sunlight lit the small room. There was one free cot. Michael placed his haversack at the base of it. He caught a glimpse of his face in a mirror. There was a dark stubble on his cheeks. This was not the standard military image. Protocol demanded that he report to his commanding officer as quickly as possible. He rushed to a hand basin and shaved.

—Ah Sullivan, welcome back, said Colonel Murphy acknowledging his salute in his spartan office. At ease, Sullivan. At ease. You know we don't stand on ceremony here. Now, I received both your telegrams. You followed military procedure to the letter in presenting yourself at Portobello Barracks immediately you learned of the emergency. This letter from Major Rosborough is quite complimentary. I'll see that it goes on your personal file. Now, there was a very bad incident in Portobello during the insurrection. Are you free to talk about it?

—Only in general terms Colonel Murphy. The officer in question is in detention awaiting military court-martial.

—I understand that Sullivan. As a matter of fact, I understand that he's a serving officer in our 1st Battalion and distinguished himself at Mons.

—He did indeed Sir. However, in my opinion he clearly suffered from shell shock or battle fatigue. Are you aware of his name?

—Yes, I've seen it in military files.
You had a longer leave than you bargained for, Sullivan.

—Yes indeed. When the insurrection began, I was with family near Bray. News was unreliable at first. Once I realized that there was an emergency, I informed my parents of my duty. My father drove me to the nearest barracks, Portobello, near the Grand Canal.

—Yes, I know it. The CO there is elderly.

—Yes. Major Rosborough. He's now been seconded to General Maxwell's staff.

—General Maxwell? The new General Officer Commanding armed forces in Ireland?

—The same, Colonel. He quelled the rebellion in six days. May I speak freely Sir?

—Of course Sullivan.

—Well Sir. This whole matter of the alleged breaches of military conduct was brought to the attention of Military Authorities due to the intervention of Major Fletcher Vane. All I can say is Thank God for officers of his calibre. I witnessed the aftermath of these events and made both a verbal and written statement to Major Vane. He later traveled to Westminster and brought the matter directly to the Prime Minister's attention. When he returned, this officer Captain Bowen-Colthurst, was placed under arrest pending trial by court martial. There the matter rests, Sir.
It could go on for months.

—Do you know anything personally of General Maxwell, Michael?

—Well, he has been assigned military control of Dublin. I know nothing of his background except that the Prime Minister and Cabinet have confidence in him.

—Do you think he'll take harsh measures, Sullivan?

—He already has, Colonel. He sent gunboats up the Liffey to shell occupied buildings on Sackville Street. He's arrested Pearse, Connolly, McBride, McDonagh, and all the principal leaders.
Let's hope he doesn't apply the full force of Military Law.

—It seems to me that he has to Sullivan. After all, these men took up arms against the government in time of war.

—Be that as it may, Sir, if the full force of the law is applied, and there are reprisals as following the rebellion in 1798 the authorities will be making a terrible mistake.

—How's that, Sullivan?

—Well, if all these leaders are summarily executed, most of them university lecturers or teachers, there could be a real change in support for the authorities. I hope this General Maxwell knows something of Irish history.

—Perhaps he does Sullivan. The question is, will he listen to advice.

—I hope he does. If he doesn't, things could go badly for the whole population of Ireland.

—Secretary Birrell, John Redmond, John Dillon and the Irish leadership are reasonable men.
Surely they can have some influence on General Maxwell.

—That remains to be seen Sir. He acted with great efficiency in quelling the rebellion. These days and weeks ahead are crucial. I agree with you that the rebel leaders will have to pay a price.
But if authorities act with vengeance, they'll make martyrs of them. Anyway, time for a little taste of Ireland.

He proffered a flask of Powers whiskey from a pocket of his uniform and passed it to Colonel Murphy.

—God this is wonderful. Your very good health, Lieutenant, said the colonel pouring two tumblers.

—And yours too Sir. What's the news here?

—Not good, Lieutenant. Even though we just received a draft, the morale of the men is bad. Last month was very difficult. I'll tell you more of it later. The last straw was in Orders of the Day today.
All leave to Ireland has been suspended because of the rebellion. Of course, this order didn't come from General Hickie. It came from high command,

probably Haig himself. Many of the men aren't aware of this order as yet. Quite a number were due leave. There could be trouble.

–Yes, there could Sir. It seems unfair.

–It is. I've called a general meeting of all officers for 16.00 hrs.

–I'll be there Sir. I'd better let you get on with your day.

–Fine, Sullivan. Thank you for your assessment. Take a little rest, but be at this meeting.

Michael saluted smartly.

Lieutenant Colonel Murphy sat at the centre of a long oak table, Captain Palin, Adjutant, and Padre Maloney on his right, Lieutenant Plowman, Transport Officer, and Dr. Morley to his left. Hawkins, Michael, Lavell, Nolan and the other junior officers sat in front, notepads and pencils in their hands.

–Gentlemen, I called this meeting to advise you of the Order of the Day cancelling all leave to Ireland. This order does not come from General Hickie. It comes directly from High Command and is signed by Field Marshal Haig himself. The reason given for the cancellation of leave is the current situation in Dublin following the events of ten days ago. Our men will be allowed to travel to London, but no further. Alternatively, they may stop in Le Pas-de-Calais, or in some cases Paris, for rest. After the difficult winter many of our soldiers will be disappointed. Some will probably be angry. I want you all to treat them with understanding and respect.

–Strictly informally, Lieutenant Michael Sullivan apprised me of the events he witnessed in Dublin over the six days he was there. The CO in Dublin, General Sir John Maxwell, has had a long and distinguished army career. He quickly quelled the rebellion, captured the ringleaders, and now holds them in detention in Kilmainham Goal. The majority of the population of Dublin are solidly in support of the civil authority. However, as Sullivan explained to me, the situation is volatile. Overly harsh measures by the military authority could have a massive effect on public morale and make the maintenance of order difficult. The coming days and weeks will tell. Here at the front I want all you officers and junior officers to be understanding of the men. My fear is that if truly harsh measures are applied in Ireland, the men will be angry. Some may even question their allegiance to the Crown and the oath they took on entering the army. So be attentive to the men and keep me apprised of the situation. Thank you gentlemen. As always, I count on your cooperation. Dismissed.

The assembly rose as one and saluted Colonel Murphy.

The battalion remained in reserve for the next four days. The draft were a mixed bunch of veterans from other Irish battalions, and new recruits. Hawkins, Lavelle, Nolan, and Michael, aided by Malone, Cunningham and other NCO's, put them through the gamut of short order drill, company drill, artillery and Mills bomb training, and hand-to-hand combat. The men excelled at all the normal training. However, judging from their facial expressions, Michael saw that many didn't see the point of plunging their bayonets into straw dummies while yelling battle cries.

At 8.00 p.m. on Saturday 6th May they left Kortepyp by company to relieve the 7th Battalion Northamptonshire Regiment. Relief was completed by 10.15 p.m. Michael's 11th Platoon, accompanied by Hawkins's 10th Platoon, occupied the front line. Enemy machine guns were active that night. There were no heavy bombardments. As usual Michael doled out a tot of rum to each man at 'stand to'.

Now that the weather was warmer there was less need of it, but still it worked its magic. At dawn, skylarks rose from the tall grass in No Man's Land. They sang their three-minute song; beauty amid such brutality.

Because of spring growth, No Man's Land was almost meadow. Enemy trenches were on higher ground about 100 yards distant.

–Look Sir. The enemy seem to be holding up some kind of newspaper, said Malone handing Michael the box periscope.

They were. It was *The Irish Independent* of some days earlier. **Rebel Leaders Executed**, announced the black banner headlines. A little further along their front trench the enemy had unfurled a long white banner with bold two-foot high headlines stating

> This is how Great Britain treats its Irish Subjects.
> Is this British Justice?
> Irish soldiers lay down your arms
> and join your German confederates!

So, it had begun. Just as Michael had feared. He quickly wrote a note informing Murphy of the situation.

PLEASE ADVISE AS TO HOW TO PROCEED, he wrote in conclusion.

–Tommy, ask your runner to await the Colonel's reply, he advised Malone.

SULLIVAN THIS IS WHAT WE FEARED, wrote Murphy in reply. ALL I CAN ADVISE IS TO KEEP THE MEN AS BUSY AS POSSIBLE WITH ROUTINE DUTIES. AVOID LETTING THEM LOOK THROUGH THE BOX PERISCOPE. I FEEL THIS IS THE BEGINNING OF A DIFFICULT TIME FOR ALL IRISH REGIMENTS.

The following days were relatively quiet. Because the grass in No Man's Land was so high, Michael, Hawkins, and the other junior officers ordered Sergeants Malone and Gaffney to organise parties with sickles to cut as much as possible of it. The enemy did likewise and adopted a live and let live policy.

Parties also worked on a new fire trench near a sap (*a tunnel dug through to the German line*) called 'Dragon Alley'.

Lieutenant A.E. Bailey, a member of the recent draft, made the mistake of letting his curiosity get the better of him. At 'stand to' on the morning of the 12th he looked over the front-line parapet.

A sniper caught him in the shoulder. He was rushed down the line and transferred to hospital near Poperinghe.

At 23.30hrs that evening they were relieved by the Northampton Regiment and returned to Red Lodge Barracks in Ploegsteert, Flanders

There were three letters and two newspapers for him at Red Lodge. Two of the letters were from Virginia, the third from his mother. Virginia told of nursing badly injured soldiers in King George Hospital and of the reaction of ordinary people to the execution of the teacher Patrick Pearse.

The general opinion, Michael, is that he was a dreamer and harmless. To think that the Military Command wouldn't even release his body to his mother. Rumours say he was buried in quicklime like a common criminal. Along with Mr. Pearse two fathers have been taken from their families Mr. Tom Clarke, and university professor John McDonagh. Hopefully this is the end of these reprisals.
Your own, Virginia.

He quickly scanned *The Independent* before beginning his reply; insurrection leaders Joseph Mary Plunkett, Edward Daly, Michael O'Hanrahan, and Willie Pearse, brother of Padraig had been executed after court-martial on Thursday 4th May. So the bloodletting was continuing. General Maxwell and the authorities obviously knew nothing of Irish history.

He began his letter.

Dearest Virginia,
Thank you for both your letters. Firstly, I want to apologize for not being able to say goodbye in person before my return here. I was simply ordered to report to a military transport at the North Wall on the evening of Saturday 29th April. I did telephone the nurse's residence of your new hospital and left a message. Forgive me. I'm back in the same section of Flanders where the regiment was before my furlough, Things have been

relatively quiet, but as always, there are several casualties each day. Colonel Murphy questioned me ' in camera' on my experiences in Portobello Barracks during the emergency. I told him everything, including my view that the authorities should be very careful as to how they deal with the over 3000 arrested. According to the latest newspaper available here, seven leaders have been convicted and executed. Perhaps it's seven too many. Time will tell.
Spring is a little further advanced here than in Ireland. Most of the little byroads in the back areas here are very pretty. The trees form a sort of arc and there is a kind of half-light just as in a thick wood on a sunny day. The whole countryside is in bloom. It reminds me a little of the Lower Rosses in your beloved Rosses Point. Remember, sweetheart? Some spring sowing has been done, shoots of barley of about two inches in length cover the fields. Yesterday at 'stand to' an 'exaltation' of larks rose from No Man's Land and sang their beautiful three -part song. We're in reserve at present. We're not sure as to how long. Please write again soon.
Your own Michael

—Gilligan, could you please make sure this goes in this evening's mail hamper? he said after he'd addressed the envelope.

—Certainly Sir, said his batsman. Anything more I can do?

—Yes. I believe Lieutenant Hawkins has a few letters also.

Later, in a small bistro near Red Lodge, he discussed the situation with Hawkins.

—Frank, how are your lot? I find that several in my platoon are very uneasy about events in Dublin.

—Well Michael, the majority of my platoon are confused. They don't know what to think. Initially, in April, they were very angry that Sinn Feiners and so-called conscientious objectors took up arms against the civil authority in time of war. Pearse, McDonagh, and Plunkett were known to some of my men as dreamers who disagreed with Redmond. Nobody thought they would take this military action. The men saw it as betrayal; a knife in their backs. Then towards the end of that week, once newspaper delivery was resumed, the men showed a kind of grudging regard for the leaders and their courage. After all, they held out against much superior forces for six days.

—My platoon seem to have a similar feeling, Frank. I just hope they'll continue to do their duty here. They're still displaying anger and confusion.

The papers of the following Wednesday brought news of the executions of John MacBride, a Major of the Irish Brigade in the Boer War, on the 5th of

May and of Cornelius Colbert, Eamonn Ceannt, Michael Mallin, and Sean Heuston on Monday 8th of May. Countess Markievicz, a labour leader, was sentenced to life imprisonment for her part in the insurrection.

Michael remembered that Constance Countess Markievicz, a woman of great beauty, was one of the Gore Boothe sisters that the poet Yeats had loved. She'd used her wealth to help the poor of Dublin and became a follower of Labour Leader James Connolly. There had now been seven executions. Were they not enough he wondered? He saw signs of hope; the commutation of the Countess's death sentence was one, and eighteen other death sentences had been commuted to penal servitude.

Michael read a speech by John Dillon, the senior member of the Irish Party, with great interest. Speaking in the House of Commons, Dillon protested against the large number of military executions.

> We solemnly warn the government that any further military executions will have the most far reaching and disastrous effects on the future of the peace and loyalty of the Irish people.

Were Mr. Asquith and his Liberal Government listening? The immediate problem for Lieutenant Colonel Murphy, for Captain Palin, and for junior officers like Hawkins, Lavelle, Nolan, and him were to convince the men that in continuing to honour their oath to the King and the Army, they were also serving Ireland. Days later he learned that John McDermott and Labour leader James Connolly had been executed at dawn on Friday 12th. Connolly, badly wounded, was dying of gangrene.

Could the military authorities not have spared this champion of labour and the poor? Michael thought angrily. Perhaps this indignity was the one that would break the camel's back and alienate the ordinary people of Ireland.

CHAPTER FIFTEEN

The Somme, August 1916

The unrest among the men gradually subsided over the following weeks. In several memos Colonel Murphy indicated how proud he was of the men and their service. In late June there were sounds of a massive bombardment some forty miles to the south-east. Then in early July came rumours of the assault of the first day of the battle of the Somme. Some of these rumours were of a great loss of life on that day.

Michael questioned if this was true.

Then the battalion moved to the rest area of Feltre Meteren towards mid-July.

'Rest' meant a general verification of equipment, followed by intensive training. The weather was fine and, despite rumours of the heavy losses suffered by the Ulster Division on July1st, the men were happy to be on the move. Twenty months earlier, they had been in the Feltre Meteren area, and the belief that they would all be home by Christmas was common then.

Weapons training involved a lot of bayonet practice, controlled rushes and Mills bomb charges. Glad to be out of the trenches, the men threw themselves into training with gusto. The battalion was almost at full strength and stood at 900 men commanded by Lieutenant-Colonel A.D. Murphy.

Michael remained in command of the 11th platoon. His sergeant was the veteran Malone.

On the 25th of July, the battalion received movement orders. At 2p.m., they paraded in front of Divisional Commander General Hickie, Colonel Murphy, and Lieutenant Plowman. They then marched to a railway siding where they entrained for the Somme. The journey to Amiens was via Hazebrouck, Saint-Omer, and Doullens by train. At 1.30a.m.they arrived in Amiens.

–Try and get this unloading done as quickly as possible Sergeant, said Michael to Malone.

–I'll do my best, Sir.

The unloading of transport vehicles took an hour. At 02.30 hrs, they marched from the station to billets in an agricultural area, about six miles away. Though tired, the men were in good spirits and sang softly as they marched.

Michael was allotted a room in a farmhouse, next to Hawkins and Nolan. The whitewashed bedroom smelt of lime, had thick walls and was cool and clean. Despite the sounds of animals and birds, he fell quickly asleep.

Gilligan, his batman, woke him at 11a.m. with a mug of tea. He had already poured boiling water into a hand-basin.

–Lovely day outside Sir, he said as he pulled the curtains.

Michael heard the cackle of geese. The pungent smell of pig manure assaulted his senses.

–Want to explore the countryside Michael? asked Hawkins, as they finished lunch.

–That would be great, Frank.

The afternoon sun was hot, yet there was little humidity. The countryside was a great improvement on Ypres.

–You know Frank, I like this scenery. It's much more beautiful than Flanders, said Michael.

Hawkins agreed. Facing them were high wooded hills and dark copses.

–These are friendlier than those filthy low mud hills of the Salient, Michael, he said, -let's explore.

They harnessed the geldings Matilda and Gina and pushed them to a gallop. They would be going back into the line shortly, but they were not back there yet. They felt the warm sunshine on their faces. It was good to be alive! They could hear the front. Yet, their minds were only on the riding. The noise in the east seemed insignificant, at least for now.

Momentarily, they reined in the horses and halted. On the horizon, far to the east, they watched clouds bulge, black and sulphur. Sometimes, a ray of sunlight would surface, making a single cloud of lustrous vermillion.

.... Seeing bombed farmhouses...They saw a house on a far off slope suddenly disappear in an eruption of smoke and dust. Were there still families in these houses wondered Michael. This was the new form of battle, the great push; at this distance it didn't look too bad. After all those horrific stories they had heard! Of course, the officers in Feltre Meteren had been trying to make them apprehensive. Trying to make them feel they had everything to learn. This offensive couldn't be worse than the Menin Road could it? It couldn't be worse than Ypres or Hooge?

The countryside was rather like Dysart, a beauty spot, near his home made up of silica sand and marl. The hill they were now crossing reminded Michael of historic Dunamase outside Maryborough. This country had plenty of cover. It could be useful for many strategic surprises.

Enchanted by the scenery, Michael fell into a kind of trance. He felt no elation and little curiosity about being back in the thick of things. He was finally over the anger he'd felt over the executions in Dublin, weeks earlier. He had always been treated well in the army. Most British Military Officials were fair, at least those he'd had contact with. The Home Rule Bill had been signed by the King and would be respected. There was still the dream. The dream of an Ireland with its own Parliament. So he was going back into the thick of it once more. The enemy had to be shoved out and now it was being done. He and Hawkins were there as part of this plan. This push would settle it. It had to come and here it was. If he had been reminded of his keenness, when he arrived in Ypres twelve months earlier, and even paused to look up in interest to the whine of shells flying over treetops, he would have been disconcerted. A lot had happened in a year.

There had been hundreds of miles of trenches everywhere. The same drudgery over and over again. Those first months were another life! Now, it was a business! The business of war!

You had to get on with it and not stop to think about it.

...Oaklands, his home on a Sunday afternoon, his father reading *The Leinster Leader*, Brian and Rosemary playing on the front lawn.

...his mother watering the geraniums in the bay window, checking the leaves and growth of the new cuttings, unaware that he was watching her. It was another life, a life that he'd return to.

—Come on, Michael, enough time for musing later, said Hawkins. Let's make for that small village on the other bank of the river.

The village consisted of just twenty houses, it was languid and peaceful. They stopped the horses on the bank of the river to allow them to drink. The Somme flowed slowly between low banks.

Standing beside Matilda, Michael saw a school of minnows dart through the shimmering water.

—We'll have to remember this place, Frank, and return here tomorrow with rods and bait, perhaps a bit earlier in the day.

—Yes, it would be a great way to spend a morning, said Hawkins.

They left the horses grazing on the river-bank and walked a hundred yards to a small bistro. Inside, it was cool with only a few farmers in blue smocks drinking Pernod, A young girl of about sixteen came from behind the zinc counter to take their order.

—A half-litre Frank? asked Michael, and Hawkins nodded.

—*Un demi-litre de blanc du pays, s'il vous plait, et aussi un bonne fromage*, said Michael in halting French.

His command of the language had improved, but he still had some difficulty.

—*Un brie* Capitain?

—*Mais oui, si c'est mur.*

—*Oui, c'est mur et bon.*

The wine was dry and cool, the brie ripe and creamy.

—Not bad wine at all. A damn sight better than that tack they serve in Hazebrouck, said Hawkins.

—Yes, it's just a perfect meal on a hot day like today.

—We'd best make the most of the coming days, Michael. These weeks ahead aren't going to be easy.

—Oh, I know that Frank, but perhaps this really is the big push, and if we get through it, we'll be home by Christmas.

—Wouldn't that be something, though? To leave here with honour. To spend the first Christmas of a lasting peace back in Ireland.

—Yes, and then, in our small way, help Redmond, Dillon, and Kettle build a Free Ireland with a Home Rule Assembly in Dublin.

—Do you really think Carson and the Unionists in Northern Ireland will allow this to happen, Michael? said Hawkins.

—They'll have to, Frank. Home Rule is the law.

—Well, I hope events prove you right and me wrong. But those Orangemen have to be accommodated one way or the other.

—They'll have their rights in the New Ireland, Frank, just as they have now. Would Redmond and Dillon lie to us? They've worked for this their whole lives.

—Indeed they have, Michael, but they may be overtaken by events. Maxwell has declared a state of military law in Dublin and has executed or imprisoned the leaders of the insurrection of this past Easter.

—I'm well aware of that, Frank. My brother Chris is active in the Republican movement. He's had to be very careful of his activities over the last three months. He loves the cause of freedom and feels that Professor McNeill and the Irish Volunteers should take any and every means to free Ireland and establish an independent country. He didn't want me to volunteer for this war, you know, and we had many arguments. Yet, he feels that Redmond is an honourable man and eventually agreed that there was a certain logic in my decision. So, I'm glad to say we're still the best of friends.

—Well, that's important. This conflict has caused enough trouble without dividing families. I wouldn't be here without the support of mine. But then it was simpler for me, my father being a Church of Ireland minister, and all.

—Oh, my parents and the rest of my family, especially my older brother Jack, supported my decision, Frank. Jack's a Surgeon Commander in the Navy. He's a member of the surgical staff in the military hospital in Tenedos, one of those Greek islands near Gallipoli. We're proud of him.

—And rightly so... what do you think our chances are of surviving this push, Michael?

—Well, with luck and the grace o' God, perhaps forty per cent Frank.

—You really think so?

—A lot of us are going to die, Frank. That's a given. But, if we can achieve some kind of a breakthrough, the war could easily be over in four months.

—Wouldn't that be wonderful? Then you could return to your banking career and me to architecture. There should be a boom in building design once this is over.

—Yes, there should be, especially if you're prepared to work for a company here on the continent. You'll probably be a millionaire before you're forty Frank, and be able to buy and sell a career banker like me.

—Yes, and you'll finally be able to realize your dream and marry Virginia. I see the way you read and re-read her letters, Michael. I can see you're deeply in love.

—Yes, I love Virginia passionately, Frank. I think of her night and day. We're unofficially engaged; as a matter of fact she offered to marry me last Easter. I hesitated because of the uncertainty here. Now I wonder if I've really done the right thing.

—I think you have, Michael. It's simply too dangerous here. I'm sure Virginia understands.

—She says she does Frank.

—That's true love, Michael. You know what Montaigne says. Let your love run free, and it will come back to thee. I can't wait to meet her.

—You will indeed, Frank, just immediately we're shut of all this. Virginia already knows you through my letters.

—Well, here's hoping we'll both come through Michael, said Hawkins after a pause.

He raised his glass in a toast. Shadows were beginning to lengthen on the small bistro wall and several of the farm workers were standing up saying their good-byes.

Michael glanced at his watch.

—God, it's after five, Frank. We'd best be on our way.

Matilda and Gina were quietly gorging themselves on long, luscious grass beside the riverbank as they returned. The horses nuzzled forward looking for a treat.

—Sorry, nothing sweet for you right now, Matilda, said Michael as he tied the cinch under her belly.

They made good time and were at the Colonel's table promptly at eighteen-thirty.

—Gentlemen, I've important news, said Colonel Murphy. Our time here has been shortened. H.Q. have informed me that the battalion is to move to Bray-sur-Somme tomorrow.

We entrain for Bray-sur-Somme at Amiens at 5a.m. Roll call will be at 4a.m. So enjoy supper and get a good night's sleep!

The expected train transport was not available, and so, two days later, after a number of delays due to narrow roads completely congested by limbers, ammunition caissons, and by the non-arrival of the train transport, the battalion arrived at Bray-sur-Somme.

Led by Colonel Murphy, the men had marched the twenty-two mile journey from Mollienes-Vidame. The men coughed as they marched because of blowing dust. Most of them had tied handkerchiefs over their noses. The countryside showed little sign of cultivation. Fields near the rutted roads had become dust. In addition to the endless lines of horses and mules, all picketed under any available cover, were many signs of the gigantic offensive in progress: large aerodromes, colossal dumps of ammunition, shells of every size and caliber. Michael noticed that many of the trees in the area were either dead or dying, as the horses had eaten their lower branches and leaves.

Once in Bray-sur-Somme, a rough track off the main road brought the battalion finally to their camp, about six hundred yards north-west of the town.

—Not a bad area at all, is it Hawk? said Michael.

—No. It's almost like a rest camp. It'll be nice to be under canvas again, especially given the weather.

It was dark when the company finally fell out. Michael shared a tent with Hawkins and Nolan. At this point he felt as close to them as to his brothers. Towards the Northeast, the whole horizon shone red, vermilion and black, because of the bombardment at the Front some four miles distant. Nearer, he noticed many sausage-balloons observing enemy gun flashes. After the long forced march and given the heat, he felt extremely tired. After lifting a back flap of the tent to create a draft and consuming a neat whiskey with Hawkins and Nolan, he pulled out his sleeping bag, got into it, and fell immediately asleep.

Due to the intense heat, duties the next day were reduced. They were on high ground overlooking Bray, a fairly large town with rustic red-tiled roofs and a Gothic church. Between their camp and the town were a number of ammunition columns with rows and rows of horse lines all in the open. Slightly to the North were hundreds of bell tents. All belonged to the other regiments of the 16th Division. Looking Northeast Michael counted thirty observation balloons. Each balloon was in turn attached by steel cable to a motor transport. If fired on the observation personnel quickly called to have the balloon hauled down.

Early that evening the heat abated a little. Michael, Hawkins, Nolan and the other platoon commanders drilled the men in the new manoeuvre of advancing behind a creeping barrage system of shell fire. This new technique of warfare made effective use of bombardment and saved lives. Officers and men learned when to take cover and when to advance as a barrage lifted. To make things more realistic, Battalion drummers sounded drum rolls to represent friendly fire.

Michael and his platoon advanced at walking pace, the men carrying their rifles at port. The Battalion advanced in waves of platoons on a two-company front. Each man had a special role and was followed by the moppers-up, those responsible for clearing all captured trenches, and killing or capturing all remaining enemy. By bitter and costly experience, High Command concluded that moppers-up were vital.

The weather continued extremely hot, so battle exercises were held only in late afternoons and evenings. Bathing outings to the river and organized games filled earlier parts of each day.

On 8th August the Battalion paraded and moved to a bivouac line at a landmark called the Citadel, some two miles nearer the front.

Their billets were in an area between a cemetery and an Indian Army Battalion. Michael shared a small tent with Hawkins. From flimsy camouflaged shelters near Fricourt, large guns kept up a continual barrage. Fields, once golden with corn, were barren and scarred with white trenches, the chalk ground showing through.

Michael recorded in his diary:

Things hum. Troops like ants are all over any open ground. In tents, in bivouacs, in the open, everywhere. The eternal chain of motor-lorries is unceasing, bringing up ammunition and supplies. One sees this throughout France, but here they block half the roads. At least the weather remains clear!

The following morning began with torrential rain. This continued unabated throughout the day. The men were wet through, but were happy that temperatures were cooler.

–At least there's a bit of a breeze and the men aren't complaining, said Sergeant Malone.

At 19.00hrs brown-haired, acne-scarred Lieutenant Lavelle led a working party. Under his direction the men laid 500 yards of telephone cable. Then the rain finally cleared, and everyone watched in fascination, a bombardment at the front.

–We're finally on the move Michael, Hawkins said, next morning, holding the order in his hand. We're to report to Battalion headquarters at the Briqueterie near Guillemont, immediately.

At the Briqueterie, the Battalion was in final preparations for the move into action. In addition to his normal munitions for battle order, each man had to carry empty sand-bags and Mills bombs.(hand grenades) The men sweated profusely; it was clear that they'd been ordered to carry too much.

Which member of the top brass had come up with these weight requirements? wondered Michael. Was it General Haig? Clearly, he'd never set foot in the front lines, otherwise he'd have seen that the men could do nothing more than walk slowly with so much equipment, and to have to carry sand-bags in addition was a further hardship.

Colonel Murphy issued each officer a small supply of morphine tablets to be used with wounded soldiers.

–This is to be used only in case of emergency. If one of the lads is in terrible pain. Understood?

–Understood Sir, replied Hawkins, Nolan, and Michael as one.

The attack wasn't simply a Divisional operation. There was to be a general advance along the whole front. On their left, the 14thDivision, and on their right the 3rd Division were advancing.

To the south at Perrone, the French were attacking simultaneously.

The main topographical feature of the area was the Guillemont Horn Farm ridge. The ruins of Guillemont stood on the highest point of this ridge, dominating the countryside. Guillemont was the key, and once captured by the Leinsters, would allow control of the region. The enemy fully realized the town's importance and had turned it into a fortress. Three previous attacks had been written off as failures. Now B and D companies were to lead the attack, with A Company and C Company - Michael's own - in support. Since he was not in the first wave, Michael found a vantage point at the top of some ruined walls near the Briqueterie. He was about a thousand yards from the jumping-off trenches, before Guillemont. He stood on a small ridge, separated from the main Guillemont ridge by a valley known as The Valley of Death. Before zero hour, the leading companies of the Battalion were moving across this valley and winding up Guillemont ridge. Now they would witness the efficacy of the much vaunted creeping barrage.

Suddenly and abruptly, a crashing roar resounded over the whole area. Even at his thousand-yard distance Michael felt his eardrums would burst. The preliminary bombardment of the enemy had commenced punctually- to the second. All batteries were firing simultaneously. Thousands of tons of munitions were raining on the enemy trenches on the skyline.

Shells came from places unthought of and unseen, so excellently were they camouflaged - from field guns in pits with a covering of rabbit wire interlaced with grass and leaves for concealment.

Behind these, ranged rows and rows of howitzers, which made the ground quake each time they fired. The noise of the explosions, the pain in Michael's inner ear, and the concussion he felt, were greater than anything he'd experienced or imagined. The acrid smoke blocked out the noonday sun. The air hung heavy with the smell of cordite and gunpowder. Even at his observation point, Michael could hardly breathe, while watching the British shells bursting over the German lines. Under this curtain of fire, Michael could see numerous German SOS rockets of every colour shooting up in the sky, signalling for return fire on the British lines from their artillery.

Behind Michael, artillery gunners at their guns were stripped to the waist. Their sweat-begrimed bodies showed the superhuman effort of endurance they were making under the blazing heat of the August sun. How long would this furious bombardment last? How long could these brave gunners continue their superhuman efforts before exhaustion set in? The flash of the shell bursts from the British guns seemed further away. The gunners were extending their shellfire further into the German lines.

The barrage lifted. Simultaneously, up rose a line of forms from the British trenches - the first wave - and disappeared into the smoke. This cloud grew denser with the debris of bricks and mortar from the ruins of Guillemont. The enemy were retaliating with a vengeance, aiming at the slopes of the ridge, in hopes of knocking out British artillery. Nearer, Michael now heard the chatter of small arms and machine guns.

Through his field-glasses Michael saw that something was happening on the right flank of the assault. Highlanders of the 3rd Division were falling back, and so were the attacking companies of the Leinsters. These were not the walking wounded, coming out of the black smoke. These men were still in tight formation. Was the assault a failure? He'd been elated, seeing the forward battalions going into action. Now, seeing them pull back, he felt despondent.

Groups of wounded, walking and on stretchers, were now drifting by: men with smashed arms, limping, some with blood streaming down their faces and eyes. All muttered about machine guns in a sunken road, which fired on them mercilessly. Father Maloney was among the stretcher cases. He'd been hit in the chest. Michael talked with him in a sheltered area. He'd lost a lot of blood, but was lucid. It was clear to Michael that the selfless priest would need many weeks of convalescence.

—I saw Lieutenant Lavelle fall as he advanced towards the first objective, said the priest, gasping for breath. He got caught in crossfire and died instantly. I knew no finer officer. You must write to his family, Michael. Over one hundred casualties just going up that ridge, without even seeing the enemy! All just fodder for enemy guns! I gave the last rites to those near me. Then as you see, I got hit.

He groaned and clutched his chest.

—Damn it, give Father Maloney something for his pain! said Michael, grabbing the arm of one of the stretcher bearers.

The soldier, a red-haired Kerryman, put a morphine tablet on the priest's tongue and helped him drink from a water canister.

—I'll take care of everything, Father. Now stop talking. Take care of yourself. Get better and come back to us if you can.

—You take care too, Michael. Try and keep yourself safe. We're all in God's hands, the priest said weakly, as the stretcher bearers carried him towards a clearing station.

As part of the 73rd Brigade, the 2nd Battalion Leinsters were to have exploited the success of the jump-off regiments. Since the attack had failed, they now had the task of replacing a disorganized battalion and holding the original front line against counter attack. On their left, the 17th Brigade had captured a strategic farm, and part of the 7th Northamptons had captured a post at the quarries near Guillemont Railway Station.

On receiving the changed orders, Michael, Hawkins, and Nolan started across country for Guillemont village. Every inch of ground they walked was completely churned up by shell fire. Here and there lay huddled stiff figures in khaki, all casualties of the morning's engagement. It was almost dark when they reported to Lieutenant Colonel Murphy at Advance Headquarters.

His face begrimed and red hair dusty, Murphy sat on the ground in a dug-out off the main communication trench. He gave orders in a clear, concise manner. Palin, the Adjutant, knelt behind a makeshift desk, an empty fruit crate lit by a candle, noting these directives on a message pad. Two signallers, completely exhausted, lay prone behind him.

–Glad you got through safely, said Murphy. It's been rough up here. Our main task now is to somehow consolidate our front line and repulse any counterattack. Right ... first things first. Sullivan, I want you to see that hand grenades and shells are brought to the front trench, from the depot at the sunken road. Hawkins and Nolan, I want you to supervise the reconstruction of the front line.

Michael reached the barricade at the sunken road towards five-thirty. He was struck by the stillness of the area after the furious pandemonium of just three hours before. Battalion bombers, bent double, carried heavy ammunition boxes up the line. Occasionally a solitary shell burst over their heads or whined, going in the direction of the transport dumps. The operation took over an hour.

Finally reaching the front line, Michael saw utter devastation. The line was no longer a line, but just a series of shell holes. The enemy trenches, a hundred yards distant, were in even worse shape.

What had been the ruins of a village six hours earlier was now a heap of red brick and mortar. The few intact trees were torn up by the roots. The pitted, ploughed-up yellow earth stank of lyddite and gun powder. Stretcher-bearers were combing no-man's land for casualties. Occasionally, Michael heard the pitiful cries of the forgotten wounded.

Nolan took out a patrol to reconnoitre enemy positions, while Michael and Hawkins helped rebuild the line. It was vital work and there was no standing on ceremony. So both he and Hawkins set to with the men.

Later, Murphy walked the still-damaged parapet. He wanted to carry out an attack that night and had sent a messenger to Brigade for permission. Despite heavy losses, morale was high and a determined attack that night could wrestle Guillemont from enemy hands.

Brigade refused to hear of an attack. The runner brought orders that they would be relieved. At twenty-one-thirty that evening the 1st Battalion of the North Staffordshire Regiment arrived in their trenches.

Michael's C Company had been ordered to withdraw to a sunken road on the left flank in support of the 7th Northamptons. The enemy attempted a counterattack, but were beaten off. C Company's help was not needed and so they were ordered to spend the night at the sunken road.

At the road Michael noticed a lot of huddled figures. They seemed to be sleeping, but there were no sounds of snoring or heavy breathing. There was a rumour that A Company of the North Staffordshires had been badly hit on this section of road. The light was very poor, everyone was close to collapse. An investigation of the immediate area could wait until morning.

Michael and Hawkins posted sentries and got their men hidden under the available cover. A light rain began to fall. Michael found an undercutting in the side wall of the sunken road. He signalled Hawkins. They both crawled into the opening and, leaving their legs exposed, tried to sleep.

Sleep came quickly, the sleep of exhaustion. *Michael was swimming off the second strand at Rosses Point, Co. Sligo, Virginia a little to his left. The sea was perfectly calm except for white caps on the horizon northwest. Swimming towards Virginia he tried to kiss her and ended up with a mouthful of water, as she playfully pushed his head under. Taking a deep breath he dove down to her legs, but she anticipating this, swam further away. He felt blissfully happy and prayed the day would never end. He now knew he loved Virginia; knew he could be happy with her. Though he was up to his neck in water, his feet seemed colder than the rest of his body... strange! Then from the beach came the sound of the five o'clock signal cannon. Yet it wasn't five o'clock, it was noon. He and Virginia had been in the water less than fifteen minutes. What was the reason for this? Why had the cannon sounded so early? As they both reached the shore, harried parents were shepherding their children, hurriedly putting away picnic items. Enemy U boats offshore, he heard someone whisper. How could this be? Virginia and he were on a remote beach on the west coast of Ireland!*

Michael woke up at dawn, wet and cold. He saw that lying on either side of himself and Hawkins were two dead men of the North Staffordshires. The whole sunken road was littered with corpses of that same regiment, at least thirty men.

His men complained that they had no food, so he ordered them to turn out the kits of the dead for iron rations. They found a couple of cigarettes as well and proceeded to light up. With the help of a little rye bread he and Hawkins had a makeshift breakfast.

At 6.00hrs, orders came to move down into the valley. C Company fell in and moved off. The undergrowth and remaining stunted trees were very wet. The men trod as warily as possible, yet many slipped and fell.

—Jesus fucking Christ, cursed giant John Cunningham, falling full on his face.

—You hurt, John? asked Sergeant Tom Malone, putting an arm under his shoulder.

—Only my pride is hurt, Sergeant, replied the corporal.

Enemy shelling was sporadic. Michael suspected that enemy gunners were dead tired. Either that or they were low on ammunition. The Regimental Sergeant Major collected a party of men to aid in the burial of the North Staffordshires. Several of Michael's company volunteered.

Some forty minutes later their company reached a reserve trench about eight hundred yards distant. Here, they found the rest of the Battalion. Under cover of a thick mist the men were making breakfast. This trench consisted mainly of fire-bays. The men stretched ground sheets from trench parapets to parados for cover, then went to sleep on the fire steps.

All day there were orders and counter-orders for the front line. At about 18.00hrs. there was terrific shelling all along the front. They expected to go up the line at any moment. No attack followed this intense barrage. Michael breathed a sigh of relief. At least they had been spared for now. Towards 21.00hrs. they were relieved by a bantam battalion. It had only recently arrived from England.

—It's rough that these poor little blighters are having their baptism of fire here at the Somme, said Sergeant Tom Malone.

The regiment moved off by company to billets in an area called the Craters near Carnoy. It formed part of the former German front and had been mined by sappers. All these mines had been blown on 1 July, forming a crater line as far as Fricourt.

The men had a knack of adapting to any situation. Within a short space of time they had all lit fires and were making up their tea. Morale was low. Through no fault of its own, the 2nd Battalion had lost a great chance at capturing a vital military target. The capture of Guillemont was to have been the star turn of their earlier engagement. Now, in divisional reserve, their orders were to hold themselves in readiness and be prepared to return to Guillemont within an hour.

Since the deep German dug-outs contained human remains, Michael, Hawkins, Nolan, and their fellow junior officers camped under canvas.

As the whole Battalion, a largely Catholic one, was in battle operations, there was no possibility of Sunday Mass next day, August 20. The men prayed in small groups. Later Michael was ordered to make a reconnaissance of the best route for ration parties going towards the front line. He led a small group of NCOs towards the front lines, past Bernafay Wood, where the Brigade artillery store was situated.

As the group moved forward, a German shell, fired on the road to sow disruption, caused a horse drawing a general service wagon to bolt, and it overtook them at great speed. The driver panicked and jumped off, running for the nearest ditch.

—Goddamn it, man! What's happened to your courage? shouted Michael, rushing forward.

The lead horse was foaming at the mouth, bucking wildly. Michael caught the reins and talked softly, trying to calm the agitated horses.

—You're responsible for these animals and the load you're carrying. Get back on your limber and give me the name of your commanding officer!

—I'm Private O'Malley of A Company in the 7th Battalion Leinster Regiment, Sir. Our CO is Major Kerwin.

—Right then. Carry on, ordered Michael, closing his notebook.

He probably wouldn't report him, but felt that under these strained circumstances discipline had to be maintained.

At Bernafay Wood, the Brigade Major responsible for the artillery store, stopped the party and recommended that they return to Carnoy Craters.

—It's too dangerous, Sullivan. You'd best try again after dark.

The small party started out again a little after ten in the evening. All went well until they entered Trônes Wood. Suddenly, the enemy put down a box barrage round the wood.

Cover was reasonable. In a communication trench named 'Leinster Avenue', A Company had a carrying party at work. They were in front of Michael and his patrol. The carrying party halted and the trench got so jammed up that nothing could move in any direction. Fallen trees and thick brambles blocked any move towards open ground. Shells rained down on them at a rate of eight to ten a minute. Michael was covered from head to toe with perspiration, it condensed between his shoulders and flowed down his back. Sergeant Malone, Corporal Cunningham, and others in the party looked deathly pale. Feeling embarrassed Michael realized that he had just soiled himself. He moved a little away from the platoon, lowered his trousers and pulling out a handkerchief cleaned the turds and threw them towards the side of the trench. As a precaution, he pushed a field dressing between his buttocks. The stench of decomposing bodies made him retch.

He sent a runner to Lieutenant Sharp of A Company, asking if it was safe to push on. Sharp replied that it was impossible. At last, towards twenty-three thirty, they moved to the front line without a casualty and returned to battalion headquarters at two in the morning.

Next day began with rumours of a return to Guillemont. By midday these orders were cancelled. C Company was ordered to rest. However, the order paper read:

Be prepared to return to action at short notice.

Moving off by platoons towards the west, they passed parties of Irish Guards mending the roads. They soon reached their destination, an encampment of large, camouflaged tents on sloping ground due East of the scarred desolate town of Albert. On the horizon they could see the figure of the Madonna suspended in mid-air from the mutilated church-spire.

Army cookers were in the area and gave them a meal of beef stew, potatoes, and strong tea. The weather remained humid and hot. Hawkins produced a flask of Black and White Whiskey and a pack of cards from his rucksack. Michael and he played twenty-one until the light failed. The whiskey relaxed him and helped him keep his mind off the ever-present sounds of war.

Next day, 22 August, was spent refitting the men with clothes, boots and equipment. The sun shone. The men spent the day washing and shaving. They were in fine shape. Towards three in the afternoon of the following day, a runner brought orders for the relief of troops holding the line in front of Guillemont.

At five the Adjutant and four commanders rode off to reconnoitre the line. At six the Battalion moved off with five hundred yards between each company. A little beyond Carnoy they rested for thirty minutes. In the near distance Michael saw shell-bursts in the line of march. There were no casualties.

Towards ten they reached their batteries, in action south of the Valley of Death. All went well until they reached Stanley Dump in the valley. There, transport were unloading rations and barbed wire. Abruptly, the enemy began a horrendous barrage. All was chaos, everyone crouching low, diving desperately for any cover. Michael knew the communication trench to the front line was quite near. It would provide some cover. Then he found himself winded, knocked clear off his feet. Shale and small stones rained down on his upper body. He checked his feet and arms there were a few superficial cuts on his jaw and hands. Nothing broken, thank God. Gingerly picking himself up, he discovered that two fine soldiers, Privates Lynch and McDonald, had been killed instantly. Sergeant Sweeney was bleeding from a flesh wound. Michael helped him to apply a field dressing.

In all the confusion and gloom, Michael heard Regimental Sergeant Major Smith bark:

—This way, C Company.

He directed the men towards Smith's voice. His face illuminated by shellfire, Smith stood bolt upright under the barrage, guiding each company as they came up. The men stood calmly with their heads bent. Then Michael led the platoon up the shallow communication trench on rising ground.

Lieutenant Colonel Murphy met them and conducted the company across open ground, behind the front line, to a sunken road junction. There they entered the trench and proceeded to relieve two Bantam Battalions of the Gloucester Regiment. The Battalion was astride the sunken road with Guillemont about one hundred and fifty yards away. A Company was on the left, in front of Arrow Head Copse. Michael's C Company on the right. Both companies joined at the barrier, where the Battalion bombers and a section of the Machine-Gun Corps were posted. B and D Companies were in support.

Nolan, commander of Platoon 9, was perspiring heavily. He was deathly pale and looked like he was running a very high fever.

—Eddy, you look like shite, said Michael. Don't you think you should go back down the line? If a bullet doesn't get you, you'll die of what looks pneumonia. We'll cover for you.

—Shut the fuck up, Sullivan. Everyone in my platoon is in as bad shape as me. The lads look up to me. I'm not leaving.

Torrential rain began to fall. The shallow trenches quickly became sodden and waterlogged. Bent double, Michael walked and slid all night, visiting the sentries, checking they had enough ammunition and making the odd joke. Shelling continued severely at half-hour intervals. Towards three in the morning he rested and chatted with Corporal Bradbent and Private O'Leary, friends from Ypres days, at a muddy fire step, the raised step on the face of the fire trench for shooting from.

He continued on, and returned ten minutes later to find a colossal shell-crater where the parapet had been. Bradbent was dead, his body badly mangled. O'Leary, the keen sentry of minutes earlier, was terribly cut about his head and body and was raving. Michael searched in his uniform, found a morphine tablet and pulling out his water canister placed the morphine on O'Leary's tongue.

–Swallow this quickly, Tom, he said. It'll take away some of the pain.

Walking as slowly and carefully as possible, stretcher-bearers Morrissey and Reid took O'Leary down the line.

Later, Michael directed the men to deepen the trench and build up the parapets. The Bantams, at an average height of five feet, had sufficient cover, but the trench was by no means deep enough to provide cover for men up to six feet. Just before dawn, Captain Palin came to inspect the line. Together he and Michael toured the whole company front, including a detached post twenty yards into no man's land. To arrive, they had to cut across the open. However, since it was foggy, they were unobserved. Conditions were deplorable. All around lay dismembered enemy corpses. Several were very swollen and about to burst. In the dark, gleaming small eyes were everywhere. Fucking brazen rats! Michael quickly checked that his trousers were tucked in. They were. The little ditch of a trench was full of mud, pieces of useless gunnery, and half buried bodies. Lt. Jameson, the commander of the second platoon in the trenches with Michael's, addressed Capt. Palin during the inspection.

–We're dying of hunger here, Captain Palin. It's twelve hours since the men ate. Can you help?

–You think I'm some kind of a miracle worker or something, Jimmy. Break out the Iron Rations for God's Sake. No ration parties are getting through this mess. What about that post to your right?

–We tried to make contact, but shelling was too intense Captain. As you can see, they're at quite a distance.

–Well, keep trying. It's in a strategic position at the boundary of Leuze Wood. But most of all keep under cover and take calculated risks only. Carry on.

–Right, Captain.

Shelling was intense that afternoon. Box barrages were put down all round the front trench. The earth was continually going up like lava from a volcano. The sun split the sky, the heat and humidity were unbearable. Crouching in the forward portion of the trench, Michael developed a craving for two things: water and cigarettes. Stones and lumps of earth ricocheted off his helmet every other minute. As large sections of trench were blown in, he felt in mortal fear of being smothered. Dear God, anything but that, he prayed. Bring us through this and if I must die grant me a quick death. He pulled heavily on a cigarette, his eighth in the last hour. Swarms of horseflies, furious at being disturbed from their breeding grounds in no man's land, filled the trench, biting any exposed skin, squirming under uniform sleeves, ravenous for salt and fresh blood. Michael's cigarette smoke at least kept them at bay. The intense bombardment reminded him of Hooge, exactly one year earlier.

The entire British line was one cloud of smoke. Evidently, the enemy anticipated an attack, as they fired all kinds of distress rockets seeking support fire from their own artillery.

—Making sure all Lewis guns were in position in their gun emplacements on the parapets, Michael ordered fix bayonets.

This simple act prepared them for the fight to come.

Dusk was falling as the shelling ceased. The platoons linked up at the centre. There the line was completely blown in; nothing but a series of smoking craters.

—Right lads. We must connect these as much as possible, said Michael, grabbing a shovel. Otherwise, we'll have no cover at all.

The men set to with a will. Several men in A Company had been killed. His C Company had got off lightly, with just a few casualties.

By five that morning they had consolidated the line, put up parapets, and deepened the trench. Michael was now the company officer in the southern end of the front line. Nolan's platoon was next in the line, but he was very ill, yet still refused to go towards the rear. Shelling was still intense, but no longer continuous. He must write to Bradbent's wife and was not looking forward to this sad task.

In the afternoon Michael reported to Murphy at Battalion Headquarters. The relief of Jameson's forward listening post was the most important matter in hand.

—Men got enough to eat Sullivan? the Colonel asked, as Michael turned to leave.

—Yes Sir. At all events we can break out the Iron Rations if need be.

—You know we're very proud of their courage under fire. I want you to recommend three men who behaved exceptionally. I'll commend them for the Military Medal. Carry on.

The Battalion was to be relieved by part of the Gloucestershire regiment, while another regiment was to furnish a platoon to relieve the detached post, opposite Leuze. Making his way back to the post, Michael recalled similar forward listening post saps (a forward leading trench into No Man's Land) in Ypres.

This was much worse - a series of linked-up shell craters. If one of his men was killed, he buried him by putting his body in a shell-hole and filling it in. All the torn-up ground around the post was lined with dead. Though he wore a handkerchief laced with camphor directly below his nostrils, he found he was continually gagging on the smell. Firing was still too intense to bury any of them. There was no protective barbed wire there, but fortunately, they were not visible from any other part of the line. Company strength was down. Only one sergeant was left with the company, and Malone with Michael at the post they'd relieved.

Michael was bathed in sweat as he took up his position with the men. He steadied two machine guns on their tripods, fixing them into battle position. The crews had been injured, but fortunately both he and Sergeant Malone had had machine gun operational training.

Throughout the afternoon Michael had the men deepen the trench. This turned out to have been wise, as at five that evening the enemy began another fierce barrage. All around their post the earth heaved and trembled with great columns of acrid black smoke and colossal clods of earth. But enemy gunners hadn't got their exact range. A barrage would land five yards in front of them and then five yards to their rear. They could hardly breathe as the dust and smoke filled their mouths and lungs. Shells kept hitting unburied corpses in No Man's Land and hurling body parts on top of them. *Oh Jesus make it stop*, prayed Michael as he ducked a dismembered torso.

—Fix bayonets and remain in crouch position under the parapets, Michael commanded.

Knowing that the suggestion to the men that they were about to go into battle would boost their morale, he then walked down the line to give encouragement.

Private Moran, once a platoon sergeant, but demote for his problem with drink, was a tower of strength during the nine hours of incessant shelling.

Michael felt his ears would burst. He abjectly wondered if he'd have a loss of hearing if he survived this offensive. But then, he'd have to survive first. Everyone was at the point of exhaustion. They hadn't slept since they left Albert three days earlier.

He was responsible for thirty lives, two machine-guns, and an important forward post. Frequently, he found himself leaning against the parapet, VERY pistol in hand, dozing. A shell would land near him in No Man's Land and he would be startled out of his semi-comatose state, coughing from the dust, fumes, and cordite.

Damn it. The relief was hours late and would not arrive now because of the bombardment. They simply had to hang on. An enemy attack was expected. So they all strained their eyes, looking across the one hundred and fifty yards of smoke-filled, churned-up earth, waiting to see waves of Boches advance in the moonlight. Star rockets were going up continuously from enemy lines to light up the area of No Man's Land. Several were more brilliant and of different colours to the rest. He questioned if these rockets signalled the attack.

Though it was now well after dark, the heat was still intolerable. Michael could hear his heartbeat. His breath came in short quick gasps. Nothing was worse than this infernal waiting.

When the hell would the attack come?

Michael held his VERY pistol at hand, ready to signal when the German attack came. Although tired, hungry, and thirsty, with their nerves on edge, he knew his men would put up a hell of a fight.

Hours were slipping by. Michael glanced at his watch. It was well past midnight, and there was no sign of the relief. One way or another they had to be relieved before daylight. They would be sitting ducks once the sun rose. If not relieved the men would be stuck in this shattered lookout post for another fifteen hours. Many were at the breaking point. He as their officer had to do something.

He waited another ninety minutes. Then taking a deep breath, he tapped veteran Private Flannery on the shoulder.

—Paddy, let's try and find that relief. You on?

—Yes Sir. Anything to break out of here.

They set off towards the left. Jumping from shell-hole to shell-hole, they reached an isolated communications trench, about three hundred yards away to the rear. Here, they found the relief, a platoon of Bantams, asleep at the bottom of the trench. Their officer sat in a deep dug-out reading by candlelight.

—I'm Sullivan, officer in charge of the lookout post to the right. We've been under fire for nine hours. Why the hell haven't you made any attempt to relieve us?

—Lieutenant Bowen of the North Staffordshires, Sir. Well, when we arrived at midnight, shells were raining down at the rate of three a minute. I couldn't risk the lives of my men going across open ground, the young officer replied.

He bit his lower lip, his book now on the dug-out floor.

—Damn it, Bowen. The barrage ended over an hour ago, Michael replied trying to control his temper. You could have relieved us then. I should report you to your CO
All I want is the relief of my men. They haven't slept in three days. Some are close to breaking. Right. Who's your second?

—That would be Sergeant Brown, Sir.

—Have him fall in the men and follow me, then. You and I can lead the party.

With the help of Private Flannery and Lt. Bowen, Michael brought the party of fifty men across the open ground, relieving his platoon.

Michael told Brown all he knew about the line and gave him the two machine-guns. As it was already getting light, he made no delay in leaving. The men were already in battle order and filed out under cover of mist.

—I hope those poor little blighters have it easier than we did, said Sergeant Malone pensively.

—They'll get through all right, Tommy, just as we have, whispered Michael. Their lack of height is probably an advantage.

They cut quickly across the churned-up open ground, making for the sunken road northeast of Delville Wood. German shells continued to fall, irregularly.

Towards five-thirty the platoon reached the Briquetierie. The men were extremely thirsty and rushed to a water dump near Brigade Headquarters. As the water had been stored in petrol cans it had the usual terrible oily taste. However, it was cold.

—Have the men wait here, Sergeant Malone. I must report to Battalion Headquarters. Have the men join us tomorrow morning at headquarters.

Battalion Headquarters was several miles to the rear, southwest of Albert. He commandeered a lorry at Montauban.

—Take me as close as possible to Headquarters, he ordered the driver. I've an important report to deliver.

—Yes Sir, said the driver putting his foot hard to the floor.

The lorry lurched forward, narrowly missing a tree on the side of the road.

—Jesus H. Christ, just get us there alive, said Michael laughing.

Though the roads were full of potholes, they made good time and arrived at the Citadel at Albert fifteen minutes later. The main square was crowded with ambulances and army vehicles of every description. Battalion Headquarters were not at the Citadel, but in a partly damaged house on the outskirts of the town. Michael reported the platoon's safe return and proceeded to the company officers' tent, then stumbled into a camp bed.

An orderly woke him three hours later with a breakfast of strong tea, fried bread and tomatoes.

Captain Palin said the CO had been worried about the platoon. Intelligence suspected that the Boche were going to attack in front of the detached post. The CO had ordered D Company to stand by and assist.

Michael's platoon had rejoined, and at three in the afternoon the Battalion paraded, and then marched to a rest area at Dernancourt southwest of Albert. On their way they passed a Battalion of the Royal Irish Regiment going up the line. The Leinsters gave them a rousing cheer.

—What's it like up there, mate? shouted a Royal Irish private.

—Been at the Salient, Private?

—Yes, almost a year ago.

—It's much worse than that. So, watch your back and trust only your mates.

They reached Dernancourt towards five. Bell tents covered an area of about four acres. Weeks earlier this had been a wheat field. Now they were surrounded by sheaves of newly harvested grain. What a contrast to where they were that morning thought Michael. He felt the tension ease out of him. The cooing of wood pigeons, the calling of swallows and swifts, and the distant thunder of the guns were the only sounds to be heard. Michael thought he could be happy there as he threw his pack on the ground inside his tent.

That evening the weather broke. The tent he shared with Hawkins withstood the first showers, but by next morning, water was dripping at the seams.

Father Doyle, their replacement chaplain, said an open-air Mass for the men, after which they began specialist training, Lewis gun, and bombing classes. The men worked well.

Towards afternoon the weather improved and at five Michael led the platoon to the river Ancre. The river was about five feet wide at this point and moved languidly through tall banks. He dove in, and after doing the breaststroke for fifty yards, turned over on his back and floated. Clusters of cumulus clouds moved slowly across the sky; the tops of several willow trees swayed in the wind. He felt the vibrations of the platoon splashing and washing in the water. Though they were less than ten miles from the Front, the war and the events of the last few days seemed distant.

He again questioned if he could go through the same frustration and tension of the last three days again. He had been a volunteer soldier and was now a junior officer—he had to do best by his men. They looked to him to bring them through. So far he had performed well taking out the forward post on the German line, and had brought his platoon back to Brigade intact. He'd been deadly afraid, but had conquered his fear. With God's help he'd continue to perform well. But he felt weary. Weary at the loss of so many good men; weary at the loss of so many brother officers; weary at the waste and filth of war. He'd use this rest period as best as he could, and continue to do his duty.

He felt ripples in the water and saw Hawkins approach, doing a strong over-arm.

—Race you as far as that willow, said Hawkins treading water.

—Right, but breaststroke. It's the only stroke I do well.

—Fine. Ready, steady go!

Hawkins swam forward, head partly submerged, gaining several yards. Michael followed, by keeping his head and torso under water as much as possible, he gained ground and beat his comrade by a yard.

—God isn't it great to be alive, Mick? Great to be here?

—Yes Hawk, we'll tell our grandchildren about this someday. We'd best swim back now and join the men.

The men were drying off. Several were lying down, taking the sun.

That evening the regimental pipers played a selection of traditional airs to the assembled company. Nolan joined Michael and Hawkins in their bell tent that evening.

He'd recovered from his fever, but looked tired and worn, his grey eyes sunken in their sockets, his fair hair unruly and in need of clipping.

Towards midnight, torrential rain moved in and continued throughout the morning. Michael, Hawkins, and Nolan got soaked as their tent could not withstand such a deluge. The straw they'd placed their sleeping bags on, their underclothes, and uniforms were sodden. The entire camp was saturated and lay under two inches of water.

Gilligan brought Michael and his companions a breakfast of sorts: cold tea, damp bread and butter, plum jam. He could not get the field cooker going properly. The men fared equally badly.

Michael, Hawkins, and Nolan were almost finished their breakfast when Murphy came by.

—At ease gentlemen! At ease! he said as they made to rise. I'm afraid I have some bad news. We're going up the line again.

—But we've only just got here, Sir. It's only been three days, stammered Nolan, his lips trembling, his face flushed. You know we've lost four officers. Two companies are commanded by junior officers. The men are badly shaken and weary.

There was a pause as Murphy eyed Nolan, coldly.

—Those are our orders, Lieutenant Nolan, said Murphy in a harsh voice. We must obey them.

Michael looked at Nolan, then Hawkins. Perhaps Nolan should have gone on sick leave when he was ill days earlier. He had never publicly questioned an order before.

How would he behave now under battle conditions? And yet Nolan was only voicing the concern of the entire battalion.

The men were happy to leave their sodden camp. Many of their tents had collapsed. As usual, they quickly formed battle order with only their ground sheets for cover.

Led by their pipers, they paid their compliments to the Irish Guards who, in turn, gave them a vociferous send-off.

Towards noon the companies piled their rifles and fell out. They were just a little outside Fricourt. Michael, Hawkins, and Nolan sheltered behind a high wall, eating wet sandwiches, while the men, surrounding the company cookers, were eating beef stew. The rain was heavy and incessant. Michael's trench coat was no longer of use. Water seeped through the seams, then through his uniform and shirt, forming rivulets on his shoulder blades and arms. He shivered. He hoped this wasn't the beginning of a cold.

—We'll be lucky if we don't catch our deaths from this, Frank, he said to Hawkins.

—Ours is not to ask the reason why, Mick, said Hawkins grinning.

—We've made good time despite this deluge, said Colonel Murphy minutes later, approaching from where he'd been eating.

—Privates Maloney and Murray, run ahead and make contact with the company in the line to see if they've cleared the way to Delville Wood. Be careful, I expect you back here in an hour or so.

—Yes Sir.

Murphy seemed elated. He always showed his best soldiering qualities under duress. He appeared to revel in these circumstances. Was this simply a show for the men? ...a means of keeping their morale up?

—Pour a drop of this into your tea, Lieutenant Hawkins, said Murphy producing a flask of Black & White Whiskey.

—You too Sullivan and Nolan. It'll keep the dampness out.

Even mixed with sweet army tea the scotch packed quite a punch.

Maloney and Murray, accompanied by two guides, returned towards two in the afternoon to report that the advance battalion was within thirty minutes of the Wood. The Battalion paraded by company and marched off to their destination – Delville Wood.

Due west of Montauban, they entered Caterpillar Valley. The rain had turned to a close drenching drizzle now. The entire valley was inundated with flash floods - completely waterlogged.

The company was quickly caked in mud above their ankles. Shells were dropping haphazardly about the valley, spirals of smoke spread upward mixing with the drizzle. As they turned right and upwards towards Green Dump they heard a threatening whisper. This quickly became a deafening roar. Jesus Christ! It was on top of them! Michael dove forward.

He felt Malone's head hit his boots, saw black soot shoot up ten feet away and felt his ears might burst because of the thunderous crash. The air was full of clods, stones, and twigs.

Michael gagged on the stink of cordite and explosives. Something hit him hard on the right arm.

—Jesus Fucking Christ! he shouted.

The pain was excruciating. He quickly checked to see if his arm was broken. Happily, it wasn't. He could still move his fingers. A rock as big as his fist lay just beside him.

—Keep moving, men. Keep moving, shouted Murphy urgently.

They scrambled up and hurried on.

Green Dump had always been an unhealthy spot and was particularly so that day. Shells were falling all round them. Fortunately, the enemy hadn't got the correct range, as a direct hit would have caused tremendous carnage among the halted companies. Captain Palin and Smith, the Regimental Sergeant Major, gave each man two hand-grenades and two empty sandbags.

—God, will you look at that, Mick? said Sergeant Malone as they moved off single file up the ridge.

An optimist had pitched an ancient bell tent beside the arms dump. It still had the semblance of a tent, but was riddled with bullet holes.

—In a way it represents us, Tommy. We survive. We'll get through this.

The Battalion took over the support line on the crest of the ridge from the 4th Battalion Middlesex Regiment. To their right the remains of Delville Wood were under heavy bombardment. The dug-outs on this line were plentiful and deep. Since they had been built by the enemy, all faced the wrong way. The trench itself was in good shape and had well-re-vetted parapets. Gas sentries were posted. The rain finally stopped, so Michael, Malone, and the men stripped and tried to dry their sodden uniforms. Wearing shirt, tie and trousers, Michael and Hawkins met Captain Palin in a captured dug-out.

–Sullivan, Hawkins - be prepared for a full-scale attack later tonight. The enemy must continue their offensive. They'd be foolish to ease up on the pressure now, he said wearily.

–Yes, we expect you're right Sir. The men will be prepared.

Michael managed to catch a few moments of sleep on the steps of another dug-out. The actual dug-out was decidedly unhealthy as it contained a number of putrefying enemy corpses.

The expected attack didn't materialize. Michael caught a few more hours of sleep.

Michael was roused by the enemy shelling Delville Wood.

Michael's C Company, on the western approach, nearest the wood, came under heavy fire. Sergeant Sheridan and one soldier were severely wounded. Towards eleven o'clock the shelling became infernal. Michael's stomach heaved. It was good that he'd only had some sweet tea as breakfast. Regimental Sergeant Major Kerrigan of the 13 Middlesex Regiment walked along the top of the parapets, yelling that his regiment was retiring. Had Kerrigan gone bonkers? wondered Michael. Minutes later Captain Palin came by and gave the order to form up. His information was that the 13th Middlesex had given ground. The units holding the front line were the Sussex and the Middlesex. The Leinsters had been in support and the 7th Northamptons in reserve.

–Sullivan, the enemy is in the Middlesex trench and have bombed them back into Delville Wood. I want your platoon and the rest of my company to go to the head of the communication trench now, said Palin in an urgent voice. Colonel Murphy is there and will give you further instructions.

The shelling was intense; a number of casualties were streaming back. Soon the small dressing station in the line was overcrowded. Father Doyle ministered there. Hearing that Michael's company were going in line, Father Doyle insisted on joining them and reporting to the Commanding Officer.

Colonel Murphy crouched at the head of the communications trench. He had his field glasses in use and was studying the ridge where Longueval stood. *What a really brave man; he leads by example*, thought Michael.

–Ah, Sullivan, he said. Glad you're here. I want you and your men to report to the commanding officer of the 9th Sussex. You'll probably find him near those shattered trees over there.
You'll take your orders from him. You and your men will be directed to make

effective use of the extra Mill's bombs you've been issued to attack and push back the German line.

Michael nodded, and then waved his men forward. They moved quite slowly. Among them they were carrying ten heavy boxes of Mills bombs. Two men carried each box. Father Doyle blessed the men as they scaled the top of the trench. They had to go through a small ravine to get to the ridge and Longueval. The enemy was shelling the area with really large shells.

There was a communication trench, but Michael chose not to use it. It was full of the walking wounded trying to reach the nearest clearing station. The going was slow. In crouch position, hampered by the boxes of bombs, Michael and the men seemed to take one step back for every two forward. Smoke from enemy shelling acted as cover. They made the most of it.

Through all the noise and confusion Michael used his whistle sparingly to direct the men. Away to the rear, stood the intrepid Colonel Murphy.

Michael's platoon continued to follow him. Arriving at a trench on the ridge he indicated a halt. So far so good. The men really needed this pause, he thought, taking a drink from his water flask.

The rest of C Company now came up, with Nolan's platoon leading, and halted at a trench called Pont Street. Across to his right, Michael saw khaki-clad figures running back from the southern end of Delville Wood and through Longueval. It must be really hell over there, he thought.

Under a hail of rifle and small arms fire, they scrambled up a small slope and into a shallow communications trench. Michael's breath was coming in short quick gasps. His face and body were bathed in sweat, but he had to hang on.

From the ridge, through breaks in the smoke cover, he could just make out the forward positions in a disconnected line due west of Delville Wood. They made their way towards them, taking advantage of the smoke and all available cover. When they arrived, the 9th Sussex under the command of their CO were already in place. Their exact position was at the junction of an area code-named Plum Street and Chesney Walk.

—Lieutenant Sullivan, said the Sussex CO, I want you to advance up Plum Street and bomb the enemy. Use Mills bombs, rifle fire everything you've got! They penetrated our network of trenches forty minutes ago.
They're at that T-junction at the end of this system in great strength.

Michael had no time to feel fear. He had a job to do. His goal was to drive out the enemy, with the least sacrifice of his own troops. His orders were clear: he was to blast the Germans from their pocket in Orchard Street by bombing them out.

—Right lads, bombers in front, then bayonets, then carriers. Let's go.

He placed himself third in line. With bent heads they advanced into the trench called Plum Street, which was at right angles to the enemy strong point. They advanced with extreme caution knowing that one hundred and fifty yards away, on a hillock, stood an enemy post. All along the left-hand side of Plum Street were shattered stumps of trees. Twenty yards into their advance they ran smack into an iron gate still upright in the shallow trench. Light shells and bombs rained down on them. They retaliated with hand grenades and small arms fire and managed to dislodge the gate. After a short, sharp exchange, the enemy pulled back. They continued to advance, hugging the ground, crawling on their hands and knees as the trench was completely caved in. Behind him, Private Mallon cried out. He had a flesh wound which he quickly bandaged. Like a swarm of wasps, rifle bullets whistled over their heads.

The screen they'd laid down with their smoke bombs was dissipating. The platoon now had the advantage of a little cover from a flattened-out traverse. To cover the advance Michael directed two men to watch the enemy from two shell holes on either side of the communication trench and shoot as many as possible. The two took up position, but had only fired a few rounds before being killed. As Michael and the platoon crawled ahead, rifle fire continued to rain down on them. Then suddenly he felt a very sharp pain at the back of his neck.

Had he been hit? No. A bullet had hit a large stone in the trench wall to his right, driving splinters towards his body. Fuck it! Fuck the pain! They had a job to do. He had to persevere.

The platoon was out of bombing range. They watched as the enemy bid a hasty retreat at the head of the communication trench. Rising to crouch position they sent a hail of rifle fire at the remaining opponents. A couple of their platoon cried out in pain; their comrades dragged them to safety. Simultaneously, an enemy Maxim gun opened up on them. Six of Michael's men died instantly. There was absolutely no question of further advance! The bodies of the slain men lay just ahead of them blood flowing from their wounds mingling with the marl and clay of the trench.

—It's suicide to continue, lads. Fall back to reserve lines, ordered Michael.

In this action he'd lost twelve good men, all killed by sniper or machine gun fire. His colleague, Lieutenant Crowe from B Company, with his platoon, joined up the remains of Michael's platoon. Together Michael and Crowe returned to the Pont Street trench to join with another two platoons and assemble at Sussex headquarters. Michael and Crowe had reached there without further casualties.

Back areas were under continuous heavy shelling. There were a lot of stretcher-cases in the deeper trenches waiting for darkness and evacuation.

They were allotted Bulge Trench, a series of connected shell-holes on the edge of Delville Wood. To get there they all had to run the gauntlet. One by one, each member of the platoon ran from shell hole to shell hole, bullets whizzing past and slapping the earth on all sides. Leinster and Sussex corpses lay everywhere. Michael shuddered. In a fold of ground, he saw two men sitting bolt upright - they looked pale but alive. Then he saw that their half-open mouths were full of black flies. He knew this sight would haunt him to his dying day.

It was a little after six in the evening when they completed the manoeuvre. Even with two extra platoons their strength was wavering. The shells now falling had a chirruping sound and landed behind them with a soft plop.

–Oh, Jesus, it was gas.
Adjust Gas Helmets now! Michael shouted.

The shells continued to land in the wood to their right. The yellow mist tended to drift towards them, as their trench, Bulge Trench, was in a hollow. Delville Wood remained under heavy fire. It was strange that allied guns were silent.

The other Companies of the Battalion engaged in bombing attacks throughout the night of August 31st. C Company, under the command of Captain Palin, attacked successfully and regained the left position of the original line. At ten that morning, A Company, who were immediately to B Company's and Michael's left, continued the advance into the part of Plum Street still occupied by the Germans.

They were unsuccessful. One of their officers, Lieutenant O'Connor, who had done basic training with Michael, died in the attack.

Towards four that afternoon there was a sudden lull in combat. To Michael this seemed odd. Artillery, machine-guns, and snipers seemed to pause for breath. Suddenly the stillness was broken by the crisp bark of an exploding bomb. Michael, Sergeant Malone, and all of C Company looked left to the ridge which B Company held. A khaki figure without a steel helmet was hurling grenades at rapid speed into an enemy advance post. The figure fell, but quickly regained its footing, continuing to toss grenades. The figure then became enveloped in smoke, screening it from view. Smoke clearing, revealed the figure still advancing and tossing Mills bombs. An enemy machine-gun opened up with deadly accuracy.

The fearless bomber fell and disappeared into a shell-hole.

–God, it looks like he bought it this time, Mick, said Sergeant Malone.

No one seemed to know who the hero was.

—He's one of B Company, for certain, and a reckless but brave man, said Michael.

Enemy planes were flying over less than a hundred feet above them, along the edges of Delville Wood. They didn't fire. They were observing and making reconnaissance, with a view to a new attack.

At five, British guns began a brief bombardment. Then the 3rd Rifle brigade and 8th Battalion of The Buffs attacked in full view of C Company.

—Hip, hip hooray! cheered Michael and his platoon as the Buffs advanced.

They fired rapidly their guns at high port position. The enemy ran like a pack of rabbits.

This attack was a perfect manoeuvre. The Buffs advanced steadily in perfect waves. Enemy shells burst among them, taking a toll. Yet there was no hesitation except in the rear, where stretcher-bearers dodged about, picking up the wounded. Throughout the attack, enemy artillery was active. Michael's platoon and the rest in C Company, and the outer edge of Delville Wood, were hit ferociously. However, spirits were high because of the forward gains. The 3rd Rifle Brigade and 8th Buffs took many casualties, but regained the line.

At dusk Michael again heard the chitter and soft plop of gas shells. He immediately gave the order to don masks. Too late. He and several of the men inhaled some gas.

They coughed, gasped, spluttered, and felt light-headed and nauseous. Several men pulled furiously at their masks trying to remove them.

—Jesus, Tierney and Mallon, for God's sake don't do that, he shouted.

He fired a warning shot in their direction. Neither quite understood. Tierney fell to the bottom of the trench, green bile spewing from his lips. He was unconscious within seconds, dead a few minutes later. Mallon, gasping and vomiting inside his mask, held on. Twenty minutes later, seeing the gas clouds sink towards the bottom of their trench, Michael gave the order to remove masks.

Because of the action and enemy fire, their ration party failed to get through. The men had already used their iron rations. Malone had them brew up some tea.

—At least it's wet and will sustain us a little, Lieutenant Sullivan, he said loudly.

—Right you are, Sergeant Malone. I wish there was something I could do.

—It's not your doing, Sir. It's the war.

The next day dawned hazy and hot. The gas of the evening before had mostly dispersed, but lingered in shell-holes and the bottom of their trench. As it was necessary to make contact with the unit on their right side, Michael set out at a run with Lieutenant Crowe. Two enemy aircraft flying low came up on their left, shooting on them with machine guns.

Jesus get me through this, prayed Michael, throwing himself forward on the ground.

Bullets ripped the earth, raising clouds of pink dust. After a very long pause, hearing the sound of aircraft grow fainter, he and Crowe picked themselves up, and after what seemed like an eternity reached B Company's trench.

–Sullivan! you, Crowe, and the men have been doing a great work. Excellent, said Murphy, beads of sweat glistening on his freckled forehead. I'm proud of their performance and will be mentioning them in dispatches.

–Thank you Colonel, said Michael. My platoon performed with great courage yesterday. My only regret is that I lost so many men.

–That's none of your doing, Sullivan. I want no regrets. We're in this fight to win and win we will. All going well, we'll be relieved this evening. Carry on and continue this fight.

Running the gauntlet a second time, Michael and Crowe returned to their units. Enemy aircraft were still active, dropping flares to mark shelling locations for their artillery. These were immediately followed by a salvo of shells.

Shells continued to fall on the outer lip of Delville Wood. The wood no longer provided any cover. It was a smoking confusion of shell holes and shattered trees.

Towards four o'clock a ration party, coming by the northern edge of the wood near Longueval, were heavily shelled. Sometime later Private O'Neill of B Company reached their trench. He carried a quart of Black & White Whiskey in his knapsack and two pints of water in the pockets of his uniform. He lacked both his helmet and rifle. From his speech and demeanour, it was clear he'd sampled the product. However, Michael and Crowe decided not to put him on report, as the whiskey boosted the men's courage and provided a real boost.

At six that evening, A Company from the 7th Northamptonshire regiment arrived to take over the line. Michael and Crowe wished its officer luck and marched off. Crowe was ahead with half of B Company, while Michael remained and picked up Lieutenant Clancy and part of A Company. By eight o'clock he reported to Brigade Headquarters that their last company had been relieved. Shells followed as they moved towards the rear, but happily, there were no casualties.

Towards nine the three companies reached an old enemy line running along a ridge due South of Mametz. Their bedding rolls had been left for them at this line. Exhausted, they slept under the stars.

Michael woke to the boom of guns a little after eight next morning. Something was afoot a little to the Northeast. It was probably another assault on the key village of Guillemont.

He remembered that they had passed members of their own Seventh Battalion when leaving the line the previous evening, but were too tired to give them any recognition. It would be a hard fight, but hopefully the Seventh would succeed where they had failed, and without too many casualties.

As it was Sunday, Father Doyle said Mass for the men in the field, wearing dun vestments. The men went to communion in large numbers.

Father Doyle used the text *If any man loves me, he will take up his cross daily and follow me* for his homily.

–All you men here to honour the Lord have shown great courage and devotion to duty over this past week. I commend you.
Continue to put your trust in Christ.
He will watch over you and keep you in his loving care.

–You've been pretty brave yourself, Father Willy, said Michael to the middle-aged priest after Mass.

–Oh, it's nothing to the courage the men have shown. If the Battalion is in the thick of it, then it's my place as a priest to be with the men.

–Well, I can tell you every man in the 2nd Leinsters appreciates that Father, and also your prayers for them.

–Will you stop that, Michael Sullivan, you're embarrassing me. I'll see you later today, if you're not moving up the line. I've a flask of Redbreast.
We'll kill it.

–Right you are, Father Willie. See you around seven.

Michael walked back to his dug-out. Looking towards the Northeast, he saw that the sky was teeming with airplanes. They appeared to be bombing enemy positions.

Suddenly whole batteries started shelling. Zero hour must be now, he thought, lighting a cigarette and straining to see the battle. Enemy guns replied, but not intensely.

Then, twenty minutes later, shelling abated. They're at hand to hand fighting now, God help them, he thought as he started another cigarette and descended into the relative cool of his dugout.

The battalion was in reserve and the men were told they might have to move into action at any moment. This would be difficult, as strength was low. The Battalion had been reduced from thirty-nine officers and twelve hundred men five weeks earlier, to nine officers and two hundred and seventy men.

In orders of the day, Colonel Murphy had authorized the men some free time. Many spent the morning cleaning their rifles, brewing up tea, or washing socks and underwear.

Some just lay in the hot sun, smoking or playing cards.

—The Connaught Rangers and our 7th Battalion under Holland have captured their first and second objectives at Guillemont, Mick, Hawkins said excitedly, at a little after five that evening, a field telegram in his hand.

—That's terrific, Frank. Perhaps it's part of a breakthrough.

—Hardly that, Mick. But you know the strategic value of that village from the time we spent in front of it and the number of lives that have been lost trying to capture it.

—Well, I've some idea Frank. Thank God we've finally taken it. You know this is a real cause for celebration.

—We'll have to postpone that 'til later, Mick. We're moving to a camp south of Fricourt. We're to be on the move by six tomorrow morning.

—Well at least we'll be out of it for tonight. I know someone who has a bottle of Redbreast. He's invited me for a drink already. Care to join us?

—I can definitely be persuaded, especially now that there's something to celebrate.

After supper Michael and Hawkins went to Father Doyle's tent.

—Father Willie, you know Frank Hawkins? said Michael.

—O' course I do, Michael. Frank, you're very welcome. Make yourselves comfortable lads.

Father Doyle motioned them to his camp bed and pulled the Redbreast whiskey from his haversack.

—Hold your mugs out there while I pour. What'll we drink to lads?

—The 7th and the good work they did today, said Hawkins.

—The 7th, God bless them, said Michael and Father Willie in unison.

The twelve-year-old whiskey was smooth to the taste. Michael, Hawkins and the genial priest passed the next two hours talking of the possibility of a breakthrough and a quick end to hostilities.

—We'll have to continually pray for that, lads. God is good and will eventually hear our prayers. Goodnight and God keep you both. said Father Willie holding up the flaps of his tent.

—Thanks for your hospitality and good counsel, Father Willie. God keep you too, they said, and set out, walking unsteadily to their tent.

Following breakfast, the regiment prepared to march to Fricourt, and assembled to hear an address by Colonel Murphy.

—Men, in the true tradition of our Regiment, the 7th Battalion commanded by Captain Vincent Holland captured Guillemont village late yesterday. There was some fierce fighting, but aided by the Connaught Rangers, the 7th broke through! Three cheers for the 7th! Hip, hip, hooray! Hip, hip hooray, said Colonel Murphy to the assembled Battalion just before their departure.

The men cheered lustily.

The heat had abated a little from prior days. The men marched with energy and covered the five miles to the camp in a little over an hour. A draft of eighty men from the Royal Irish Battalion joined them at Fricourt. It looked like they might soon return to action.

The Battalion were under canvas again. The weather had turned muggy and dull with a hint of rain.

A steady drizzle moved in overnight. The Battalion was to parade for inspection by the Divisional Commander. It continued to rain as they fell in and formed a hollow square. The draft was on their left flank, well turned out in their new uniforms. Most were wounded veterans returning to service.

The Divisional Commander, Major General Capper, made a short inspection. He then addressed the men.

—Officers and men of the Leinster Regiment 2nd Battalion, I deeply regret your severe losses, but I'm proud of your bravery and valour. Colonel Murphy, Captain Palin and all the junior officers should be really pleased with your courage. I always knew I could depend on the Leinsters, and I know it more than ever now.
Make the most of your time here, since it's probable you'll be moving up the line again this evening.

All day long the expected orders hung over the Battalion like a dark cloud. When the orders hadn't arrived by ten that evening everyone went to bed.

Next morning, orders were received to advance to Dernancourt in the back lines. The Battalion struck camp at two in the afternoon and marched towards Dernancourt. The weather had now turned cold and foggy.

The road was now a quagmire. Their march was broken as they stood by to allow infantry and ammunition columns going to the front to pass. This was standard procedure, and rightly so. Finally arriving at Dernancourt at eight that evening, they broke up into smaller groups and filled several camping sites. They were to be on the march again at dawn, and therefore had an early night.

At four the next morning they marched in darkness from Dernancourt to the railhead. Entraining took more time than usual, as the horses and mules had to be loaded without a platform. In the half-light the rumbling of guns continued.

–Well at least we're moving away from the front, said Hawkins, noting the strain on Michael's face.

–Yes, thank God for that, said Michael with a sigh.

Munition trains moving towards the front, made the journey to Amiens a series of long delays as their troop train was repeatedly diverted to sidings. They finally arrived at Longpré Lès Amiens, a suburb of the city, at eight-forty-five that evening. Detraining was quicker than entraining, and they found their way to an overnight campsite. Towards ten a.m. the next morning they started marching northeast, along endless dusty roads, bordered with familiar poplars, to a hollow surrounded by woods.

Poulainville, the town nestled there, was to be their base. Companies were to be billeted in houses about the village, which seemed peaceful after the carnage of the past month.

Now that they were finally away from the sound of the guns, Michael felt the need to relax. He knew he had miraculously survived the most difficult five weeks of his life.

Better men than he had died. Lavelle, with his puckish sense of humour, and also O'Connor and Siddons. Yet because of luck or providence, he had survived. He had lunch with Father Doyle at the local small bistro.

–Sure we're all in the hands o'God, Michael - he takes care, was the priest's only comment.

The following morning, Friday 8th September, Captain Palin read Battalion orders to the men on parade. When the troops were dismissed, Palin signalled to Michael that they needed to talk. Palin reminded Michael that previously, because of his experience as a banker, he'd been asked to act as Paymaster for C Company.

Michael was pleased that Palin remembered this, and his orders were to proceed with Corporal Sharp to the cashier's office to accept the pay packets, and set up a pay table to distribute their pay to the men. He's also get Sergeant Malone to help them.

The entire company was in the street, waiting to be paid. Michael noticed the restlessness of the men and hurried inside the cashier's office to fetch the money.

A table and army blanket were taken from the house and placed on the footpath along the street. The green felt blanket was smoothed and spread. Sharp went back into the house and returned with two chairs. Sergeant Malone detailed two men as witnesses.

Immediately afterwards, Michael and Sharp settled at the table. Malone called the company to line up in front of the table to attention, and saluted. Michael acknowledged the salute and told the men to stand at ease. Michael, Sharp and Malone began to count the notes and arrange them in bundles.

Sergeant Malone was the first man to be paid, followed by Sergeant Walsh and Sergeant Duffy. The rest of the men were paid in alphabetical order. As each man's name was called, he came forward, saluted, and was ordered to take his cap off so that it could be seen if he needed a haircut. Standing orders stated that the men must have their hair cut very short as a help to medical services, in the event of head wounds. Michael noticed that three of the Company were a bit long-haired and ordered immediate haircuts.

The company were well housed. The men were happy to be out of the line and showed it, engaging in pranks and practical jokes. Lewis Gun classes were held in the town square under some ancient chestnut trees. Sergeant Finnegan, a specialist instructor, joined the company. He took the men to an open field where he had set up straw dummies and led them through bayonet practice. He shouted the usual phrases—*The only good German is a dead German, Get the fucking bastards in the guts then twist and pull.* Michael felt his stomach heave at this phrase. It brought back everything he was trying to forget. He quickly left the area. Late that evening he had a note from Captain Palin, asking if he'd accompany him on a ninety six hour furlough to Paris.

> Lieutenant Sullivan,
> As you're probably aware there has been a change in protocol with regard to furlough in Irish Regiments. Now officers and men are allowed to visit Paris and Pas-de-Calais if they wish. Because of your performance over the last two weeks, and the fact that your recent visit to Ireland was a holiday only in name, Colonel Murphy and I as Adjutant would like you to have the opportunity to visit Paris. A group of officers from assorted regiments leave tomorrow on a ninety-six hour furlough.
> Please come to my quarters for further instructions.
> A.C.S. Palin
> Adjutant 2nd Battalion Leinster Regiment.

Paris. The very name excited him. He remembered how his mother had talked wistfully of a visit she'd made to the city as a young woman, in 1882. This was before the erection of the Eiffel Tower. Now he was finally to visit the City of Light. He finished up the work in hand and went to Battalion Headquarters.

–Sit down, Sullivan, said Palin, indicating a chair. Apart from the trip, I have some good news. Colonel Murphy is happy with your conduct as commander of C Company's leading platoon in the action at Delville Wood. He congratulates you on it and will mention you in dispatches.

–The men behaved very bravely, as I've mentioned in my report. Especially Sergeant Malone and Private Flannery.

–Yes, they'll be mentioned in dispatches particularly, and Flannery will be promoted.

–Fine; Michael heard his voice crack.

He was having trouble keeping his emotions in check. He'd lost half his platoon in this action and remembered their bravery.

–Now, there will be four others joining us on the furlough, Palin continued. I've arranged for a mess cart to bring us to Brigade H.Q. in Abbeville. From there we'll catch a 2:00 p.m. train on to Amiens, and then on to Paris. Can you be ready by noon?

CHAPTER SIXTEEN

Paris, mid-September 1916

Palin had arranged a driver to take them to Brigade headquarters. There they were joined by an officer of the 7th Hussars. At Abbeville three officers of the 7th Northamptons joined their group. The train was crowded with French poilu, French soldiers, but since their seats had been reserved by headquarters they had a compartment pretty much to themselves. *Mefiez-vous, Taisez-vous. Les oreilles ennemies vous écoutent* was plastered on both sides of their compartment.

Palin produced a bottle of Martell Cordon Bleu and asked the steward for the bill of fare, some soda and glasses. There was a good leek and potato soup and escalope of veal on the menu. All five of them decided to have it with dry white wine.

The other officers had been through the crucible of the Somme. They wanted nothing more than to relax.

As the train sped through the countryside, Michael saw farmers harvesting potatoes and turnips, making the best of the weather. One of the Northumberland officers took out a pack of cards and suggested they play whist.

–Oh, great, said Palin. Just the thing to shorten the journey. How about Sullivan and myself against two of you?

–Perfect, said Captain Olson of the Northumberland's, and Johns here, can join us.

–So then it'll be you two against us. But that leaves you out, Crawford.

–Oh, that's all right. I haven't played for years. I have some letters to write in any case.

Michael only knew the game in theory from rule books, but he felt it was better not to say so. The cards came his and Palin's way. The fact that all had consumed a fair amount of alcohol made them enthusiastic players.

Evening sunshine filled La Gare du Nord as the train arrived as scheduled. Picking up his haversack, Palin told him that their first and only duty was to report to the Provost Marshall's office, sign in and then park their luggage at the hotel.

Their journey by taxi from the Provost Marshall's was less than five minutes. Situated on Boulevard Malesherbes, L'Hotel Florida was a small YMCA-run facility.

–Sullivan, you know we're only ten minutes walking distance from Place Vendôme and the Ritz. What I suggest is that we freshen up a little, then go to the bar at the Ritz for a pick-me-up. Then, go to Le Moulin Rouge and see La Miss.

—Who is she, Sir? asked Michael, a little puzzled.

—Why Mistinguett, the greatest star of French cabaret. Her admirers are legion, you know, and having seen her in Les Folies-Bergere when I last visited here in 1912, I can't wait to see her on stage again. You'll adore her, Sullivan. I'll give two to one you fall in love with her.

The subdued lighting in the new bar at the Ritz was reflected in a large ornate mirror. It showed a rectangular room decorated in velvet navy blue wallpaper crowded with officers - British and French. Palin had white wine and soda, Michael a champagne cocktail. He felt the tension of the previous week ease out of him. He was relaxed, not drunk. Conversation with Palin flowed easily. Pascal, the elderly barman, complimented him "for holding so many, for one so young." Impressed by Pascal's attentiveness Michael gave a fifteen percent tip.

Palin hailed a taxi to take them to Montmartre.

—Somehow, I expected the lights of Paris to be a lot brighter Captain, said Michael.

—You forget we're only fifty miles from the front as the crow flies, Sullivan. A good percentage of the population have been evacuated. Paris is a city at war. But it's still Gay Paree.
Let's explore.

As he entered the cabaret restaurant, Michael remembered the poster reproductions he'd seen of the work of Toulouse Lautrec. The high-ceilinged room had private booths in its alcoves and was covered wall-to-ceiling in maroon brocade. A stage with heavy velvet curtains dominated the further end. The floor had more than eighty elegant tables with silver settings and maroon linen. The audience was composed mostly of French and English officers. Following a meal of veal and red *vin du pays*, the French officers became more and more vivacious. Cries of *Garçon, une autre bouteille de champagne!* and *Garçon, quatre cognacs!* rang out on all sides. Then a concerted cry of *Miss, Miss, Miss, on veut Mistinguett* arose amidst the din. Interspersed with a banging of cutlery on glasses, the shouts and cat calls continued for several minutes.

Finally, the velvet drapes at the rear of the oval restaurant parted slightly and a small auburn-haired woman in a cream hip-hugging satin dress walked toward the footlights.

She raised her hands. The hall became hushed.

—It's the great lady herself, whispered Palin.

—*Alors. Bienvenue à tous, a cette magnifique salle de théâtre. J'espere que vous avez bien mangeaient, et que vous allez encore boire du vin ou du cognac.*

Switching to English, the diva continued.

—We're proud that our French volunteers and their English comrades have come here to Le Moulin Rouge. We've prepared a very special programme for you.

She retired quickly behind the curtains.

The screens opened to a depiction of Montmartre with people at sidewalk cafés, walking and browsing on the boulevards. Then, toward the back of the stage, a waif-like creature clad in a torn dress entered. She was accosted by a brutish man. Together they began a rhythmic waltz, brutal and tender, a dance of flight and pursuit. In mime style, the man sometimes struck the gamine, yet she continued to return to him. The rhythm picked up, pulsating through auditorium. The dance movements became more erotic, ending in a soulful embrace.

—That was *La Chaloupée*, a dance Miss developed a few years ago with her partner, Max Dearly, said Palin. Passionate, isn't it?

—Yes, extremely. I see what you mean about Mistinguett, said Michael.

The curtains parted again to reveal a duplicate of Le Moulin Rouge, with tables identical to the ones where they sat, spaced at intervals. Women in costume of the 1890s and men in top hats and formal wear sat at the tables. Some heavily rouged, and scantily clad, women sat at one of the tables. A small man with a sketch pad moved through the crowd.

Michael took him to be Toulouse-Lautrec. Offenbach's *Gaietie Parisienne* filled the theatre. The dance company danced the can-can, the Quadrille and *La Groule*. Then the lights dimmed, and the company had a change of costume. The stage became a huge moving chessboard of Latin couples dancing the tango. Lights dimmed again. The couples wore costumes of the day and danced to the strains of *Alexander's Ragtime Band*. The scene ended, with Mistinguett and her partner, reclining on a park bench after dancing slowly to *Moonlight Bay*.

—In effect, Miss and company have given us the history of this music hall. and music, over the last twenty-five years, in a fifteen minute sequence, said Palin, as the audience erupted in applause.

Then Mistinguett and Dearly danced a poignant sequence to the strains of *After the Ball is Over*. Later Mistinguett sang the enormously popular *Le Cri du Poliu* with its rousing refrain '*Our soldiers in the front, what do they want, a woman!*

A *woman!*' She followed this with *Mon Homme*, and then involved her predominantly English audience in singing *After the Ball* and *Till We Meet Again*. Michael felt the tears flow freely down his cheeks as he sang the verse. He attributed this to the prodigious amount of alcohol he had consumed, or perhaps the poignancy of the words of this song and its memories. He sang:

Smile a while, you kiss me and adieu,
When the clouds roll by I'll come to you.
Then the skies will seem more blue.
When I'm close to you.
Down in Lover's Lane, my dearie...
Wedding bells will ring so merrily.
Every tear will be a memory.
So wait and pray each night for me,
Till we meet again.

—I think perhaps we should leave Captain, he said, as he wiped his eyes.

—Well perhaps we should, Sullivan. It's been a long day. There now, there's nothing to be ashamed of man. We've all got sweethearts or wives at home. Half the audience here have wet eyes. But let's get back to the hotel and have some bicarbonate of soda. I'll show you the sights tomorrow.

Michael luxuriated in the cold stiff linen sheets and down pillows of L'Hotel Florida, a drastic change from the vermin-filled cotton sheets of a day earlier. Exhausted, he was quickly asleep.

The faces of the two grey-clad soldiers he had seen near Delville Wood loomed before his eyes. He knew this was a nightmare, yet he couldn't wake up. He knew he had somehow to get away from that place, or be killed himself.

He awoke suddenly to the sound of a boom. He was in a lather of sweat. The shell sounded like it was less than a hundred yards away. He was wearing pyjamas for the first time since being in Ireland, yet he couldn't remember where he was. Was he still at the front? No, he had travelled to Paris with Captain Palin. He jumped out of bed in the half light, reached for his trousers, and ran for the door. Palin was already in the corridor. -

—Not to worry, Sullivan. That's a Boche long range shell. It fell about a half mile east of us. The enemy use them all the time to demoralize the Parisians. The next one won't be for at least two hours. So go back to bed and get some more rest.

Palin knocked on his door some time later.

—Rise and shine Sullivan, he said, pulling back the heavy brocade curtains.

Brilliant sunshine flooded the room. The sound of morning traffic resonated in Michael's head.

–What time is it Captain? he asked.

–It's eight thirty. You've had three hours extra sleep. Right, we have a heavy day ahead of us. I want to show you all the sights. Paris is a beautiful city, even in wartime. There's one thing I'd like to make clear, though: We're here on a well-earned break. I don't want to stand on ceremony. So why don't you call me by my first name? It's Colin and I'll call you Michael. Camp and the line are a different matter.

–Thank you Colin.

–So now it's up and at it. Finish your toilet as quickly as possible. We'll have croissants and coffee in one of those sidewalk cafés near here.

As Michael munched on a brioche some forty minutes later, Palin presented his plan for the day. Fresh air and strong coffee had renewed and revived him. He was on furlough in the City of Light with someone who knew the city well. The autumn sun felt warm on his temples and hands. He intended to enjoy the day.

–Right, Michael, did you know we're just round the corner from La Madeleine? I don't suggest that we visit it right away. After all, you'll probably be worshipping there on Sunday.
What I suggest is that we take a bus, or the Metro, to the nearest point of the Eiffel Tower. Go up as far as the second platform. There's a terrific overview of the city from there.
Don't worry, we won't have to climb on foot. There are high-speed lifts.

They decided to walk to Place de la Concorde. The view was tremendous: the square itself, with its Egyptian monuments captured and transported by Napoleon a hundred years earlier, and the broad sweep of the Champs-Elysées stretching all the way to l'Étoile, dominated by L'Arc du Triomphe. There was little traffic on the avenue.

At the Round Point of the avenue, souvenir sellers had set up their stalls.

–Do you wish to buy La Croix de Guerre, enemy armaments, a Boche sabre? they asked aggressively.

Palin and Michael politely replied that these decorations had been earned and that they felt it was wrong to trade in them.

Arriving at L'Arc de Triomphe, they climbed the internal staircase and took in the view from the summit. The whole city lay like an architect's blueprint below them, resplendent in the autumn sunshine.

–It's intricate, isn't it? said Michael.

—Yes, magnificent.

To their left, the Eiffel Tower dominated the skyline.

—Well, we'd best be on our way Michael, said Palin after they'd taken in the view from all angles.

They took an avenue going west and were at the base of the Tower some fifteen minutes later.

— *Je suis desolé, messieurs, mais l'ascenseur est fermé depuis le début de la guerre pour économiser du courant*, said the care-taker.

—Well we've come all this distance, we can't turn back now, can we Colin? said Michael, taking a deep breath.

—No we can't. I'll race you to the top.

—I'll win.

He ran towards the staircase on his right, Palin towards the one on the left.

After climbing a hundred and fifty steps, he got a violent stitch in his side and had to stop for several minutes. Resuming, he climbed the remaining steps slowly.

Palin was waiting for him at the stair exit, observation level.

—You all right, Michael? You look a bit piqued?

—Oh, I'm well Colin, I'm just not as fit as I thought I was.

—Which of us are, after the trials of the last three months? But look at the view. It's ten times better than the view from the Arc.

Telescopes and a description of what they were watching were placed at several points on the platform.

—Look here, Michael. If we go in a clockwise direction, we can see Champs de Mars and L'École Militaire directly in front. Then there are several bridges. I'm sorry I forget their names. If you look to the west, you'll see the Palais de Chaillot. There's L'Arc de Triomphe as we look north, and way north in Montmartre, do you see that mass of granite?

—Yes.

—That's to be a national monument dedicated to Christ. I think it's to be called Le Sacre Coeur. It's been years in the building and work was postponed at the outbreak of hostilities.

It's being built at the highest point in the city. It's a pity construction had to be delayed.

—Yes, even at this level we have all Paris at our feet. Thank you for insisting that we climb the stairs.

The once elegant restaurant at this level was now more of a bistro. They had Coq au vin and talked of their plans for the rest of the day.

—We can't leave Paris without visiting Les Invalides and Napoleon's Tomb. And you know what, Michael?

—What, Colin?

—It's only a little out of our way, as we walk back to the hotel. Then this evening we'll return to the Ritz, or we could explore another part of Montmartre.

—I'm open to either, Colin. In fact, let's do both, if our livers and energy hold up.

—That's the spirit Michael. Well, shall we climb down?

The dome of Les Invalides gleamed magically as they walked across Place Vaupan.

—You know, this was originally a church, used by the last kings of France, said Palin. Then, following Napoleon's death and the return of his body from St. Helena, the government decided to make it into a monument to him.

—Yes, but he was indeed a great man, apart from the Russian Campaign. France could certainly do with his likes right now. The only one who might remotely be compared to him is that General who rallied the French army at Verdun.

—Pétain.

—Yes. He seems like a good man. He respects the ordinary soldier and won't allow him to be abused.

Beneath the three-hundred-foot-high dome, in a crypt of the same circular dimensions, lay the man who had made France a great power. The red porphyry sarcophagus rested on a base of green granite. Around it stood statues of twelve goddesses of victory, with swords on their shoulders. So ends earthly life even for great men, a simple memorial to their deeds while here.

The only thing is to use the time we have as best we can, thought Michael.

He said a brief prayer for the great statesman and for all the comrades he had lost in the last three months. Shafts of sunlight highlighted the sarcophagus and its guardian angels. There were but a few other people in the church.

—Well, what did you think of that Michael? asked Palin as they left the hushed monument.

—It's a sort of defiance of defeat and death. After all, Napoleon was France. He summed up its values in his life and soul.

They were in the main restaurant of the Ritz. The music of a small orchestra vibrated in the background. An aged tenor held a megaphone to his mouth and croaked:

At seventeen he falls in love quite madly
With eyes of tender blue.
At twenty-four he gets it rather badly
With eyes of a different hue

—He's singing the story of my love life, Michael, said Palin. I've been unlucky in love more than once.

—I simply don't believe that Colin. I'm certain there's an English, or perhaps an Anglo-Irish, colleen that has a great love for you.

—There is someone in Midleton. However, she's of your religious persuasion. Her parents are making things quite difficult. I hear from her occasionally and write her at the address of a mutual friend.

—The real thing is how she feels about you, Colin. These religious differences can be reconciled. After all, Anglicanism is very close to Roman Catholicism. Don't give up. Didn't Shakespeare say something about that?

Beneath frescos of Diana and Bacchus, and below large floor-to-ceiling windows, danced a dozen British officers, all with their arms around semi-dressed young women, many of whom had bangs and bobbed hair. The Parisian style for 1916 seemed determined to conceal nothing. Yes, these coquettes were physically beautiful, but could in no way compare to his Virginia. There was a certain hardness in their facial expressions that he couldn't quite understand.

He and Palin were nearing the end of a four-course meal and had consumed almost two bottles of Château Mouton Rothschild 1900.

—You know Michael, 1900 was a vintage year for many French wines, said Palin.

—This is certainly a great Bordeaux Colin. Do you think we should have another bottle?

—Why the devil not!

—You know, the French have come up with a rather nasty term for what we're experiencing now, Michael. They call it *la guerre de luxe.*

—An interesting term Colin. Still, we may as well enjoy it.

He had the strange feeling that someone or something was watching him. He cast a furtive glance through the potted palms on his right and saw a tall blond in the company of an overweight French officer. Everything about her was soft, sinuous, feminine. She was obviously bored. Catching his glance, she held it and gave him a half-smile.

—You know there are available women here, said Palin. Many are girls whose husbands or fiancées have died or are missing in action. Some are members of the oldest profession.
That girl you noticed lost her husband at Verdun. The elderly officer she's entertaining is a relative. Still interested?

—Yes, very. But I'm more or less engaged. How do you know these things anyway?

—Oh, I have my sources. Don't forget this isn't my first wartime visit here. I can introduce you if you wish. We must wait for the right moment. You'd like that, wouldn't you?

—Yes, very much.

He heard the heavy sound of a chair being pulled back and looked again to his right.

—*Tu veux m'excuser un instant, Diane, mais il faut que je lave mes mains. Ça sera pas long.*

—*Mais volontiers, Oncle Paul.*

—Now's our chance Michael, said Palin, rising.

—*Diane, quel plaisir de te revoir,* Palin said, kissing her on both cheeks.

—*Mais comment ça va, Colin? Depuis combien de temps êtes-tu à Paris sans me dire bonjour?*

—*Trente-six heures, Diane, mais j'ai toujours eu l'intention de te revoir. Je te présent mon collègue Michael Sullivan. Nous sommes du même régiment.*
Nous avons fait la guerre ensemble a la Somme.
Je l'amené ici pour un peu de repos et pour voir Paris.

—*Enchanté, Lieutenant.*

Michael kissed her hand. Diane invited them to join her and they continued to talk animatedly in a mixture of French and English. Michael looked at the beautiful vision opposite him.

—*Vous aimeriez dansez, Diane?* he asked, rising.

—*Mais volontiers,* Michael.

Palin also rose, and they excused themselves courteously.

They danced the next three dances, Diane light as a feather in Michael's arms. She told him of her husband Martin's death the previous February and how now, after seven months of mourning, she had decided to resume her life.

—*Les morts sont morts, Michael, et même qu'on regret ça, nous, le vivants, doivent continuer à vivre.*

—I'm glad you feel like that Diane, Michael said softly. I've lost many close friends at Ypres and the Somme. I've never really had time to mourn them properly. But in a way, by trying to stay alive and continuing the struggle, I'm honouring their memory.

The orchestra were playing *La Composita* now. As they moved sensuously to the tango, Michael felt the full length of Diane's body press close to his. Palin was right. This beautiful girl likes me, he reflected, feeling a strong physical response. He wanted to spend the night with her. To forget the horrors of the last three months in her arms; to make passionate love to her until the first birds sang. Then, to have a leisurely breakfast in her room and make love again until noon. He began to feel a sense of guilt; he questioned if he wasn't being untrue to Virginia in simply wanting to spend time with this beautiful person.

—*Tu sais que tu es la plus belle femme ici, Diane,* he said hoarsely.

—*Et tu es le plus beau jeune homme,* Diane replied, smiling.

He asked about her male companion and was told he was her uncle, and late husband's commanding officer.

—*Mais il y'a rien entre nous. Nous sommes juste des amis.*

—*Alors ont peux passer du temps ensemble?*

—*Oui, tu peux m'accompagne après le départ du colonel, mais soyez discret.*

The orchestra were beginning *Moonlight Bay* now and she suggested they return to their table, where her uncle had returned. Diane introduced both Michael and Palin to him.

—*Oncle Paul, il me semble que nous allons visité un restaurant dans le quartier latin un peu plus tard. Tu voulut nous accompagner?* Diane asked.

Explaining that he was already tired and had to travel to Amiens early next morning, her uncle excused himself.

—*Prends soin de toi, Diane,* he said, kissing her.

—*Que le Bon Dieu te garde, Oncle Paul.* Till you return.

Palin ordered a bottle of Mumm's Cordon Rouge and three glasses. They passed another hour in growing giddiness.

—My goodness, it's already eleven thirty, Palin exclaimed as he finished the last of the champagne. You know Michael, I'm really not up to too many late nights

anymore.
I think I'll return to Boulevard Malesherbes.

—*Mais restez avec nous Colin. Ce n'est pas tard,* Diane entreated.

—*Non, merci, Diane. Tu vois que je suis un peu ivre.*

He rose unsteadily.

—Michael, take care of this beautiful lady. I'll see you in the morning or perhaps a tad later. Don't get up. I'll find my own way. You should have a Grand Marnier or Café Cognac together.

—*À bientôt, Colin,* Diane said.

—Be good, old friend, said Michael.

Michael signalled the waiter.

—*Oui monsieur?*

—*Deux Grand Marniers, et la note s'il vous plait.*

They drank their liqueurs slowly, Michael holding Diane's left hand. She smiled warmly, her light blue eyes aglow. He wanted to kiss her, but sensed that this grand restaurant was not the place for open expressions of affection. The restaurant was now almost empty; only two other tables were occupied. He looked furtively at the bill.

It was much less than he'd expected. Palin, the romantic, had paid for everything including the champagne; the only item outstanding was the Grand Marnier. Michael left a five-franc note under the bill, enough to cover the last drinks and a tip.

—*C'est l'heure de partir, Diane,* he said, rising.

—Yes I think so Michael, it's past midnight, she said in slightly accented English.

—But you speak English, said Michael with surprise.

—Yes, several of the nuns in the convent I attended in Nantes were Irish. My parents insisted I study languages in my final years there. I also speak Spanish and some German.

—You really are a wonder, Diane, he said as helped her with her silk wrap.

—One does what one can. Languages are the keys to so much beauty.

—Yes, that's so true.

Two ancient taxis lingered in Place Vendôme. Michael hailed one and held the door open for Diane.

— *J'espère que je peux t'accompagner jusqu'à chez toi,* Diane, he said hesitantly.

—Certainly, Michael. It's near Place Malsherbes, your hotel is about one mile away. Listen, I think it's best we speak in English for the rest of the evening.

—Thank you Diane. It's certainly easier for me.

She leaned close to him and kissed him gently on the lips, He returned her kiss and then kissed her on the neck and cheeks. She put her fingers gently on his lips.

—We're almost at my building, Michael. *Il faut attendre juste un petit moment.*

—*Deux cent Place Malesherbes*, said the elderly driver.

—*Merci mille fois Monsieur*, said Michael giving a two franc tip.

Diane's apartment on the third floor was spacious. The living room was dominated by an ornate mahogany bookcase replete with leather-bound books, a small concert-style walnut piano, chaise-lounge and two brocade easy chairs. An oil portrait of a young man in full formal military uniform filled the wall above a marble-topped fireplace.

—Is that your late husband, Diane?

—Yes that's Pascale, Michael. The portrait was completed late last year.

—He's very handsome.

— *Oui, mais on a rien trouvé de son corps*, Michael. It was a direct hit.

She sobbed, throwing herself into his arms.

—There, there, Diane. I can see that you're still in very great pain. I know it's no comfort, but at least he didn't suffer. You must be very proud of him. He died for peace and his country.

He led her gently to the chaise lounge and held her as she recounted the details of Pascal's death in a small outpost at Bois des Caures on the 21st of February, the first day of the Battle of Verdun. Their position had been hit early that morning. None of his platoon had survived; Diane and Pascal's parents had grieved together. Then in July, Diane had decided to try to resume her life working as *aide infirmière* in a hospital at Port de la Muette in the western part of Paris.

—I work as a volunteer, just six hours a day, and finish at three in the afternoon. Perhaps we could meet then. The hospital is very near Le Bois de Boulogne. I know the weather will be good. We'll enjoy the day. *Maintenant il faut que je dors Michael. Je dois être à l'hôpital à neuf heures. A demain chéri.*

—A *demain chère Diane*, said Michael, kissing her on both cheeks.

Adjusting his uniform he rose and walked to the apartment door. He closed it quietly behind him. It was clear that Diane was still in mourning, yet she was a kind, generous person and could be his muse and guide for the remainder of his all too short leave.

He reached his hotel within ten minutes. Palin was in a deep sleep as he entered their room. Not wishing to disturb him, Michael removed and folded his uniform by the dim light of the open window. Then, pulling back the covers of his bed, he fell immediately asleep.

—Wake up Casanova, said Palin, shaking him next morning. I've strong coffee, fresh croissants, and marmalade here.

—Is it already morning, Colin? asked Michael. His head throbbed, his mouth was dry.

—I thought you might have spent the night with Diane, said Palin.

—No, Colin, she's not really that type of girl. Besides that, she's still mourning the loss of her husband.

—Lieutenant Pascal Du Vivier, a brilliant engineer in civilian life. I knew him slightly before hostilities.

—Yes, and also a brave man who behaved with courage on the day of his death.

—You're not sorry I introduced you two?

—No, on the contrary. She's a beautiful, kind, and thoughtful companion. She does volunteer work in a hospital east of the city. I'm meeting her at three this afternoon. Want to join us?

—You're naive, Michael. Three is always a crowd. Enjoy Diane's company. Let her show you her Paris and have fun. Want the paper? There's good news for a change.

Le Matin, reported on the British successes in Africa, but also on the German capture of Kavala in Greece.

—It took Romania a long time to make up their minds. I believe the Queen has both Boche and British cousins. Thank God they committed to our side. Hopefully it will shorten the war.

—Oh I'm sure it will. Get a move on now. Perhaps we could have a quick look at the Louvre before you have to leave to meet Diane.

—That would be wonderful Colin.

They walked from their hotel to the Louvre in brilliant sunshine. Sand-bags covered the exteriors of most of the structure to a height of eight feet. In spite of this the beauty shone through. Michael was impressed by the sheer size and grandeur of the gallery.

–It was once a palace, but began to fall into ruin after Louis XIV moved the court to Versailles, said Palin. Napoleon restored it and established it as a museum. It's unfortunate that many of the great treasures have been moved because of hostilities, however, many of the great works including the Mona Lisa remain.

–It's truly fantastic, Colin. And these gardens are beautiful.

–We don't have that much time, so why don't we just look at the Renaissance period, and some recent French paintings by Paul Cézanne and August Renoir? They're all in the Grande Galerie.

–Fine, I'll be guided by you.

They marvelled at the freshness and detail of *The Coronation of the Virgin* by Fra Angelico, and spent close to ten minutes enraptured by the *Mona Lisa.*

–It's a much smaller painting than I thought it would be, said Michael. Reproductions don't do it justice.

–No, they really don't. Then there's the question of who the Mona Lisa was.

–What's the best evidence?

–That she was the wife of a wealthy Florentine merchant, although some experts say that that it might be a self-portrait of da Vinci in disguise.

Rembrandt's *Pilgrims at Emmaus* and Vermeer's *The Lacemaker* also impressed them, but it was the realism of Renoir's *Girls at Piano* and *Mademoiselle Legrand* that truly took their breath away.

–It's almost as if the subjects were alive, said Michael. I've never seen painting like this.

–William Orphen and John Lavery are good, said Palin.

–Yes, but they're not in Renoir's league. Not by any measure.

–I agree one hundred percent, Michael. By the way, hadn't we better watch the time? It's one thirty now. You'd need to leave here in about thirty minutes to be in time for your meeting with Diane.

They looked at *Water Lilies* and *Regatta* by Manet and paintings by the troubled van Gogh.

–It's really quite sad so many of these artists were paupers. It's only since their deaths that they've been appreciated, said Palin.

–Perhaps that will change once this war is over, said Michael.

–I do hope so. Goodness, it's time you left. It'll take an hour to cross the city. I'll continue my explorations here. Please give my love to Diane.

–I will indeed Colin. I expect I'll see you sometime this evening.

—You will. Now be good and if you can't be good, you know the rest.

The tram was less than half full. Most of the passengers were factory or munitions workers, their faces fatigued from lack of sleep and the long hours required by the war effort, The munitions workers had sallow yellow faces, a side effect of working with explosives.

Michael again admired the beauty of the city and picked out landmarks he'd read of. He saw a sign for Boulevard Lannes and knew that Port de la Muette was nearby. In fact, it was the terminus. He inquired from the driver as to where the Anglo-French Hospital was and learned that it was just three hundred yards to his right.

Diane had just finished her shift as Michael arrived.

—You've arrived exactly on time, Michael, she said kissing him on both cheeks.

—Oh Diane, you look so beautiful in your uniform, he said.

The uniform was almost completely white, quite a lot different from Virginia's uniform of sky-blue and white.

—*Je ne suis qu'un étudiant*, Michael, an apprentice. Is that correct? There are so many things to learn. I won't be very long. Perhaps you could wait here.

—Yes certainly.

The hospital was formerly the home of a successful medical scientist. He had willed it to the state as a research institute. The grounds contained formal gardens which were now a little overgrown because of lack of labour. Michael sat on an iron bench and read *Le Matin*. The paper said that there was great enthusiasm in Paris because of Romania's successful occupation of Orsova in Hungary. It also reported riots in Hamburg: The authorities were taken by surprise, and before they could intervene crowds had taken over the centre of the city. Only strong military measures succeeded in re-establishing order, Marshal law was now in effect. The demonstration was made because of hunger and in favour of peace.

It was clear the German civilian population were suffering as much as the people of London and southern England, thought Michael, remembering the Zeppelin raids of a week earlier.

He felt it extremely unjust that civilians suffered not only from food shortages and other privations because of hostilities, but directly from shelling and bombings. This all-out warfare had no justification. The question was whether these decisions were made by commanding generals or by politicians. Michael's thoughts were interrupted by the sound of crunching pebbles. He saw that Diane had changed into a light green diaphanous dress. He could see her long lithe body through the chiffon.

–My God you're a vision, Diane, he gasped, his heart pounding. What would you like to do? It's such a beautiful day.

–Well, we're just minutes away from *le bois*. It should be cool there. There are several things I'd like to show you.

–Excellent. It will be lovely to visit places you love, Diane.

–Le Bois de Boulogne is unique, said Diane as they entered. I doubt if you have a similar city park in Ireland.

–Oh, yes we have Diane. The Phoenix Park in Dublin is probably a little smaller, though it contains a zoo, lots of shaded walks, and the Governor General's Residence.

–Yes, but are there amusement areas for children?

–No, apart from the zoo there aren't. Of course there are lots of picnic areas, tennis courts, and football fields, but there isn't an amusement park as such. Oh, I forgot, there's a race course with races throughout the autumn and early winter.
It's beautiful to be here, Diane. Especially with you as my guide.

He kissed her lightly on the cheek. She leaned into the crook of his chest and shoulder. They walked hand in hand through an open area. The long grass had not been cut and had turned to seed.

–The city isn't really able to keep this or any of the parks in order because of the war, said Diane. So many men are in the army. There are two race courses here, L'Hippodrome de Longchamp, where they used to compete for Le Grand Prix de Paris each spring, and L'Hippodrome d'Auteuil, which is more for steeplechases like Aintree.

–How do you know about Aintree, Diane?

–Both Pascal and my father loved horse racing and followed it both here and in England. I don't know if there'll ever be racing here again Michael.

–Of course there will Diane. Of course there will, *quand la guerre est finis.*

–Yes, everyone says that. But when?

–Probably by the end of this year or early next year. Things will go more quickly once the Americans join us.

–They haven't so far.

–Yes, but they will. It's just a question of time. They're already supplying arms to Britain.

Children playing catch ran across their way from time to time. Several other couples, the men nearly all in uniform, walked in the shade of giant oak trees, or towards the café tables near La Porte Maillot.

They walked on a bridle path by the banks of Le Lac Inferieur towards Le Lac Superieur and the village of Saint-Cloud. The foliage was like a canopy above them, blocking out much of the sunlight. About fifty yards behind, four horses and riders cantered two abreast. Suddenly, with a piercing shriek one of the horses reared up, almost toppling its rider.

It then bolted at breakneck speed. Their spurs hitting their steeds sides, the other riders followed at great speed. Michael and Diane moved to one side. The startled steed fled directly beside them, fear filling its eyes. Michael stopped and stood rooted to the spot. The horse was in distress, possibly dying. Where were the enemy? Where? He was surrounded by trees.

The Boche used trees as cover. Where were the Boche? His hands were moist. He felt cold beads of sweat congeal between his shoulder blades. His breath came in quick short gasps. Who was this person beside him? Where was his weapon? Crouching, Michael broke into a run. He had to find cover, some kind of cover. He was on a sunken road; this wasn't enough cover.

He ran off the bridle path and seeing some low briers threw himself beneath them. Enemy shells wouldn't reach him there.

–Michael! shrieked Diane running after him.

Michael seemed extremely distraught, totally different from the gentle humorous man she'd just been accompanying. His cap lay at the base of a tree. She picked it up and continued to run.

–Michael, Michael, she shouted, to no reply.

Eventually she found him, cowering below some briers, his face pale, eyes full of fear, his auburn hair matted and knotted with twigs.

–Michael, Michael, she said, as gently as possible. There was no recognition. She took his hand, and putting pressure on his right arm, helped him stand up. His eyes were still fearful. She had seen some patients in the hospital like this. Sometimes they remained in this state for weeks, but Michael was on leave he'd have to return to his regiment in days. She'd overheard one of the senior nurses say that sometimes pain or another shock helped. Against all her instincts, and with a silent prayer, she summoned her strength and slapped him full in the face. The result was instantaneous: fear seemed to leave Michael's eyes; colour returned to his face.

–Where am I? he said slowly and drowsily, as if awakening from a dream. Diane? I heard a horse shriek as if it were dying. I don't remember anything else.

—*Mais tu es ici avec moi au Bois du Boulogne, Michael. Loin, loin de la Somme. Loin du champs de bataille*, she said cradling his head.

—You need a cognac, she said moments later, taking him gently by the hand towards the bridle path in the direction of a nearby tearoom.

Two Martell Cordon Bleu restored his strength, but he was still agitated.

—The enemy are here, Diane. Don't you see them? They're in the shadows at the back of this bistro, he said in a loud voice.

—They're not, dear, they're not, she replied calmly. Perhaps we should return to your hotel. You've had a lot of excitement today and a good night's sleep would do you good.

—Perhaps, Diane. I'm in your hands.

Diane called the waiter, paid the bill, and asked if the *patron* could find them a taxi.

By sheer chance, Palin was in the lobby of Le Florida when they arrived. Even before Diane spoke he had divined the situation.

—I've seen soldiers and junior officers like this before. Usually after their first time in battle.

A good night's sleep helps, but not always, Diane. Right, Lieutenant Sullivan, you've had a bad break, but nothing a meal and a good night's sleep won't change.

Let's have supper now. Diane will meet us both again tomorrow evening. All right?

—Yes Captain, said Michael slowly. *Au revoir*, Diane. Thank you for all your kindness and for taking such great care of me. À *demain.*

—A *demain, cher Michael*, she replied, moving quickly towards the front door.

Palin ordered a light meal for them both from the limited hotel menu. They finished with cheese and washed everything down with a litre of *vin ordinaire*.

—Goodness, it's after nine, said Palin, as they ate the last of their cheese. Let's just have brandy now. We'll sleep better if we don't have coffee, Sullivan.

—As you say Captain, said Michael wearily.

It had been a long eventful day. He could only remember certain parts of it: the visit to the Louvre, seeing Diane at the hospital where she worked, and the beginning of their walk. Everything else was confused, like a bad dream.

He woke a little after eight next morning, refreshed, and invigorated. His sleep was completely unbroken, his dreams, visions of Virginia and their days in Rosnua.

—Perhaps we should return to the Louvre Michael, said Palin, as they ate their croissants. There's an exhibition of sculptures from the Middle Ages and the Renaissance that I missed yesterday. Then later in the afternoon we could visit La Sainte Chapelle and Notre-Dame. Then we're to meet Diane at about six-thirty. She has planned something of a surprise.

—That would be wonderful Captain. Let's enjoy the day.

—Michael, I thought I told you not to stand on ceremony, and to call me Colin.

—Yes, but what about last evening, you wanted to be addressed by your military rank then.

—You were in shock then Michael. I used military discipline and my rank, as a way of bringing you through it. Thank God it appears to have worked.

—Yes, it has Colin. I feel well today. Listen, I want to apologize. I can't explain what happened.

—There's absolutely no need for that, Michael. We've both been through hell, seen sights and sounds that we'd never thought we'd encounter. We came through it, Michael. We're better men for it. But somewhere or other there's bound to be a toll. I've seen veterans crack under this kind of pressure. Yesterday you had a minor incident of crisis. Tomorrow it may very well be me. Please don't mention this again, Michael. As far as I'm concerned it never happened. You're a brave man and an excellent junior officer. Right? Enough said!

The exhibition was extensive and covered works from France, Switzerland, and Italy. Most of the works were of a religious nature, which puzzled Michael.

—Well, historically, the church was always a patron of the arts, and many of these artists were in fact members of religious orders like Fra Angelico whose work we saw yesterday, said Palin. Then for those who were secular it was a way of making a living.

They reached La Saint-Chapelle just as it was reopening for the afternoon. As in the Louvre and Les Invalides, sandbags were piled to a height of six feet against the exterior walls. Sunlight flooded the upper chapel, highlighting scenes from the Bible.

—What a witness to an age of faith, Colin, said Michael.

—Yes Michael. Prior to the building of Versailles this was the private chapel of kings.

—Could you give me a moment, Colin, said Michael as he spotted the sanctuary lamp to the right of the high altar.

He prayed silently for two minutes.

An organist practised Vidor's *Toccata* as they entered Notre-Dame by its main portico. The sound filled the body of the cathedral, reverberating from the walls. As in La Saint-Chapelle, sunlight flooded the nave, shining through the stained-glass windows. There were only a few worshippers in the massive cathedral, so Michael felt free to walk quickly down the centre aisle to the front aisle to look back at the rose window.

He then turned and looked back towards the rose window dedicated to Mary, with a statue of the Virgin directly in front of it. Palin joined him. They stood transfixed. It had taken years to make this window: probably months to make and place the stained glass in it. What a testament to an age of faith and to man's mission to honour God and His creation. He remembered little of Notre-Dame from his visit of fifteen years earlier save its massive size. He was only eleven at the time. He remembered lighting a candle with his parents at one of the side altars, and how impressed they all were by this tribute in stone to Christ's mother.

—It's more impressive than Westminster Abbey, isn't it Michael? said Palin.

—Yes, I'd say so Colin. Both were built in an age of faith, but this is the more impressive cathedral. There's a great feeling of beauty and light here, the Abbey is more sombre.

—Yes. Do you know it took almost ninety-seven years to complete. Have you seen Chartres? If anything, it has an even greater feeling of brightness. But then this is perhaps France's greatest church. Did you know that all distances from Paris to the borders are measured from Notre Dame's square and that all French roads run towards this church?

—No I didn't. Isn't this unusual given what happened here during the Revolution?

—Yes, but then Napoleon staged his coronation here and in the last century the cathedral was returned to its former preeminent position by both church and state. Let's explore some more.

—Could you excuse me for a moment, Colin? asked Michael noticing an alcove with a bright light burning at eye level.

The blessed sacrament chapel was in simple gothic style, with several small clear windows. Michael remained for less than three minutes, asking God's blessing on the remainder of their stay.

—I expect you've read Hugo's *Hunchback of Notre Dame*, Michael, said Palin as they walked towards the left side of the apse.

—Yes, of course, when I was about fourteen.

—I don't suppose they'd allow us to visit the bell towers, but perhaps they might allow a visit to the level of the rose window.

Walking quickly, Palin found a sacristan and requested permission to mount to this level.

—*Oui, volontiers, mais seulement là-bas*, he indicated the first balcony. *Il y a deux cent marches, faite attention.*

He lit a gas fixture at the entrance to the stairwell. The view of the interior from the choir loft was magnificent. Outside, looking towards the east, Michael saw Île de la Cité and Sainte-Chapelle immediately below him, then the complete length of the Seine, and beyond that Le Bois de Boulogne merging into fertile farmland.

—It's almost as great as the view from the Eiffel Tower Colin, he said.

—Yes, it's a pity we don't have a camera, but then a camera could never do justice to this panorama. It'll be something to tell our grandchildren. Look at these buttresses and gargoyles behind us. Can't you see Quasimodo in that tower above us pouring boiling water on the crowds below?

—Yes, I believe I can Colin. I must re-read the novel. I expect we'll be able to pick up a copy here.

—Probably not in English. Is your French strong enough to read the original?

—Well, I studied the language for four years in secondary school. I do get stuck for a word from time to time. Reading a heroic novel will be a challenge, but what an escape from the war.

—More power to you. Diane is meeting us here in about fifteen minutes so we'd better descend those stairs.

Dressed in a pink taffeta, with an ivory wrap, Diane met them moments later.

—You absolutely take my breath away Diane, said Michael.

He kissed her on both cheeks.

—You're a vision, Diane, said Palin. But why so formal?

—That's part of my surprise, Colin. We're going to a semi-formal event. We'll have to eat quite quickly, as we have to be at this venue at seven forty-five and it's a little after six at present. The theatre is a little north of here. It will take about fifteen minutes to reach it.

—Tell us more Diane, please, pleaded Michael.

—No Michael. Otherwise it won't be a surprise. Now let's eat.

Palin found a bistro near Pont Notre-Dame. They chose veal from the table d'hôte menu and had a half bottle of Rose de Provence. At seven-fifteen they drank their coffee.

Palin asked for the bill and paid it, complimenting the patron on his excellent service.

—We're doing alright on time Diane. Can we walk to this theatre? said Michael.

—No, it's a little too far to walk. It's best we take a taxi.

—Consider it done, Diane, he replied and walked towards the centre of the street.

After a wait of several minutes he managed to flag down a battered landau cab. Though the open car was in need of paint it still had vestiges of its former grandeur. Smiling, Diane whispered their destination to the elderly driver. Within minutes they arrived at a very busy intersection with an enormous greco-roman building filling all of one side.

—Diane, you shouldn't have done this, said Michael and Palin together as she signalled the driver to stop.

Place de L'Opera was a hive of activity, with caleches and taxis arriving on every side.

—*Mais c'est vraiment un plaisir Michael, Colin. Un grand plaisir.*

She took each of them by the arms and quickly crossed to the formal staircase. Apart from some light at the entrance, the building seemed to be in darkness. By the waning sunlight, Michael saw large posters announcing Berthe Lamarre was performing in *Madama Butterfly* by Puccini.

—Oh Diane, what a great souvenir of Paris, he whispered.

—Yes, I'm glad to be able to offer this to you both.

The main foyer of the opera was full to capacity. Officers of all ranks from the allied forces, many in formal uniforms, were much in evidence. Civilians, mostly elderly, were in black tie and tails, their wives in silk gowns. Several people spoke to Diane, enquiring about her parents.

An actor in eighteenth-century costume beat a large formal gong signalling that the performance would shortly begin. Michael, Palin, and Diane mounted the large marble staircase to the atrium.

—I've never seen a theatre like this, said Michael.

He'd once seen a formal room at Dublin Castle, but this foyer alone was almost three times its size. Surprisingly the auditorium, five tiers high of plush red velvet and gold leaf, dominated by an enormous chandelier, was intimate.

Diane had found seats in the centre of the parterre, about twelve rows from the stage.

–How on earth did you manage this, Diane? asked Palin.

–Connections Colin, she replied, smiling.

The houselights dimmed. The pit orchestra played *God Save the King* and followed with *La Marseillaise*. The entire audience joined in on the latter. Then the lights dimmed completely. The grand curtains parted, revealing a light-timbered wooden Japanese-style house surrounded by cherry blossoms in full flower. All were set on a hill overlooking a harbour with an American naval vessel. Pinkerton, played by tenor Alessandro Bonci, entered.

–Oh, I've seen Bonci in *Don Giovanni* at Covent Garden, whispered Palin. He's got the same voice and breath control as our own McCormack.

–Well let's see how he'll do in the unsympathetic part of Pinkerton, said Michael.

To great applause tiny Berthe Lamarre, dressed in a pink kimono, entered as Cio-Cio-San, singing of her wedding day.

–She's from Lorraine. This is her greatest role to date, said Diane.

Suzuki, Cio-Cio-San's maid, was played by contralto Louise Kirkby Lunn, also of Covent Garden. Pinkerton's character as a naval man with a girl in every port is made very clear, yet as evidenced by the love duet at the end of the first act, he seems to genuinely fall for the petite Cio-Cio-San. Michael, Diane and Palin were profoundly moved. Berthe Lamarre took five curtain calls.

–What beautiful music, said Michael. I saw *La Boheme* in Dublin a year ago. The production was beautiful, but not as moving as this.

–*La Boheme* is tragic, but not as tragic as *Butterfly*, said Diane, her eyes sparkling.

–I don't know what Puccini can write to top this; Palin agreed. God really smiled the day this composer was born. He's as great as Verdi.

They had moved back to the atrium and were drinking white wine.

–You know you really are the most beautiful person here, Diane, said Michael.

–Yes, and I've the two most gallant escorts, she replied laughing.

–We'll try to live up to your estimation, said Palin.

–Colin Palin, I've heard rumours about you and some of your amorous adventures. Could they be true? said Diane with mock indignation.

–Diane, these are lies. Lies, I tell you. I'm not a Lothario. I've always treated my paramours with kindness.

A gong sounded and they returned to their seats. The setting was the same as before except that Cio-Cio-San's villa was a little more to centre stage. Three years have passed, Cio-Cio-San still waits for her husband's return. Suzuki shows her the little money they have left and is told to have faith, in the aria *One Fine Day*. The American consul Sharpless comes with a letter from Lieutenant Pinkerton, but before he can read it to them, a marriage broker comes with the latest in a long line of suitors. Cio-Cio-San dismisses the marriage broker immediately, insisting that her American husband has not deserted her.

Tactfully. Sharpless again begins to read the letter, and to suggest that Pinkerton may never return. Cio-Cio-San rushes into the house and picks up her young son, insisting that when Pinkerton knows of his child he'll surely return. Sharpless hasn't the heart to tell Cio-Cio-San of the lieutenant's remarriage.

He leaves. Cio-Cio-San is distraught, but hears the sound of a cannon; taking a spyglass, she sees Pinkerton's ship enter the harbour. Overjoyed, she orders Suzuki to help her place flower petals throughout her house. Then as night falls she begins her vigil.

Again, Michael felt emotional and drained. He saw that Diane was in tears.

—It's just melodrama Diane, he said squeezing her hand.

—I know, Michael. It's just so moving and true.

The last act followed without intermission. As dawn breaks, Suzuki insists that Cio-Cio-San rest. Humming a lullaby to her son, she carries him to another room, then rests herself.

A little later, the consul, Pinkerton, and his American wife Kate, enter. Suzuki realizes who this woman is and agrees to help in breaking the news to Cio-Cio-San. Overcome with remorse, Pinkerton bids an anguished farewell to the scene of his former happiness and rushes away. Cio-Cio-San rushes from her room, expecting to see Pinkerton, but finds only Kate. She quickly realizes the truth, and courageously agrees to give up her son if only the father will return for him. Then, sending Suzuki away, she takes out the dagger with which her father committed suicide so her son is not tormented in his adult years by his mother's abandonment. As she raises the dagger the cowardly Pinkerton is heard calling her name. The curtains close to a reprise of the final chords of *One Fine Day*.

The audience rose as one and applauded for over two minutes. Berthe Lamarre came forward, and took three curtain calls alone; then, accepting a bouquet of red roses, she gestured to Louise Kirkby Lun and Allesandro Bonci to enter. All three took calls together; then the curtains parted completely and the chorus and lesser players came forward and took several more minutes of applause. Michael's hands were sore. His arms were becoming tired.

Finally the house lights came up. Michael and Palin helped Diane with her wrap. Others in their row, still enthralled, picked up their belongings and moved slowly to the aisles.

—Diane, this is one of the greatest experiences of my life, something I'll tell my grandchildren, said Palin. Thank you, thank you. The company here have far more passion than Covent Garden.

—I second everything Colin says, Michael whispered. Everything was superb, especially in comparison to the production I saw of *La Boheme* in Dublin. Puccini's music was especially heavenly. I'll carry this production and this evening with me as long as I live.

—Goodness, it's after eleven, said Palin. Do you have time for a nightcap Diane? It's all very well for Michael and I. We're on furlough and don't have to report for duty until Saturday morning. We keep forgetting about your nursing duties.

—Yes, certainly Colin. We're all still young, and it's too early to say adieu.

Michael found a small sidewalk café at the corner of Boulevard des Capucines and Place de l'Opera and ordered champagne and brie. The weather had turned quite humid; Michael loosened his tie and undid the top button of his shirt.

—It looks like we'll have a thunderstorm in an hour or so, Diane. Still, Colin and I can't complain. We've had perfect weather throughout our stay.

The brie was ripe, the champagne well-chilled.

—Even though it's wartime this is the most enchanting city in the world, Diane. Thank you for being our guide, said Michael. Imagine what's ahead when peace comes.

—Yes I hope so, said Diane. But first the fighting must end. There must be a peace with honour because without that, we'll sow the seeds of future conflicts.

—Of course you're right, Diane. A lasting peace can only be achieved if the Imperial German Forces are treated with dignity. Germany is France's nearest neighbour and should be treated with respect. Don't you think so, Michael?

—Yes, of course. The German people are already suffering greatly because of the naval blockade. Remember that story in *Le Figaro* just the other day about food riots in Hamburg?

Ordinary people in either Germany or Austria didn't vote for this war. I'm sure if they were asked now how they felt about the conflict they'd want their soldiers to come home.

Remember that diary we found some months ago written by an enemy soldier, Colin? He was suffering as much as we were and just wanted to see his wife and children again.

—We all do. Diane, I'm beginning to feel quite tired, and you have an early start tomorrow.
So I think I'll return to the hotel. Tomorrow is our last day here. We must catch a train at eight in the evening. Michael, please see Diane to her apartment. Then I expect you'll return to the hotel later.

—*A bientôt, Diane, et encore merci pour ta gentillesse.*

Rising, Palin kissed Diane and hailed a passing taxi.

Michael reached into the wine cooler and replenished both his and Diane's glass.

—Let's linger a few more minutes, Diane. It's so wonderful being here with you.

Michael leaned into Diane, with his hand on her neck, and kissed her. Her lips were soft and tender. He kissed her deeply. He wanted to be completely alone with her once more. Yet somewhere in the back of his brain, a voice kept saying that it was too soon after Diane's loss, that to try to seduce her now would be unfair to her and utter selfishness on his part. Michael leaned back into his chair.

—Well perhaps we should go in the direction of your apartment Diane, he said. It's after midnight and you have to be up in six hours.

—We can walk home, Michael. I know a shortcut, as you say in English.

Michael settled the bill. Walking arm in arm they turned to the right on Boulevard des Capucines, continued to the right past the imposing bulk of La Madeleine and found the beginning of Boulevard Malesherbes.

—Diane, I feel a little like Lieutenant Pinkerton, Michael said when they reached her apartment. I haven't been completely honest with you. I have a sweetheart back in Ireland.
Like you, she's in nursing. We've been walking out together for over a year now. I'm sorry I wasn't honest earlier.

—*Mais ça ne fait rien*, Michael. I guessed as much. We can be friends. This is my address here.

She gave him a small card from her make up compact. Reaching in the pockets of his uniform, Michael found a note pad and an indelible pencil.

—If you write to me care of this address and regiment of the British Expeditionary Forces, your letter will reach me regardless of where we are on the front. Please write Diane.

Your letters will mean a lot to me. Now I'll say adieu, Diane. I do hope to return. *Merci mille fois.*

Again he kissed her. Then, turning away from her door, he walked resolutely towards his hotel.

—*Michael ce n'est pas adieu. Ce n'est qu'au revoir*, he heard Diane say, her voice breaking.

The weather broke overnight. Rain was persistent, with heavy squalls.

—How should we spend our last day? asked Michael as he and Palin ate breakfast.

—Do you know anything of the sculptor Rodin, Michael?

—Yes, of course.

—Well, there's a museum on rue de Varenne which features his art and that of some of his pupils. It's just beside the church of St. Louis des Invalides. We could spend several hours in the area.

They left their rucksacks with the concierge, then, to save time, took a taxi to the Rodin Museum.

—This is amazing, said Michael as they admired *The Kiss*. It's so lifelike and sensual, It would be interesting to know who posed for it and if they're still alive.

—Oh, they're probably quite old or dead by now.

The museum contained the work of several of Rodin's pupils, including pieces by Camille Claudel.

—This is really wonderful, Colin, said Michael examining one of Claudel's smaller sculptures. Is she a relative of Paul Claudel?

—Yes, his sister. She fell in love with Rodin, but was rejected. I understand she couldn't cope and became eccentric. Paul and her family had to take control of her affairs.
She's now in a private hospital. It's all very sad. So much for great artists.

The rain had eased a little.

—Shall we walk in the gardens, Colin? asked Michael. There are several large works there.

They went through a side door and found the massive *Gate of Hell* and replicas of several sculptures kept in other museums.

—Colin, thank you for suggesting we come here.

—No, it's been a pleasure. The last time I visited here I was quite rushed. It's been good to have had more time. What would you like to do now?

—I know this is difficult Colin, but do you know of a good bookstore? I've read all the books I brought from Ireland.

—Yes, there's a shop on rue de l'Odeon. They have some English books.

The bookstore was in the same area. Palin found it without too much difficulty.

—This is terrific, Colin, said Michael. Here's a copy of Hardy's *Jude the Obscure*, and *Far from the Madding Crowd*. There's even a copy of *Of Human Bondage*.

They spent more than an hour there. Michael bought *Of Human Bondage* and several titles by Joseph Conrad.

—I see you really like Conrad, said Palin.

—Yes. For me he's as great as Tolstoy or Dostoyevsky. His characters are real and he probes the depths of the human spirit. Also, many of his books are set in Cambodia and the Far East, places I'll never see.

—So it's a break from the daily routine at the front.

—Yes. His descriptions of life at sea and the Far East are so vivid that they transport me to those worlds.

—We'll have to move along now Michael. We'll just have time to cross the city, pick up our bags, and get to Gare du Nord. We can eat at the station.

It seemed like the whole French army was in the station when they arrived a little after six. Soldiers were everywhere, some with their wives or girlfriends, others alone.

—I'm famished, said Michael. We'd better eat something now. This train will be so crowded we'll be lucky to get even coffee in the dining car.

The Café de la Gare was very full, but they happened on an efficient waiter and on his recommendation chose the simplest item on the menu: French Sausages and sauerkraut.

—*Il faut une bonne bière avec ça*, said the waiter.

They ordered two liters of Stella Artois and paid the bill at the same time. Despite the weather, the beer was cool and an excellent complement to their meal.

—That's quite a beer Michael, a little lighter than Blanc de Bruges. I suppose it might qualify as a lager, said Palin draining the last of his glass.

—Yes I think it is, Colin. Well we'd best be off. We'll be lucky to find any space on this train.

They managed to stake out a small area in a carriage full of French officers, and slept on their rucksacks.

Chapter Seventeen

Back to the front, October 1916

The regiment had moved to the village of Bienvillers, eleven miles south of Arras. Arriving in Arras at seven thirty in the morning, Palin and Michael found a place in an army transport.

The countryside was only slightly damaged by warfare. They were surrounded by lush fields where harvesting was in full swing. Arriving in Wailly, the roads became rutted and bumpy; the transport made slow headway. L'Alouette, the next village en route, was a shambles. It had been the focal point of the bitterest fighting between the French and Germans.

The inhabitants were long evacuated; trench rats and other vermin had swarmed in. Most of the houses were red brick, built some fifty years earlier; walls and roof-tiles were of the same faded terra-cotta; surrounded by the dark green of elms, the view was tranquil and pleasant.

Arriving in Bienvillers, Palin and Michael made their way to battalion HQ to report to Lieutenant Colonel Murphy.

–Perhaps you'd both like to rest up for an hour or two after you've had some breakfast, said Colonel Murphy after they'd reported to him.
We've been here for three days and don't go back in the line for another four. Routine training each day. I know you've both had a relaxing time in Gay Paree. While we prepare to go up the line, make the most of this extra break.

–We will indeed Sir, said Palin.

They found an unoccupied red brick cottage, spread their sleeping bags on the floor of a room partly shaded by a large elm, and slept soundly.

Michael sensed that someone was standing over him and woke with a start. Palin's sleeping bag was neatly folded in the far corner of the room.

–So, I take it you had quite a time in Paris, Michael, said Hawkins with a broad smile.

–Paris is Paris, Hawk. Even in wartime. Palin knows the city well and was an excellent guide.

–Had any little adventures?

–Yes, one. I'd rather not go into details. Suffice it to say that I remained a gentleman.

–I'd never doubt that. Can't you give some details? Palin told me that Mistinguett was on stage.

—Yes, we saw her at Le Moulin Rouge. She's a great artist and a patriot. The audience applauded for almost ten minutes at the end.
What's happening here?

—Well, we've just received a draft of eighty. They're a mixed bunch. Only thirty are Irish. The rest are from Liverpool or London. They spent the usual week in the Bull Ring, but are still green. Malone has been putting them through their paces and has been tough on them. He's got to be, after what we were through last month. I've just been on manoeuvres with them. They're shaping up all right.

—Good. There's no space for any slackness given what we've been through and are going back to.

—Yes, we're moving up the line in four days.

That evening there were semi-finals in a soccer tournament between soldiers from East Cork and men from other counties. Michael played for the others. His team won, three goals to two.

—Damn it, Hawk. All those East Cork players are in great shape. I felt short of breath several times during the game. We won by a lucky goal, said Michael later.

They were in a small bistro on the outskirts of the village. Sergeant Malone, Corporal Cunningham, and several enlisted men were at the other tables.

—Well, you haven't played for over six weeks, and perhaps you got a bit out of shape while on furlough.

—Perhaps. I've said all I'm going to say about Paris, Hawk. Have another pint?

—Yes, this is almost as good as the beer in Belgium.

—*Patron, c'est quel marque du bière?* asked Hawkins of the elderly owner.

—*C'est Kronenberg, Capitain, de la région de Alsace. C'est comme une bière Boche.*

—That explains everything, Mick. The French in the Alsace/Lorraine region follow the same brewing process as the Bavarians.

—Yes, and the hops and the malting techniques are probably not that different than in Flanders. Remember how a lot of the lads got involved in hop picking near Poperinghe this time last year?

—Yes and ended up with a few free firkins of beer by way of payment. The Ulster battalion got a bit out of hand.

—Yes, they broke up a bar trying to get free beer after the owners had run out of change. The top brass had to be diplomatic there.

—Yes, they calculated what was owing and paid le patron some cash and the balance in horse manure. They gave him about half a ton.

—That proved acceptable?

—Yes, they're farmers as well as shopkeepers. They've little or no manure now because of hostilities. Horse manure works well in the loamy soil of Belgium.

The following day was spent in short rushes, rapid fire on the rifle range, Mills bombs training, and hand-to-hand combat.

—Goddamn it lads! Show some gumption! Me grannie could do better than you lot, said Malone in mock frustration.

Privately he felt the new recruits were shaping up well.

Following a five-mile route march Michael felt suddenly tired. He made excuses to Palin, Hawkins, and Nolan and retired early.

He felt pressure on his right shoulder and awoke instantly. Everything was pitch black in his billet except for a stream of light from a hand-held carbide torch. Gradually he discerned a shadowy form.

—Lieutenant Sullivan, you're to form a squad with Sergeant Malone and your most trusted men for an operation two miles from here. Secrecy is of utmost importance both now and later. Understood?

—Yes Captain Palin, said Michael, buttoning the top of his uniform.

He knew he'd have no trouble in getting a squad of trusted men together, but questioned what the reason for the secrecy was. Palin wouldn't have emphasized it if the operation was not of great importance.

—You know where Malone is billeted?

—Yes, I do sir.

—Go there, but wake only him.

—Tommy, I need you and six men for a special mission, said Michael, moments later.

Malone chose Corporal Cunningham and battle-hardened Privates O'Riordan and Mullins as part of the squad. They reported to Palin.

—Men, you're required to do one of the most difficult duties you'll ever perform as members of the armed forces, said Palin in the village square. You're to proceed as quietly as possible to Souastre three miles from here; you don't need your weapons. There you'll meet a stick from the 7th Leinster Battalion with a prisoner in custody. You must reach Souastre before four hundred hours, as you have a difficult job to perform at exactly four hundred hours, fifteen minutes. No one is to talk of this now or in the future. Understood?

—Yes sir, all responded.

Looking at map coordinates from time to time, they proceeded southwesterly in complete silence. The sky was starless, lit only by a red glow in the east. As a group they proceeded by a narrow muddy road for forty minutes. They made good time and reached the town square of Souastre at three- fifty hours. An athletic man wearing captain's insignia awaited.

—I'm Stephen Gwynn of the 7th Battalion, he said quietly. We have a prisoner, PFC Michael Butler, in custody. Proceed this way.

Michael, Malone, and the rest of the squad followed. The dark streets were heavily rutted. They stumbled along for almost five hundred yards. Captain Gwynn turned sharply to the left. They found themselves in a semi-enclosed courtyard. In front of them were four stacks of rifles, three to a stack.

—Attention, said Gwynn.

Michael sensed the tension in the captain's voice.

—Unpile arms.

Each soldier in the squad including Malone and Michael took a rifle.

—Men, you are here on a very solemn duty. You have been selected as a firing squad for the execution of a soldier, who having been found guilty of a grievous crime against King and Country, has been regularly and duly tried, convicted, and sentenced to be shot at four hundred hours fifteen this date. This sentence has been approved by reviewing authority and ordered carried out. It is our duty to carry on with the sentence of the court. There are twelve rifles, one of which contains a blank cartridge. Every man is expected to do his duty and shoot to kill. Take your orders from me.
Squad - 'Shun!

The squad came to attention. Captain Gwynn left. Michael's mind raced, filled with a thousand thoughts. His heart beat rapidly, his knees seemed made of jelly. This was the most difficult thing he'd been ordered to do since his enlistment. Yet he was a serving officer. He'd sworn an oath. He had to honour his commitment.

After standing at attention for what seemed like a day, though in reality it could not have been more than five minutes, Michael heard a low whispering to the rear and footsteps on the stone flagging of the courtyard.

Gwynn reappeared and in a low, but firm voice, ordered:

—About - Turn!

The squad turned. In the grey light of dawn a few yards ahead Michael could make out a brick wall. Against the wall was a dark form with a white square pinned to its breast.

They were supposed to aim at this square. To the right of the form Michael noticed a white spot on the wall. This would be his target. Given what he'd witnessed in Dublin in the Easter Rising, he could not bring himself to shoot a fellow Irishman.

—I serve no King or country but Ireland, shouted this form, standing to attention at his full height.

—Ready! Aim! Fire! commanded Gwynn.

The dark form sank into a huddled heap. Michael saw his bullet hit the whitish spot on the wall; he could see some splinters fly. Someone else had held the rifle containing the blank cartridge. His contained live ammunition. While he supported military discipline and would never know the details of the case, his mind was at ease. At least there was no fellow Irishman's blood on his hands.

—Order - Arms! About - Turn! Pile - Arms! Stand Clear, said Gwynn.

The stacks were re-formed.

—Quick - March! Right - Wheel!

They left the scene of execution behind them. It was now daylight. Gwynn accompanied them. After marching for about five minutes he dismissed them with the following instructions:

—Return alone to your respective companies, and remember, no talking about this affair, or else it will go hard with those who do. Understood, Lieutenant Sullivan?

—Understood, Captain Gwynn.

They marched back to Bienvillers in complete silence. To the east, dawn was breaking, clouds becoming grey then white.

What had caused this volunteer to be sentenced to death? Had he deserted in face of enemy fire? The 7th Leinsters had had a very difficult time at the Somme. True, they had finally taken the strategic village of Guillemont some two weeks earlier. He wondered if that soldier had been affected by the events of the Easter Rising.

There was quite a lot of unrest in mid-May when the ferocity of General Maxwell's response to the rebellion became common knowledge. Perhaps the most heinous miscarriage of military justice was the execution of labour leader James Connolly. The social activist was within days of death from gangrene infected wounds suffered in the armed action. Yet British Military Justice was not to be thwarted. Connolly was propped up in a chair and summarily executed. No wonder Virginia and his family were writing him about new sympathy for extreme republicanism in Ireland. As for himself, he'd given his word to serve the King in the action in Flanders. His word was his bond.

He lay down and tried to sleep. Again, his mind raced; he kept hearing the shout of the executed soldier, the priest rushing forward to bless him and anoint his forehead, lips, and hands.

Well at least the unfortunate bugger had had the comforts of religion. Of course, in order to protect the man's family, he would be listed as killed in action. How many times had he wanted to leave his post himself? Far too many to count on all his fingers. Fighting seemed to be interminable, with no clear victories. Even when they were in support trenches, one or more of their number regularly died from sniper fire. He questioned whether the conflict would ever end, and if the end would be something of a pyrrhic victory. He searched his kit bag, found a flask of Bushmills and drank deeply.

–Rise and shine, Mick. We're going up the line at two this afternoon, said Hawkins shaking his shoulder some ninety minutes later.

–What time is it, Frank? he asked in a sluggish voice.

His head ached. His eyes hurt. He had trouble focusing.

–Nine thirty. Jesus, what the hell has happened to you? You look like death warmed up.

–Oh, I'm all right, Frank. It's just that I've only slept about three hours.

–How's that? said Hawkins, concern in his voice.

–Malone and I had to get a stick together well before dawn for a special action.

–What was that Mick?

–I'm sorry Frank, I'm not at liberty to say. It may be mentioned in the battalion diary or orders of the day.

–One of those top-secret affairs. I understand. Mum's the word. Right, you'd better get with it Mick. Time's passing.

–Yes, I'll shave and have a bowl of oatmeal and some strong tea. That should do it.

–It should indeed. Now get with it, otherwise I'll have to pull rank with a smile in his voice.

They moved out by company at fourteen hundred hours. Colonel Murphy was in good form as the men boarded the transport. London Transport buses, now painted light brown, but still carrying names like High Chapel, Westminster, and Soho on their canvas signs, picked them up. The drivers were French, and knew the lesser roads well. They arrived at Mericourt-L'Abbé at midnight. The weather was quite cold. Billets were not as good as at Bienvillers.

That afternoon they marched to the Citadel halfway between Bray-sur-Somme and Albert, a rest area along the way. Michael was not glad to be under canvas again. Even in his greatcoat and sleeping bag he felt extremely cold. Perhaps they were experiencing the first hoar frost of winter.

Towards five-thirty in the morning, enemy planes flew over their transport wagons, dropping two incendiaries. Fortunately neither exploded.

They went east in the direction of Mametz Woods and Trônes, using cross-country tracks. The men slithered on the higher parts and sunk to the tops of their boots in mud. Transport wagons kept getting stuck and had to be pushed from behind. They left most of the wagons at Carnoy and continued by sunken road to Trônes Wood, a ruin of branchless and fallen trees, broken by shell holes and sodden trenches. Using damp branches as kindling the men huddled around smoky fires and brewed tea. They fell in again at midnight. In pitch blackness and with many stoppages they continued.

The roads were narrow, and carried many French and British ammunition wagons. Their route was by Guillemont and Ginchy, both now just coordinates on a map, having been completely obliterated in earlier offensives.

Night shaded into day. There was no dawn, no brightening, no sunshine. What was once fertile wheat land was now a grey, broken, barren landscape. To their right Leuze Wood, trailing into Bouleaux Wood, seemed less damaged than the woods to the rear. Its main feature was grey-green stubble stippled here and there with chrome-grey shell holes and scarred with shattered trenches. Beyond Ginchy Corner the road became less crowded. They were now able to march in fours. By mid-morning they reached Serpentine Trench, part of the recently captured Flers Line. It was in a hollow between Ginchy and Morval.

A misty cold rain was falling, the ground completely waterlogged. The only real shelter was occupied by artillery, whose field guns were in a line fifty yards to the rear. Nearer was a shack of empty shell boxes, six feet high by five feet long, open on one side. It was better than nothing.

The Battalion had been loaned to the 4th Division, now in action on the Morval–Lesboeufs front. Their mission was to improve the line prior to an attack on a key tactical point on the Perrone-Baupalme road. It was a joint operation with the French. They were to be in support in this attack.

The attack began at exactly zero-two-hundred hours. Again, Michael's eardrums, bursting, marvelled at the savage beauty of the barrage. The majority of shells hit their targets.

The early walking wounded reported that they had secured their objectives. Later accounts were not as good; it appeared that the attack, like many in this same area, had failed. A cold rain began, and continued throughout the predawn gloom. The only relief was by changing posture or shifting weight as one remained in crouch position. The rain continued.

Undaunted, the men slung their macintoshes across the tops of their trenches and broke out their iron rations. Nerves were frayed.

—You goddamn Micks are going to give away our position with your bloody fires, shouted a burley gunner in a Yorkshire accent.

—What about you lot? You're far more exposed than us and your breakfast fires are double ours, countered Moran.

—Perhaps you're right. We're starving here. Nothing like a good fight to increase the appetite. If we're going to get hit we'll be hit.

—That's the way we see it too. We've a hard couple of days ahead of us, said Moran with his mouth full.

The line had only advanced seven miles since they were last there in mid-August. Much of the advance was on a day in mid-September when, in their first use by the British, at Flers-Courcelette during the Battle of the Somme, tanks rolled over everything that didn't get out of the way. The Germans had sent in more troops and withdrawn their lines, favouring strategic positions. The muddy ground created by the wet weather hampered the heavy tanks.

The evening of the 21st September, they were on the move again. Their route was through fields by a beaten track entered about a half-mile behind the village of Morval. Hawkins grabbed the only trench map and raced ahead. The 9th Platoon under Nolan and the 11th Platoon under Michael lost touch with Hawkins in the twilight. As they advanced they met stragglers from the morning's engagement. The men were carrying far too much in equipment and ammunition. They were sinking well over the tops of their boots on the waterlogged track. At the sunken road designated as their reserve position, several men of the Yorkshire Regiment were stuck fast. Michael delegated Prendergast, O'Riordan, and Mullins to assist.

—Hop to it lads, these Yorkies look all in. The sooner ye get them out, the better for us all.

—We'll do our best Sir, said O'Riordan, removing his shoulder bag and pulling out his short entrenching shovel.

A shell burst overhead. Three men from Hawkins's 10th Platoon were badly injured.

Several of Michael's 11th Platoon had been lost. Wet, weary, caked in mud, they arrived at the reserve trench at dawn, knowing they might be called at any time up to one of the support trenches, or indeed the frontline, fire trench.

The Regiment lay ready on a two-company front in relief of the 11th Brigade. A Company were on the right, in the village of 'Slush'. They were in touch with the French 125th Regiment in the adjoining town, 'Antelope'. All the communications about many of these locations, for security purposes, used coded names rather than names from the maps. The French were also to their rear, in Sailly-Saillisel. Michael's C Company was on Hawkins's left, in 'Frosty'. There was quite a gap between them and the 20th Royal Fusiliers in the village of 'Snow'.

The trenches were a maze. All the forward companies had to wend their way around the dead and wounded of the 11th Brigade. There were over two dozen stretcher cases. Since there were no communication trenches, stretcher bearers could only work in dusk and darkness. It took them all night to remove the wounded to the aid stations in the rear.

C company moved up to the fire trench and by daylight the men worked tirelessly to deepen the series of shell-holes serving as trenches marking out the forward line. These were so undefined that at dawn on the 25th, Colonel Murphy and his adjutant, Captain Colin Palin, almost crossed over to the enemy line while inspecting C Company's open side.

—That was a close call Sir, said Michael to Murphy.

—Not to worry Sullivan. It goes with the territory, doesn't it Colin?

—Of course it does, said Palin. Think nothing of it.

While working feverishly to deepen trenches, the men were jumpy and the soldiers defending the parapet fired at anything that moved. O'Riordan was claiming to have shot three Germans in one shell hole when a head was raised in another shell hole, and a tired voice pleaded.

—Don't shoot at me sir. I'm a wounded Hant's of the 11th Brigade.

This soldier was a Newfoundland Colchester and Hant's soldier and they helped him to their trench.

The day continued in deferred expectation of some kind of action while they continued improving the trenches. They were to attack with the French, who fixed an hour, then cancelled it.

Towards nineteen hundred hours, Michael's C Company was withdrawn to the support line so that six-inch howitzers could bombard enemy positions at 'Hazy'. This was in preparation for a combined attack with the French.

The attack was again cancelled. Returning to the front trenches they found them obliterated.

Finally they were ordered to advance against the German trenches. A steady cold drizzle continued to turn the ground very muddy, making each step an effort. As they advanced, shells continued to fall on the German trenches. The noise was horrendous, but somehow Michael was able to block it out as they sheltered in a small dugout.

Prendergast passed with an enormous kettle of tea. Michael raised his enamel cup to his lips only to have it filled with mud displaced by shells. He tried again, finally feeling the scalding mud-flavoured liquid filling his throat and warming him.

The order to go over the top never came, so Michael, leaning against the front of the trench, fell into a waking sleep. He had a vivid, fearful nightmare: someone had grabbed him at the base of his neck and was about to plunge a bayonet into his ribs. He awoke with a start, shouting, punched the assassin's hand and found he had killed a mouse which had run down the front of his shirt to escape the barrage. A cold sweat beaded on his forehead. He needed a drink - whiskey, navy rum, anything.

Late that evening they received orders to build a cruciform strong point at a map reference twenty yards to their right. A cruciform strong point consisted of two trenches, each some twenty yards long, crossing at right-angles in the middle and heavily wired all round. It reminded Michael of a hot-cross bun. They were to hold these trenches with a Lewis gun and the four platoons of C Company manning each quadrant.

They had just deepened and fortified this strong point when they came under heavy sustained fire from German batteries. They decided to move back fifty yards to the support trench at a rush. As they did, an eight-inch shell burst in the open ground between the German and British trenches behind Michael. He heard the explosion and felt as though he'd been punched hard between the shoulder blades. He had been knocked to the ground and could feel he'd received a wound in his backside, and blood was trickling into his eyes. He felt weak.

—Tommy, I've been hit.

He turned towards Tommy. Things were confused.

—Hold on Lieutenant. Hold on. We'll see you through here, shouted Malone.

Malone was standing over him. He'd cut Michael's trousers up to the waist and was applying packing to the deep wound on his backside. The pain Michael had felt between his shoulders was more than just the blast impact; he had a wound there from shrapnel. It was lodged below his right shoulder blade, but the bleeding was limited. The wound on his backside was on the right, very near the back of his testicles. It was the worst pain he'd ever experienced, almost unbearable. He ground his teeth. He had to somehow hang on and remain calm despite the pain.

If he cried out he'd only be making things worse for Malone and the platoon. He lost consciousness. Next, he heard Doctor Morley's voice.

—Jesus, you're a lucky man, Sullivan. Another quarter inch and you'd be singing soprano.

—Christ, clearly I was lucky Doctor, he replied laughing weakly.

With the start of the shelling, Dr. Morley had decided to move closer to the front. He'd come up the line with a stretcher party. The doctor dressed Michael's wound in his backside and gave him a shot of morphine.

—Sullivan, we'll have to probe a bit for the lead near your shoulder blade. It's best we do this at the clearing station. The bullet in your backside hasn't exited. We may not be able to remove it for some time. All right?

—As you say, doctor.

Malone helped the stretcher bearers place him on the litter.

In a drowsy haze, Michael saw the clearing station, a cellar smelling of dried blood, urine, and methylated spirits crowded with groaning wounded. Morley and another doctor moved methodically between cots doing what they could for the injured men. Father Doyle followed behind them offering confession to those who requested it, anointing those whose respiration and pallor indicated that they had died or were about to.

—Would you like to confess Lieutenant Sullivan? he asked.

—Yes Father Willie, he replied semi-consciously.

He confessed as best he could.

—Well now. You're prepared, whatever the outcome. God grant you his peace, said the priest moving to the next litter.

He appeared to be moving in and out of consciousness, his sleep confused. He had a dream of being in a deep dug-out which suffered a direct hit. Covering his face and nose he was frantically trying to claw his way out with his right hand. Encountering heavy timber and earth, he cried.

—Help me. For God's sake help.

Awakening, he saw a pert, dark-haired nurse, a glass of water in her hand, by his stretcher.

—That's just a bad dream, Lieutenant, she said in a gentle Scottish voice, placing a damp towel on his forehead and forcing him to drink.

—You're an angel, nurse, said Michael.

—We'll be moving you by ambulance to Albert later this morning, she said quietly.

The pain of being jolted on a back road near Albert with a shell hole every ten yards woke him. He screamed and was given a morphine tablet. He lost consciousness again.

In the main square of Albert, across from Allied Headquarters, were eight hospital tents with a red cross prominently painted on the roof panels to dissuade enemy bombing. They brought him to the tent nearest to the municipal offices and placed him gently on a corner bed. Both his upper leg and back wounds throbbed. The shooting pain in his backside was just bearable. Presently, the duty doctor came to Michael's bed; he looked as though he hadn't slept for days.

–Can I have something to drink, doctor?

–They have tea with condensed milk.

Michael's stomach convulsed.

–Sorry doctor, I just can't stomach condensed milk.

–I'm afraid there's nothing else.

Tears welled up in Michael's eyes: he expected better of a hospital well behind the lines.

–How about some water?

–Not if it's that boiled stuff.

–It is. We've run out of Perrier and Vichy.

–Perhaps you have some apples or grapes then?

–I haven't seen any for days. I'll check.

He returned ten minutes later with two red apples and a bunch of green grapes.

–Come visit me in Ireland and I'll give you an apple orchard, Doctor, said Michael.

Despite gas heaters in the centre of the bell tent, the next two nights were cold and very uncomfortable. Early on the morning of the third day the doctor returned.

–Doctor, you must send me on to Rouen. This cold weather will kill me, said Michael.

–Stick it out, Lieutenant Sullivan. Your best chance is to lie here and not be moved. You'd not reach the base alive.

–Can't we risk it? I'll be all right, you'll see.

An hour later the doctor returned.

–Well, you'll have it your way. I've just had orders to evacuate every case of the lightly wounded in the hospital, and you'll accompany them. Apparently a Welsh Regiment has really taken a beating at Trônes Wood. All the wounded will be coming down tonight.
We'll need every available bed here. We're taking a calculated risk in your case, but if you're willing, we'll move you.

Michael didn't feel he would die; now it was enough to be recovering from his wounds, with the prospect of returning home.

A senior officer in the next bed gave him news of the battalion.

–The 2nd Leinsters behaved admirably throughout this action. Sometimes it's difficult to work with our esteemed Allies. It appears, however, that all objectives have been taken and secured. They're at rest in Guillemont or what remains of it at present.

Orderlies were afraid to lift him from his stretcher to a bunk on the hospital train to Rouen, for fear of starting a haemorrhage. So they lay the stretcher above the bunk with the handles resting on the head-rail and foot-rail. The long journey was very painful, his back sagged through the stretcher. He couldn't raise his knees to relieve the cramp as the bunk above him was just inches away. A German flying officer with a compound fracture of his leg from a plane crash, groaned and wept without pause. Though the other wounded shouted at him to be quiet, the German continued, keeping everyone awake.

Michael called out to one of the nearby orderlies, saying he wanted to write a letter to his family. The orderly brought Michael an indelible pencil, and a notepad. Michael simply wanted to give his family some reassurance.

I have been wounded, but I am all right.

He addressed the note and gave it to the orderly. It proved to be fortuitous that he sent the letter, as a letter from Colonel Murphy saying that he was gravely wounded, and not expected to live, arrived at the same time. His father, confused, sent a telegram from the RIC barracks in Rosnua asking for clarification, and permission to visit.

After a four-hour journey, Michael found himself in Hospital No.8 at Rouen, Normandy, a stately home high above the town. That evening a very tall, thin, auburn-haired woman in her mid-forties nursed him.

There was something about this beautiful lady: he'd seen either a photograph or portrait of her sometime in the recent past.

–I feel I've seen you before, Michael said.

–My former husband, a native of Westport, was one of the leaders of the Easter Rising. He was executed in early May.

The penny dropped.

–Oh, you're Madame Maude Gonne, Major John MacBride's widow. My deepest sympathy on the loss of such a brave man.

–One has to do something, Lieutenant. I don't disparage what you and so many Irish soldiers do. My daughter Iseult and I live near here. We volunteer at several hospitals. Keep well, Lieutenant. Give my love to Ireland. It's never far from my thoughts.

–Or mine either. As it happens, I was on leave at the time of the take-over of the General Post Office and other buildings last April. One way or another, Ireland will be free very soon.

–*Le cunadh Dé (God willing).* Well, I must leave now Lieutenant. See you again.

–I hope so Madame.

William Butler Yeats's muse, working as volunteer nurse in an army hospital. It was known that she'd lived for many years in Paris. She and her daughter must have left the city late the previous year. Would she get actively involved in the Irish Cause? It remained to be seen.

The following days went quite quickly. The wounds at his shoulder and in his backside now itched continually, as did other smaller wounds.

–The itching means that it's healing, said Dr. Byrne, resident surgeon, the following Friday. I think you'll be able to continue your journey in a couple of days, and be sent back to hospital in London. I want you to eat a full breakfast every day, and everything we lay before you. You've lost an awful lot of weight.

–Of course doctor. I wish the food at the front was as good as here.

–I think the army does its best, Lieutenant. Here we try to help our wounded.

–Certainly, Doctor. Thanks for your care.

Michael inquired about the trip back to London and sent a cable to his Father to tell him he'd soon to be back in England.

```
DR SULLIVAN, OAKLANDS, ROSNUA, QUEENS COUNTY,
FATHER THEY ARE SHIPPING ME BACK TO HOSPITAL IN
LONDON
ARRIVING WATERLOO STATION-DATE TIME TO FOLLOW
STOP MICHAEL
```

Four days later, an army ambulance left the hospital for Calais, with Michael and five other patients. Orderlies carried his stretcher with care onto the towering white hospital ship. The close, cold drizzle was refreshing. It was typical November weather. Michael hoped they'd have a halfway decent crossing as the orderly strapped him into a bunk bed.

Despite squalls and four-foot waves, they made the Calais-Dover crossing in a little over four hours. Quite good time. A fleet of ambulances awaited them at quayside.

CHAPTER EIGHTEEN

London, Kingstown, Dublin, November 1916

He had telegraphed his father that he would be arriving at Waterloo Station, on his way to the hospital. The pathway from the hospital train to waiting ambulances had been roped off. A small crowd waving both Union Jacks and Irish Green Ensign pennants stood behind the barrier. Michael was surprised to see a middle-aged man gesticulating, waving an umbrella, detaching himself from the throng.

It was his father.

–See you at Queen Alexandra Hospital, Son! his father shouted.

The hospital, a regency house loaned to the army for the duration, was in Highgate, well north of the centre of London. Travelling by both the underground and bus, Dr. Sullivan arrived at the hospital at almost the exact time as the ambulance. Partly through his father's influence, Michael was given a private room.

After having his dressings changed and a sit-bath Michael finally was allowed to meet his father.

–I never thought you'd come all the way from Ireland Father, he said, swallowing hard.

–Your Mother insisted I travel here, son. We're so proud of you. You don't seem too much the worse for wear.

–I've some shortness of breath, and haven't walked any distance without assistance since the incident, but the doctors reckon I'm healing well.

–I'm so happy that that seems to be true. Your job now is to take care of yourself and simply recover your strength and health. From what I've heard you've more than done your bit.

–Nonetheless, I think continually of the men much braver than me still fighting over there.

–Have it your way, son. We're still very proud of your conduct. Oh by the way, I've a drop of the Redbreast here. Have a sip.

–Gosh, I don't think I should, Father. The doctors in Albert and Rouen told me to swear off it for now.

–O' course, they're right.
I don't want to tire you, so I'll see you tomorrow afternoon. Get a good night's sleep.

–I will indeed, Father.

The dream was always the same: he was running, running as fast as his legs could take him in an almost collapsed trench. There were dismembered bodies every ten feet, some recognizable, others just fragments. Though he was three feet below the brow of the trench, bullets flew past his head like angry hornets. They smacked into the opposite trench wall sending clods and stones into the acrid air. Finally, rounding a corner, he fell flat on his face into two inches of freezing mud. Gagging, he rolled over on his back and spat spittle and mud.

Corporal Cunningham and Private O'Riordan had followed him. They just managed to keep their balance.

—We've no choice but to withdraw Sir, said the red-haired Corporal.

—You said it, Cunningham.

He woke, unsure of where he was. Painted white ceiling, ornate filigree at the corners, dim winter light from a window, damp linen sheet against his body. Cold sweat beaded his forehead and face, trickled down his back. His heart raced, breath came in short quick gasps. He was out of danger. Where? Wind blew softly through leafless trees. To his right a clock ticked. Five-thirty. He was unsure if it was morning or evening. He heard a rooster crow somewhere. So it was morning. He suddenly remembered that he was in a regency house on the outskirts of London. They would probably bring morning tea at six. His breathing became more regular.

His father arrived towards eleven.

—Did you sleep well son?

—Not too badly Father, he lied.

There was no point in troubling him.

—Well, I've good news Michael. The hospital are releasing you to my custody for the journey from Euston to Holyhead and then to Kingstown. You'll spend four weeks in King George V Hospital for tests and physical therapy. Then, all going well, you'll be allowed home for Christmas. Something to look forward to, son.

—Yes, very much father.

—It's wonderful that you'll be in Virginia's hospital for your treatment. I'll send her a telegram to tell her that that's where we're headed.

```
TO NURSE VIRGINIA MARTIN
C/O THE KING GEORGE V HOSPITAL DUBLIN IRELAND
STOP MICHAEL AND I ARRIVE KINGSTOWN EARLY THIS
AFTERNOON STOP WILL BE MET BY MILITARY
AMBULANCE AND TRANSFER TO YOUR HOSPITAL STOP
```

I MUST LEAVE IMMEDIATELY FOR MARYBOROUGH AND
ROSNUA STOP
AFFECTIONATELY TF SULLIVAN MD STOP

Two army ambulances met them at Kingstown. There were six patients to each ambulance. Except for Michael, everyone in the conveyance was mildly sedated. Two army volunteer nurses had accompanied them. Nurse Muldoon and his father sat in his ambulance.

An industrial building with a broken roof and blackened walls bore signs of the fighting in the recent uprising; apart from this, Kingstown was as he remembered it. The wind was sharp and cold, with weak November sunlight.

Nestled on a wide green plain about three miles from the port, King George V Hospital consisted of a large red-bricked Georgian house, sitting between two large hospital wings. Nurse Muldoon and his father signalled two orderlies to carry his stretcher from the ambulance to the admitting office.

–We're in luck, son, given the number of injured in care here. They've found a bed for you in the rehabilitation wing, said his father. Now, I'll see that you're settled in. Then, if it's all right with you, I'll ask them at the Admittance desk to let Virginia know that you've arrived. I'm sure she'll want to visit you as soon as she has a break, or at the end of her tour today, depending on her duties. I'm sorry, but now that you're settled in, I'll have to rush to Kingsbridge Station and take the first train to Maryborough and Rosnua. I couldn't find anyone to take care of the practice. Many things will have accumulated and of course your Mother will be anxious for all your news.

–That'll be fine, father. As you can see I'm all set here. Everything is bright and clean, a very modern facility. Such a change from the Somme.

–Get plenty of rest, son. Follow every instruction of the specialists here. You've more than done your bit. All you have to do now is rest and get well. Great to have you home again in Ireland, Michael.
I'll be off now.

–God bless you, Father. Give my love to Mother and Brian, said Michael, pulling the stiff linen sheets up to his neck and hearing his voice waver.

Virginia came for a visit early in the evening, after Michael had dinner, and the ward nurse allowed her to sit with him for twenty minutes. She was delighted to see him looking better than she had feared, and gave him a warm kiss and embrace when she had to leave.

–I'll be back to visit you tomorrow, although not sure when. Sleep well.

Heavy rain mixed with hail woke him from a light sleep towards six that evening; his brow was damp, his leg still ached. Breathing was still difficult. He pressed the room bell. A nurse in her early twenties answered.

—Nurse, I'm still having trouble breathing, could you please put an extra pillow behind my back?

—Certainly, Lieutenant Sullivan. May I also bring you some lemonade or apple juice?

—Apple juice would be lovely, nurse. What's your surname, you already know mine?

—It's Coleman, lieutenant. You'll have to call me Nurse Coleman. That's how Sister Daly our head nurse wants it. It's a military hospital. Sister feels that rules work.

—Of course they do Nurse Coleman. Anything that helps maintain discipline in the difficult work you do will help in my recovery and that of the other patients here.

Virginia visited first thing in the morning. He noted now that she looked thinner than he remembered, and a little drawn. Despite the fact that she'd worn a scarf her ash-blond hair was wet. She kissed him. Michael felt a sensation of languorous pressure at the top of his spine; his chest felt tight, his legs weak. He wanted to be completely alone with her, but was conscious of the others in the ward.

—Let me just go for a towel, Michael, Virginia said in a tired voice. As you can see I got wet running the short distance from the bus stop.

—Not to worry, love. I believe there are towels in the drawer under those basins behind you. But first let me look at you. You're a vision. A little thinner than last April, but still a vision. How are things here at the hospital?

—The work is very interesting; mostly surgical cases from the front. Those with facial injuries require many surgeries and skin grafts. It's a whole new type of medicine. I'm learning a lot. As a practical measure we remove all mirrors from the wards.

—Why is this done, love?

—Some patients are horribly disfigured, with broken jawbones and holes where their eyes were. If they were to see their injuries they'd become terribly depressed, even to the point of suicide.
We treated very similar injuries at the North Infirmary in Cork. Especially after the July offensive at the Somme.

—What brought you to King George's? Weren't you happy at the North Infirmary Virginia?

—Yes, I was Michael, but apart from Norah McCarthy and Dr. O'Hara, I hadn't made many friends. Train connections to Sligo and my parents' home are very poor from Cork, so it made sense to move here.

—How often do you get home Virginia?

—About once a month. It's a five-hour journey passing through Athlone, then Roscommon and Longford.

—To get back to your patients, you had patients with similar injuries in the North Infirmary. Did you follow the same procedures regarding mirrors?

—Yes, we did Michael. It was the only way to avoid reminding the men of their terrible injuries.

—So not seeing their reflections is probably best. What about facial hair and shaving?

—We shave them several times a week. We have to be extremely careful given the seriousness of some of the men's facial damage.

—I'm sure you do love. But how is it that you've lost so much weight?

—I might ask the same of you, you imp. It's the war, for God's sake. There are food shortages here. I grab my meals when I can and work nine hours a day, six days a week. I'm usually off on Saturday, but that's not guaranteed.

—So you're making lots of sacrifices too.

—Yes, I suppose so. It's nothing compared to what you and the lads have been through at the Somme and Guillemont.

—It's very hard for me to talk about that, love. It's still very painful. All I can say is that we did our best. As a Regiment, the Leinsters acquitted themselves with honour.

—The newspapers reported some of this, especially Captain Holland's bravery at Guillemont.

—By all accounts he was fearless and deserves his V.C. We've lost what's left of the village since then. It doesn't take away from his feat. But enough about the war love. How are your parents?

—They're well. I was home for two weeks in late September. Father's import business is still doing well. There's difficulty in getting provisions from Scotland because of U-boat activity, most shipments get through.

—Did you get to Rosses Point?

—Yes, we were there for four days. The weather was glorious. There were many fewer people than usual because of the war.

—Naturally love.

Virginia stayed for thirty minutes, then noticing that Michael seemed to be tiring, kissed him quickly and promised to return later in the day.

—Tomorrow is a busy day for us, Michael. We have reconstructive surgery beginning at eight in the morning. . I learn something new every day. However, I have to get at least seven hours sleep, otherwise I'm no use at all.

—Of course love. I'm sure it's intense and precise work. Well, see you this evening. Bye my love.

—All my love, Michael.

Next morning was bright and cold. Michael noticed ice crystals on the window to the left of this bed. At seven thirty, a maid of about fifteen brought him a full Irish breakfast - oatmeal, bacon, eggs, black pudding and strong tea.

—Gosh this is fantastic. Thank you very much, dear. Sorry, I don't know your name.

—It's Monica, Lieutenant.

—Thank you Monica. We'll meet again.

—Of course Sir. I'm here every morning.

He'd just finished his breakfast when a grey-haired nurse of about forty-five approached his bed. She picked up his chart.

—Did you sleep well, Lieutenant Sullivan? she asked in a strong Cork voice.

—Quite well, nurse. Is it Corcoran? He squinted at her name tag.

—Lord, you have great eyesight, Lieutenant. Most soldiers can't read that tag. Right then. My instructions are to bring you to the x-ray department. They'll look at your backside.
Then, depending where that bullet has moved, Surgeon Nolan will remove it. He thinks he'll be able to do this simply by anaesthetizing the whole area. I have a wheelchair here. So simply put on this gown and we'll be off.

—Fine Nurse Corcoran.

The x-ray room was small and lit by two strong bulbs.

—Can you stand up, Lieutenant? Then could you just walk into this booth here. I'll take two x-rays, one from the back where the bullet entered, the other from the front of your groin. Just come in here. It won't be long.

She was as good as her word.

—Now you can sit in your wheelchair again. I'll have the pictures to your doctor as soon as they're available.

An hour later she returned.

—They're quite clear Lieutenant. I'll fetch Surgeon Nolan.

—Lieutenant Sullivan, said a thick-set man of about fifty, moments later. I'm Nolan. These x-rays are clear.
With this good view of where it's lodged, it will be a short procedure to remove it. You'll be anaesthetized. We can't begin physiotherapy until we do this procedure. Are you up for it, Lieutenant?

—Of course Mr. Nolan.

The operation went well. Within an hour, Michael, mildly sedated, was back in his hospital bed.

—We'll have to sleeping on your side with the wounded area raised. Pillows between your legs will prevent you rolling onto it until it heals.

—Thank you Nurse Corcoran. I think I'll sleep a bit now, said Michael groggily.

Virginia visited him late the following evening. She looked a little less drawn than on her first visit.

—We had a light day at the hospital, Michael. A specialist in skin grafts visited from London. He complimented the personnel of King George's on their professionalism and compared us favourably to several hospitals in Britain.

—Great, Virginia. I always knew that medical staff who graduated from Trinity or the College of Surgeons were as good as those from the U.K. It's quite a kudo for you. I hope it means larger budgets.

—Perhaps. Enough about work. Are you strong enough for a tour of the corridors here? I'll help you to your wheelchair. We'll proceed slowly.

—Of course love. I'll have to lean on you to get to the chair.

—Oh, that's fine Michael. I've plenty of practice of supporting patients from my training in Vincent's.

—If you go in the other wards don't make noise Lieutenant, cautioned Nurse Coleman.

—That goes without saying nurse.

There were six other wards similar to his. Most of the patients suffered from leg or arm wounds and were partly mobile. At the very rear of the second floor was a locked ward.

—That's probably for soldiers suffering from shell shock, whispered Virginia. Some have no visible injuries. They simply tremble all the time, or do certain actions over and over again.

Many keep repeating the same phrases over and over. Most have lost the ability to understand language, except for army words of command. They never get through the night without morphine.
They're liable to harm either themselves or others. A doctor Tyrell from Edinburgh is doing a lot of with them.

—How do you know all this, love?

—Oh, he visited the King George about six weeks ago. He's associated with Dr. Rivers of Craiglockhart Hospital outside Edinburgh. Actually Dr. Cameron was a psychiatric resident of The North Infirmary for several weeks in 1915. He and Rivers are fighting to get shell shock seen as a medical condition, not as cowardice.

—And it isn't. I've seen men who were formerly very brave, freeze and become unresponsive when sent up the line too often. I've seen others just begin walking away from the support, or the reserve trench, and continue walking until captured by Military Police in Rouen or Bordeaux. Usually they can't explain their actions apart from saying that they want to go home.

—It's a mess over there?

—It is love. I've seen horrendous things, things too painful to talk about.

—You can talk to me, Michael. I've some training in the matter from both Dr. River's in Cork, Dr. Cameron's lecture, and my work in King George's.

—I know love. It's not that I don't want to confide in you. I will sometime. I'm still only putting these things into some kind of perspective myself. Perhaps we can talk of them later in my visit?

—Yes, there's nothing I'd like more Michael. Perhaps we should go for a sandwich and tea in the cafeteria now.

—Let's.

The cafeteria was near the front entrance.

—Two ham and cheese sandwiches and a large pot of tea dear, said Michael to the waitress.

—Would you like dessert Sir?

—I don't think so dear. We'll let you know.

The surgical wound at the back of Michael's knee healed quickly. Some ten days later Mr. Nolan his surgeon examined him.

—Lieutenant, I think you can begin physiotherapy and exercises to strengthen your knee tomorrow. Take it easy at first. Nothing too strenuous. Be guided by the therapist. I'll see you in a couple of weeks. All right?

—Fine, Mr. Nolan.

Days now followed a fixed routine. Breakfast at 7.30a.m. Massage therapy from 8.30 to 9.15. Exercise on a stationary fixed bicycle at a low tension from 9.15 to 10. Group exercises with several other recovering soldiers from 10 to 11. Then a shower followed by lunch at 11.30. A further period on the exercise bike followed from 1 to 2p.m. In the afternoons he was free to walk in the grounds, read, or write letters. Virginia visited as her schedule permitted.

—Lieutenant Sullivan, you've made excellent progress, said Mr. Nolan in mid-December. We try to let as many of our patients spend Christmas with their families as possible. So I've authorized a pass for you from the 24th of December to 7th of January. We'll give you a checkup again around the 9th, and if that is satisfactory, I'll allow you to spend the remainder of your convalescence at your parents' home in Queen's County. Your father's a doctor isn't he?

—Yes Mr. Nolan.

—Good. Keep up the good work. I'll see you in the New Year. My best to you, and your family.

—Thank you Sir.

Michael told Virginia his good news that evening. They walked, nestled in each other's arms, in a wooded area at the outer limits of the grounds.

—That's really wonderful Michael. I have over Christmas free ...not enough time to visit my parents in Sligo.

—I want to marry you Virginia. It's something that's been in my mind and heart for months. We've been seeing and corresponding with each other for over two years now and have talked regularly about marrying.

—...almost three, dear.

—I love you, Virginia. You're the first person I think of in the morning; the last person at night. I've loved you from the first time I met you at that benefit dance at Palmerston Tennis Club, remember? This is like nothing I've ever known. It's unselfish love, grown up love. You know it is. It's mature, absolute, thrilling love. I've hesitated to ask this leading question because of hostilities and what we're both going through. I can't wait any longer. Will you marry me, dear Virginia? We don't have to wed right away. Hostilities will probably end sometime next summer. We can marry then.

He was conscious that his voice trembled. His hands were moist. Tears welled up in his eyes.

—Of course darling. Of course. I've loved you forever. There's never been anyone else.

She flung herself into his arms, kissing him on the mouth. He responded with equal passion, clinging to her for seconds, minutes. He lost track of time.

—Gosh, you literally take my breath away, love. Perhaps we should go into Wines Jewellers on Grafton Street this coming Monday?

—Yes darling, yes, she sobbed.

—No need for tears, my love. Please no tears.

—These are tears of happiness, you imp. I've never been so happy in my life, she said, her voice still trembling.

—When will you tell your parents, love? Perhaps they could travel to Rosnua for the holidays, said Michael, his voice wavering.

—I'll telephone them once I get back to the Hospital Residence.

—I'll telephone Mother and Father from here, love.

Hugging closely, they walked back to the main entrance. The military orderly directed them to a closed phone-booth at the rear of the hall.

—Can I have long distances charges charged to my account here? asked Michael.

—Certainly, Lieutenant Sullivan.

—Rosnua 42, a person to person call to Doctor and Mrs. Sullivan, said Michael to the operator.

The phone rang four times.

—Rosnua 42, said a female voice.

—Mrs. Sullivan? asked the operator.

—It's my mother, operator, said Michael. Mother, it's Michael. I've wonderful news. Virginia has accepted my proposal of marriage. I'm the happiest man alive. Yes, we're going to Louis Wines on Grafton Street on Monday to pick out a ring. God willing, we'll get married sometime late next year. Is father there? He's on a maternity case? Virginia is with me here, Mother. I'll hand her the phone now.

—Mrs. Sullivan. Yes, I'm so happy. I've loved Michael from the very first time we met. Separation has only deepened my feelings. No, I haven't told my parents yet. I'll telephone this evening.
I'll mention what you're suggesting. I don't think they've any firm plans for the holidays. Perhaps they could telephone you? Grand Mrs. Sullivan. Annie, I'll tell them that. I'll pass you to Michael again.
See you soon.

—Great news, Mother. I'm glad you're happy. I'm over the moon. See you in a few days.

His father arrived in the Model T on the afternoon of Saturday the 23rd. The weather was clear and cold.

—We've decided to treat ourselves and the Martins, Michael, he said. The Royal Marine Hotel, where we stayed last spring, have a special rate for the Christmas period. So, I've booked a two bedroom suite with parlour for us, and a similar suite on a different floor for Virginia and her parents. Mr. and Mrs. Martin are arriving at Amiens Street Station late this afternoon. Virginia will meet them there. Then together they'll continue here by suburban train. They should be at Kingstown Station by seven. I thought you'd be happier here than in one of the city hotels. A lot of the central city is still in ruin. God knows you've seen enough of rubble and destruction.

—That's very true father. Thank you very, very much.

—Think nothing of it, son. We'll have a lovely celebration.

—We will indeed, father.

Michael's father quickly drove the short distance to the fortress like hotel and brought him to their suite.

—Michael, Michael. We were so worried about you, said his mother, kissing him on both cheeks.

—Well, I'm here Mother. Almost as healthy as I was last April. God has been good to me, said Michael trying to control his voice.

—Let me look at you, love, she said holding him at arm's length. A lot thinner, very heavy shadows under your eyes. All things considered you're walking quite well. We'll get you healthy and fit over this weekend and later in Rosnua. Won't we, Tom?

—Of course Annie. All he needs is lots of rest and moderate exercise.

—What do you think of the suite, son?

—Oh, it's beautiful, especially that small Christmas tree in the corner and that upright piano. Is this not the same suite you had in April?

—It is indeed, Michael, except for the addition of the piano and the Christmas tree. The piano is pretty much in tune. I played a little Chopin on it a few minutes ago. Now you and Brian will share a room as you did in spring. Deirdre and Rosemary will have the second bedroom here.

—That's fine, Mother. Where is Brian?

—Well, Castleknock College only broke for the holidays at five yesterday evening. He'll come by bus across the city. We expect him here at about six thirty. Deirdre went out to Rathfarnham to fetch Rosemary. They should arrive here fairly soon. Deirdre is earning a very small salary even though she's still training in the Mater. I think she went out to Rosemary's school by bus, but is taking a hackney cab from there. It's a bit costly, but it saves time. They're both so happy that you're home.

—As am I. It will be great to see them. Well perhaps I'd better go to my room, mother.

—I think it's the same room you had in spring. Father will guide you there.

—You see, Michael, it's the same room with the addition of this Christmas tree, said his father opening the door. Now get yourself installed and come back to our suite as soon as you're set. I'll come along with Brian when he arrives.

—Right you are Father, said Michael giving him a quick hug.

His possessions were few. He placed clean shirts and underwear in the top drawer of the ornate dresser, his army greatcoat and hold-all in the closet, and his toiletry in the large bathroom. Feeling tired, he removed his Sam Brown belt and upper uniform and lay on the bed closest the window.

—May we come in, Michael? said his father knocking softly some twenty minutes later.

—Yes, of course.

He rose quickly and opened the door. His father and younger brother faced him.

—Well, what do you think of Brian? He's even taller isn't he?

—Indeed Father. Let's have a look at you, Brian. You've put on weight. It all appears to be muscle. I expect you're playing a lot of rugby. I hope you enjoy it. It can be a rough game. Give us a hug.

The strong hug showed that Brian's weight gain was indeed muscle.

—Yes, I do enjoy it Michael. I play scrum half and I'm really in the thick of things. I'm part of 'Knock's junior team.
We just beat Clongowes.

—I'll leave you two to catch up, said his father. You know where we are. Come to our suite in a half-hour or so.

—We will, father.

—Do you still enjoy study, Brian?

—Yes. I find Greek difficult. But then so much philosophy begins with the Greeks. I like Latin, especially *The Aeneid*; parts of it are very beautiful.

—Yes, Virgil was one of the great poets. Stick with Latin, Brian. It's the basis of most European languages. It's been quite a help to me, especially since I joined the war effort. My French has improved a lot.

—I'm sure. I got the card you sent from Paris. You appear to have had a great time.

—Yes Captain Palin and I had fun. It's still a beautiful city even though it's only sixty miles from the front. The population behave as normally as possible. Palin and I needed the break after what we'd been through in late August.

—Can you talk about your time at the front Michael?

—I command a platoon of fifty men and much of time has been spent in trenches at the front – often remarkably close to the German front lines. I can say that it was hell on earth in late August. So many painful deaths. Grown men in tears, crying for their mothers as they died. Perhaps I'll be able to describe more details once we win and have peace. Hopefully sometime when the war is over.

—Let's hope there's peace in 1917. We're very proud of what you've been doing in Flanders, and what Jack has been doing at the British military hospital in the Aegean Sea, caring for the wounded from Gallipoli and Salonika. That being said, we want to have you both home.

—Mother and Father have not talked at all about Chris since I arrived, and I can understand that, given the trouble he's put himself in since leaving his position at Hickman's and going on the run; his views of the Rising and Republicanism have put him cross-ways with the British authorities. It's ironic given two of his brothers are fighting for the British.
We can only hope that he's not found and arrested.

—The last I heard from Father was that Chris was somewhere in the wilds of West Cork. The authorities want to question him because of his Sinn Fein sympathies - his views on the Rising and Republicanism have put him in trouble. There's a warrant for his immediate arrest. He has to keep moving

—How does he survive?

—People in the area look out for him and a number of others. He never spends more than a day in any given town.

—I see. I do hope to see him before I have to return to Flanders, but lord knows how he can manage that safely.

—Don't worry, you will Michael. He knows about your injury. He'll find a way of contacting you. He's in touch with our parents every few weeks.

—Good. You know if I continue to do well, the medical people are going to allow me to complete my convalescence in Rosnua.

—Chris will reach you there. Well, perhaps we'd better go to Father's suite.

—Yes, it's time.

Michael put his jacket back on and they went to their parent's suite. Their Mother greeted them.

–Father will have to leave soon to collect Virginia and her parents at Kingstown Station. Why don't you both have tea and cake here? asked their mother.

–That'd be lovely mother, they replied.

The Orange Pekoe tea was strong and refreshing, the strawberry cream sponge cake quite light.

–You made good time across the city, Brian.

–I did mother. I was lucky with the buses and train.

–You were indeed Brian, said their father. Well I'm off. I'm going to allow twenty minutes leeway for the suburban train at Kingstown Station. It's cold and damp down there.
I don't want them to wait. There is no need for you to come, Michael. You're convalescing. The Martins will be three people and probably have a bag each. I may have to place a bag on the back seat. So stay here, Michael. Keep warm. Doctor's orders.

–Right you are, father. See you anon.

–We'll all be back shortly.

Deirdre and Rosemary arrived some moments later.

–We're so happy that you're home again, Michael, said Deirdre. We had some idea what you went through last August. Mother told us of the break you had in Paris. Then you were in thick of it again. I'm just so glad you're here, she said quietly.

–Come here the two o' ye. You know you're always in my thoughts.

Michael hugged them both for several seconds.

–And you Rosemary, you're not so little anymore.

–I've grown an inch and a half in the last six months, Michael. Rathfarnham is a wonderful school as regards our courses. However, since early October it's been very cold inside.
There are drafts in the corridors. All the girls have chill blains. The sisters give us ointments. The sores clear up, but begin again a week or so later if the cold persists.

–A lot of my company in France have chilblains and of course very sore feet. This has been the case for about a month.

–Oh, I'm sorry Michael. Here I am complaining, and I was forgetting completely about what you and all the soldiers go through nearly all the time.

You know the sisters in Loreto Rathfarnham do one Novena after another, praying for peace and all the soldiers at the front.

—Including the Austrians and Germans?

—Yes, of course. They're suffering as much as the Allies.

—Of course they are Rose. The average German soldier is as brave as any of us Allies. They had little choice as to whether or not to join the army. I'm sure most of them don't want to be in France and Flanders. All these decisions were made by Kaiser Wilhelm and his generals. But how do you know so much about the war?

—Oh, Mother Fidelma reads the *Irish Independent* with us each day in European history class and explains the small maps included with the reports.

—She seems to be a gifted teacher.

—She is Michael. She hardly ever talks about herself, but the other students and I think she spent the last year of her secondary education in Belgium; we believe her strong command of French was the result.

—...like your Mother.

—Exactly.

—It's great to have teachers like that. And you Deirdre, are you still working a lot of night shifts? You look tired.

—I've been on night duty for the last two weeks Michael. However, I'm off now and don't have to work again until the 2nd of January.

—Aren't you the lucky duck. So you'll have lots of time to enjoy the Christmas.

—Yes and being with the family, you, the Martins, and Virginia. I hear you have wonderful news for us. Tell, tell.

She lunged at him, tickling him on his left side.

—Michael winced and pulled away. That's the side I was wounded on. You're dealing with an invalid here. If you must, tickle on the other side.

—Oh gosh. Sorry Michael. I completely forgot. Mother did describe your injuries.

—Don't worry, love. It's almost healed at this point. Sit down, why don't you? Have some tea. Do you want a full cup or should I leave room for milk?

—Yes, leave a little room.

His father arrived with Virginia and her parents, some ten minutes later.

—They arrived just as I finished parking at Kingstown station, said Dr. Sullivan. Just great timing, even if I say it myself. Isn't that true, Teddy?

—You said it, Tom.

–You must all be famished. How about a sherry for you and Virginia, Marie? …and a nip of Tullamore Dew for you Teddy? Brian will take your luggage to your suite, won't you Brian?

–Yes, of course Father, said Brian rising.

–Marie and I made good time on the journey up, Annie. Virginia was there to meet and join us at Amiens Street. There was a delay of about ten minutes, then the train continued on.
I expect it's really a boat-train. We didn't have to change trains at all.

–Yes, I think it's one of several trains that connect with the evening mail-boat. So you're surviving the present crisis Teddy? asked Dr. Sullivan.

–I can't complain Tom, except that it takes longer to get supplies from Glasgow and the North of England. It's a bit of a worry.

Michael noticed that both Virginia's parents were greyer than when he last met them almost two years earlier.

–Well, perhaps we should go down for dinner. Teddy, Marie, and Virginia, I'm sure you've got good appetites after your journey.

–We have indeed Tom. Lead the way.

With subdued lighting, a small Christmas tree in the entrance area, and holly and mistletoe sprigs on the tables and on the walls, the dining room was warmer than Michael remembered it. It was about two-thirds full. A piano trio played a mixture of carols and semi classical pieces.

The pretty waitress who served them at Easter remembered them.

–It's Doctor Sullivan isn't it? she asked tentatively.

–Triona isn't it? Are you well?

–Yes, very well doctor, good to see you again. You were with us last Easter …before all the trouble began.

–We were indeed Triona. Well there are even more of us this time. We'll be nine. Perhaps you could find a table for us towards the back of the room.

–With pleasure, doctor. It will be just a brief minute; could you wait here?

–Certainly, dear.

Triona returned as promised. Michael remembered that she was kind and attentive during their last visit.

–There we are, doctor. Here are the menus. If I might, I recommend the sole, either grilled or meunier. We also have a very good steak and kidney pie. The soup of the day is seafood chowder. We also have Dublin Bay Prawn Cocktail as entrée tonight.

—And those prawns were caught late last night or early this morning. Weren't they Triona?

—They were indeed, doctor. I'll be back in a moment.

—Don't go too far, Triona. We'll decide quickly.

Everyone looked at the menu.

—I'm for the chowder and the sole. What about you, Virginia? asked Michael.

—Yes, I'll have the sole with the prawn cocktail.

—Well that's everyone Triona, said Dr. Sullivan.
The steak and kidney pie will be much appreciated by that strong young man over there. Could you also bring two bottles of red wine and two flagons of your best white wine.

—Fine Doctor Sullivan. Enjoy your meal.

—We will, Triona. We will.

Following dinner, they returned to his parents' suite. Someone from hotel housekeeping had turned down his parents' beds and put extra coal on the fire. The living-room had a warm comfortable feel. His father produced bottles of Martell Cordon Bleu and Cointreau.

—A little liqueur to end the evening Marie? he asked Mrs. Martin.

—That would be lovely Tom, she replied. I believe Teddy will have a little brandy. Won't you, Teddy?

—Yes indeed. Tom, how did you manage to procure a VSOP in this time of shortages?

—That'd be telling, Teddy. I've had this cognac for years and been keeping it for an occasion like this. Annie will have Cointreau. I expect you'll have Cointreau as well Virginia?

—I know Michael will have cognac. So that leaves just Deirdre, Rosemary, and Brian. I think the three of you should continue with wine. These liqueurs are strong
...a bit too strong for young people.

—Father, said Deirdre pointedly.

—Yes, I know you're twenty-one Deirdre. But you're better off staying with wine. Trust me, love.

—You know I do Father.

—Michael, smell and taste the Martell first, please. You must be a connoisseur of cognacs at this point ... after your time in Amiens and Paris.

–Hardly Father. A lot of the brandy we've had is really young and raw. You know, the stuff that makes you gasp for breath. However, this is a VSOP, it should be smooth.

The aroma was fruity and strong.

–No need to taste at all, Father. This is absolutely beautiful, like a mid-summer's day.

–Great, son. One can't go wrong with a brand like Martell. Well, good health everyone. Happy Christmas and God's choicest blessings in 1917.

–Amen to that. Again we're so happy to share this holiday with you and your family, Tom and Annie. *Go mbeirfimid beo ar an am seo aris* (That we may live to see this time again next year), said Teddy Martin.

–That's our wish too, Teddy ...and a just end to this terrible war.

Michael's mother asked if they'd like to play cards.

–We can play canasta, or even bridge.

–Oh, that would be wonderful, Annie, said Mrs. Martin.

The vote was to play canasta. Annie produced a double pack of cards and shuffled the two packs together.

–Michael, said Brian, would you like to play chess?

Michael agreed and Brian went to their room, and returned shortly with a chess board and pieces.

–Michael, have your chess skills improved or not? White or black, Michael?

–White Brian. I'm afraid I'm still rusty. We only have a chance to play when we're way behind the lines. The last time I played was over three months ago while I was in a rear area.

–We have a chess club in Castleknock, although I'm in the lower ranks.

–We're well matched, then, said Michael

Brian turned out to be much better than a beginner, and better than Michael. They played several games. Brian was an expert in opening moves and usually had his brother in a defensive position within five minutes. One game ended in stalemate, the others in victory by Brian. Towards ten thirty Michael began to feel very tired. He looked over at his mother engrossed in her card game. She sensed his glance and smiled.

–Are you all right Michael?

–Just a little tired Mother.

–Perhaps you'd better retire then. There's no real bedtime here.

–I don't want to break up the evening.

—You're not doing that, love. Father and I will probably head to bed in a half-hour or so. There's no reason to feel guilty.

—Right then. Goodnight everyone. He kissed Virginia lightly on the cheek.

The next morning was again bright and chilly. They had lunch in The Swan Restaurant near the Pavilion Complex.

—Let's check the film programme at the Complex, said Dr. Sullivan at the end of the meal.

The programme was *Birth of a Nation.*

—I hear this is already a classic, said Dr. Sullivan. It's three hours, but it will be time well spent. Do you think you'd like it Teddy?

—Yes, I know Marie would like it. I'm sure we'll have to wait at least three months before we get it in Sligo.

—Or in Rosnua, or even Maryborough.

The film was preceded by a newsreel featuring King George V distributing military honours at Buckingham Palace, and footage of the Somme front filmed months earlier.

One of the decorated soldiers at Buckingham Palace looked familiar.

—I think that's Captain Holland of our 7th Battalion. He won a VC for his bravery last September at Guillemont, whispered Michael to Virginia.

When the battle footage came up Michael felt his heart race and sweat bead on his neck and forehead.

—Are you all right Michael? asked Virginia.

—It's very difficult to watch this love, even without sound. It brings back sights and sounds that I've been trying to forget. Things were very much worse than described in these captions. Oh God!

He buried his face in his hands.

—Just breathe deeply, love. Breathe. Hold the breath for a few seconds. Then you'll feel a little better. Alright?

—I suppose so dear, he replied.

The epic story of two American families during and after the Civil War, *Birth of a Nation* held the packed audience spellbound. The resident pianist played short passages that matched the action on the screen.

—That was quite wonderful, as gripping as a live drama. The camera really shows facial expressions, something you don't see as clearly in the theatre, said Teddy Martin.

–Yes it's quite a change from Chaplin's short comedies. I suppose it will become one of the great inventions of this century, said Dr. Sullivan.

–Time will tell. Thank you Father, said Michael.

St Michael's was completely full when they arrived for midnight mass at 11:00 p.m. Though altar, choir, church decorations, and the ceremony were very beautiful, Michael kept remembering Christmas 1915 at the front, and Frank Hawkins, Sergeant Tommy Malone, Corporal Cunningham, and Privates Mullins and O'Riordan. Were they safe or in the line of fire? *Dear Lord, keep all my friends and battalion in your loving care.*

–What's the matter Michael? whispered Virginia.

–Nothing really love. I just can't help thinking of the men. I pray they're all safe and sound on this special night. I commit them to God's loving care.

–We're all in His hands, Michael. I'm sure they'll have a safe time at Christmas.

Monsignor Byrne's homily was short. He reminded the congregation of God's great love as shown at Bethlehem almost two thousand years ago:

–Through God's mercy we pray for the safety of our soldiers in Belgium and France and their safe return to their homes and families. Hopefully in this coming year

God bless you all. Thank you for coming to this Mass and celebrating Jesus' birth. Safe home. I hope many of you will also celebrate New Year's Vigil with us.

–It's been a long and happy day, said Dr. Sullivan on their return to his suite. Speaking for myself and Annie, I confess to being a little tired.

So I bid you all goodnight and a very Happy Christmas. See you all around noon for Christmas lunch. God bless us all. Marie, Virginia and Teddy, and all my children.

Michael quickly fell asleep, and had a recurrence of the dream in which the dug-out collapsed on him, and he had to use his left hand to dig himself out. Towards 5.00a.m. he woke in a lather of sweat.

Brian slept peacefully in the adjoining bed, his breathing regular and silent. The traditional candle they had placed at the window, to light the way for the Holy Family, was in a dish surrounded by water so there was no fear of fire. There was a glimmer of light every three minutes from The Bailey Lighthouse. Michael found this comforting. He finally fell into a deep sleep some thirty minutes later.

–Up and at it lads, said his father, knocking on their door at a little after 11. We've reserved a table for 12.15. I don't want to be late.

—Right you are Father. We'll be on time won't we Brian? said Michael.

—We will, said Brian sleepily.

—Go on. Get up out of that, Brian, said Michael pulling the covers off his bed.

The restaurant was arranged in buffet style with a crown roast, leg of lamb, mint sauce, carrots, parsnips, roast potatoes, and a large tom turkey surrounding a massive ice sculpture of Howth Head and the Bailey Lighthouse. Three chefs in white hats and full regalia stood behind the massive table.

—Isn't this really beautiful! Marie and Teddy? Weren't we right to come here? exclaimed Michael's father.

—Oh, it's sumptuous Tom. I never knew the Royal Marine did such a fantastic Christmas presentation. We're having a great time, said Mr. Martin.

As on their first night, they sat at a large table in an alcove. Below lay Kingstown, the harbour, the clear blue water of the bay, and Howth Head covered in a light dusting of snow.

Michael felt a great sense of peace. It was good to be with loved ones again.

—Standing up from the table, Michael said, we're both delighted that Virginia's parents have travelled up from Sligo to share our joy at our forthcoming marriage.
God willing we hope to marry in about eighteen months, or at the end of hostilities in Europe.

Michael tried to control his voice.

—Perhaps Virginia would like to say a few words, he said as he motioned towards her.

—I've nothing really to add, said Virginia. I'm very happy that Mother and Father and Michael's family, with the exception of Jack and Chris are here. God willing we hope to have a long and happy life together.

—A toast to Michael and Virginia. May they be very, very happy, and grow more in love as the years go by, said Mr. Martin.

—I second that, said Dr. Sullivan. Let's all return to our hotel suite for some Christmas carols.

—A song, Michael. A song, shouted Deirdre, Rosemary and Brian.

—I'll do my best. Michael cleared his throat. This very old ballad is a favourite of mine. Here goes.

Dear thoughts are in my mind

And my soul soars enchanted,
As I hear the sweet lark sing
In the clear of the day.
For a tender beaming smile
To my hope has been granted
And tomorrow she shall hear
All my fond heart would say.
I shall tell her all my love,
All my soul's adoration.
And I think she will hear me
And will not say me nay.
With its joyous elation,
As I hear the lark sing in the clear air of the day.

Michael finished and began tearing up.

—Excuse me everyone. Thank you for sharing our happiness.

Michael pulled a handkerchief from his pocket and dabbed his eyes.

—Father, sing something happy.

—Yes, of course Michael. Annie, let's try *Love's Old Sweet Song*. Everyone please join in on the chorus.

Once in the dear dead days beyond recall
When on the world the mists began to fall
Out of the dreams that rose in happy throng
Low to our hearts love sang an old sweet song,
And in the dusk where fell the firelight gleam
Softly it wove itself into a dream
Just a song at twilight when the lights are low;
And the flick'ring shadows softly come and go,
Tho' the heart be heavy, sad the day and long
Still to us at twilight comes love's old song
Comes love's old sweet song.

Michael was in control again. He and Virginia joined heartily in the chorus. Mr. Martin sang all three verses of *Mountain Dew*, set in his native Sligo.

—I have a flask of good *poitin* here Tom, he said, reaching in the pocket of his jacket.

The liquid was clear as gin.

—It was distilled near Ballysadare about eighteen months ago, so it should be fairly smooth. You'll have a nip, Michael?

I've got this small pitcher of milk if any of you need to cut the aftertaste. I think it's a bit too strong for the ladies. Here's health.

Michael gasped as the *poitin* hit the back of his throat. Tears came to his eyes.

–Gosh I think I will have a little milk, Mr. Martin.

The *poitin*, unusually, had a peaty taste.

–This is really good stuff, Teddy, said Dr. Sullivan. It does need to age a little more, but it's the best moonshine I've had in years.

–Oh, it'll put hair on your chest Tom. I always have a pint or two in the house. Do ye know who gives it to me?

–Who, Teddy?

–The R.I.C. sergeant from Ballysadare. The police are supposed to destroy it. They do destroy the stills, but keep most of the liquor for their private use.

The evening continued with songs by Percy French and songs popularized by John McCormack. Michael's mother sang *I Know Where I'm Going*. Deirdre sang *The Last Rose of Summer*. Only towards ten did they sing *Silent Night*.

–*Moi, je vais au lit*, said Michael's mother rising from the piano at a little after eleven. I'm a little tired. Even though we slept in, it's been a long day. Don't forget the pantomime we're going to tomorrow at one o'clock in the Gaiety. We'll have to leave at noon to be on time. Its *Cinderella*. It was supposed to be a surprise. Now you know. It'll be great fun.

–Good night everyone.

Virginia's parents, Deirdre, Rosemary, Brian, Virginia and Michael took their leave of Dr. Sullivan some minutes later.

–Wasn't that a great night and a Christmas to remember? See you all about 10.30 for breakfast, he said as he closed the door.

Returning to their room after breakfast, Michael and Brian packed quickly. They were leaving the hotel and plans were to deliver the Martins to their train after the pantomime.

–I haven't been to a panto in years. This should be great fun, said Michael.

–Yes, it should. I think the last pantomime I was at was about eight years ago in Maryborough. It was *Puss in Boots*. Rosemary was eight, I was six; we laughed until our sides hurt.
The actors made the odd mistake. For us that made it even funnier. The cast today are local comedians. They've played Christmas pantos for years. Even when they forget lines, they turn it to their advantage. They'll probably be

commenting a bit about the war, the Kaiser, and our lads at the front. I hope they don't get too serious. Everyone wants to laugh in these hard times.

–I'm sure the cast are aware of it, said Michael.

When they arrived at the front, his father was loading up the Model T. Virginia, Mr. and Mrs. Martin, Deirdre, and Rosemary stood at the back of a large hackney cab. The driver was arranging luggage as instructed by Mr. Martin.

–Joe, our driver, will place the Martin's luggage in his cab, Dr. Sullivan said. When we get to the Gaiety, Mr. Martin and you can go quickly to Amiens Street Station and leave the large bags in the baggage room there. You'll see it will all work out.
Brian, could you, Deirdre, and Rosemary go in the Model T?
Teddy will sit with Marie, Virginia, and Michael in the back seats of the hackney. Right then, I'll help with the starting crank, Joe. We have plenty of time. The road might be a bit slippery.

The weather was warmer than the day before; a light drizzle mixed with sleet made the road slick.

–Could you stop here, Joe? said Mr. Martin as they arrived at the corner of Grafton Street opposite St. Stephen's Green, with the Gaiety a short distance ahead. I believe that's Dr. Sullivan pulling in just ahead of us.
Michael, help Virginia and the girls carry their bags to the check room at the theatre. Once this is done Joe and I will travel on to Amiens Street. Won't we, Joe?

–Certainly Sir.

–Right. We'll away now. See ye all in about fifteen minutes, said Mr. Martin.

Twenty minutes later the hackney driver dropped Mr. Martin off at the far corner of Grafton Street at the entrance to the theatre where Virginia and the others were waiting.

–There's Father now, said Virginia. Father, you made great time.

–Why wouldn't I, darlin'? Joe, our driver knew every single short cut in the area. We got our bags stashed away all right. The only thing is we'll have to be at the station about a half hour before departure time to pick them up.

–Even with intermission the pantomime is less than three hours, Teddy, so you'll have time to get to your train, said Dr. Sullivan.

As a farce, *Cinderella* moved very quickly. The jokes were topical and poked fun at The Viceroy, John Redmond, Secretary Birrell, Lord Mayor Sherlock and the R.I.C. The three principal roles appeared to be played by members of the same family; strikingly beautiful Rita O'Dea as Cinderella, and Joe and Jim

O'Dea as the Ugly Sisters. Having been out of the country for over six months, Michael failed to understand several of the quips about recent events. Towards the end, Jim O'Dea, in heavy makeup, impersonated the beloved character Molly Malone. Then the entire cast sang *There's a Long Long Road a Winding* for the honour of our Dublin Fusiliers and other service men home on leave. With the singing of *God Save Ireland* by cast and audience the lights came up.

Michael looked at his watch: it was 5.30p.m. Mr. and Mrs. Martin were leaving in a little over an hour. Brian, Deirdre and Rosemary were to leave by train for Maryborough at 7.00p.m.

Despite the mixed weather, his parents expected to make good time in the Model T. They would probably also begin their journey at seven.

—So you're away Marie and Teddy?, asked Dr. Sullivan.

—Yes, we should be at home by about 11.30. I often think that in winter, train travel is quicker than by motor.

—You might be right there, Teddy. We only took the motor with us for convenience, staying in Kingsbridge and with the several members of Annie's family we had to call on, it was easier. I hope you're as lucky with your hackney driver as you were earlier.

—Oh, I more or less arranged for him to be in this area between five-thirty and a quarter to six. There he is ...Joe! Well thanks for a lovely Christmas, Annie, Tom. We look forward to meeting you and the family under very happy circumstances in the New Year. Michael, we love you very much. Virginia, we've loved you forever. Take care and be good. God bless and Happy New Year to all.

They both rushed through misty rain to the cab.

—Because of our luggage there's room here for just one apart from your mother and me. Rosemary, come with us. Deirdre and Brian. you'd best take a hackney to Kingsbridge.
Do you have enough money for that and your fare?

—We have indeed, Father. Don't forget I earn a small stipend now, said Deirdre.

—Virginia, God Bless. Take care of this soldier boy here. He's beginning to look a little more like himself. Don't you think?

—Yes, he is Dr. Sullivan. Michael and I thank you both for your wonderful generosity and being part of our celebration.

—Stop being so formal, girl. Annie and I have always considered you family. Now you are. We'll see you very soon.

–That you will, Father. Now be off. You're losing time. I'll telephone in a few days. And I'll be sure to tell you when Mr. Nolan allows me to travel, said Michael.

–Fair enough son. Dr. Sullivan hugged them both.

–Well love, perhaps we should have at least a coffee in Bewley's. We can catch a suburban at Harcourt Street in about an hour. That will leave us at the hospital in good time.

–Good idea Michael.

It was a fine late February morning. Michael felt quite well as he lay in bed. His vertigo and headaches had all but disappeared. As he washed and shaved, he saw that his face was fuller, his colour better. Goodness it was already 9.30! He had best have his breakfast and prepare for the full physical that was scheduled.

Michael's doctors concluded that his recovery was going well, and as his father was a doctor, he could continue his convalescence in Rosnua, at his parents' home. The trip home on the train was easy, and his Dad was at the station with his Model T to pick Michael up.

Michael's Mother greeted them at the door and they sat down for a tea. After they'd eaten, Michael took his cup of tea out onto the verandah and settled down to relish the country view.

Blackthorn bushes were already budding and should flower in the next ten days. Finches hopped from branch to branch on wayside hedges already beginning their spring song. High in the sky Michael saw a lark soar, listening hard he heard its three-part song. His thoughts immediately returned to Flanders where despite the ever-present odor of cordite and sulfur, larks sang over the trenches at 'stand to' each morning.

Gradually his strength had returned. Over the last five weeks, he went first for short walks through the farm. Then round the lake at the lower end, and later to beauty spots like Dysart. He seldom wore his uniform now, partly because of the political situation, and in order to keep it in good condition.

Rosnua and its town-lands had suffered over fifteen casualties since the beginning of the war. The mood of the town and countryside had changed completely since his visit a year earlier, but not because of the casualties. This was principally because of General Maxwell's actions the previous April. The blatant disregard for justice in the execution of sixteen of the leaders of the rebellion including the dying union activist James Connolly; and the death by hanging of the diplomat Sir Roger Casement, knighted by the Crown for his humanitarian work in the Belgian Congo, had angered most Irishmen and completely changed public opinion.

Michael's convalescence continued well under the careful watch of his Father.

—I'll check your heart and blood pressure after we've eaten Michael.

—Thank you Father.

—Your blood pressure is quite good, said his father minutes later, reading the mercury index on his instrument. Now let's listen to your heart and lungs. Your lungs seem relatively clear. That infection you had earlier seems to have pretty much cleared up. Your heart beats quite steadily .Let me take your pulse. 78 beats a minute .That's okay too. How are you sleeping? Better, the same, worse? Be honest. Do you still have nightmares ?

—Yes, I do, Father, but they're less intense and frequent now, he lied.

—Listen son, you've seen, and had to do things, your mother and I can't conceive of. Your commanding officer, Lieutenant Colonel Murphy, has written to us of your courage and example to the men. You've more than done your duty. If you were to do light duties here in Ireland, you'd have nothing to be ashamed of. I'm not sure if your constitution will stand another eight to ten months in the front lines. We understand however that you must do what you think is right. Your mother and I are proud of you. We'll support you whatever you decide. Now give us a hug. I know you'll make the right decision.

—I miss the men, Father. Things have changed so much here I don't feel completely at home. I know that you and mother, Brian, Deirdre, and Rosemary love me very much, as does Virginia. Nonetheless, I feel I have things to do and that I must continue to fulfill my oath.

—You've done your duty and more, son.

—I feel I've more to do, Father. I think I'll have to return.

—That's fine but you need more time. It's not just that I'm your father; I don't think an Army doctor would pass you as 'fit for active duty' at the moment. Take more time, Michael. Colonel Murphy will understand.

Later in the drawing room Michael tried to read the novella *The Man Who Would be King* by Rudyard Kipling but found he had trouble concentrating. Kipling's poem *If* had given him an added perspective to live by while in Flanders. He had written the poem out and carried it in the top pocket of his uniform.

He found the action and descriptions of the Indian Frontier in the novella fascinating but by 9.30 p.m. was very tired."

—I think I'd better have an early night, Mother, Father, he said rising.

—Perhaps you should son, said his father. We'll see you in the morning.

He was in a deep sleep when he felt a hand on his shoulder. It was his mother.

—Michael, Chris is here. He very much wants to see you. He came under cover of night and can't stay.

—I'll be right down Mother, said Michael in a groggy voice.

He poured some water into the wash-stand basin and splashed it on his face. Then, pulling on a dressing gown, he quickly descended.

Chris sat at the head of the kitchen table eating bacon and eggs.

—Michael, you look a sight, he said, between gulps of tea.

—So do you, you devil. You're like something the cat dragged in. Stand up and give us a hug.

—I'll let you lads catch up, said their mother, her hair in bobby pins. Chris, be sure and come into our room before you leave.

—I will for certain Mother. Now back to bed. I'm sorry I can't stay; it's to protect you and Father.

—You look gaunt, Chris. Do you manage to eat at all? asked Michael.

His younger brother was badly in need of a shave; his auburn hair was unwashed and touched the collar of his soiled, open shirt.

—We eat when we can, sleep where we're safe, and where we won't endanger family. It's not easy, living off the land. I know I needn't tell you that. You've experienced much worse in Flanders.

—Perhaps I have. I don't want to talk about it now. Tell me how you are.

—Well, you know how I tried to get up to Dublin from Cork, when Pearse, McDonagh, and Dev were fighting last April?

—Yes I know about that.

—Well, there didn't seem to be much point in continuing to work on small land claim cases at Hickman and Brother with all this happening, so I've taken a leave of absence. Uncle Maurice was quite good about it.

—Why would he object? Aren't both he and his brother Tim, nationalists?

—True, but they both also support Redmond's desire to achieve it through Parliament, as do you and Jack.

—We do, Chris. It seemed the right course of action two years ago. But I'm not sure any more. The behaviour of General Maxwell was terrible, deploying troops against our own Irish. Most of the troops in Belgium were very angry when they heard about the executions. I felt it was really wrong myself -

applying military law to civilians.
Of course the British had a right to be angry. The insurrection was a stab in the back, but the execution of the leaders, especially Connolly, was entirely wrong.

—You feel that way? ...as a British officer? asked Chris.

—Yes, I do. Most of the Irish at the front feel the same. But we feel strongly about the war also. I'm constantly worried. The Germans seem to have extra troops at the moment. But at least, from what I've read in yesterday's *London Times*, the extreme cold at the front is having an effect, slowing their advance, and apart from raids, there are no major battles at present.

—What about yourself, Michael? You've served with honour. I'm terribly proud of you. Surely you don't really have to go back? You could ask for an honourable discharge, or do home service here.

—I won't do home service. Not in this present situation.

—An honourable discharge then? ...health reasons?

—Perhaps. Father and I have discussed this. I'm not sure. Anyway, I can't remain in Ireland right now. Not with the army acting like a repressive force.

—Resign then and join our struggle.

—Damn it, Chris, you know I can't do that. I've given my word. In spite of everything I believe in the dream I had in summer 1914; Freedom for Belgium and small nations.

—Our dreams are the same Michael. It's just the means we're using to realize them that are different. One way or another, Ireland will have its own parliament within three years.

—Yes, Home Rule is law. If the Government has any honour, they'll have to implement it. Your way is going to involve a lot of fighting here. Are the people ready for that?

—I think they are, Michael. Nationalism is like a tide that can't be stopped.

—John Mc Neill is a good man and I respect the many who are in prison for political reasons. However, I feel I can't join the fight here at present.

—I respect that. So you've decided that you'll be returning to Belgium?

—As soon as I'm medically fit. I really don't feel I can stay here at present. I miss the action and being part of something greater than myself. The war in Belgium and France is just. However, it has dragged on far too long. The offensive at the Somme was to have been a breakthrough. But after all those acts of bravery and sacrifice, things are still the same. The ordinary soldiers go through the same hell each day, shellfire, mud, rats, and lice. It's a miracle that there hasn't been mass disobedience or desertions. The thing I miss most is the men. Their humour, daily sacrifices for each other, and bravery.

–I understand that Michael ... Well! I must be off. The safe house I'm staying in tonight is two miles from here. I won't say goodbye. I hope I'll see you again before you start your journey back.

–Right, don't forget to say good night to Mother and Father.

Chris put his empty dishes in the sink and moved quickly to his parent's bedroom, then left quietly out the rear door.

There were two letters in the mail next morning. Both were in buff ONHISMAJESTYSSERVICE envelopes. Michael recognized the writing on one as being his brother Jack's. He put the envelope to one side. He would read it later. The handwriting on the other was irregular, and not familiar. He opened the envelope quickly.

Dear Lieutenant Sullivan
I hope your convalescence and recovery is going well, and that things are now more peaceful in Ireland. As you may have read, winter this year in Flanders is the coldest in living memory. Temperatures hover at zero most days and rarely rise above ten degrees. All rivers and streams in the front line areas are frozen, as are shell holes. Then when temperatures rise to above freezing the whole front becomes a quagmire. Ration and meal convoys arrive late. The men sometimes go 12 to 14 hours without food. They never complain, and bear everything with stoic good humour. Needless to say there are many trench cave-ins and the incidence of trench foot, chilblains, and blood poisoning is high. But then, to quote Shelley, If Winter comes, can Spring be far behind. There are some milder days and the men seem to have less colds than in past years. Perhaps the intense cold has killed some viruses.
Captain Hitchcock, Sergeant Malone, and Corporal Cunningham wish to be remembered to you. The men as a whole enquire constantly regarding your recovery and your return. Your good humour and courage has been an inspiration to them.
With sincere wishes for your good health,
A.D. Murphy.
Lieut. Colonel, Commanding 2nd Battalion the Leinster Regiment.

So his comrades missed him! It was certainly good of Colonel Murphy to say this. For his part, as he had said to Chris, he missed the comradeship of his colleagues. Yes the front lines were hell, but it was a hell he, in a sense, understood. He had been tested in that crucible of horror and pain. Somehow he had survived and emerged a stronger man, and with his courage proved. He had tried to adjust to the new situation in Ireland without success. He had no home now but the front.

Chapter Nineteen

Arras, Le Bois-en-Hache, 12 April 1917

A cold northeast wind bit into Michael's face. He walked quickly up a shingled pathway to the turreted house serving as battalion headquarters. He was on his way to meet with Colonel Murphy and get his new assignment. One of the few still standing, the house was on the outskirts of Arras, five miles from the Crater Line and about six from Vimy Ridge.

—Good to see you again, Sullivan, said Colonel Murphy. At ease. I hope your journey hasn't left you too tired. We're here as part of a joint force. The Canadians want to have a crack at dislodging Fritz from The Ridge. Byng, CO of the Canadians, made a personal presentation to General Haig. We're to be part of a combined operation under General Byng. The whole offensive is part of a grand plan the French have devised. We can only hope it's more successful than the Somme. We're here as backup. H.Q. has devised several new military manoeuvres. The coming days and weeks will be a time of intense preparation. If this offensive is successful, and the Canucks take the Ridge, the war could end this year. Care for a whiskey, Sullivan? You look like you could use one.

Murphy reached for a bottle of Black & White and two tumblers.

—Thank you Sir. It will keep the cold at bay.

The scotch warmed his throat, his chest, and upper body.

—Sit Sullivan, sit. First things first, I want you to go to quartermaster stores immediately and pick up a lambskin jerkin. You may wear it either beneath or outside your greatcoat. The French tell us that the current cold snap is the coldest it's been in thirty years. The men were issued jerkins weeks ago. Anything to keep this arctic weather at bay. Now the battalion is in billets in the Souchez area, and if you hop a transport, you can join them in fifteen or twenty minutes. Pick up that jerkin first.

—Yes Sir, as you say, Michael replied, draining the last of his scotch.

—One more thing before you go Sullivan. I'm very happy you responded positively to my letter of last month. You needn't have returned you know.

Michael noticed that the Colonel's voice shook a little.

—Yes, I know that Colonel. I could have applied for duties in Ireland. As you probably know things have changed greatly there. The army has become an arm of the civic authority and sometimes acts against ordinary citizens. I simply feel I can't be part of that type of action. However, as I said in my letter of reply, I feel my duty as an Irishman and a serving officer is here at the front.

—I appreciate that Sullivan. These weeks you've been recovering from your injuries haven't been easy. However, I think we're gaining the upper hand. We need more officers like you. Best of luck, Sullivan.

—Thank you Sir.

The afternoon sunshine was fading fast as Michael boarded a transport towards the north and Souchez. The wind was still icy, but he felt a little warmer because of the jerkin. He wore it outside his greatcoat. It came up to his collar. Beneath it he wore his scarf wrapped double under his greatcoat.

So there was to be another big push, which if successful would shorten the war. How often had he heard that?

Though the 7th Leinsters had taken the strategic village of Guillemont the previous September, the gain had been short-lived. Now the Somme offensive was over. It was at best a pyrrhic victory.

So many of all ranks had died. The top brass were guarded about the real losses, yet for him as a serving officer there was no choice. He'd given his word. His word was his bond.

—We've arrived, Lieutenant, said Private Murray bringing the transport truck to a smart halt. A, B, and C Companies are here in reserve. You've got many good friends here.

—Indeed I have Murray. Thank you.

Michael jumped from the back of the truck, his rucksack on his right shoulder. Officer's quarters were solid wooden huts some fifty yards distant. He walked smartly towards the nearest one and knocked on the door.

—Welcome Michael, welcome, said Hawkins with his hand outstretched.

—Thank you Frank. It's good to be back. My God you're awfully thin; gaunt even.

—It's the terrors of command, Mick. It hasn't been an easy winter. The Hun control the Ridge. We lose men whenever we're sent on a sortie. Then there's the goddamned weather. Minus twelve one day, plus five the next.

—Colonel Murphy filled me in on the planned offensive. We all hope this offensive will be successful.

—We can only hope, Michael. One good thing is we've got quite comfortable billets. Come and see.

The billets contained beds made of rabbit wire strung over the bedframes.

—Gosh, this is a gift Frank, he said, throwing his rucksack on a nearby bed.

—Yes indeed Michael. The French built them. They're quite dry and we have little in the way of vermin.

–Here's to our allies and the entente cordial, Frank said to Michael, as he pulled a flask of Jameson from his kitbag and poured drinks out for both of them.

–Your good health Mick, said Hawkins drinking deeply from his tin mug.

–And yours Frank.

–Now there's quite a good small bistro in Champlain l'Abbee, a village about a half mile northwest of us. We should have a bite to eat there.

–Great idea Frank.

The restaurant was in the cellar of a building that had been shelled several times. The patron, a native of Normandy, had lamb on the menu. There were only ten other customers, all officers from other regiments.

–Oh this is wonderful Frank. I haven't had lamb yet this year, said Michael.

–Yes it's great, and he serves a fresh mint sauce with it. By the way the white wine here is really dry and will go well with the lamb.

–We'll have a litre of that then, said Michael.

–And a hearty potage St. Germain to begin with. A good fresh pea soup will hit the spot.

Hawkins was right about everything. The meal was excellent.

–How did you discover this place, Frank?

–Well, when we came to take over the line a few weeks ago, a couple of the French staff took Colonel Murphy, Palin, Nolan, and myself here.
This restaurant exists because George, le patron, just dug in his heels and decided he wasn't going to be forced out when the war started. As a businessman, at the outbreak of hostilities, he just decided to carry on. He uses whatever local produce he can get his hands on. The French army also help as regards supplies.

–Yes, it's in their best interests to have a place where one can relax a little.

–Now you have to have a café cognac to end the meal, Michael. George has a cognac from 1900.

–I'll forgo the coffee Frank. Fatigue has really hit me. If I have coffee I won't sleep.

–Fair enough Michael. We'll have coffee when we come next time. But do have the cognac.

–With pleasure Frank. Oh this is really beautiful. Very, very smooth.

There was shellfire from the front as they walked back to their quarters in the starless night.

Next morning Michael borrowed Hawkins's field glasses to have a closer look at the ridge. Michael advanced to the munitions rail lines, at the foot of Vimy Ridge.

The ridge, a seven-mile long cliff of grey mud, rose softly from a plain below. Bombarded hundreds of times since the outbreak of war, it was now completely devoid of shrubbery or grass. Every inch of its surface was pitted from two years of constant siege. At this distance it didn't seem too terrifying, yet Michael knew that many had already died in efforts to capture it.

It reminded him of a beached basking shark he'd seen some years before in Achill Sound. The high crest of the escarpment lay between two rivers: the Souchez to the left and north, the Scarpe several miles to the south.

Four divisions of the Canadian army were in the valley directly facing the ridge. It was designated as their objective. At the southern boundary, the Canadians were four thousand yards away from the highest point. At Souchez village where the Leinsters were encamped the distance was just seven hundred. Towards the middle of the low mountain a ragged line of gigantic craters marked the site of earlier mine explosions in failed efforts to capture the fortress. Beyond the crater line, three parallel rows of German trenches zigzagged along the lower slope. These were protected by forty-five-foot rolls of heavy barbed wire, and concrete pillboxes every twenty yards containing machine gun nests. Facing the Leinsters was a small sparsely wooded knoll which looked like a fissure on a shark's snout and was called the Pimple. To the left and immediately north lay the Loretto spur, site of the ruined Abbey of Notre Dame de Lorette.

The area to the west at the foot of the ridge had been wrested from the enemy at horrendous cost. Evidence of the struggle was everywhere. Through field glasses from the reserve trenches, partly blanketed by snow, Michael could clearly see the remains of gun carriages, tangles of barbed wire, broken rifles, rusting bayonets, dead mules, and hundreds of tattered uniforms, some blue French, others grey German, each holding their grim consignment of bones. He shuddered involuntarily. This carnage was as bad as the Somme.

—Yes, the French have paid dearly to hold this area, Michael. *Mort pour la patrie* and all that. The area seems as sacred to them as Verdun.

—Certain places can have a religious significance in the memory of a nation Frank. Think of Tara, or the Rock of Cashel at home in Ireland.

—Well, we'd best be off Michael to the Vimy Ridge model. You have your stopwatch with you? You'll need it for timing the precision manoeuvres we'll be putting the men through.

As they arrived back, they saw Nolan waiting for them. The back manoeuvre area was given over to a four mile long area, duplicating the German trench system with the trench positions marked out by miles of coloured tape and thousands of flags. The tapes laid out a full scale replica of the German trench system. Suspected mine positions, camouflaged gun positions, and other features were marked, thanks to information gleaned from captured prisoners and photographs taken by the Royal Flying Corps.

Every pillbox, every barbed wire entanglement known to military intelligence was marked and labelled. Large signposts named enemy trenches; coloured pennants outlined German positions - red for trenches, blue for roads, black for dug-outs, yellow for machine gun nests. Michael had seen sections marked out for mock offensives before, but never with this attention to detail.

—This is really something, Frank, he said in wonder.

—It's hoped that this attention and precision planning saves lives Michael, and leads to a victory.

Mounted on the chestnut mare Peggy, Colonel Murphy joined them , with a second office on horseback.

—Men, this is Captain Duncan MacIntire of the Canadians, he said dismounting and introducing a stocky, sandy-haired man of about thirty.

—Glad to meet you again. We were frequently in the same sector at Ypres, said MacIntire.

He shook hands with Michael, Hawkins and Nolan in quick succession.

—Right then, said MacIntire. General Byng, and Major General Currie are pleased with preparations to date. However, practice really does make perfect.

Murphy reminded his lieutenants that they would be advancing on the 'trench' represented by the blue tape. Murphy and MacIntire remounted their horses, and advanced, carrying red flags representing the advancing screen of shellfire - the creeping barrage.

Behind them Michael, Hawkins, Nolan, and other junior officers led platoons of men, not in military line, but in groups, carrying their rifles, bayonets fixed, walking at a measured pace, ready to shoot or lunge at the enemy once the tapes were reached. They practiced this movement, timing their advance to the advance of the creeping barrage, over and over again, walking at the rate of a hundred yards per minute and a half.

Michael and his colleagues checked their stopwatches, halted the troops to allow the imaginary creeping barrage to lift, then signalled them forward again. Murphy and MacIntire meanwhile pointed out strong points in enemy defences, and devised strategies to conquer them.

–Men, timing is absolutely essential, said MacIntire during a short break. If you march too quickly you'll be killed or injured by our guns. If you move at a slow pace you'll lose the element of surprise and give Fritz time to regroup. When you arrive at this trench, represented by the blue tape, the hope is that the Germans will be in disarray.

–...and we should be able to overrun them, said Hawkins.

–Correct. And what are you going to do now? asked McIntire.

–Consolidate our hold on his part of the line.

–Right again. At ease. You can have tea or whatever you have in your flasks.

–Christ, we need something stronger than tea right now, something to get the blood flowing, don't we O'Riordan, whispered Mullins giving his comrade a dig in the ribs.

–I'm sure Lieutenant Hawkins will arrange for an extra tot of rum once we get back to base, said Malone.

–We've heard that one before Sir, said O'Riordan dubiously.

–I'll do my best, lads; the men deserve it given the weather we're having, said Hawkins. Sergeant Malone, we'll break for today. Best get the men back to base. They should rest a little There'll be many fatigues moving shells closer to the front, once the sun goes down. Those shells they'll be moving weigh more than 120 lbs each. *('fatigues', aptly named by the troops, were tedious, consisting mostly of moving heavy shells and boxes of ammunition for distances of half a mile, from dumps in the back trenches .It took two men to move shells because of their weight)*

–Yes sir.

Narrow gauge railway cars, laden with shells of every calibre, were arriving towards the back of their base camp every twenty minutes. Working in twos, the men quickly unloaded them and then carried the heavy ammunition, first by hand truck, then again in pairs through the maze of back trenches to the front lines. It was dangerous work, but by this time all the men were battle-hardened.

–We'll be a long-time dead Dan, Michael overheard Mullins say to his chum O'Riordan as he bent to his task.

The routine of measured military operations, and the disciplined work of unloading and carrying munitions to the front lines, continued over the next three days. Then it was their turn to return to front line combat.

Colonel Murphy came up the line on the second night they were there moving munitions.

–Hawkins, Sullivan. I've a special task for your lot. As you know there's to be another big push in the next week or so. H.Q. is anxious for as much intelligence about the enemy as possible. So, we need to send raiding parties into German lines on almost a nightly basis. The Canadians have been conducting many raids with varying success. Tonight, send a party into enemy lines. Capture a couple of prisoners and check if previous reports of strength and other factors are correct. Sullivan, you'll lead this raid. You'll need about twenty volunteers. So spread the word and meet here in this dug-out at 21.40hrs. Orders for this raid have come down from G.H.Q.

Michael had a queasy feeling, but was elated that Murphy had given him this task. He saluted and climbed the steps from the dug-out to the communication trench.

–You'll be with me on this Tommy, he said to Malone.

–I'll always be your back-up, never you fear Mick. Now let me see if I can pull together a party.

Malone had little trouble gathering a group. Michael noted that Mullins, O'Riordan, and Corporal Cunningham, all hardened veterans, and extremely brave in battle, were part of the stick. Michael marched the sortie group to Murphy in his dugout. Murphy looked up from his small desk, a telephone beside him.

–At ease, men, he said. The burnt cork you applied to your hands and faces will work well to hide your presence as you cross no-man's-land. Cast a glance at these charts. Here, in this section of enemy trenches, there are two or three machine gun nests which our artillery has been unable to knock out. So, caution and cunning are the watch-words. As we're going over the top in a matter of days, I want to capture two or three men from these machine gun crews. From them we'll learn the exact location of the German gun emplacements behind their lines. Our artillery will then plaster them before the attack, and thus save the lives of many of our crowd. Now I want you to follow these instructions as if they were gospel. Take off your identification disks, strip your uniforms of all numerals and insignia.
Leave your papers here. I don't want Fritz to know what regiments are against them and I don't want any of you to be taken alive. Take your trench knives and knuckle dusters. Each of you are to carry four Mills bombs. These are to be used only in emergency. Sullivan here is in charge, ably assisted by Sergeant Malone. So put lots of that burned cork on your hands and faces and for God's sake look out for star shells. Best of luck. I want to see you all back here at midnight-thirty. Understood?

–Yes Sir, they replied as one.

Michael indicated to the men to apply burnt cork to their faces and hands. The blackening would make them less visible in the intense light of star shells and would make them less visible once they gained enemy trenches.

Minutes later they were in the communications trench, named Wicklow Street. This led to the fire trench at the point where they were to go over the top. The distance from the enemy's barbed wire was about six hundred yards.

—Listen, lads. I want to explain the tap system we'll follow while in no man's land again. We used it a couple of times in Ypres. Several of you were not part of the company then. A single tap means that a signal has been understood and will be obeyed. Two taps means that those in front should crawl forward very slowly for five yards then halt and await further instructions. Three taps when within striking distance of a German trench means rush it, inflict as many casualties as possible, capture a couple of prisoners, and then get back home at all speed. Four taps means that each man is on his own and should return to home trenches as quickly as bloody possible.

A party of Royal Engineers had cut a lane through the barbed wire of No Man's Land in front of the German trenches. Michael signalled his sortie party to climb out of the fire trench and start the advance towards the German line. The squad took up extended order format and stayed about one yard apart as they advanced to the break in the barbed wire. Michael gave the two-tap signal. Seconds later he received a one-tap signal, meaning that the soldier on his extreme left had understood his order and was crawling forward five yards at a time.

The hard-packed snow and earth froze his hands and saturated the knees and legs of his uniform. A cold clammy sweat beaded between his shirt and underpants. His helmet kept falling forward, partly obstructing his view. He pushed it back and adjusted the chin-strap. His breath came in short quick gasps. He tried to control it, holding it in his lungs and counting to three, then letting it out slowly. Listening intently, Michael continued his crawl towards the German line He fondled the breach of his rifle. It lay folded in his arms, ready for use.

Michael and his men collapsed into prone position as German star shells appeared over them. The party started advancing again once the illumination died out. One of the men sneezed. Michael cursed the soldier under his breath. He waited silently for the rifle fire that generally followed when the enemy heard noise in No Man's Land. Nothing happened. He tapped two times. The squad crawled slowly forward another five yards. By being careful and motionless when a star shell went off over them, they reached the enemy's barbed wire without incident. Perhaps Intelligence and Murphy were right, and that part of the German trench was unmanned.

Now the most difficult part of the operation began: cutting through the enemy's barbed wire at the lip of their trench. The soldier on his extreme left, a man in the centre, and Michael as leader, were equipped with wire cutters. Michael indicated to Mullins that he should grab the wire about a foot to his right. Then he grasped the barbed wire about two inches from its iron stake and cut between the stake and his hand. They had cut a lane about halfway through the massed entanglements of wire when, down the centre of the line of advance, twang! went some wire that hadn't been properly held. Michael, sweat now running down his forehead and face, his stomach a tight knot, awaited the enemy challenge and machine gun volley.

There was no reaction from the German trench, and finally, stealthily, they managed to get through the enemy barbed wire. They were within yards of the trench. Michael gave the three-tap signal, meaning rush the line.

–Halt!

The word rang out from the enemy in English, followed by a barrage of rifle fire.

They had lost the element of surprise. Machine guns spattered bullets. Several bombs were thrown to their rear. Slightly winded, Michael found himself on the floor of the trench. He sensed the presence of a giant of a man inches away. In the fall he'd lost his rifle. He knew it was somewhere near his feet. He fumbled for his holster, drew his Webley pistol and fired three shots in succession.

With a groan a middle-aged, heavyset soldier fell forward, his mouth and eyes open in wonder. His face was within a few inches of Michael, who heard the death rattle and crawled over the now prostrate figure. Beyond him, a German guardsman and his comrade were on top of each other, a puzzled expression on the guardsman's face, both his hands pressed against his right side, his grey uniform in shreds, his intestines hanging out. O'Riordan had got both with a Mills bomb. A figure in grey, a massive block of Prussian bone and muscle, came running towards him, his arms in the air. Tom Malone and Peter Mullins followed, their trench knives drawn.

–*Achtung!* Halt! shouted Michael raising his pistol.

–*Kamerad, Kamerad*, the soldier cried, sliding to a halt.

–Yes me friend, over the trench ye go now if ye don't want this in yer back, said Malone. Are you all right Lieutenant Sullivan?

–None the worse for wear, Tommy. Listen, there isn't much time. The enemy are probably regrouping in the reserve trench. We'd best be out of here. How many prisoners are there?

–Two others at the far end.

–Casualties?

–No deaths. Gleeson and Nolan slightly wounded. The medic is tending to them.

—Pass the word back Tommy, the men are to make their way back across No Man's Land with all speed.

— *Hände hoch oder wir schießen*, Michael said to the large Prussian as they mounted the parapet near the opening in the barbed wire.

The soldier nodded and raised his arms. The enemy were regrouping. Within minutes they sent up more star shells and re-manned a machine gun post. They hit the ground, Malone in front, the Prussian soldier behind him, Michael in the rear. They moved back towards their home trench, crouched over and going prone with each new star shell. After what felt an eternity, they regained their own barbed wire. A jumpy West Corkman challenged them. They gave the password—Red Lion's Pub—managed to traverse the parapet and re-entered their trench and found Hawkins waiting for them.

—I hope the interrogation of these Krauts goes well. It was pretty hairy for a while there, said Michael. It could have been much worse.

—Yes it could have, Michael. We'll miss Gleeson and Nolan. Well at least they're out of it. Have Duggan get them to a clearing station.

—He's already seeing to that, Frank. Is there a dugout with a writing desk nearby? I'd better write the Intelligence Summary of this action now.

—Of course, let me show you.

—I think Sergeant Malone and Private O'Riordan should be commended. Malone captured those prisoners and O'Riordan killed at least four of the enemy. He's absolutely fearless in battle.

The battalion remained at the front for three more days. Michael's sortie party made one more trench raid, but were less successful in capturing prisoners. It looked as if the enemy had moved men from the front trenches due perhaps to casualties or capture. The weather changed slightly. Daytime temperatures were a little above freezing. The trenches again became quagmires. It was necessary to place another layer of duckboard throughout the first and reserve trenches. Artillery continually shelled the enemy with heavy guns and trench mortars. The Germans countered with similar fire.

The battalion was relieved by the 7th Northamptonshire Battalion. The relief was orderly; during this time, the enemy repeatedly shelled the relief trenches. Four men were lightly wounded during this action.

Three days later the battalion celebrated Saint Patrick's Day. Dressed in green vestments, Father Doyle said High Mass in the parish church of Sains-en-Gohelle, taking as his theme the gospel words: *Well done, good and faithful servant, because thou hast been faithful over a few things I will place thee over many: enter thou into the joy of thy lord.*

– You soldiers of the Leinster Regiment have been faithful to Ireland at Ypres, and shown great bravery at the Somme. You will be tested again in the coming weeks. Cast your cares upon the Lord as Patrick did. Remain true to your faith, to your King, and to Ireland. Then regardless of whether you win or lose in battle, you will win the main prize and enter his Kingdom.

Happy Saint Patrick's Day, men, and many, many more.

The men sang *Let Eirinn Remember*. Then, as Father Doyle moved among them distributing shamrock following mass, several broke into a bawdy version of *Father O'Flynn*, substituting O'Doyle for O'Flynn.

Here's a health to you, Father O'Doyle,
Slainte, and slainte and slainte again,
Powerfullest preacher and Tenderest teacher
and Kindliest creature in ould Donegal.

–You're embarrassing me now lads, ye really are, said the flush-cheeked priest. Go on about your training. I'll see you and Colonel Murphy at the supper this evening.

Training continued after lunch with a short route march. The men then repaired to quarters, concentrating on pressing their best uniforms, polishing brass buttons and buckles in preparation for a visit by General Byng, Major General Arthur Currie, and their own Commander, Lieutenant Colonel A.D. Murphy. The men were happy to be inside as the weather, though milder, was a mixture of rain and sleet.

At 17.45 hours the men paraded by company to the damaged main square of Souchez. General Byng, Major General Currie, and Lieutenant Colonel Murphy arrived at precisely 18.00hrs.

Murphy conducted both Canadian commanders on an inspection of his men.

–This man's uniform is the worse for wear, Colonel Murphy, said Byng pointing to O'Riordan.

–So it is, Sir. I'd like it noted that Private O'Riordan is one of the bravest men in the Leinsters. In a trench raid two evenings ago, he killed four of the enemy and helped capture two valuable prisoners. He's been mentioned in dispatches and recommended for the Military Cross.

–Point taken Murphy. Just out of the line, is he? His worn uniform is understandable then. Keep up the good work O'Riordan.

–Thank you Sir, said O'Riordan with emotion in his voice.

The battalion then marched by company to the damaged Hotel de Ville. Several municipal officials were already in the oak-panelled grand hall. With no electricity, lighting was by lamp and candlelight. Led by Lieutenant Colonel Murphy, General Byng and Major General Currie proceeded to the long head table. There they were joined by Father Doyle, Captain MacIntire, and several middle-rank Canadian Officers. MacIntire was the only one Michael recognized.

—Tommy, could you keep an eye on O'Riordan and Mullins that they don't get out of hand, said Michael to Malone as the companies came in.

—Right, I'll do my best, but you know those two, Malone replied.

After the playing of *God Save The King* and *God Save Ireland* Lieutenant Colonel Murphy addressed the gathering.

—Reverend Father, General Byng, Major General Currie, Monsieur Le Marie de Souchez, officers of the Canadian Expeditionary Force, Officers of the British Expeditionary Force, Members of the Leinster Regiment, Mesdames et Messieurs. It seems especially appropriate that our guests of honour this evening should be General Sir Julian Byng, commander of the Canadian Corps, and his Adjutant General Currie.
The Leinster Regiment, known by everyone as an Irish regiment, is also known as the Royal Canadians, in that the original 100th Regiment was raised in Upper and Lower Canada in the last century. In the Battle of the Somme and throughout the Ypres offensives we've frequently counted Canadian officers and men as comrades in arms. Now, in forthcoming action, we will again take the field of battle together. So, it's a very great pleasure to have members of the Canadian army as our special guests on our national holiday.
Cead mile failte. Welcome. *Bienvenue*. Father Doyle, could you say grace?

—With pleasure, Colonel Murphy. *Bless us oh Lord and your bountiful gifts as we celebrate the feast of our patron saint*. Enjoy the feast, men. I certainly will.

The meal —leek and potato soup, spring lamb with peas and roast potatoes followed by sherry trifle— was served by members of the North Staffordshire Regiment. Each soldier was served two glasses of red burgundy; brandy and liqueurs were served only at the head table.

— I'd like to thank everyone in the Leinster Regiment 2nd Battalion, and especially Lieutenant Colonel Murphy for his gracious invitation to celebrate Ireland's National Day with you, said the heavy-lidded, prematurely aged General Byng. As the Colonel has pointed out, your battalion has strong Canadian connections. In the coming offensive we'll be acting as one cohesive Corps. This is why the military exercises we've been pursuing in recent weeks, and the precision of our creeping barrage is so important. In the next few days I'll inform Colonel Murphy of the regiment's plan of action in the coming offensive. The main attack on the ridge is being handled by the four Canadian Divisions. However, your contribution as part of the Canadian Corps is very important. We're among friends here, but I can't emphasize enough how important it is to be guarded and secret regarding the details of this operation. The Hun know that something is afoot. The less they know about actual plans the better for our offensive. Loose lips sink ships, to quote the naval saying. We'll be in action quite soon. Keep up the good work. Thank you all again for your hospitality.

The commander walked slowly to his seat. Michael looked at his watch. It was after ten. Even though they were relief, reveille would be at six the next morning. Members of the head table were leaving. It was time to return to quarters and rest.

The days melded into one another: intensive training each morning and well into the afternoon. Then, immediately it became dusk, back-breaking fatigue continued for each company, offloading shells of every calibre from the narrow-gauge railway, then transporting them in teams of two to munition dumps just to the rear of the front lines.

–Christ Lieutenant Sullivan, the Canadians and ourselves had better beat the shit out of Fritz to make this worthwhile, said Corporal Cunningham as he carried a crate of mid-sized shells with O'Riordan.

–If all goes to plan, we will Corporal. An awful lot of planning has gone into this action. We only know a part of it as yet. The Canadians are chafing at the bit. They're quite disciplined, but they're angry with the Hun. They've lost an awful lot of men in Ypres and at St Éloi.

–Let them have their day then. We'll act as back-up, said the giant Cunningham.

–I think that's the plan, Corporal.

A mixture of rain and high winds blew across the whole Arras and Vimy area on April 1st.

–April Fool's Day indeed, said Hawkins. Goddamn it Mick. This action had better be successful. The men are getting restless.

–Aren't we all, Frank?

Overnight wind still blew at gale force, rain now turned to wet snow, covering trenches and the back areas to a depth of four inches.

–The Canucks are used to this, maybe they can use it to their advantage, said Michael.

–God I hope so Mick, said Hawkins.

At nine the following morning Major General Currie and Colonel Murphy addressed all the officers of the Leinsters.

—Gentlemen, the main offensive on The Ridge is to be conducted by the First, Second, Third, and Fourth Divisions of the Canadian Corps. The Leinster battalion will form part of the First British Corp and assist the Fourth Canadian Corp in the assault on the hill, called the Pimple, and on the wood, called Le Bois-en-Hache, near Barlin here in the North East on this map. As you can see, these two enclaves are relatively close to each other and are almost as heavily fortified as the Ridge itself.
Whether you attack at the exact same time as the other divisions remains to be decided. Detailed here are the first, second, third, and fourth objectives to be attacked. I've arranged that copies of these plans be available to every officer. Study them closely, especially the objectives to be attained. I want each of you to know these objectives like the back of your hands and to make sure that the men are thoroughly familiar with them.
Softening-up operations by our big guns are to begin at midnight tonight and to last for five days. Many of you will be in dug-outs in the bowels of the earth and will manage some sleep. The rest of you will simply have to bear up. The precise date of the offensive is still to be decided. Remember the saying about loose lips. Good luck to all of us. Dismiss.

—Well Michael, we'll be in the thick of it soon, said Hawkins, as they left the assembly hall. What did you think of Currie?

—Very much to the point. I hear he actually drew up all these plans with General Byng and has made a study of some of the mistakes made eight months ago at the Somme. I'm a bit puzzled by his accent.
Is he Scottish, Frank?

—Perhaps a generation or so ago. The standard English- Canadian accent has a bit of a burr to it.

—How's that, Frank?

—I'm not quite sure. I think it has something to do with the number of Scottish immigrants to Canada following the Highland clearances a hundred-and-fifty years ago.

As at the Somme, the noise of the guns in the days following was ear-shattering. Short on sleep, the men moved more slowly.

—Will this be over soon, Lieutenant Sullivan? asked Corporal Cunningham on the third day of the bombardment.

—Major General Currie did say five days, John. I know that everyone is on edge, but look at it this way—there are only another two days to go, and if we feel like this, think of how the enemy must feel.
They're receiving the full force of our barrage.

–We'll all soldier on. The important thing in front of us is the start of the attack.

–That's the spirit, John.

The weather continued blustery with a mixture of snow and sleet. Detailed plans given to all officers on the 6th of April, called for the Battalion to attack and hold the enemy trenches in the Bois-en-Hache Spur in cooperation with the 9th Battalion Royal Sussex Regiment. The Royal Sussex Battalion were to be on their left. A and B Companies of the Leinsters were to capture the enemy second line, and were to establish a strong point in this line, and hold as the Line of Observation. C Company, that Michael's 9th Platoon were part of, were to capture and hold the enemy front line and establish a strong point to protect the 4th Canadian Division on their right. The enemy front line was to be consolidated and made the Line of Resistance.

D Company were to be in General Reserve in a tunnel to the rear.

The battle plans were signed by Colonel Murphy:

> Immediately each objective is gained patrols will push forward under our creeping barrage. Bombing Posts are to be established to cover the work of consolidation. Connecting posts to keep touch between Companies and the Battalion on the left will be established between Strong Points and between the two objectives. Before dawn both the line of observation and line of resistance will be thinned out as far as the situation permits. From that time the defence of the captured trenches will devolve on the commander of C Company. Companies will commence to assemble outside our own barbed wire at ZERO minus 60. This assembly must be carried out slowly and carefully. From ZERO minus 60 to ZERO our artillery will carry out a slow bombardment of the enemy front line over an extended front.

The next day and a half passed quickly. The entire Battalion assembled in Souchez for final inspection at 17.00 on the evening of 9th April. Colonel Murphy moved quickly through them to the front of their ranks, his voice sounded out strongly as he addressed the men.

—Well men, the time has finally come. All our precise and repeated maneuver movement practice of the last six weeks have been towards this offensive. I know you'll all behave with bravery and honour. You'll remain true to Ireland, Belgium, and all small nations. God be with you in the hours ahead. I'm proud to be in command of this great regiment. God bless and keep us all.

—Short and to the point Frank, said Michael. When do you move out?

—Right now Mick. We get our tea and rum first – Christ I'm looking forward to that...something to warm the gut in this kind of weather.
Then we move to relieve the 7th Northamptonshire Regiment at Kellet. We'll just have one platoon in line. The rest of the company will be in that large dug-out fifty yards behind and the very deep tunnel a little further back.
When do you march?

—Not until 20.30. I suppose we'll also have time to eat.

—Make the most of it. You probably won't eat again for at least twelve hours. Then it'll probably be only hard tack. Best of luck Mick, I'll see you after this is over. You've been a good and dear friend.

—That goes for me too, Frank, said Michael feeling his throat tighten. You know how to reach my family if things go badly?

—I do indeed. You know how to reach my father at the Deanery in Birr?

—Yes I do.

They shook hands. Hawkins marched smartly towards his company.

The meal consisted of bacon and cabbage washed down with Smithwicks Ale and hot syrupy tea. It was a change from recent fare.

—Christ, this is quite an improvement Lieutenant, said Malone softly. They're fattening us up for slaughter.

—Don't say that, Tommy. Even in fun.

—We have to find humour somewhere Sir. We're into the mouth of hell again, as the poet would say.

—The sooner the better. This eternal waiting is the worst part, said Michael.

—Indeed 'n it is. After thirty years of soldiering I can never get used to it.

—Nor can I, Tommy.

He'd experienced fear before, at Ypres and at the Somme. This fear now was part of a sudden paralyzing awareness of where he was, of what was happening, that this time he might well die. He tried breathing deeply, counting to a hundred under his breath, going over the battle orders in his mind once again. All he could think of was that zero hour was fast approaching, that he might die savagely and with horrendous pain – fear, yes, but something more, something atavistic, primitive, the instinct to run. He told himself to snap out of it, get a grip on things. No fucking good. All he could think was that he was pinned down by gunfire with no escape. He was scared shitless. So, he tried something else. He pretended he wasn't really there. That he was moving through this time and place, had to, could not avoid it, but soon he would come through it and beyond it to another part of the story. He thought of a lark he'd heard singing early one morning while beginning training shortly after his return. The lark lived in the moment; Michael was beset by his memories of being under fire. Pinned down and shit-scared he was. This was what made him human and set him apart.

B Company left billets at 19.00 hrs, moving by platoon at five-minute intervals, Then A Company proceeded in the same order at 19.30. Presently it was 20.30hrs, time for C Company to deploy. Father Doyle appeared at the door of their mess tent, dressed in his greatcoat. The priest seemed impervious to the inclement weather.

He made the sign of the cross over them.

—God bless and keep you all, men, he shouted into the wind and sleet.

As planned, they were joined by six tunnel experts, or sappers, a little past the church. They proceeded by a sunken road to their forward headquarters, arriving at a little after 22.30hrs. To everyone's delight, company cookers were already there. They were quickly served more scalding syrupy tea and a double tot of rum.

—Great stuff and thoughtful of the brass Lieutenant, said Malone.

—Let me see, said Michael swallowing the last of his tea, downing the double Army issue in one gulp.

His throat burned with the harsh rum, his heart raced, he felt the magic potion warm every blood vessel in his neck and upper chest.

—Fuck it, I hope there'll be more of this before we go over the top, said Malone.

—That would be very well received.

Helmer Crater trench was congested. Michael left his platoon with another there, and returned to a deep dug-out immediately to the rear. There were easily twenty-five men already in the cave. The air was thick with a mixture of smoke from open braziers and the cigarettes most of the men smoked. Two storm lamps and several guttering candles gave a dim light. There were only three chairs: two at a makeshift table, one in front of a field telephone. Two camp beds stood to the rear of the cave. The other men there, crouched on their knees against the walls, or were lying against the sides of the dug-out. Some wrote hasty final letters to family or sweethearts. The centre of the floor held two inches of muddy water; Michael's platoon took off their spare bandoliers of ammunition and stacked them near the entrance as they came in; next to that they piled their rifles and the white bags containing their iron rations. They then tried to find a dry corner and hunker down.

—More eternal waiting Lieutenant, said Malone.

The sounds of battle to the south were dulled. The impact of each shell reverberated through the earth, causing those closest to the walls to reach out to steady themselves. Regardless of whether they were to be there for a few hours or much longer, it was clear no one was to sleep that night. Michael's temples begin to throb. He'd have given his last crown for two aspirins.

He pulled out his notebook and an indelible pencil.

Dearest Virginia,
I'm writing this letter in a deep dug-out on the eve of an attack. I'm confiding it to Sergeant Tommy Malone, a friend and guide who's been with me from the beginning. He'll only mail it to you in the event of my death. My dearest love, as I believe I've told you, I have no fear of death itself. I do fear shell-shock or a devastating injury which would make me a burden to you and my family. I'm happy to die for a cause for which I've already given up almost three years of my life. The Dream of an Ireland with its own government in Dublin is still as valid as it was in July 1914. It remains my dream. Father Doyle has given us a general absolution. I'm completely at peace. I only hope that if I meet death it will be with the same bravery as so many of my comrades have. I hope that God will bring me through this and that we'll have a long life together. Thank you for loving me my own true love. Always yours,
Michael

He found a brown HMS envelope in the bottom of his haversack, addressed it, and gave it to Malone.

—Tommy, only mail this in the event of my death or a devastating injury. It's to my fiancée Virginia. I have a funny feeling about this action. My luck was severely tested the other evening. Maybe I've run out of lives.

—For God's sake Lieutenant, you'll see us all under. Don't think or talk like that. Here, have a slug o' this. It'll keep the courage up.

Malone passed Michael a small bottle of clear white liquid.

—What's this Tommy?

—Findlater's best ten-year-old pot still. Cunningham brought a few flasks back from Dublin. Be good now. Think happy thoughts.

—Point taken, Tommy. *Go raibh mile maith agat.* A thousand thanks.

Michael lay against the wall of the dug-out, his tin helmet over his eyes and nose, his breath coming in quick gasps. He'd have to control this, otherwise he wouldn't be worth tuppence when the order to advance came. He took a breath, held it deep for as long as he could, let it out slowly.

It was Easter Monday. His mind couldn't help going back to the Easter weekend of 1916. What a lovely day they'd had on Holy Saturday at Bray, and then their visit with Rosemary at her secondary school and their Easter Sunday afternoon in the Dublin mountains. Then their golf at Greystones. All this was before the emergency in the city and the terrible events he'd witnessed there.

Captain Bowen-Coldhurst's case was still working its way through the system. Was he a victim of battle stress, or was it irrational hatred of pacifist journalists whatever their nationality? Major Vane had remained true to his principles. Truly a noble man.

The field telephone rang. Michael moved quickly to answer it.

–Lieutenant Sullivan, the action of the Battalion as a whole has been postponed for twelve hours. Let the men stand down until further notice, said Colonel Murphy.

–Understood, Sir.

–Lads, break open the iron rations, said Michael. We're to stand down until further notice.

Relief filled his chest and stomach. The men gave a collective sigh. Corporal Cunningham had found a kettle and placed it on one of the braziers. He poured the contents of his water flask inside and asked Mullins, O'Riordan and others to do the same. When it was ready, they all had Maconochie beef, hot tea and a hard biscuit. Two men shared each tin. Malone shared his with Michael.

–Really hits the spot sir, said the veteran Sergeant.

–It's almost as good as the fare in Ireland, agreed Michael.

They ate quickly, then each returned to his chosen niche.

Short of a direct hit they were relatively safe for now. Michael's thoughts returned to Virginia. He pictured her working a night shift at the military hospital near Islandbridge. Had he been right in insisting that she remain in Dublin to try and help the war effort from there? Was this simply selfishness on his part? But then human love itself seemed a kind of selfishness. There is no point in suffering guilt. Time for happier thoughts. What a wonderful four days he and Virginia had spent that August Bank Holiday in 1914. That evening they spent at the small lake at the bottom of his parent's property; then the day he spent helping his father thresh and harvest their wheat; then his journey with Virginia to meet her parents in Sligo and the telegram from Vincent's Hospital recalling her.

Most blessed of all was their engagement in Dublin. He loved her with every fiber of his being. Would he ever see Virginia again? God willing. If he was careful, and cloaked in good fortune, he would see Virginia.

He was still beset by his fear. Fear gripped his chest and the pit of his stomach. He wanted to live, not just for himself, but for Virginia and the future they would have together. He had to push away these thoughts and concentrate; he had a job to do.

His men were depending on him and on his direction. Their cause was just. He was convinced of that. With God's help he'd do his duty and fulfill his promise.

He looked across the dug-out. The men seemed in a kind of collective trance, their eyes glassy, their features pale. The way their mouths were set, gave him a quiet confidence. They'd do him proud.

Again, he tried to sleep. He pushed deeper and deeper into the chalky wall of the cave behind him. He knew his uniform would be soiled. What did that matter? It would probably be filthy and caked in mud if the inclement weather persisted. It was spring, sowing time in Ireland. Even when he left at the beginning of March there were many signs of the new season. Before he worked at the bank he'd been a useful hand around his parents' farm. After Eddy their farm hand had ploughed the land, Michael worked the harrow, making the broken ground ready for wheat and barley seed.

Later Michael and Eddy would spread the seed grain. His great joy was seeing the new shoots sprout a week or ten days later. He drifted into a light sleep and was again in Queens County and Oaklands.

He woke with a start to the ringing of the field telephone. He stole a quick glance at the luminous dial of his watch. It was 17:00 hrs. Colonel Murphy was on the field telephone.

—Sullivan, said Colonel Murphy.

—Yes Sir.

—The attack on Le Bois-en-Hache Spur arranged for this morning will now take place tonight. Zero hour will be at 02.00. The 4th Canadian Division will attack the Pimple in cooperation with the attack of the 73rd Battalion. The 50th Canadian Battalion will be operating on our immediate right. Sorry about the change in plans. That's war. Remain where you are for now. Keep yourself and the men safe. You'll have written confirmation of these changes within the hour by way of a runner. Best of luck. We'll be in touch.

—And good luck to you Sir. Thank you.

The runner arrived almost an hour later in a state of collapse, his uniform and puttees caked in mud, his boots already almost worn through.

—Lieutenant Sullivan? Private Milligan with dispatches! He was bent over, hands on his knees, catching his breath.

—Sit down against the wall, Milligan. Sit down. You must be famished. Sorry we've nothing to offer except tea. Oh wait a minute. Sergeant Malone, is there a drop of that white whiskey left?

—There is indeed Sir.

—Get that inside you, Milligan. It'll do ye good.

Malone poured a generous tot of whiskey into the runner's tea. Michael watched Milligan smile with pleasure and saw the colour returning to his cheeks.

—How are things on the ground, private?

—Covering fire continues in our sector, Sir. To the south a fierce battle is being fought. The Canadians have attacked the southern and middle part of Vimy Ridge. There's great confusion, but the word is that they've broken through in sections. Our guns have cut a lot of the defences, but the Huns are dug in and giving as good as they get.

—Those Canucks have a great fighting spirit. More power to them. We're being held back for now. Your dispatch confirms this. Take your ease, Milligan. When you get back to H.Q. tell Colonel Murphy that the lads are itching to go.

—Yes Sir. Could I have another drop of that whiskey?

—You can and welcome; Sergeant Malone!

Milligan drank slowly, savouring each drop. Some fifteen minutes later he rose from the chair.

—Is there any other message, Sir?

—No. Mind how you go Milligan. My compliments to Colonel Murphy. Tell him the men will do him proud whether it be sooner or later. Dismiss.

Milligan saluted, did a quick about-turn and, bent double, sped away.

They received a later order with a further postponement. Zero hour was now 05.30. At 5.00 Michael signalled Sergeant Malone.

—Sergeant, before we move I want one final word with the lads.

Michael swayed stiffly on his feet.

—Now men, what is our first objective? O'Riordan?

–Sir, after we've got across No Man's Land we're to capture and hold the enemy front line. We're to establish a strong point to our right to protect the Sussex Regiment.

–Great, said Michael. Then we'll move on to attack blockhouses and other strong points in their defences. After that we'll take Le Bois-en-Hache Spur. Well, up and at 'em lads. Colonel Murphy is counting on you. I know you'll all do him proud. Let's go.

The men adjusted their helmets, replaced their heavy bandoliers of ammunition, picked up their rifles and proceeded to the reserve trench. A snowfall of heavy wet flakes had begun. To the south, the horizon was a deep dark red, flaked with hues of indigo and occasional puffs of white. Then the intense bombardment began.

Michael's was deafened. He felt he was in a silent world. The trench had been specially dug for the second wave of attack. It was easily ten feet below ground. Snow and sleet fell heavily at the top of the trench; lower down it melted, forming rivulets, adding to the mud at the base. Every twenty yards were wooden ladders. Four or more men were grouped round each ladder, hugging the trench walls. As before, Michael was impressed by the control of the men. Like him they felt a deep fear, but from their demeanour he knew they would behave with courage. Minutes seemed like hours now. Michael prayed silently.

O Lord give me the courage to do my duty this morning and today. Grant that all the men under me may behave with honour. If it be your will bring me through this and restore me to my fiancée and family. If not, grant me a soldier's death and a place in your Kingdom.

He was looking at the luminous dial of his wristwatch every few minutes.

His hearing returned. The sound was not a series of whining shells or succession of explosions; it was the disjointed dissonance of a massive untuned orchestra, but ten times the volume.

It hung over them. The only thing like it that Michael had experienced was the sound and barrage of a spring tide at the Cliffs of Moher in County Clare when he was a child. The bombardment was like massive waves of a sea of death. He cast a quick glance at Malone and saw that his face was pale. He looked again at his watch. 05.25. Five minutes to Zero. The men were bunching closer to the ladders now. In the half-light he could see many move their lips in silent prayer. All eyes were now on him. 05.29. He moved the whistle to his lips and blew a long hard peal. All along the trench, in an orderly fashion, the men began to climb the ladders.

Regaining his balance after going over the top Michael saw a line of men, rifles at the port, bayonets glistening in the light of exploding shells. There was a soldier every two yards. Way over to the left, Hawkins's 10th Platoon advanced under the same fire. All moved with caution, following the creeping barrage, like toy soldiers moving forward mechanically.

—Steady on the right, he shouted. Don't bunch up.

He knew the men probably couldn't hear him and indicated with his hand that they should spread out a little more. The ground quaked under his feet. Everything appeared to be moving along with him.

He felt the rush of another company behind. Ahead, the first waves of men were shrouded in smoke and sleet. Shell flashes made everything wobble. Bullets from small arms' rapid fire whizzed past his head. Yet he felt exhilarated and somehow invincible. He indicated again that the men should move forward, then lost his balance and fell into a shallow shell-hole. Breathless, he was hardly conscious of anything. Yet he was an officer, he had to be an example to the men. He took a deep breath. Then, digging his nails and fingers into the mud, he pulled himself into a semi-upright position and waved Mullins, O'Riordan, and Cunningham forward. To his right, several men had advanced too rapidly. He heard a horrendous scream and saw a headless torso gushing fountains of crimson blood arching through an amber cloud, landing almost at his feet. Jesus H Christ, he cursed, flinging himself forward again.

A tributary of the Souchez river now confronted Michael's platoon. They moved forward at a measured pace. The water flowed over the top of Michael's gumboots. It soaked his trousers. It was ice cold. Fuck it. His hands were frozen to his rifle, held at shoulder level. Gaining the opposite bank they again came under rapid rifle fire. A bullet whizzed past Michael's head.

He hit the ground, taking refuge in a shell-hole. Ice cold mud caked around his mouth and nose. He brushed it off with the back of his hand. An enemy shell exploded in front of Mullins, blasting him into the mouth of a nearby crater. O'Riordan and Michael rushed to him. Mullins' back was twisted out of shape; Michael knew that it was broken. One arm and leg were broken, a shinbone protruding through the flesh, shell-fragments sticking out of his head. I was clear that Mullins was a goner. God be good to him prayed Michael. As Michael cradled Mullins' head in his arm, something inside him snapped. He choked and sobbed. It was clear the wounds were mortal. Michael whispered a short prayer in Mullins' ear and forced a morphine tablet under his tongue.

—Stretcher bearers, stretcher-bearers! he shouted at the top of his lungs.

Finally, four figures wearing red cross armbands rushed forward. He recognized one as Corporal Morgan.

—Listen Morgan, Mullins here has been badly hit. Do the best you can.

—I will, said Morgan, placing Mullins gently on a stretcher.

–Give me a second Sir, said O'Riordan.

–Hold on Morgan, said Michael.

–Well Gerry, said O'Riordan to Mullins, we've been mates since we joined up in '14. We've been through everything together. Now you're going on a journey. I can't go with you right now.
Hold a spot for me. Wherever you end up.

–Ye can count on that, old friend, whispered Mullins.

–Mullins, O'Riordan and I have to move on now, said Michael.

They hit the earth again, moving forward inch by inch in a hail of machine gun fire. An enemy pillbox was the origin. Motioning O'Riordan to give him some covering fire, Michael doubled behind the emplacement and threw two Mills bombs through the rear embrasure. There was an instant explosion and cries of pain.

Now they were coming under fire from another emplacement. They dove into a shell-hole. A skeleton, wearing a ragged blue uniform, lay beside them. Michael shuddered. If they didn't break out of there they would surely die. No doubt about it. He checked the number of Mills bombs he still held. Six. Then, breathing deeply, he signalled O'Riordan that they should jump ahead. Finally, they reached the enemy's front line. It was largely unoccupied, with bodies scattered along the trench showing the effect of the creeping barrage. Hawkins and his 10th Platoon were engaged in hand-to-hand combat at the far-left end.

A thick-set grey-clad soldier lunged at Michael. They struggled together for several seconds, the German's hands in a stranglehold around Michael's neck. Michael knew that unless he broke the hold he'd lose consciousness and die. Gasping for breath he tried dislodging the hold with both his elbows. Miraculously, he felt the grip relax. The soldier fell backwards, a baffled expression on his face. O'Riordan, with a grim smile, withdrew his bloody bayonet.

–Thank you Dan, you saved my life, said Michael hoarsely.

Relief and gratitude filled his being.

–Think nothing of it Sir, said the wiry mud-spattered soldier.

The creeping barrage continued over their heads, now aimed at the enemy's second line. The immediate work was to consolidate this former front line as a line of defence. Michael and Hawkins directed their men to the work of strengthening and rebuilding broken trenches. Michael looked at his watch. 05.50 hrs. Suddenly they came under heavy rifle and machine gun fire from the direction of Le Bois-en-Hache, the enemy's rear trenches. Michael, O'Riordan and Malone hit the ground and hugged it for dear life. Bullets hit the snowy earth with a hard plop, a ping when hitting a stone.

It was hard to pick out the actual site of the machine gun nests. The enemy had held the area for two years. The emplacements were well camouflaged by scrub and soil.

—Jesus Christ. Is there no fucking end to this messing?

Beefy Corporal John Cunningham was grabbing a heavy Lewis gun, running towards the second trench. He bobbed and weaved, firing all the way. Though hit several times in the torso he continued his advance. Reaching the trench he tossed several grenades then jumped down.

—Let's help Corporal John, shouted Michael over the din.

They reach the second trench without losses and find Cunningham propped against the near side, firing his Lewis gun in quick sharp bursts. At least twenty grey bodies lie dead around him.

—God John, you're a holy terror, I'll see you're mentioned in dispatches and given a medal for this, said Michael. Now let me see that wound.

Michael quickly opened Cunningham's heavily stained uniform and shirt.

—Hold this here.

He pulled out the largest of his bandage pads and presses it against the corporal's chest.

—It's a clean wound, John. The bullet doesn't appear to have exited. You've already lost a fair amount of blood. We have to get you to a dressing station now. Are you in pain?
I still have a morphine tablet left.

—It's nothing I can't take Sir, said Cunningham in a weak voice.

Stretcher bearers arrived within minutes to take the NCO down the line.

They came under sustained fire again. Clearly the enemy were trying to counterattack. As a company they'd stand their ground, it was what they'd been ordered to do. The enemy counterattacked in groups of ten, and since there were no intervening defences, the advance was steady. C Company machine-gunners kept up a heavy hail of bullets. Enemy soldiers fell, but they advanced unrelentingly.

—We're getting low on ammunition Sir, yelled Malone. Machine gunners have only one belt of shells left, riflemen only ten or fifteen clips. There are only a few grenades left. They're for emergency only.

Reluctantly Michael ordered a pull back to the former enemy front line. This was to be a line of resistance. At 07.30 hrs, Michael sent runners to make contact with the 9th Royal Sussex Regiment on their left, and to H.Q. now occupying their old front line. A reserve company was advancing to fill gaps between the Leinsters and the Royal Sussex. Consolidation of the line of resistance was proving difficult due to heavy chalky mud, water seepage, and the battered state of the captured trench. The men worked mightily and quickly, sweat beading on their foreheads. Fair progress was being made. By 09.30hrs the line was consolidated. Enemy rifle and machine gun fire had practically ceased.

—Tea break lads. Make sure you give me a cup, said Michael.

—Christ Tommy. Thanks a million. This hits the spot. The men are working like Trojans.

—It's the way they've been trained and are led.

—That's not the whole of it Tommy. Ye bloody well know that.

—No. They're a brave bunch. They've proved this again and again. Drink up, Lieutenant.

As before, the tea tasted of paraffin.

Stretcher bearers came up from the rear, attending to the wounded. Michael directed several from his company to help. Many of those who'd fallen were past help. They'd died either from direct impact of a shell, from concussion, or simply bled to death. Michael and his men carefully place each survivor gently on a stretcher and move towards the dressing stations. Each step was extremely difficult because of hundreds of small shell holes, the melting snow, and the glutinous mud. The injured often cried out in pain as the carriers slipped or hit a treacherous spot.

Michael had to report to Colonel Murphy and he helped carry one of the stretchers as that would take him in that direction.

The dressing station was in the dimly lit basement of a half-demolished building in the rear lines. It smelled of disinfectant, vomit, and dried blood. Michael helped O'Riordan placing Private Lawlor on a camp bed. Twenty other beds, most of them occupied, filled the makeshift hospital. Lawlor, hit in the legs and chest, was moaning in pain.

Dr. Morley, his forehead beaded in sweat, his white surgical gown stained with blood, stepped forward from the oil-lit gloom. He quickly examined Lawlor.

—You've lost a lot of blood Private. The bullets that hit your legs have exited. You'll walk again, possibly with a limp. I'm worried about the bullet in your chest. We'll try and fish it out. I'll have to put you under and do that work right away. You've got a Blighty anyway; you'll be going to hospital in England. Ye happy about that?

—It's a chance to see the family, whispered Lawlor.

—Nurse Casey, I need you now, said Morley. Bring the chloroform and my instruments.

—We'll see you in Ireland, Jimmy. Be brave now, you fought well and with courage, said Michael.

—Yes Jimmy, say hello to all the lads in Cork and Kilworth for us. Take care of yourself, said O'Riordan.

—I'll do my best, Dan. We'll place a few bets at the Mallow Races when this is over.

Lawlor slumped back on the pillow, his face deathly pale.

—Dr. Morley! shouted Michael and O'Riordan.

They both knew that Lawlor had died.

—Listen O'Riordan, I'll have to have a word with Colonel Murphy at the new H.Q. on our way back, said Michael as they left the casualty station.

—Right you are Sir. I'll continue to the line of resistance.

They covered the two miles to the rear trenches in less than thirty minutes. The sleet of the morning had changed to heavy misty rain.

—You continue on now, O'Riordan, said Michael, as they reached the former front line now serving as H.Q.

Colonel Murphy sat on a wooden chair behind an overturned tea-chest serving as a desk. He seemed deeply engrossed in a tattered trench map.

—Welcome Sullivan, said the Colonel as Michael entered. At ease. This is a trench map captured by the Canadians. It gives details of every enemy gun position in Le Bois-en-Hache Ridge.
It'll be of great help to you and Lieutenant Hawkins in mopping-up operations. I can't make copies. Come here, study it closely. Know any German?

—The gothic alphabet and a few catchphrases; it's six years since I last studied or spoke it.

—Fair enough. Memorize as much as you can.

He could see from the map that, as he had suspected, the area of the ridge near the top was heavily fortified, with the area in front containing five well-camouflaged blockhouses.

—Has Hawkins also seen this, Sir? asked Michael.

—Yes, he was here about half an hour ago. Try to take out as many of these gun nests as possible. The Canadians have done well in their attack on the centre part of Vimy Ridge. If we can knock out these fortifications, we could have a breakthrough and probably shorten the war.

—We'll do our best, Sir.

—I know you will. C and B Companies have already done the Regiment proud. Dismiss. Keep up the good work.

—Thank you Sir.

As he got back to the line Michael noted that the work of consolidation and re-vetting had been largely completed. The men were taking a well-earned break; having rigged canvas covers atop their rifles, they had broken out more emergency rations and were cooking bully beef and tea. The enemy were now shelling their former front and support lines. It looked like they were trying to stop munition and supply wagons from getting through.

—We'll be all right unless they mount a counterattack, Michael told Malone.

—Don't worry Sir, they're in far worse state than we are. This is only diversionary fire. We'd better content ourselves with this hard tack as food. They're not going to allow anything to get up here tonight. If there's to be a real counterattack, it will probably be tomorrow at dawn.

—You're right there, Tommy. We'll just have to make the best of it. We've come through a rough day, but our losses haven't been too high. Post sentries at the weak points in the line and have the balance of the platoon form a wiring party. We need to lay down barbed wire in this new stretch of No Man's Land to slow down any German counter-attack they may throw at us. We'll go out as soon as it's dark.

Michael called for Sergeant Malone to join him.

—I want you to go out in advance of the wiring party and set stakes along the line where we'll lay down the barbed wire. Do a stretch to the left, and then return and do the right. I'll assemble the party at the parapet, and then you'll go out.

—Ready, Lieutenant? asked Malone.

—As ready as we'll ever be, Sergeant, whispered Michael.
Good. The rain has finally stopped Sergeant, and there's no moon.
Off you go now.

Sergeant Tom Malone advanced towards the new enemy front line the Germans had retreated to, every sense and nerve straining to detect danger. It was like being suddenly completely naked, alone, without cover, completely vulnerable. Malone halted about fifty yards from their own trench and began traversing the line where he'd drive the marker stakes.

Michael gave Malone ten minutes to start to mark the line, and then ordered the party to climb out of the trench, leaving men in position, ready to cover their return if the worst happened. Michael picked out each man as he ascended the parapet, everyone a dark shadow, their faces blackened with burnt cork.

Corporal Nick Madigan was at the rear, joining the others assembled at the top of the trench.

–Listen now. Corporal Madigan and I will advance to the post positions marked by Malone, and we'll use the silent screw pickets to drive in the barbed wire posts, whispered Malone. The rest of you just ply out the wire and attach it to them. We'll withdraw after we've done the wiring to the left and the right.

They moved away from the trench, Michael with pistol in hand, the others with their rifles at the ready; Madigan carried the 'silent screw' and several of the posts. Some of the other men, crouching, carried the spools of barbed wire and the remaining posts. The drums of barbed wire, with a stout spar through the middle and with leather gloves for protection, were carried by pairs of men.

Malone could faintly hear the rest of the wiring party moving up to his position in unison, but couldn't see them. He continued to traverse No Man's Land, laying out white pine stakes to mark where each barbed wire post should be driven in.

–Michael came up to the first of Malone's stakes and said, Madigan, punch in a post here.

The 'silent screw' drove in the post soundlessly. The enemy were still sending up occasional star shells over No Man's Land. Madigan marked the post with a piece of white tape, then crept another twenty-five yards to the next stake and drove in another post. The soldiers behind them plied out the barbed wire and attached it. A star shell exploded, turning night into brilliant daylight. Malone and Madigan fell to a prone position. Their comrades also hugged the earth.

Malone, traversing to the right saw a wounded German in front of him, his eyes like stars in the drifting flare. The soldier looked about sixteen. Malone saw the gaping wounds, black as the star-shell light faded.

–Goddamn it, die why don't you? he whispered.

The boy's mouth moved. Malone heard nothing. The boy was too weak to talk. Then he raised his hand as if to seize Malone's uniform. The hand fell back. It was clear to the veteran sergeant that the boy was in great pain and near death. Rules of war didn't apply. Malone reached for his bayonet, fearing that the boy would cry out to the German line.

Malone crept back to rejoin the wiring party. At the flash of another shell, Michael could see a strange dark expression in the veteran sergeant's eyes.

Michael dispatched another part of the wiring party to work along where Malone had been driving stakes to the right. The troop reassembled in the centre, the barbed wire spools now almost empty. The enemy sent up more star shells, and everyone hit the ground again.

Michael cried out as he felt a tremendous blow at the base of his ribcage on the right side of his back. His mouth filled with blood. He tried hard to breathe, but breath wouldn't come. He felt himself rush out of his body, out and out. He had a transcendent sense of peace. Was he dead? Then he floated and felt himself slide back into his body. He breathed deeply and was conscious of Malone, Madigan and the others bending over him.

—Hold on Lieutenant. Hold on. We'll get you back to our lines and to the aid station. Do you think you can walk? asked Malone.

—I'll do my best, Tommy.

It was difficult to get the words out. His legs felt like bricks. His breath was coming in short swift spurts now. Even with Malone and Madigan holding him up on either side he felt he would fall at any moment. He had to hang on, had to somehow remain conscious.

They finally reached the back of the line of resistance. Malone jumped into the trench first. The others passed Michael to the sergeant.

—Jesus fucking Christ, cried Michael, feeling pain in every pore of his body.

—Sorry Lieutenant, said Malone.

He laid him at the base of the trench and cut through the front of his uniform with his trench knife. The bullet had hit the very base of his rib cage. Already there was very heavy loss of blood. Time was of the essence. Malone realized that if he couldn't somehow stop the blood flow, Michael would die. Pressure on the wound might work. He was conscious that the nearest stretcher station was a half mile away.

—Sir, you've lost an awful lot of blood. You'll lose a lot more if we try to move you. Here's my field dressing. Madigan will give me his also. We'll press hard on them to begin with; then you have to try to apply pressure yourself. In fifteen minutes or so we'll try moving you. Your blood will have coagulated a bit by then and there'll be less chance of you bleeding to death.

—I see Tommy. Do your best.

—You can count on that, Sir.

—I always could Tommy. Right from my time in Formoy and Kilworth.

—Enough ould talk now. You have to keep your strength. It looks like you have a Blighty here Sir. You'll be going home.

—Right, Tommy. I hope that happens.

Michael closed his eyes. He could hear his breathing. It seemed shallow, like that of a six- month-old child. He saw Virginia smiling serenely. He smelled her skin and hair. Lily of the Valley.

That was her perfume. She seemed to be in his arms again. Was she? He had to survive. Virginia was his life. He remembered her last words to him just a month earlier.

Return to me, Michael.
Keep safe, don't take unnecessary risks. Please return to me.

My love, my beautiful girl. I'll come home to you. We'll have a long and happy life together.

The sounds of battle became distant. He was in a lush summer meadow full of wild poppies and cornflowers, the air heavy with the scent of woodbine and laburnum. Co-co-co-rico, went a wood pigeon chanting the only song that it sings, that it never tires of calling. High in the clear blue sky, larks soared, singing their twelve-note melody. Lower down, a school of swallows swooped, following summer midges.

How could this be? Was he not in the thick of battle near a French village? He caught snatches of conversation.

–Sergeant the bleeding at the base of Lieutenant Sullivan's ribs has stopped, he heard Madigan say in a West Cork voice. Perhaps it's safe to move him.

–Let me see Madigan, he heard Malone reply. Yes, you're right Corporal. The blood has congealed. We'll have to take a chance. It looks like the only one we'll get. Lieutenant, we're going to try to move you now. Brace yourself as we lift you onto the stretcher and lift it up. We'll try to walk as evenly as possible on the way to the dressing station. Alright?

–Yes Tommy, Michael whispered.

His lips felt very dry. He would have given anything for a glass of cold fresh lemonade. He felt a quick jolt of pain, then his mind drifted again. He was back in that warm summer meadow, foxgloves and hollyhocks in full-bloom at its edges. Co-co-co-rico, sang the wood pigeon. Sparrows and finches flew to their nests in a bordering hedge, their beaks full of worms, midges, and grubs for their nestlings. Again, Michael had an overwhelming feeling of peace. He sensed acceptance. Warmth. Love.

He wanted to remain in that peaceful place.

Tired and fatigued, Malone and Madigan arrive at the dressing station. There was less activity than two hours earlier.

–Dr. Morley, we've just brought in Lieutenant Sullivan. He's been badly hit. A wound to his rib cage on the right side. We were afraid to move him initially because of the bleeding. I hope we're not too late, said Sergeant Malone noticing the lieutenant's pallor.

–Let me see Sergeant, said the surgeon.

—Sorry lads. This brave man has bled to death. I hope he wasn't in great pain. He was here just ninety minutes ago ferrying wounded. How did he die?

—He was out with a wiring party as we consolidated a captured trench, and was hit there Dr. Morley.

—Well, he's in a better place now. Another life for a dream.

—Yes. Freedom for Belgium and small nations. What we've been fighting for, said Sergeant Tom Malone with no attempt to hide his bitterness.

—It will happen sooner or later. Mark my words, Sergeant.

Lieutenant Colonel A.D. Murphy at General HQ in Arras. sat wearily at his desk towards 8a.m. on Saturday 14th April. Morning sunshine showed dust mites in the air and highlighted a pastoral scene in the beige wallpaper. The official reports of the Leinsters' actions over the previous thirty-six hours lay in front of him. The battalion had captured and consolidated all their objectives. The Canadians had been badly bloodied, but had captured Vimy Ridge. Would this be the battle to shorten the conflict? Time alone would tell. The fight for Le Bois-en-Hache and The Pimple appeared to have been costly; perhaps not as costly in men or resources as in the Battle of the Somme, but nevertheless great in casualties: four junior officers killed, six wounded, fifty-one soldiers killed, one hundred and fifty-five wounded. As with the battle of the Somme he would write personally to the families of all his junior officers, delegating the equally difficult task of writing personally to the families of enlisted men to several of his adjutants.

Murphy thought of Lieutenant Michael Sullivan, a junior officer he'd seen just thirty-six hours earlier, shocked again that he was among the dead. He picked up the telephone.

—Get me Lieutenant Frank Hawkins as quickly as possible, Private Miller.

Minutes later the phone rang back.

—Hawkins, can you tell me anything more of Lieutenant Sullivan's death? I'm about to write his parents. It was a wound to his chest; was he in pain? I see. Thank you Hawkins.

Not good; best to not relay that part to the family, too hard for them to bear. He started his letter to Michael's family:

Dear Dr. and Mrs. Sullivan,
You no doubt have already had a telegram from the department of defence telling you of the tragic death of your son Michael on the morning of 12th April. He died instantly and bravely from a wound to his chest. He will be treated with full military honours. Notification of his burial and the location of his grave will follow. I've known your son for almost two years. He was the bravest and most courageous of officers. The men loved him and appreciated his humour and fearlessness. On a personal level I feel a deep sense of loss. It was at my request that your son returned to action in the middle of last month. He need not have returned, but felt that his duty was here. May God keep him in His loving care.
Yours very sincerely,
A.D. Murphy, Lt. Colonel Commanding 2nd & 3rd Leinster Battalions

Afterword

As I wrote this novel about Michael Sullivan in the Great War, and his beloved Virginia, behind him always was the shadow of my Uncle Michael Higgins. A letter, like the letter to Michael's family at the end of the novel, was also received by the Higgins family:

April 1st 1917

Dear Dr. Higgins,
Will you accept my deepest sympathy in the great loss you have sustained in the death yesterday of your son. He was killed instantly by a bullet through the chest at 10.30 last night whilst watching a bombardment on our flank.
It is only a fortnight since your son joined us for a second time at my special request and I am deeply grieved that this should have been the result of my efforts to get so fine an officer to my battalion.
His cheerfulness and his energy and good humour have made him popular everywhere, and there is no one in the battalion who has known your son who has not good things to say of him. He will be buried tomorrow by his comrades and his grave will be clearly marked and preserved.
Once again let me assure you of my heartfelt sympathy as well as that of all his comrades in the second battalion.
Yours sincerely,
A.D. Murphy,
Lieut Col. 2nd Battalion
Leinster Regiment

Acknowledgements

First and foremost my family:

Philippa & Kevin McPhillips

Helen & Enda Cleary

Patricia & Sean Clohosey

John & Annie Kirby

Denis & Ann Kirby

for their love through my life.

I also wish to thank:

Arthur & Nonna Broes

Dermot Bulger

Ingrid McCarthy

Maeve McPhillips

Kevin McPhillips Jr.

Author Peter Kirby

Brian & Jean Moore

Christopher & Elaine Plummer

Gordon Snell & Maeve Binchy

Kevin Myers of RTE

The late Abraham Ram

Leslie Hoban Blake

Michael Kenneally of the Dept of Irish Studies, Concordia

Derek Webster and Ian McGillis for their constructive comments

Dear friends

Jack & Jane O Hare

Paul & Vivi Loftus and

P.J. O'Donnell.

And especially Antoine Maloney
for his patience, technical expertise, and kindness.

Sources / Citations / Bibliography

My main source for my novel is *Stand To: A Diary of the Trenches* by Captain Frank Hitchcock, published in 1937. Captain Hitchcock mentions a maternal uncle seven times in his narrative. Both that maternal Uncle, Lt. Michael Higgins, and Hitchcock were members of the Prince of Wales's Leinster Regiment 2nd Battalion.

Hitchcock, F. C., *Stand to: a Diary of the Trenches 1915-1918*, Gliddon Books, Norwich UK, 1988

The books appearing with an asterisk at the end of the entry were also important sources:

Whitton, Captain, *The History of the Prince of Wales's Leinster Regiment (Royal Canadians) Vol 2* *

Denman, Dr. Terence, *Ireland's Unknown Soldiers: The 16th (Irish) Division in the Great War*, 1992 *

———, Dr. Terence, *A lonely Grave: A Biography of Major William Redmond*, 1993 *

Dungan, Myles, *Irish Voices from The Great War*, 1993 *

———, Myles, They shall not Grow old, 1997 *

Dunn, J.C., *The War the Infantry Knew*, 1938 *

Fitzpatrick, David, (Ed.), *Ireland and the First World War*, Lilliput Press, Dublin: Trinity History Workshop, 1988 *

Gibbon, Monk, *Inglorious Soldier*, 1968 *

Kee, Robert, *Ourselves Alone*, 1972 *

Lyons, J.B. *The Enigma of Thomas Kettle, Irish Patriot, Poet, Essayist, British Soldier 1880-1916* *

O'Rahilly, Dr. Alfred, *Father William Doyle SJ*, 1918 *

The remaining entries are a general bibliography:

Ballard, Robert D., Spencer Dunmore, *Exploring the Lusitania: Probing the Mysteries of the Sinking That Changed History*, 2003

Barbusse, Henri, *Le Feu (Journal d'une escouade)* translated as *Under Fire*, Penguin Books, 2003

Berton, Pierre *Vimy*, 1986

Bird, William, *Ghosts Have Warm Hands: A memoir of the Great War*, 1968

Blunden, Edmond, *Undertones of War*, 1928

Bolger, Dermot, (Ed.), *Selected Poems by Francis Ledwidge*, 1992

Brittan, Vera, (autobiography), *Testament of Youth*

———, Vera, *Account Rendered.* a memoir

———, Vera, *Letters From a Lost Generation: Letters of Vera Brittan and Four Friends*, 1998

Celine, Louis Ferdinand, *Voyage au bout du Monde* translated as *Journey to the end of Night by a French soldier*, 1932

Christie, N.M., (Ed.), *Letters of Agar Adamson 1914-1919 Lt. Colonel Princess Patricia's Can. Light Infantry*, 1997

Crowley, Deborah, (Ed.), *George Vanier: Soldier: The Wartime Letters and Diaries 1915-1919*

Curtayne, Alice, *Francis Ledwidge, a Biography*, 1972

De Rosa, Peter, *Rebels*, 1990

Fannin, Alfred & Adrian Warwick-Haller (Aut.), Sally Warwick-Haller, (Ed.), *Letters from Dublin Easter 1916: Alfred Fannin's Diary of the Rising*, Irish Academic Press, 1995

Ford, Ford Maddox, *Parades End Tetralogy*, 1928

Frazer, Donald, *The Journal of Private Frazer Canadian Expeditionary Force 1914-1918*, 1985

Gardiner, Brian, (Ed.), *Up the Line to Death: The War Poets 1914-1918*

Glover, John & John Silkin, (Eds.), *The Penguin Book of First World War Prose*

Graves, Richard Percival, *Robert Graves: The Assault Heroic 1895 -1926*, 1990

Graves, Robert, *Goodbye to All That*, 1929

Griffin, Gerald, *The Dead March Past, A Partial Memoir*, 1937

Griffin, Peter, *Along with Youth: Ernest Hemingway The Early Years*, 1985

Harrison, Charles Yale, *Generals Die in Bed*, 1930

Harvey, Dan & Gerry White, *The Barracks: A history of Victoria/Collins Barracks, Cork*, 1997

Healy, Timothy, Q.C., *Letters and Leaders of My Day*, 1920

Hoehline, A.A. & Mary Hoehline, *The Last Voyage of the Lusitania*, 1956

Hogg, Ian V., (Ed.), *The Guns of 1914-1918*, 1971

Jeffries, Keith, *Ireland and the Great War*, 2000

Johnstone, Thomas, *Orange, Green and Khaki, the story of Irish Regiments in the Great War 1914-1918*, 1992

Kelly, Jean, (Ed.), *Love Letters from the Front*, 2000

MacBride, Maud Gonne, *Gonne-Yeats Letters, 1893-1938: Always Your Friend,* 1993

Manning, Edward, *Her Privates We*, 1930

McClintock, Alexander, D.C.M., *Best O'Luck: How a Fighting Canadian Won The Thanks of Britain's King*, 1917

McDonald, Lyn, *Somme*, 1983

———, Lyn, *The Roses of No Mans Land*, 1980

———, Lyn, *They Called it Passchendale*, 1984

McGill, Patrick, *The Red Dawn*, 1916

Messenger, Charles, (Ed.), *Trench Fighting 1914-18*, 1972

Mottram, R.H., *The Spanish Farm Trilogy* 1914-1918, 1927

O'Connor, Ulic, *The Times I've Seen: A Biography of Oliver St. John Gogarty*, 1983

O'Flaherty, Liam, *Return of the Brute*, 1929

———, Liam, *Shame the Devil a Biography*, 1934

Remarque, Eric Marie, *All Quiet on the Western Front*, 1924

Sassoon, Siegfried, *The Complete Memoirs of George Sheraton*, 1937

Taylor, Alice, *To School through the Fields*, 1996

Tuchman, Barbara W., *The Guns of August*, 1962

Vaughan, Edward Champion, *Some Desperate Glory: The Diary of a young Officer 1917*, 1981

Winter, Denis, *Death's Men: Soldiers of the Great War*, 1978

Winter, Jay, PhD., *The Great War and the Shaping of the 20th Century*, 1996

Biography

Anthony Kirby was born in Dublin on the 25th February 1940. His father, Dr. Anthony Kirby, d. 10 Nov 1953 was the dispensary doctor in Kiltimagh, Co. Mayo from 1927 to 1953.

His mother nee Patricia Higgins d July 1969 was a member of the Sullivan-Higgins (O'Higgins) family. Members of her family have contributed to the initial government of Ireland.

Educated at Castleknock College and St. Joseph's, Temple Rd., Blackrock. Anthony graduated with a B.A. in English literature and film from Concordia University, Montreal, Canada in 1978.

He contributed a comprehensive filmography to *Contemporary Irish Cinema from The Quiet Man to Dancing at Lughnasa*, ed., James MacKillop, Syracuse University Press 1999.

His film criticism appears regularly in *filmireland.net* His journalism has appeared in *The Irish Times*, *The Irish Literary Supplement*, *The Cork Examiner*, *Irish America Magazine*, New York, *Music Magazine*, Toronto, and *The Christian Science Monitor* (Boston).

Fascinated by the history of his mother's family, especially from 1910 to 1927 Anthony began research on his World War I novel *For a Dream* in the 1990s.

Research began in Arras, France, and continued at the National Library of Ireland, The Public Record Office U.K., The Library of Congress Washington, New York Public Library, and McGill University. This research included visits to Ypres, the Somme Battlefields, and Vimy Ridge.

As a tie in with Canadian Celebration Commemorations of the Battle of Vimy Ridge in 2017, Anthony authored an essay on the participation of the 2nd Battalion of the Leinster Regiment in this battle. This was published in a Montreal Irish newsletter and formed the basis for a PowerPoint Presentation he gave at the Canadian Conference of Irish Studies Meeting in late May 2019.

Anthony has spent much of his life in the hospitality industry and is working on a novel and memoir based on his experiences.

About the typeface

Goudy Old Style (*also known as just Goudy*)
is an old-style serif typeface
originally created by Frederic W. Goudy
for American Type Founders (ATF) in 1915.
Suitable for text and display applications,
Goudy Old Style matches the historicist trend
of American printing in the early twentieth century,
taking inspiration from the printing of the
Italian Renaissance without a specific historical model.
Eccentricities include the upward-curved ear on the g
and the diamond shape of the dots of the i, j,
and the points found in the period, colon and
exclamation point, and the sharply canted hyphen.
The design is relatively light in colour.

from Wikipedia

Printed in Great Britain
by Amazon